Bitter Haven

BITTERROOT MONTANA VETERANS

BOOK 1

ANNE M. SCOTT

Dedication

To all those damaged by war.

Stay with us — we need you.

Cover designed by MiblArt
Developmental Editing Lia Huni
Proofreading Paula Lester, Polaris Editing

This book is a work of fiction. Names, characters, places, and incidents either are products of the author's imagination or are used fictitiously. Any resemblance to actual persons, living or dead, events, or locales is entirely coincidental.

Anne M. Scott
Visit my website at www.amscottwrites.com/romance

First Printing: May 2021 on Kindle Vella
Second Printing as Love, Coffee & Cars Mar 2022
Third Printing as Bitter Haven Dec 2022
Version 3.0
Lightwave Publishing LLC

Author's Note

Content Warning: A military sexual assault survivor is a supporting character in this novel. Details are minimal, but her terrible experience is integral to her character. Some readers may think her reaction is unrealistic, but every survivor's coping mechanisms are different, and they are all equally valid.

If you are a survivor, I hope you are getting the support you need. In the US, the Veteran's Administration is finally taking the issue seriously. If your branch of the VA isn't, complain to your congressional representatives. If you feel unsafe at your local VA, call and ask for an escort before your appointment. You earned your benefits, and you deserve them.

For every sexual assault survivor, reaching out for help is brave, not weak! I hope each and every one of you receives the help you need. Same with anyone struggling with trauma, physical and/or emotional, depression, or any mental health struggle. We need you here—please ask for help. See the Author's End Note for some resources.

Note: This story was originally published as *Love, Coffee & Cars* on Kindle Vella, then heavily revised and printed as a novel. Since then, the title and series name have changed; the story remains the same.

Chapter 1

Mom: Another Word for Trouble

Sweat trickled down Erin Moore's back. Air-conditioning her four-bay auto repair garage in Marcus, Montana was too expensive and unnecessary most of the year, but she regretted the lack in July and August. Especially when battling stubborn bolts under a car. "Blast it all, what behemoth tightened this thing?" She latched both hands on the oil-slick wrench again, jerking with her entire body.

"I don't know, dear. A man, maybe?" a woman scoffed.

Erin jolted but miraculously didn't hit her head on the car's undercarriage. She hadn't heard the door. She bent her knees to take a peek. "Funny, Mom."

Sharlene Murphy wore one of her many perfectly tailored designer skirt suits. Emerald green with a high-necked white silk blouse, the luxurious, jewel-toned material complemented Mom's dark auburn smooth chignon and showcased her beautiful porcelain features. Her carefully applied makeup disguised the tiny signs of age she couldn't prevent, despite a meticulous and expensive maintenance schedule.

In distinct contrast, Erin's mass of bright-red curls, pulled back into a messy bun, was coated with dirt, and she never bothered with makeup at work. What was the point? The cars wouldn't be impressed. Nor would her too-few customers, mostly older women who trusted her, either despite or because of her mother. She clamped her lips together and wiped her hands on her stained, baggy, heavy-duty gray coveralls. Far from designer wear—and she loved it.

"Yes, yes, I am. You know what else I am, dear?" Her dulcet, superior tones didn't lessen the never-ending, well-worn criticism.

"Yes, Mom." It wasn't a question—Erin knew exactly what she'd say, but answered anyway, unwilling to receive the rudeness lecture. Good thing the car on the lift hid Erin's expression.

"Clean. I'm clean and I'm wearing beautiful clothes. Oh, and jewelry. And nail polish. As a matter of fact, I look absolutely stunning today." Her voice was maliciously cheerful, echoing slightly in the too-empty eight-car garage.

"Yes, you look lovely and professional. Don't you think you should leave before some bit of grease or gunk comes flying off when I finally break this bolt?"

Erin held her breath, hoping her hint might work for once.

"Dear, I'm thirty feet away from you; I think I'm safe. Although I don't enjoy having to yell at you." Her toe, encased in conservative designer heels, tapped impatiently on the clean but oil-stained concrete. Her arms were certainly crossed, fingers tapping too.

"I don't know about that. Turn around and look at the wall behind you. That dent? That came from a car part." True, but only because she chucked it at the wall. Expensive material swished with a sharp intake of breath. *Huh.* Mom actually did something Erin asked her to do. She should mark the day on her calendar and celebrate it every year. She held back a snicker.

"Fine, Erin, I'm going to work. You can wallow in grease and guilt all you want. But you're coming out with us on Saturday night. This is not a request." Mom's voice was back to commanding and exasperated, her normal tone with her only child.

Erin shrugged. "Fine. I'll see you Saturday." She'd get a decent meal anyway—Mother dined only at the best restaurants.

"Good. Dress nicely. We'll have dinner and then attend the show."

"Show? What show?" At least a performance would save Erin from constant criticism. Snide remarks about her shortcomings would accompany dinner. She bit her lip. Retorting would backfire.

"The Marcus Playhouse is putting on *Boeing,*

Boeing. It has very good reviews." The toe tapped louder and faster.

"Okay. What's it about?" She was stupid to ask, extending the painful conversation.

"It's a comedy. I'm sure it will be delightful. Or as delightful as this tiny town can be."

Mother didn't sound sure at all, but Erin didn't bother to push the point. "Sure,. I'll see you Saturday evening at six-thirty?"

"Six-fifteen."

"Okay, Mom. Have a good day at work." Erin waved.

"Of course, dear. You too, although I doubt that's really possible."

Heels clipped sharply across concrete, then the heavy shop door clicked open and sighed close. Erin slumped, resting her head on her forearm, giving up on the bolt to indulge in her own sigh of relief. The bolt abruptly released, the crosshatched grip of the wrench rasping across her palm, and she went down, banging one knee on the concrete, hard. "Ow." That was gonna bruise.

The bolt had waited for Mother to leave, scared stiff like everyone else in town. Erin chuckled. She wasn't being fair. President of the most successful local bank in town, Mom was admired and sometimes absolutely adored. Marcus City Bank was safe, respected, and thriving because everyone in town knew they were extremely fiscally conservative.

An equal number of people hated Mom. Her conservative approach to banking meant a lot of foreclosures. Many believed a bank should give them more chances to catch up on their loans, but Erin wasn't so sure. Foreclosures cost money—money Mother would rather have in the Bank's accounts. Mom secured the Bank's investments, no matter what the impact was on the people involved.

One of many reasons Erin joined the Air Force after high school and started her business after Michael's death. She could never work for her mother. Despite the heat, ice shivered down her spine.

Rats. Mother said "us," which meant she'd already invited a man or two to accompany them. Forcing Erin to socialize with "eligible bachelors" was an excellent use of her time. Marcus City Bank sponsored a lot of local charities, so Mom probably got the play tickets for free. Her biggest customers got dinner and a show, plus "here's a chance at my lovely daughter," was seen in public with said daughter, enhancing her "family-friendly" image, and got Erin to do what she wanted, a personal triumph.

She only needed a feathered purple hat to fulfill the pimp stereotype. Erin chuckled. Mother would be horrified at the comparison. And the hat.

Erin stood and removed the bolt. Especially when Mom's idea of an eligible gentleman was far from hers. Usually they were ten to twenty years older than Erin, a stuffed shirt who'd never left the town, their brains as soft as their bodies. None of them had any desire to go, do, or see anything new or different.

Sure, Marcus, Montana was a beautiful and wonderful place—that's why she'd come back after everything fell apart. The gorgeous Bitterroot Mountains, the rushing streams, the miles of hiking, the fantastic skiing, the amazing fly-fishing; it was the perfect place to call home. But everyone should experience some of the wonderful, beautiful, and terrible things in the world so they'd appreciate what they had. And if they couldn't physically leave because of financial or physical limitations, the desire should still exist. Erin couldn't connect with people who lacked the longing to learn. She'd experienced so much and knew there was more.

Thank the heavens, there were plenty of people here who wanted to widen their minds, even if they couldn't leave.

Lately, though, Mom's dating pool had widened, and not in a good way. Men from out of town, with expensive suits and entitled attitudes. Wealthy, self-absorbed, rough and tough despite the designer duds, like movie mobsters. A couple carried weapons—she could smell the gunpowder and if she looked closely, see the bulge from a pistol. Some of those had slight accents; Russian, if she had to make a guess. If she had to deal with slime, she preferred the local losers. Like Chaz Cust. Bad enough Mom dealt with him; these new customers and associates made Erin nervous.

Whatever it was, it wouldn't pay her bills. She clinked the wrench into place on the next bolt and pulled. She might need the impact wrench, but then she risked rounding off the bolt's head, making her job harder.

"Hey, Erin," a gruff male voice said.

Her tense shoulders relaxed. "Hi, Pete, what can I do for you?" She ducked, shooting a smile at him, then went back to work. Pete Borde, local rancher and Vietnam vet, wouldn't mind. He knew time was money.

Pete hadn't known what to make of her, an Air Force veteran who'd become a military spouse and then a widow. But he'd warmed up to her quickly when she offered him the coffee shop next door for their veteran meetings. He insisted on paying for the coffee.

"I'm checking your schedule. Are we still clear to use the coffee shop on Tuesday afternoon?"

"You bet, Pete. You're always welcome, you know that." He made sure the shop was cleaner than he found it, too.

"Appreciate it. See you later."

"Bye. Have a great day."

"You too."

The door sighed again, and she echoed it. Pete's group was getting smaller. They should reach out to the younger vets moving into Marcus. Many of them had severe wounds, often hidden, like traumatic brain injuries and post-traumatic stress. They'd come, just like she had, to rest and recover in a friendly place. And sometimes, just to hide. Marcus was a good place to hide. A small town but large enough to not know everybody, with mountains on all sides.

An easy place to hide in plain sight. Vietnam vets did the same, years before. The survivors learned hiding didn't work. The new guys—and gals—could use some mentorship, and the Vietnam guys needed new blood.

Erin closed her eyes. Michael would have integrated the two groups, but he was a one-of-a-kind man. She'd been lucky to have him as long as she did. Wishing for more was futile.

Enough memories. She had work to do. The last bolt broke and spun out. To finish the job, she needed the transmission rebuild kit, which should have been delivered already. She wiped her greasy fingers on a shop rag. She rarely remembered her mechanic's gloves until dirty grease blackened her fingernails.

Her boots thudded across the twenty feet of concrete to the auto shop counter. Opening the connecting door behind the counter, she breathed deep. Dark, rich espresso overwhelmed the sharp scent of burned oil. But her pleasure was short-lived. No one stood at her very expensive espresso machine or behind the cash register next to it. Or at the drive-through window. She scowled. Tiffany was gone. Erin edged behind the counter, pulling her greasy coveralls against her body, keeping the dirt away from the surfaces.

Halfway down the long, narrow dining area, Tiffany giggled and batted her eyelashes at the men who came in every morning. From the sawdust left under their chairs, Erin was pretty sure they were loggers. "Tiffany!"

She jumped and turned, her big brown eyes open wide, lashes fluttering with too much mascara, pink lips pouting.

Great. Sad puppy dog eyes first thing in the morning. "Tiffany, did you order that transmission rebuild kit for me like I asked?"

"I think so!" She shot a smile at the loggers, then sauntered away, hips twisting like a model on a catwalk.

That phrase meant the opposite—she hadn't ordered the parts or finished any of the other tasks Erin had asked her to do. Erin checked the computer next to the cash register. *Yup, no order. Rats.* A shiny expanse of red caught her eye. "Tiffany, the drive-through. There are customers waiting." Erin kept her tone flat, even though she wanted to yell.

"I'm so, so sorry. I didn't notice them, Erin!" The cute little blonde scurried to the window.

Of course not. She clamped her lips shut. Customers in the drive-through weren't nearly as interesting as the muscle-bound, bearded loggers in the dining area, even though the drive-through customers tipped, and the loggers generally didn't. Erin needed a decent employee, somebody who would work and could learn new skills. So far, the hours and pay she could offer made it impossible. Her business plan was a good one—mother's bank wouldn't have approved the loan otherwise—but finding the right person was mission impossible so far.

Erin waited until Tiffany was back on the job and returned to the garage. She hit the quick dial on the garage phone, gripping it tightly to keep the slightly greasy plastic from slipping out of her hand.

"Kelly's Auto Parts, lowest price always, how can I help you?"

"Hi, William. It's Erin at Coffee and Cars. Got a 2010 Pontiac G6, four-cylinder automatic, and I need a transmission rebuild kit. Tiffany was supposed to order it, but..."

He snort-chuckled, the tapping of computer keys underlying his mirth. William understood how hard it was to find good help. "We've got one. I'll have it to you shortly."

"Thanks, William. Appreciate it."

"No problem. Have a good one."

Erin took her frustrations out on the bolts rusted into the tranny. At least the car problem was solvable.

Her mother wasn't so easy.

Chapter 2

Misdirection and Memories

"Hey, kid!"

"Yeah?" Ryan Walsh hated the moniker, but since Jim was older than the hills, he put up with it. Besides, complaining brought more of the same. Ryan learned that lesson in a far tougher place than Kelly's Auto Parts. He missed the guys from his unit. They could be rough but not mean.

"Take this tranny rebuild kit to Coffee and Cars." Jim held the box high; it shook in his trembling hand.

"Coffee and Cars?" Must be a new repair shop. The tiny town of Marcus had changed a lot in the years Ryan had been gone. Kelly's Auto Parts was still the same, though. A standalone store at the north end of town, jammed with parts, cases of oil, and antifreeze stacked in the aisles, making it hard to move if they had more than two or three customers. The mix of oil, grease, and antifreeze hit his nose like a baseball bat every time he walked through the door.

"Yeah, kid. They're down the highway about a mile on the left. Ask for Erin." Jim gave him an evil grin, dropping the box and paperwork in Ryan's hand. Shuffling to the tiny office at the end of the back parts counter, Jim's gimpy leg made his shoe squeak on the concrete with every other step.

"Aaron?" He always asked; with his lousy hearing, he missed things.

"Yeah, kid. Erin. Pay attention!"

Ryan frowned. Jim knew cars, but he was such a grouch. Rude, even to the customers, did as little work as possible, had one foot in the grave, and brayed like a jackass. Ryan quickly learned to question almost everything Jim said, except actual mechanical car information. That, Jim knew like the back of his hand. Probably better—his liver spots seemed to multiply daily. Ryan checked the address on the receipt, then plugged it into his phone.

Yeah, it was a mile away on the left, but it was a mile north, not a mile south as "down" the highway would imply. His mouth twisted, holding back the comment he wanted to make so badly. Jim was trying to send him on another wild goose chase. Good thing William knew the score. Ryan checked the delivery counter. Jim "forgot" to tell him about deliveries, too. No boxes waited on the table, so he grabbed the delivery truck keys. The job definitely wasn't his dream job, but it kept him busy and gave him spending money. His hands ached to hold a wrench. But that wasn't possible anymore.

Ryan followed the directions to a big beige metal building with a green roof, like many of the other commercial buildings along the highway. Strange he hadn't noticed the big 1960s style sign proclaiming "Coffee and Cars" on top of the building. But he'd missed a lot of things since he got back.

He drove into the parking lot. Smaller signs directed him right for "Coffee To Go," along a slightly rutted gravel road leading to what must be a drive-through window; another pointed left for "Cars & Dining." He went left and pulled into a parking spot. Two human-sized doors about twenty feet apart broke the expanse of metal siding, with four big double-high garage doors beyond on his left. Coffee and cars seemed like an odd combination, but maybe not if people waiting for car repairs bought expensive drinks and snacks.

Ryan tugged down the long sleeves on his bright green shirt, then hopped out with his box. He opened the door in front of him, assuming it led to an office. Strong, slightly scorched coffee scent blasted him. A long, narrow dining room stretched ahead with an eclectic collection of tables and chairs. On his right, a group of hulking guys surrounded a big round table in dirty T-shirts and jeans. The rest of the tables were empty. The walls held a collection of early-era car memorabilia, including the entire front end of a 50s Chevy, the headlights and blinkers shining. A cute little blonde with big brown cow eyes, too much makeup, and lots of curves stood behind the counter at the far end.

Ryan walked to the counter, attempting to smile. "Hey, can you tell me where to find Aaron?"

The girl blinked at him for a few seconds. "Sure. Go back out the door and in the door next to this one." She looked him up and down. "And come back and get some coffee after you drop that off. I'll be happy to serve you." She leaned on the countertop, deepening her cleavage with her arms and smiling sweetly, fluttering her eyelashes at him.

"Thanks." Ryan turned on his heel and stomped away. She'd be happy to serve him until she discovered all his damage. Then she'd run away screaming. He'd learned that lesson. She was too young anyway. He entered the next door, stepping into a small foyer. In front of him, a door labeled "Private;" the door to his left held a smaller version of the "Cars" sign. He opened the left door.

His feet stopped. A huge garage, with four bays, but it could easily fit eight cars, with plenty of room between them. At the far end, two classic muscle cars—one a primer gray shell with boxes piled around it, the second a big silver beauty with the hood propped open. In front of him, two lifts, one with a car up high. Big red rolling tool cabinets stood against the back wall, bright stickers plastered across them. It was hard to tell from where he stood, but some of those stickers looked familiar. His shoulders tightened and rose to his ears; he rolled them.

The stickers were probably racing stickers, not military unit stickers. The sharp smell of citrus hand cleaner mixed with a little burnt oil, but the shop was clean. A long, narrow office counter on his right was empty. A pair of gray coverall-clad legs stood underneath the car on the lift, the car hiding the upper body and face. The only vaguely human-looking thing in the garage, it must be Aaron.

Ryan walked closer to the car. "Aaron? I've got a delivery from Kelly's."

The coveralls ducked out from under the car. Ryan faced a pair of brown eyes, totally different from the cow eyes on the girl next door. No, he knew these caramel brown eyes, flecked with gold, surrounded by a gorgeous, freckled, heart-shaped face, a radiant smile, masses of wavy red hair, and the hottest figure to ever grace the Elmendorf Air Force Base flight line. Shoving the box into Erin's outstretched hands, he spun, sprinting for the door, escaping to the truck. Somehow got the underpowered piece of junk to spin out in the gravel and reached the highway. His heart hammered.

Holy... Erin Moore. I'm going to kill that old coot. Jim did the whole name-confusion thing on purpose. Jackass. His fury grew with every mile. He pulled into the parking slot, threw the truck into park, and jumped out. Banging the door into the wall, Ryan marched behind the counter, throwing the keys at their hook. He pushed past his coworkers to the office door, his jaw aching.

"You! I've had enough of your jokes!" Jim's wrinkled face grinned up at him, but the silly smile disappeared when Ryan raised his right arm, bringing it back to punch Jim's smug face. A grip of steel clamped Ryan's wrist.

"Stop," the equally steely voice said. "Jim, get out front, and do some actual work."

Jim scuttled below Ryan's arm, still held back by William's hand, and scampered away like the rat he was. William let go and pointed at a chair. "Sit."

Ryan sat. *Jerk.*

William closed the door and sat, gazing at him for a long time. "Want to tell me what that was all about?" Mild interest sat on his slightly round face, the long, slightly edgy flattop haircut above it contrasting with his looks and his manner. William was one of the calmest guys Ryan had ever met—and far from edgy. He was pretty sure William's wife insisted on the haircut.

Ryan forced his jaw open. "I've had enough of the not-funny jokes. I know I'm the FNG, so I've sucked it up and taken all the crap, but I've had enough. It's been two months and today was the last straw." He owed William for giving him the job, despite his handicap and post-traumatic stress.

"FNG?"

"Freaking new guy." Sometimes it took real effort not to swear, but he'd given that up along with the military.

"Thanks for the translation. Think I heard that one from Craig too, but I couldn't remember it." William frowned. "What did Jim do this time?"

"Sent me to Coffee and Cars thinking Erin was a man."

He laughed. "I think he's pulled that one on everyone. And Erin is about as far from a man as you can get."

"Yeah."

William sobered and looked at him again, head slightly tilted.

The staring was freaking Ryan out a bit. It was also giving him time to calm down and think about what he'd almost done. His stomach churned. He'd almost decked a sixty-something-year-old guy who could barely work with all his medical issues. His shoulders tightened. "Guess I over-reacted. Sorry."

William leveled a serious, narrow-eyed look at him. "Just a little. Glad I was here, or you might have ended up in jail for assault, if not manslaughter. I'm not too sure Jim would survive a hit like that." He paused again, then frowned. "So far, you've taken all of his crap pretty well. Why now?"

Shoot. "I know Erin Moore." *Weak excuse.* He was dirt. Lower than dirt—desert sand.

"From the Service?"

"Yeah."

"And?"

"And she's had a rough time and shouldn't be the butt of some jackass's jokes." "Rough time" didn't begin to cover it. It was devastating—for all of them. Ryan trembled and clenched his hands on his thighs, trying to stop the shaking.

"Hmm. I know she lost her husband in Afghanistan. Is that what you're talking about?"

"Yeah." He hunched.

"Was there more to it?"

"Yeah. I can't talk about it." *Won't talk about it. Don't want to talk about it.*

"Okay." William nodded, lips pursed. "Look, you get a pass this time. I know Jim can be a real pain, but he knows his stuff, and he needs the health insurance. Can you work with him? He won't know who you knew in the Air Force."

Ryan took a deep breath, then blew it out, trying to regain control. "Yeah, I can do that. Look, I know I completely over-reacted. Coming face to face with Erin, with no warning, was bad." He scowled. "Guess I owe Jim an apology too."

William shook his head. "Don't bother. He's been riding you hard. Now maybe he'll remember that actions have consequences." He snorted. "Eh, probably not; Jim never learns." He pointed a finger at Ryan's chest. "But you pull something like that again, and I'll fire you on the spot. Understood?"

"Yeah. Sorry." Ryan couldn't stop shaking, but he kept eye contact.

William's mouth twisted. "Stay here until you've got it under control. I'll tell everyone to leave you alone." He stood but stared down at him. "Unless it's better to have someone here? I can ask Craig to hang out with you."

He was too perceptive. "No, it's better if I'm alone. Thanks." Craig didn't have a clue; he'd been in the military but never deployed, let alone to Asscrackistan. Lucky guy. When the door clicked, Ryan dropped his head into his hand. He'd learned to get all the emotions out, rather than try to hold them back. No sense in making everything suck more.

But instead of pain, he remembered the first time he saw Erin Moore. He was a shiny-new Airman, working in the gigantic C-17 cargo plane hangar on a bright, sunny and—unusual for Anchorage, Alaska—downright hot day. Ryan smiled. The entire crew was moaning about the heat. Technical Sergeant Moore told them to shut their traps because it was way better than Iraq or Afghanistan. He'd been over there plenty, so he knew.

Then she sauntered in, and it got real quiet.

Erin wore a bright yellow sundress, tight on the top and tied behind her neck, hugging her perfectly. The skirt flared out, but the material was thin and wrapped around those very long, very sexy legs. She broke into a run, right toward him, an enormous smile on her pretty face, long red hair waving behind her. Ryan thought he'd died and gone to heaven until she launched herself at Sarge, kissing him like there was no tomorrow.

Ryan chuckled. Clearly, he'd been caught in a fantasy.

Erin gave the Sarge something he'd forgotten at home and walked away with a swing in her step. The Sarge caught them all staring, but he didn't yell. He laughed like they were the funniest thing ever. He wiped his eyes and said, "There are many women out there, but this one is mine. Get your own!" in a parody of the Marine Rifleman's Creed.

After work, the guys filled him in. Mrs. Moore used to be Airman Murphy, public affairs. While deployed in Afghanistan, she'd done a story on C-17 operations, interviewing then-Staff Sergeant Moore. They'd hit it off right away and gotten married six months after returning to Elmendorf. Erin left the Service at the end of her commitment.

Sarge got Ryan through his first deployment without a scratch. He and the rest of the crew knew exactly where to go and what to do in every possible circumstance downrange. Sarge trained them relentlessly. It paid off for all of them. Especially for Ryan—Sarge's training saved his life, no doubt.

Maybe it would be better if it hadn't.

Come on, Walsh, don't go there today. Ryan rolled his shoulders and forced his thoughts back to the Moores.

All that training didn't help the Sarge. After the Moores transferred to McChord Air Force Base in Washington State, Sarge went back to Afghanistan. A month later, a suicide bomber blew himself to pieces in the chow hall, killing Master Sergeant-Select Moore and twenty-two others. Ryan moved to McChord only a week before the attack. The next time he saw Erin Moore was at the funeral. She wore all black and a grimly determined expression. At least Sarge hadn't left kids behind, but that probably wasn't a comfort to her.

He'd heard Erin moved to Montana after the funeral but didn't know she lived in Marcus. She was a few years older than Ryan, so they hadn't gone to high school together. She must have entered the Air Force right after high school, or he would have run into her. That's why her tool chests and stickers looked so familiar. They were Sarge's. Ryan had the same stickers on his tool chest. The stab of loss and longing hit him in the heart. He endured it, fists clenched, until he could breathe again.

Sarge had a hot classic car he'd restored himself. He must have taught Erin, or maybe that hobby brought them together. The garage was a great tribute to Sarge's memory. Ryan heard Erin was good at public affairs, and she was certainly still beautiful, so it seemed strange she wasn't working on TV. But those jobs were far and few between, especially in Montana.

Either way, thinking about Erin derailed his reaction, so he should probably get back to work. Ryan pried himself up and out of the chair. Had she married again? Sarge was killed four years ago. William knew who Erin Moore was, so if she had remarried, she'd kept Sarge's last name. Ryan shook his head. War took and took, giving nothing in return.

War took everything from him, and it just kept on taking.

Chapter 3

Small Town Trouble

Erin frowned at the door, the rebuild kit in her hand sagging toward the floor. Strange. The Kelly guys were usually pretty friendly. Other than Jim. William had hired a new guy for the early shift, so she'd expected someone different. But shoving the box at her and running seemed odd.

She shrugged and turned back to the blasted Pontiac G6. Why did people buy these? They were junk. The pan was clean, so Erin slapped the new filter in place, along with the new seal, and bolted it back up. Without torquing the bolts so hard they'd be impossible for the next mechanic to get off. With any luck, this thing would go to the great junk yard in the sky before it needed another tranny fluid change. But Mrs. Cust loved this car, and she was too mean to die, so Erin would be stuck changing it again.

Probably sooner rather than later because rich old lady Cust drove the car like the legions of hell were on her tail. Maybe that was why she didn't have an expensive Mercedes or BMW—she was too tough on them. Hard to get those serviced in the area, too; parts were special order, and some of the tools were, too.

As Erin tightened bolts, she considered the new Kelly's guy. He'd looked vaguely familiar. Medium brown hair, a little long and hanging across a rugged, sharp-edged face, pale lines crossing one cheek like a mountain lion clawed him. He was younger and a little taller than she was, and his bright green Kelly's shirt stretched tight across a powerful set of shoulders, down into a narrow waist and nicely fitted jeans. She snorted a laugh. *Get a grip, Erin. Really.* She didn't have time for everything she was doing now. She definitely didn't have time for a man.

But she couldn't shake the feeling that she knew him.

Erin torqued the bolts on Mrs. Cust's Pontiac transmission one more time, filled it, and double-checked everything else. At the sink, she scrubbed her hands thoroughly, the pumice rough on her hands and the citrus sharp in her nose. Carefully peeling off her coverall, she wiped her hands again, checked herself all the way to the soles of her boots for any leftover grease or dirt, eased into the car, and started it. She'd hate to get anyone's car dirty, but old Mrs. Cust wouldn't hesitate to raise a fuss if she found even a tiny smudge. She wouldn't pay the bill, either. Erin clicked the garage door opener and drove out. After a quick test drive, she parked in front of the coffee shop, pulled the plastic off the seat, and walked inside.

Mrs. Cust had been drinking coffee with her rich society friends earlier. Such a shock—they usually haunted classier places than Coffee and Cars. They must have been providing mutual support. Old lady Cust couldn't lower herself to the slums alone, after all. Erin smirked at her own cattiness. No sign of them; one of the posse must have taken her home. Or to their next stop, wherever that might be today. Probably some charity luncheon where they could sit around, sip tea, and tell each other how generous they were. Which was fine, because a charity got money and didn't have to find them "jobs" they'd be willing to do.

"Tiffany, please call Mrs. Cust and let her know her car is ready."

"Sure, Erin. I'll do it right after I finish cleaning Izzy."

Amazingly enough, Tiffany was cleaning the Italian espresso machine. Erin usually ended up doing it, cursing the entire time, because the longer it sat dirty, the harder it was to clean. After Tiff left, she would double-check. Last time she "cleaned" Izzy, Erin almost got the milk foaming wand through her foot. Erin sighed. At least she was here and trying. Sort of.

"Thanks. I appreciate it." Erin checked the clock. One hour before Tiffany left—enough time to get something on the 'Cuda. She'd call Mrs. Cust later; the easily distracted girl wouldn't remember.

Skirting Tiffany, she headed for the 1968 Plymouth Barracuda, her latest project car. Erin preferred to buy a car and restore it her way, but sometimes it was easier to give in and take the money from a customer than argue. This one belonged to Chaz Cust, old Mrs. Cust's son, one of the richest men in town. He was rich thanks to his grandfather, who'd made a fortune investing in the 1950s housing boom, then the 1970s oil boom, and the subsequent bust. Granddad made out like a bandit, literally—many compared him to one of the robber barons of old, like Marcus Daly the Copper King, the town's namesake.

Unfortunately, Chaz didn't have his granddad's brain or style. Chaz had looks when he was a football star at Marcus High, but that was the pinnacle of his greatness, other than in his own mind. He blew through Mommy's money, but she had lots, so it wasn't really a problem for anyone. Except Erin. Since she'd agreed to work on his car, Chaz had decided Erin was desperately in love with him but couldn't get over the guilt of her husband's death. Chaz thought he could wine, dine, and/or badger his way into her heart.

Or bed, which is all Chaz really wanted. Erin shuddered.

Equally unfortunately, Chaz was five years older than she was, five inches shorter, had a brain a fifth the size of hers, about five hairs left on his head, a gut five inches deep, and, most importantly, was fifty times slimier than anyone she'd dealt with before. Adding insult to injury, the Custs were very good customers of Mom's bank, so she couldn't offend the idiot too much. She really hoped Chaz wasn't the "gentleman" Mom set her up with on Saturday. She'd told Mother she was walking right back out the door if she ever invited Charles "Chaz" Cust again. Erin shook her head. But Mom never listened to her.

This time, though, she would walk out. She'd had enough. She would not sit through another production fending off Mr. Hands after the lights went down. Her lip curled, remembering the last time. She'd really wanted to watch the acrobatic act, but no, she hardly saw any of it because she was too busy deflecting Cust. Mother could go pound sand. Erin would buy her own ticket so she could enjoy the show. Maybe she'd invite the new guy from Kelly's. Her laughter echoed through the garage.

Despite the ugliness of her owner, the 'Cuda would be a beauty. Erin ran a hand over the fender, the primer catching the calluses on her fingers. Chaz probably paid way too much money for it. Erin smirked. He'd keep paying top dollar. She was charging him her highest rates, plus storage fees, plus an extra annoyance percentage. Not that she labeled it that way. No, that was an "energy surplus" or some other nonsense she'd come up with when she wrote their contract. And if he got really annoying, she could add recycling fees, research fees, and the ever-popular handling fee. Each expense was stated in the contract he'd signed. She wasn't cheating him, but she'd already used most of his ten-thousand-dollar deposit. Erin sighed.

If she wanted Cust out of her life, she had to get his car finished.

She'd already stripped everything off the car, had the body and frame professionally prepped, and the new wiring harness was in place. Picking up the brake line she was working on, Erin contemplated the six foot long, three-sixteenth inch diameter tube of stainless steel. Adjusting the odd curves and bends was a bit of a challenge—these aftermarket lines never fit quite right. And she had to check every single change, making sure it didn't interfere with any of the other necessary pieces and parts mounted on the car. It was a difficult, fussy task but satisfying.

Surprisingly, Chaz wanted a car he could drive, not a show car. Erin upgraded the working parts to a higher safety standard, like using stainless steel brake lines rather than the original mild steel. Stainless was much harder to bend. And expensive, if she messed up.

As she tested the fit of her latest change, the door to the coffee shop opened. Tiffany called, "Erin, I'm out of here. I've cleaned Izzy and everything else. I'll lock the door on my way out."

"Great. Thanks a lot, Tiffany. I'll see you in the morning."

"Sure. See you then."

Erin sighed, put the brake line down, cleaned her hands, and took the time to put some moisturizer on, too. With the beating her hands took, every little bit helped. Then she stripped off the coveralls and returned to the coffee shop. First, she checked the front door; Tiffany had locked it. The drive-through window was not only unlocked but wide open. She locked it, then started on the closing checklist she'd written when Tiffany started. Not that a checklist seemed to do much good, since Tiffany checked the step off as "done" no matter what.

She wiped counters, the scent of bleach warring with coffee. The idea was perfect. An employee in the mornings to pull espresso while Erin rebuilt classic cars. In the afternoons, Erin would man the coffee shop and use the time between customers to order parts and do research. In reality, Erin spent most mornings in the coffee shop because Tiffany wasn't reliable. Or fast enough.

Or anything enough.

If only Erin could find someone who would take the apartment above the coffee shop in exchange for working in the mornings, as she'd originally planned. But, as long as she had to pay Tiffany a salary, Erin had to take outside work like the maintenance on Mrs. Cust's car to pay the bills. And that meant closing the coffee shop after noon to work on her classics. Even when the coffee shop was officially "closed," it was rarely empty. Organizations used the shop for meetings, paying a flat fee for coffee and snacks and serving themselves. Unfortunately for her, they were all non-profits, so Erin earned nothing but goodwill.

Eventually, she'd like to hire a couple of reliable high-school kids for the after-school crowd and moms desperate for an afternoon pickup, but that hadn't happened yet either. Not enough hours in the day. Erin counted out the till, set it up for tomorrow morning, and took the bank bag for her afternoon rounds. Peering out the window, Erin grinned at the bright sun and blue skies.

In the garage, she clicked the far-end door opener and hopped in Smoky, Michael's 442. She grinned when the engine turned over with a roar. It quickly settled to a high idle, pushing fluids through the engine and joy through her heart.

Michael loved this car, and it showed. The 1968 Peruvian Silver Hurst/Olds 442 wasn't a popular muscle car, like a Mustang or a GTO, but it could scream off the line much faster. Especially this model—one of only five hundred and fifteen produced. When Michael was still too young to drive, he pulled it out of a field and restored it to driving condition. Every time he had a little extra money, it went into the car, along with a lot of elbow grease and love.

Erin ran a hand over the velvety dark gray upholstery. She'd learned on the 442, too. As she helped Michael with his project cars, she became a better mechanic. Eventually, she got good enough to keep working while he was deployed. In Michael's limited time at home, he concentrated on his favorite part, rebuilding engines. Erin did or arranged for everything else. Other than the bedroom, their favorite place was the garage. The neighbors commented enviously on their "made in car heaven" relationship.

A classic car restoration shop was their post-retirement dream, but dreams became plans and then reality when Mother commanded their presence for a big bank anniversary celebration. Driving around Marcus to avoid spending time with Mom, they'd spotted the property. The main building was nothing but a shell, a huge open room with nothing inside. They watched the listing and scooped it up after the price dropped dramatically. When their realtor complained about the lack of good espresso shops north of town, they decided adding a coffee shop with a drive-through would be a good second revenue stream. They both loved coffee and knew the car business wasn't steady or stable. But adding the coffee shop plus the upstairs apartment meant getting a loan—they couldn't do it with just their savings. Especially when they'd planned on having kids. So Erin took some small business classes and wrote a business plan.

Then Michael was killed. She tightened her grip on Smoky's steering wheel. She'd run back home to grieve and hide. But only two months later, her loving mother decided it was time for Erin to stop mourning, whether she was ready or not. Mom invited single men over for dinner and held parties each weekend. Mom's house no longer a haven, Erin updated their business plan, making an appointment to discuss the loan while Mother was traveling. After a glowing report from the loan officer, Mom had no choice but to approve it. Erin grinned. Especially after she reminded Mother how bad it would look if Erin went to a rival bank. Angered, she approved the loan but stepped up her campaign on Erin's love life. Erin moved into the bare-bones apartment above the coffee shop, doing much of the finish work herself. That didn't stop Mom from trying to set her up with the "right kind" of man.

Most of the time, it wasn't worth fighting about. She would go, be polite, and never think about that particular guy again. Then Chaz told Mom that Erin was the love of his life, and the war began. To Mom, he was the perfect man, simply because he was rich. Perhaps that was the appeal of the new people Mom was associating with—sheer wealth.

Erin shuddered and hit the accelerator to kick the engine down to its normal low rumble. Her entire body rumbled with it. Cust and company could go pound sand; she had Smoky. She pulled out of the garage, driving slowly down the gravel driveway to avoid dinging the paint. At the highway, she stepped on the gas, hard, and laughed. Pure, old-fashioned horsepower never got old—the heart-pounding thrill ran right over the depression, loneliness, and guilt.

Slowing as she rolled into town, Erin made her deposit at the bank, then drove sedately through town to Deb's Bakery. She and Deb graduated from high school together, but when Erin entered the Air Force looking for adventure and money for college, Deb stayed in Marcus and married her high school sweetheart. After Deb's sleaze ball husband decided dealing drugs to kids was better than working a real job and ended up in jail, Deb started a bakery. In the mornings, the active, retired set hung out when they weren't out fishing, hiking, or gardening, and kids dropped by after school. Deb had a delivery service, but Erin wanted to see her friend—and the sun.

Erin entered the bakery's back door, knowing Deb would be madly mixing, baking, and decorating. About once a week, Erin got to taste test a new recipe—a wonderful experience for her mouth but terrible for her hips. Which led to her next semi-regular stop, the late afternoon Crossfit class. But not today.

Inhaling deeply, cinnamon, chocolate, and delicious browned butter filled her senses. Her tummy rumbled in response. "Deb?"

"Decorating!"

Erin passed the still-hot ovens, the cooling racks, and the huge stand mixers, to the decorating table. Before she said anything, Erin peeked around the corner, into the shop's small eating area. Erin did not want to run into any of her would-be boyfriends, especially Chaz. Fortunately, only Deb's regulars sat there. "How's it going?"

Deb never looked up from the cake, piping elaborate silver figures across pristine white fondant with a big pastry bag. A white cloth cap contained her long strawberry blonde hair, and bright frosting smeared her white coat. "Today's a good one. Lots of orders for the next couple of weeks, but spaced so it's doable, and plenty of customers, but not too many. Perfect, all in all, which makes me wonder when the cheesecake will crack."

Erin snorted. "I figured the pessimism was coming eventually, but really? In one sentence, you go from 'it's great' to 'the world will end'?"

"It does, ya know?" Deb chuckled.

Erin laughed. "I know. Got another command performance with Mom on Saturday night. If it's Cust, I'm turning right around and walking out."

"Ew, yes." Deb's nose wrinkled. "He's slimy."

Erin nodded. "But his money isn't, and I've got a lot to make on restoring his car, so I guess I'd better get back to it."

"I still can't believe you agreed." Deb shook her head.

"I agreed before I knew Mom was trying to set me up with him. I never dreamed she'd keep trying so hard for so long with so many losers. Especially Chaz." Erin shuddered.

"Maybe if you leave her with the losers, she can hook up with them. Your mother would be the quintessential cougar if she'd loosen up a little." Deb grinned.

Erin laughed. "Wouldn't she? I think that's why she picks them; she's looking for somebody who'd be right for her, not me. But Cust's simply a money thing. I don't think Mom likes him at all, personally." She stared at Deb's display case. "I'm not sure what's really going on. She's made comments about him being a spendthrift loser in the past, and I think she'd hate having him for a son-in-law, so why is she giving into his pressure?"

"Lots and lots of lovely money?" Deb chuckled.

"Maybe, but it's still Mrs. Cust's money, not Chaz's."

"Maybe mommy dearest is pressuring your mom. Or because it will be Chaz's money eventually."

"True. Unless he runs through it all." Erin frowned.

"Wouldn't surprise me. If anyone could, it would be him. He's an idiot." She drew another figure across the cake. "Hey, Erin?"

"Yeah?"

"There's something else going on with your mother. She's sent a couple of people to talk to me about investing in my business. I pay my loans on time, and I've never expressed any interest in having investors, silent or otherwise." Deb's shoulders hunched, then she shook them out and looked up at Erin, her brows wrinkled. "I politely send them on their way, but they're persistent. And a little scary."

Erin grimaced. "I don't know what's going on there, Deb. You know I stay away from Mom's business as much as possible. But she's inviting some strange men to her dinner parties, and they make me nervous, too. I'd rather deal with Cust. I can ask her to stop sending them to you."

"No." Deb returned to piping. "No, I'll send her a formal letter. That way, it's all on record. Sorry, I shouldn't have brought it up."

"No, you should." Erin patted Deb's shoulder

gently, so she didn't smear the cake. "You and I have always been there for each other. Don't hesitate to vent or ask for help. I'll always do what I can."

Deb flashed a smile. "Same here. We need to get together for a longer session sometime soon."

"We do." Erin sighed. "But for now, I need to get going. My stuff's in the back?"

"Yup, on the cooling rack like usual. See you tomorrow? Maybe I won't be stuck staring at a cake the entire time you're here." Deb piped another figure.

"It would be nice to see your face a little more, but I get it. Got to make dollars when you can. Bye!" Erin headed to the back and grabbed her big box. Carefully loading the box into the trunk, she drove back through town, right at the speed limit. With the north-south main street also being a state highway, it meant Marcus City Police, the County Sheriff and the State Patrol were all looking for speed violations. And they'd love to pull over Smoky.

Rumbling along, Erin arrived at the last light in town. *Yes, red!* Most people weren't happy about red lights, but this one was Erin's favorite—if she was first in line. When the light turned green, she dropped the hammer. The tires squealed, then caught, pushing her body back into the seat. Grinning, she reached the speed limit and let off the gas. So much fun.

A mile down the road, a horrible thrashing and thwacking came from the engine compartment. Her smile fell off. Turning off the engine, she coasted onto the highway's shoulder, the racket decreasing. She hopped out and opened the hood. As expected, Smoky had broken a fan belt. Noisy and annoying but an easy fix. Erin always kept an extra in the trunk; these old cars were touchy. Opening the trunk, she pawed through the duffle bag holding her tools and spare parts. No belt. Erin slumped. She must have forgotten to replace it last time.

She sighed and pulled out her phone. Hopefully, Kelly's could bring her one, since she really didn't want to bother anyone else, especially Mother. She did not want to hear any whining about her job. Not today.

Chapter 4

Car Problems

Ryan snatched the phone on the third ring. "Kelly's Auto Parts, lowest price always, may I help you?"

"Yes, please. I need a fan belt for a 1968 Chevy Olds/Hurst 442, with the W-45 engine," a brisk female voice announced over a lot of background noise.

Wow. Year, make and model, and engine type, without being asked. Ryan typed the information into the parts database, and the listing came up. "Do you want the basic one or the better one, ma'am?"

"The better one, and I want two, please."

His day was getting better. A pleasant voice using the word "please." Miracles did happen. "Sure, we've got them." He scribbled the part number on a note pad.

"Charge them to Coffee and Cars, please." A heavy sigh followed. "And is there any chance you can deliver them? Now?"

Blast, a delivery to Erin Moore. "Sure." Ryan's shoulders hunched.

"And... I need them delivered to—oh, this is embarrassing—the side of the highway about a half-a-mile north of town. The car is silver with black stripes. I don't think you can miss it."

"I guess not. Be right there, ma'am." If she needed a rescue, he was on it.

"Don't call me 'ma'am.' It's Erin. Ma'am is my mother." She laughed.

Ryan smiled; her laugh sound exactly the same. "Yes, ma—Erin. I'll try."

"Thanks."

"You're welcome. I'll be right there."

"Thanks again."

He hung up the phone, printed out the receipt, found the belts, and grabbed the keys to the delivery truck. "William, got a delivery. Might take me a while; Erin Moore is stranded on the side of the road."

William glanced at the belts and chuckled. "Nah, you give her those, she'll have one on before you can say 'Party on, dude!'"

"What?" What did fan belts have to do with parties?

He chuckled. "Never mind; you're too young. Take your time."

Ryan slid his sunglasses on. Maybe this time he wouldn't act like a complete idiot. Driving north, he looked for a big silver muscle car, and despite his anemic truck, he found Erin's car quickly. He pulled up behind her, put his hazards on, and hopped out with the belts and receipt. He squinted. The sleek silver beauty was almost too shiny in the bright sunlight. Erin obviously took good care of it, which he'd expect from Sarge's wife.

Walking up the side of the car, buffeted by the wind, noise, and fumes of passing cars and trucks, he held the belts out. "Here you go, ma'am—I mean Erin."

Wow. A tight T-shirt and tighter jeans outlined sexy curves, leaning into the engine compartment. More gorgeous than the car. She was smoking hot. Erin straightened and turned toward him. He'd forgotten how tall she was, only an inch shorter than his six feet. Her face was equally beautiful, even with no makeup, her hair pulled back in a ponytail and dusky purple circles under her eyes. Lack of sleep from owning her own business, or was she still mourning the Sarge? Maybe both—grief took time.

Erin grabbed a belt and turned back to the car. She tossed it on the air cleaner and yanked the wrench in her hand. "Thanks a lot. Can you throw the other one in my trunk?"

Ryan pulled his eyes off her backside. "Sure." Shoot, he didn't want to leave her here on the side of the road by herself. "Uh, do you want any help?"

Erin spun, hands on her hips. "You're kidding, right? You realize I'm a mechanic?" She bit off the words.

He raised a hand, remembering at the last second

to leave the left one down. "Yes, ma—Erin. Just trying to be polite."

"Oh. Sorry." She grimaced. "Guess I'm a little sensitive about it."

"No problem." He stepped away but stopped to admire Sarge's car. It must comfort Erin to have something real, something solid to hang on to. He wished he had something real from his lost squadron mates. Most of them hadn't lived long enough to own anything but a few clothes and a beat-up car.

"What's your name, anyway?"

He turned back. "Ryan. Ryan Walsh." He held out his hand, and she shook firmly.

"Nice to meet you, Ryan. You already know I'm Erin, I guess." Her eyes narrowed, and she seemed to examine his face. "You look familiar. Have we met?"

He swallowed hard. "Yeah, actually we have. A while ago. A long while." He grimaced, unsure how she'd react. His right hand clenched, his left tried. "I was on your husband's crew at Elmo."

Erin leaned closer. "Oh! I remember you. The long hair threw me off."

Ryan forced a smile. More likely, it was the scars across his face. "Yeah, had enough of the military thing."

She chuckled. "I get that. Wore mine long and down for a couple of years after I got out."

"I remember." He recalled it all too well.

"You're not working for an airline?" Erin tilted her head.

He definitely didn't want to talk about his issues.

"No."

She gave him an impersonal, polite smile, probably reacting to his abruptness. "Next time you bring something out to my shop, grab a cup of coffee first—on the house, of course—come back and talk. I'd love to know what you've been doing."

"Sure." Ryan nodded once. "See you then." *No way.* Erin Moore made him want things he couldn't have. She was way out of his league, even without all his damage. He trudged to the truck and drove to the shop, trying not to think about Erin. He failed miserably. In the shop, he put the keys on their hook and grabbed his soda.

"Ryan, can you get the phone?" William yelled from the office.

Jim was missing again. "Yeah, sure." He fumbled but scooped it up before the fourth ring. "Kelly's, lowest price always, can I help you?"

"Uh, yeah. There's something wrong with my car. Can you help me?" a high-pitched female voice whined.

"Maybe. What's the problem?"

"It's making a funny sound. Here, listen."

All Ryan heard was static and a clicking noise, a pause, and more clicking. "Ma'am, I'm sorry, but what am I listening to?" Expecting a diagnosis of a car problem, a noise, over a buzzy cell phone connection with no idea of what it might be, was asking way too much.

"Can't you tell? There's something wrong!" Yikes, that was a nasty squeal she had going on there, but

Kelly's didn't sell vocal cord lubricant.

Ryan lowered his voice in an effort to get her to lower hers. "What part of the car am I listening to, ma'am? What part of the engine are you putting the phone near?"

"It's not the engine, it's at the back of the car!"

He winced at the even higher screech; his tactic clearly didn't work. "Ma'am, where at the back of the car?"

"Like, it's where you put the gas in!"

Ryan frowned. "The gas cap? You're turning the gas cap?"

"Well, yeah!"

"Ma'am, it's supposed to make that noise. That lets you know it's fastened."

"But I'm at the gas station and it won't come off!"

"Ma'am, you have to push in and turn at the same time."

"It worked!" -click-

Ryan hung up the phone, shaking his head. He muttered, "You're welcome." What he really wanted to say was, "Take the car back; you're too stupid to own one," but that would get him fired. Besides, he was being uncharitable; maybe she couldn't read. Still, a thank you wasn't too much to ask.

He wasn't at the shop long; he made delivery after delivery, and his shift extended. Their other delivery driver didn't show up or even call in. Ryan felt bad for William, although he appreciated the addition to his paycheck. When the end of the day finally rolled around, he was wiped, and his arm ached.

After work, Ryan hit a drive-through. His stomach gnawed on his backbone, and he didn't feel like cooking. At his mom's house, he let himself in and padded down the stairs. He didn't want to talk to anyone. Not today—too many people for too many hours. No workout either—he needed pure couch potato time.

Plopping down on the full-size bed, he sighed. His old bed was a little saggy. He'd get a queen or king whenever he got his own apartment. He'd looked, but there wasn't much available in his price range, not where he'd feel safe living. And "safety" wasn't physical safety—overall, Marcus was quiet and peaceful. He couldn't live near a bar—the noise and commotion would drive him crazy or trigger his post-traumatic stress, and the temptation to drink himself into oblivion would be too much. He'd done enough of that at Walter Reed Army Hospital. He'd learned excessive alcohol made everything worse.

He didn't want to live downtown for the same reasons. But he didn't want to live in the middle of nowhere because it would cost too much in gas and time to get to work. He stuffed a French fry in his mouth. A place of his own was a problem that wouldn't get solved today. Scrolling social media was boring. So was his email and e-reader. He didn't feel like watching TV either.

Restless, he thought about Erin Moore. "Smoking hot" didn't begin to describe her. She was beautiful, with a generous laugh and happy smile. And legs that went on for miles, plus all that red hair...

He dropped his head, groaning. He was lusting after the Sarge's wife. That was so wrong.

But the Sarge was gone. He'd been killed... almost four years ago. Erin should have a boyfriend or be remarried, have some kids, maybe. But the rumor mill said she was single. The guys in Marcus were dumb. Beauty, brains, her own business—she was a catch. Ryan sighed. Owning a business wasn't easy, so maybe she didn't have time to date. Maybe she didn't want to date.

Ryan sniffed. He could understand that. Dating was hard. For someone like him, it was impossible. Maybe she was tired of sorting through the duds; it would take a lot of time and effort. But if he were dating her, he'd find things to do that wouldn't take time away from her business, like bringing her a picnic dinner, or taking her to a classic car show, or offering to help work on the cars or do research on the cars, or just about anything, as long as it was with her. Not that she'd want anything to do with him; he was too damaged. His mouth twisted. He'd given up on a lot of dreams. Erin Moore was one more.

Chapter 5

The Future Is Milky

Erin leaned into the Barracuda's engine compartment. Where was the master cylinder mounting point? Disc brakes were a factory option in 1968, so it ought to be easy to find, but... Like so many other things that ought to be easy, it wasn't. Not on a classic car. The metal crease of the fender bit into her legs.

High-pitched screeching penetrated the shop wall. Erin jumped, dropping her wrench with a clatter on the concrete floor. *Trouble.*

Sprinting into the coffee shop, Erin stopped just inside the door. *What in the world?*

Tiffany and another girl screamed at each other, arms waving around wildly, milk running down their faces and clothes. Milk was *everywhere*—sticky white coated the floor, the walls, and the countertops. Izzy was covered too; scorched milk hung in the air and steam hissed wildly out of the wand, with nothing to catch it. Erin cranked Izzy off and turned on the two women. "What is going on here?!"

Silence rang for a split second, and then both girls turned toward her and screeched, waving crazy arms again. The loggers at the end of the room grinned, enjoying the show. Not surprising; not only was it a girl fight but a wet T-shirt contest too. Erin glared at the two girls—definitely not women. *Wait a minute.* They both wore the exact same T-shirt, some custom air-brushed hot pink thing with a guy's name in fancy writing. *Aw, rats.* Teenage girls and boys. Too many hormones, not enough brain cells.

"Stop! Sit down and shut up!" Erin barked in her best Michael imitation, pointing at both of them.

It worked. Sort of. The girl on the far side of the counter plopped into a chair and cried. Tiffany turned to Erin with big puppy dog eyes and pouting, trembling lips.

"Tiffany, start cleaning up this mess. I want every bit of milk mopped up and the whole place sanitized." Erin snapped the commands but didn't wait to see if it worked. She grabbed a wet cloth and a dry one, handing them to the other girl. "Here, get yourself cleaned up."

Erin's boots were already sticking to the floor. Good thing she'd sealed the concrete. She called to the loggers, "One of you gentlemen want to tell me what happened?" It wasn't really a request. The show over, they were retreating. They looked at each other and one shrugged.

The bearded giant came over, stopping before he stepped into the milk splatter, and took off his beat-up ball cap, staring down at her. "We're not sure how it got started, but there was a lot of yelling and screaming and using the 'B' word, ma'am, if you get my drift."

Erin nodded at him to continue.

"Then this girl here—" he pointed at the girl crying in the chair "—she grabbed the milk container on the counter and threw it in Tiff's face, so Tiff grabbed the other one and threw it back, and ma'am, that's when you walked in." He backed away. "Gotta get to work. Sorry, ma'am."

"Thanks. Appreciate you telling me. Have a good day, guys." She waved as they turned tail and ran. If only she could do the same. Erin glared at the two girls. "I will not tolerate reckless and destructive people in my place of business. You." Erin pointed at the girl sitting and crying. "What's your name?"

The girl sniffled. "Kaylee Adams."

"Kaylee Adams, I am officially notifying you that I am refusing you service. If you come back to my place of business, I will have you charged with trespassing. Is that understood?"

"What?! That's not fair! She started it!" Kaylee pointed an accusing finger at Tiffany and then swung it to Erin. "You'll be sorry!" Kaylee jumped up, wobbling on her ridiculously high heels, threw the dishcloths on the floor, and stormed out the door.

"Good riddance." Erin turned to Tiffany. "And what do you have to say for yourself?"

Tiffany was scowling. "She called me a loser because I was wearing the same T-shirt she was. She's the loser! He's mine!"

"This is about a T-shirt?"

"This was my favorite T-shirt! Brad gave it to me!" Wailing, she dropped into the chair Kaylee left.

Erin rolled her eyes. She'd been right. "And precious Brad gave her the same T-shirt?"

"Yes!!!"

Erin couldn't help it. She laughed. Tiffany's face crumpled into hurt disbelief. "Why are you laughing?! Brad is the love of my life!" Tiffany rose, stamping her foot on the floor like a three-year-old.

"He gives all his girlfriends the same T-shirt? What an idiot." Erin shook her head.

"He's not an idiot! I didn't know Kaylee had one too. I'm going to kill Brad when I see him!" Tiffany looked murderous. If a brand-new baby calf could be murderous.

"He's an idiot." Erin laughed harder.

"I can't believe you're laughing at me! This isn't funny! My life is over! I quit!" Tiffany threw down her towels and stomped out the door, leaving it open. Then she stamped back in, ducked behind the counter, grabbed her purse and coat, and slammed the door. The rest of Erin's customers followed, with commiserating looks and unconcealed laughter.

Erin kept laughing, but her chuckles turned to despair and finally died entirely as she surveyed the mess. *Rats.* White splotches of milk tracked across the dining area floor, all the way to the door. She wrote two signs: "Temporarily closed due to equipment malfunction. See you tomorrow," and taped them to the drive-through window and the front door, which she locked. At least the morning rush was over.

Erin pulled out buckets, soap, and bleach, cleaning the bottom of her boots first. She had a long day of scrubbing and sanitizing ahead. Erin laughed gloomily. Next, she'd have to find a replacement for Tiffany.

Yup, a very long day.

By the middle of the next week, the long day had turned into a series of never-ending days. Yet another potential employee hadn't bothered to show up for their interview. Not even a phone call. A week of spreading the word and she'd had little luck. Guess she'd have to post the position with the Job Service, which meant sorting through a hundred applications, most of them totally unsuitable. She yawned.

Between getting up early to run the coffee shop, staying up late to work on the 'Cuda, and making phone calls in the afternoons to set up interviews, Erin wasn't getting much sleep. She rarely slept well these days, but now that she was tired enough to sleep like a log, she was too short of hours to sleep in. And she couldn't even visit her friends; not enough hours in the day. Deb's delivery person brought her pastries, and the bank courier picked up her deposit.

As the door opened, she yawned again. William from Kelly's Auto Parts entered with a blast of highway noise. Erin forced herself to her feet. "Hi, William. Get you some coffee?"

He waved a big silver and green travel mug. "Brought my own mug. I'll get it, thanks." He loaded his mug at the drip coffee station and crossed to her. "I'm out doing my regular sales calls. I heard a rumor about you having some sort of girl-fight here, so I thought I'd stop in and get the actual story." He huffed a laugh but looked sympathetic.

Erin sat at a table, waving her hand in invitation. "It was a fight over a guy. A stupid guy. This idiot gives all his girlfriends a custom air-brushed T-shirt." She rolled her eyes. "The same T-shirt, of all the dumb things to do in a small town."

William laughed, shaking his head. "That's hilarious. What a doorknob."

"Yep, but when I said that to Tiffany, that's when she got upset and quit. I thought she'd calm down and come back, but no such luck. I've got to find somebody reliable, preferably somebody who will do the job in exchange for the apartment upstairs."

William sipped his coffee and tipped his chair back. "We may be able to help each other out. Corporate is telling me my payroll is too high. They think I don't need another part-time driver. Technically, they're right. But only until someone gets sick or doesn't show up. Then I need that extra guy. My new guy, Ryan, is reliable, an outstanding worker, and I don't want to lose him, but if I cut his hours too much, he'll find something else." William scowled and shook his head. "He's totally wasted as a driver anyway—he's way too smart, and he's good with the customers, if a little, hmm, quiet."

"So, we can help each other out how?"

"I know Ryan's been looking for someplace to rent. He's living in his mom's basement, and I think it's driving him nuts. It's hard to tell because unlike most of the guys, he doesn't talk much. He's got some issues left over from the Service too, but you'd understand that better than I would." William shrugged. "Anyway, if he takes your job, then I can cut his hours and maybe not lose the guy entirely."

Erin wasn't so sure. Ryan seemed awfully skittish. "It's a good thought, but I've invited him to come out and talk, and he won't. I don't know if it's me, or him, or both." She shrugged, chuckling. "I'm pretty sure his tips won't be as good as Tiffany's."

William laughed. "Or maybe you'll get an entirely new clientele. The little old ladies love him because he's nice and helpful." William cackled. "Put him in a tight T-shirt and you'll have cougars filling the place."

Erin laughed with him. *I wouldn't mind seeing him in a tight T-shirt. Does that make me a cougar?* She considered William's proposal for a moment. "I think you should bring it up to Ryan first, and then send him out here." She grimaced. "If he's even willing to talk to me, let alone work for me."

"Sure." He grinned. "I'll tell him corporate's cutting my hours, but I know a great deal that will make it up to him." He looked at her, raising his brows. "You'd want him working, what, six to eleven?"

"If he's taking the apartment, I'd want him to work six to ten for the apartment and preferably ten to eleven for pay. What hours do you need a driver?"

"I'd like one to four." He grinned. "That gives him time for a sandwich, a nap, and the drive to Kelly's. Now, if we can get him to see what a great deal this is, it will work out perfectly."

"We'll have to line up vacation too. I'll be shutting the shop down for a couple of weeks in September and taking a couple of long weekends this summer. Of course, he's free to work for you during those periods or take vacation when I do." She smiled and shrugged. "That's paid vacation, sort of, since he'll still be in the apartment."

"I'm sure we can make that all work out. My other part-timer will take extra shifts occasionally, although he warned me they were taking a long September vacation too." William waved a hand. "It'll work. I'll make it work." He frowned, then added, "But you need to get Ryan to tell you about his issues and limitations before you hire him. Maybe test him out on the espresso machine to make sure he can do it."

Erin frowned, puzzled. "Oh? What issues?"

William shook his head. "I can't share any medical stuff with you. You know that, right?"

"Ah." She shrugged one shoulder. "Okay, we'll do some test drinks and talk. If you can get him to come here at all."

"I'm pretty sure I can sell this deal." William stood and raised his mug to her. "Thanks for the coffee."

"Anytime. Get a fill up whenever you're here. Or passing by." William was one of the good guys. He waved as he left, and Erin locked the door behind him.

She didn't remember Michael saying much about Ryan, probably because he was a good, hard worker and did his job right—Michael complained about the troublemakers. Although, now that Erin thought about it, Ryan had been over to their house a few times in Alaska. Michael hosted plenty of parties and backyard barbecues in the summer, and there were tons of people at those things—everyone loved him. Erin remembered the drunks she'd driven home better than the rest. She'd never had to drive Ryan home.

Ryan seemed awfully standoffish, though she really wasn't sure whether it was because of Michael, or if it was her, or maybe just the way he was. She couldn't ask about the medical issues, but hopefully he'd open up on his own. He should be an airplane mechanic—Michael would have made sure Ryan was an expert. Even if he couldn't find a position with an airline, Marcus had plenty of open automobile mechanic positions. Sure, there was a learning curve, but he had the basics; he'd catch up in no time at all. But maybe the medical issues William hinted at were severe enough to keep him from being a mechanic.

Knocking sounded from the door. She called,

"We're closed, sorry!" but they kept rapping. She tromped to the door, her boot heels thudding in contrast to the fast, annoying knocking, and opened the door a few inches. "Yes?"

A short, stocky man in beat-up, dirty canvas overalls held up a big manila envelope. He peered up at her from under an equally dirty baseball cap. "Are you Erin Moore?"

Kind of a sketchy looking delivery driver. She didn't let go of the door and blocked it with her foot. "Yes, I am. What can I do for you?"

He pulled papers out of the envelope and handed them to her. "You're hereby served. You've got copies there of the official filings. I have the original if you'd like to see it."

Erin looked at the paperwork. Sure looked official. "No, that's okay. I'd say thanks, but I'd be lying." *Great.* She was being sued.

"Just doing my job."

"Yeah." She closed and locked the door, sat down at the nearest table, and started reading. The thing was in legalese, but it seemed Kaylee Adams was suing her for mental distress and some sort of damages, plus attorney's fees. Great. Erin sighed. Good thing she had a brilliant lawyer. *This puts the topper on a cake of sucky.* Shaking her head, Erin pulled out her phone.

Late the next afternoon, Erin finished her story about Tiffany and Kaylee, sat back, and gazed wistfully at her friend and lawyer, Samantha Kerr. Impeccably dressed as usual, in fitted black slacks, a beautiful ruby-red silk top, chunky silver jewelry, and her long, honey-colored hair wrapped into a tasteful updo. Erin was underdressed and outclassed. Sam was elegance personified. Fortunately, her insides matched the outside.

Sam frowned. "You won't like what I have to say, but I'll say it, anyway." Erin nodded. "It will cost you more to fight this than to settle it. I'd recommend we file an answer with the Court and schedule a settlement conference right away. I think they're trying to punish you for a spoiled brat's tantrum, but since the Adams have money, and Kaylee's their precious youngest child, they might not be willing to settle. I know their lawyer, and I'm guessing he tried to talk them out of this already, but..."

Erin nodded again, glumly. *Figures.*

Sam tapped the papers. "Do you think Tiffany will give a deposition in your favor if it comes to that? And can you find that logger?"

Erin sighed. "Tiff, maybe, maybe not. She was pretty angry when she left. The logger comes in at least a couple of times a week, but I don't know if he'd be willing to get involved."

"That's what I figured." Sam shrugged fatalistically. "Hopefully, James can get Mr. Adams to see sense once I file your answer, but Adams is a bit of a hothead. Especially when it comes to his kids." She grimaced. "I'll get a draft to you this week. If you can review it right away and send it back, that will be helpful. I'll also send you an attorney-client agreement for your signature, and I'll need a thousand-dollar deposit. If this goes before the judge, you can expect to spend five times that, easy." Sam's face was grim.

"Great." Erin sighed again. "Just what I need. I can do a thousand, but five? That will take an extension of my loan, which means Mom can put more pressure on me to date her sleazy clients. Wonderful."

Sam clamped her lips together for a second. "Sorry to ask you for the deposit, but being a small-town lawyer isn't exactly lucrative. I've got too many pro-bono clients and too many people who won't pay. I can't extend credit to anyone, not even you."

Erin held up her hands. "I understand. I'd never ask. It's tough being a small business owner."

Sam snorted. "You know how this goes. Still, this really isn't an appropriate use of the law, so I'm sorry."

"Seems like legal extortion to me." Erin sat up straight and put her nose in the air, imitating her mother. "I'm angry, so I'll sue, knowing you don't have the money to fight me. And I'm connected with all the judges in town, so they'll be on my side too." She slumped.

Sam shrugged again. "You know I can't agree with you, but..."

"I get it. But it sucks." Erin sighed.

"I will agree with you there." Sam gave her a commiserating smile, then nodded sharply. "I'll get a draft to you soon, probably tomorrow."

"Thanks, Sam." Erin left Sam's office, confirmed

her contact information with Sam's secretary, and walked out to her car. At least Smoky was reliable. More reliable than hired help anyway. And far easier to fix when he broke down.

Chapter 6

Putting out Fires

"Ryan, got a minute?" William beckoned from the office door.

"Sure. You're the boss." William pointed at the door, so Ryan closed it, the hinges squealing.

William plopped into his chair. "I got a problem."

Ryan waited. Figured he wasn't getting a pat on the shoulder. Not with a closed door.

"Corporate is hassling me about our payroll. They want me to cut it. But I've got everyone on the minimum hours now, except you. I have to cut your hours." William held up a hand to hold off the protest Ryan wouldn't bother making. Neither of them could do anything about the situation. "I don't want to because you're an outstanding employee. You show up, you're a talented mechanic, and you're calm and polite. But I have a proposal for you that might fill the gap."

"Yeah?" Since he trusted William, Ryan was unusually curious.

"Yeah. You know Erin at Coffee and Cars, right?" Ryan nodded and William continued. "Her girl got in a catfight with another girl and then she quit. The girl was a lousy employee, but now Erin's stuck. She needs someone to work the early shift at her coffee shop for her from six to eleven. Then you could come here and work one to four, if you're willing to do that." William gave him a brief smile—Ryan wasn't sure what it meant, but it didn't help the anxious tension creeping up his spine. "Erin's got some other incentives, like a private apartment, in trade for hours, but she'll talk to you about that if you're interested."

The automatic "No" for anything concerning Erin Moore abruptly changed to a "Maybe." Ryan frowned at William. "An apartment, huh? Where?"

"Right above the coffee shop." William's smile turned smug.

"Really? Now that might be interesting." It would be the perfect location, except for the proximity to Erin. Ryan's shoulders tightened.

"I can set up an interview for you. Either way, I can give you only twenty hours a week, at most."

"I don't know if I'm the right guy." Ryan snorted. "I'm not really a coffee guy. I mean, I drink it, but not that fancy stuff."

"Drip's good enough for me too, but Erin's is fantastic." William raised his brows. "She'll want to give you a test as part of the interview. I didn't tell her anything about your medical issues, of course."

Ryan scrubbed his hands through his hair, dropping the left arm immediately. "I'll have to tell her, won't I?"

William shook his head. "Not legally." He held up his hand and tipped it back and forth. "Not if you can do the job. But if you need some sort of accommodation to do the job, you'll have to let her know what that is."

"Huh. I have no idea if I can make flashy coffee drinks. Don't know how those machines work." Ryan shrugged. "Can't say I'm thrilled about the whole idea, but I definitely need my own place."

"There might be other benefits too." William smiled with a sly edge.

"Like?" William couldn't be implying anything romantic because that was patently ridiculous.

The smile grew wider. "Like space to work on your own car and use of the tools."

"Huh. Good thought." Ryan had his own tools but no place to put them. They were in storage, along with a bunch of other stuff. "I've always wanted a muscle car. Or an old truck."

William was almost grinning. "Erin's good. She could help you find one and walk you through the restoration too."

Tempting but troubling, too. "Huh. Can I think about it?"

"Sure." William shrugged. "How long?"

"I'll let you know by the end of the day."

"Perfect. Thanks." William turned to his computer.

Ryan returned to the counter. Nobody waiting for a change. A pleasant change—it'd been a busy day. He straightened the flyers near the register. He'd heard corporate was always riding William, so the cuts weren't a surprise. Better than he originally thought, which was a layoff. Sure, he could find a wage-slave job in half a dozen other places around town, but he liked Kelly's for the most part. Except Jim.

Coffee was just coffee to him, but he'd learned to appreciate micro-brewed beer, so he could learn to appreciate espresso. He liked the smell, so living above the shop would be okay. Ryan wrinkled his nose. Although, after a while it might get old. Or maybe he'd get nose-blind. Guess he'd have to talk to Erin and see what the place looked like.

His shoulders hunched and he swallowed hard. He'd have to talk to Erin. Have to tell her about his injuries, and his post-traumatic stress, and talk about Michael. And she wouldn't want to stop there, no— she'd probably insist he go back to therapy, and join a support group, and talk to her about his feelings, and... Ryan sighed. *Shoot.* And he'd be around her all the time. She was too attractive in every way, shape, and form. Working with her every day would be torture. Or maybe not. Maybe he'd hate working for her. Maybe she'd turn out to be terrible. He snorted. Not a chance. She was an awesome person. And in a tough spot, trying to hire someone decent in a tight market.

He was gonna do it. He was *such* an idiot. Ryan would smack his head on the countertop, but he'd taken enough hits. Erin Moore would *never* be interested in him, but missing the chance to spend time with her made him scream "no!" inside. At least he'd work for someone who spoke his language—they'd lived the same places, they were both Air Force, and they'd seen some of the same stuff.

William emerged from the office, clipboard in hand.

"Hey, William!" He was so dumb.

He stopped. "Yeah?"

"I'll talk to Erin. Can you set it up?" Ryan couldn't quite put a name on the mix of emotions, but hope was part of it, along with a little excitement, and a whole lot of... worry. Yeah, worry. He wasn't scared.

"Sure." William nodded. "One afternoon this week, okay?"

"I'm free other than working here." He needed to get a life.

William smiled smugly. "I'll let you know." He chuckled and returned to the office.

"Thanks. I appreciate it." Ryan stacked another case of oil on the hand truck. Stocking oil probably wouldn't take his mind off of the coming interview, but he could try. The bell on the door rang, so he walked to the counter.

"Welcome to Kelly's, can I help you?" A scruffy guy, clothes and face smeared with black streaks shuffled toward him; a normal occurrence since working on cars was a dirty job. Body odor gusted across the counter. Ryan tried to hold his breath. Showers were a good thing.

"You got a screwdriver I can borrow?" The guy tapped nervously on the counter.

"Sure, we've got some loaner tools." Ryan turned to the tool cart, taking a big breath when he got farther from the guy. "Phillips or straight?"

"Straight, man."

Ryan handed him the tool. "Here you go. Anything else?"

"Can you give me a jump?" The man jerked his head back toward the front door.

"Sure, we can do that." At the battery rack, he pulled their jumper battery. The phone rang, and he couldn't find Jim again, so by the time he got free, more than a few minutes had passed. Ryan finally got the battery and jumper cables out the front door. The guy he'd loaned the screwdriver to was working on his car's fuel system—with a cigarette in his mouth. *Brilliant.* "Uh, excuse me, sir, but could you put out the cigarette?"

"Why?" Scruffy sneered over his shoulder.

Really? Ryan kept his tone even if no longer respectful. "Because spark and fuel are a good way to start a fire." Military life could be dangerous, but customer service might get him killed at home.

"Guess so." The man put out the cigarette on the sidewalk and placed the stub inside the big rusted hunk-of-junk car through the open window. Somehow, the cig stayed intact, even with all the kids screaming and tussling inside. Then Scruffy unscrewed the connection between the fuel filter and the carburetor, reached inside the car, and turned over the engine. Fuel sprayed across the engine, carving little canyons in the built-up oil and dirt.

"Hey, turn it off. You're blowing fuel everywhere!"

"Huh." The man leaned into the engine compartment. "I thought the filter was clogged, but I guess not."

"No, guess not. Your battery is working too, since you're spraying fuel everywhere." Ryan stayed away from the disaster zone.

"But the car won't start. And the battery's getting weak."

"It's not the fuel filter." With the engine coated in leaking oil and grease, it was hard to say what the problem might be.

"Got that." Scruffy reconnected the filter and got back in the car, pushing aside a kid or two. He tried to turn it over, but sure enough, there wasn't enough juice left. "Give me a jump?"

"How much fuel is on this thing? You could start a fire, you know." It was more than probable with all the junk coating the engine.

Scruffy shook his head. "Nah, it's not that much, man. Just give me a jump."

Ryan sighed and hooked up the battery. Nothing like experience to teach someone the error of their ways. He backed away from the vehicle, ready to run inside and call 911 if it went really bad. "Okay, it's hooked up."

Scruffy turned over the engine. *Surprise, surprise.*

The engine caught on fire. Ryan circled wide around the engine compartment. Keeping his voice calm, he leaned toward the window. "Your car is on fire."

Suddenly, kids streamed out of the car, one almost knocking him over. The man turned the engine off.

Ryan twisted his hand like he was starting a car. "No, keep turning it over! It'll suck the fire back in and put it out!"

The guy actually listened and kept turning it over. The carburetor sucked the vaporized fuel down and burned it inside the engine. And the car finally started. Ryan cautiously stepped up to the vehicle. Some flames still flickered, but they were dying. "Better keep an eye on it. Make sure nothing happens until it's all out. You're probably going to need a battery."

"I don't have any money. Gonna have to make due until payday."

Ryan unhooked his battery and cables, carrying them to the door, but returned to the car. "Hey, I need the screwdriver, please."

Scruffy scowled but handed it back. Then he started yelling at the billion kids running around the parking lot to get back in the car or they wouldn't go swimming.

Really? The car was unreliable, but Scruffy was taking an unnecessary side trip. And, once again, Ryan didn't get so much as a simple thank-you. *Figures.* Snorting, Ryan walked inside. Everyone in the store, customers and employees alike, stared at him. "Yeah, yeah, show's over folks."

Chapter 7

Shocking Revelations

The bright Coffee and Cars sign seemed ominous. Ryan wiped his sweaty hand on his jeans and rotated his shoulders, trying to calm his nerves. The job didn't worry him, but the woman sure did. His new boss. Maybe. Ryan took a few deep breaths and tried to calm himself, but it really wasn't working. Time to get it over with.

A sign on the door announced a temporary hour change. Ryan entered the coffee shop, the rich, smoky scent smacking him in the nose. He trod the long, quiet room filled with empty tables, his tennis shoes squeaking slightly on the concrete.

Erin perched on a stool behind the counter, typing on a computer. She flashed a smile. "Hi, Ryan. Have a seat. I'll be right with you." She tapped at the keyboard. "Just got to finish this order."

"No rush. Not doing anything else today." He slid into a chair, gripping the seat tight to keep himself from running out the door. He didn't want her scrutiny. Or her pity.

But he didn't want to be anywhere else, either.

Erin wore jeans, a form-fitting "Coffee and Cars" logo T-shirt, her hair tied back in a ponytail, without a bit of makeup, and she was gorgeous. She bit her lip. He wanted to kiss it, make it all better. *Down, boy. You're here for a job, not a date.* Ryan shifted, uncomfortable on the hard chair.

Erin got up and sat at the table across from him. "Thanks for coming out, Ryan. What did William tell you?"

"He said your girl got in a fight and quit and that you needed someone to run the coffee shop in the morning. He also said you might exchange rent on an apartment for work and that I might get some space to work on a car." *Slow down! You sound like an idiot. You're going to blow this, Walsh.*

Erin smiled slightly. "That's the basic facts. I need help making drinks and serving folks in the mornings, so I can work on cars. I'd like to find someone who will trade work for rent on the apartment upstairs. Frankly, I'd like someone who'd work full time, but since William brokered this deal, I'm willing to compromise. Do you know anything about coffee or espresso?"

Ryan shook his head slowly. "I drink regular old coffee, not fancy drinks with stuff in them, but I can learn."

The corners of Erin's lips rose slightly. "If you're willing to learn, that's all I need. Does the trade for an apartment interest you?"

"Yeah. I've been looking, but most places that I can afford aren't places I want to live. I'd be okay living out here; it's not too far away from town, and it's pretty quiet."

Erin tilted her head and shrugged one shoulder. "There is a lot of highway noise, especially if you have the windows open. The apartment, and the rest of the building, has air conditioning and gas heat. There's also a propane fireplace."

"Wow. Nice." Nobody jumped on the deal? There had to be a catch...

"It is." Erin nodded sharply. "Tell you what—let's see how you get along with Izzy first. if you feel like this is something you can do, I'll show you the apartment. Then we'll discuss salary and compensation. Work for you?" She rose.

"Sure. But..." Ryan swallowed hard. *I do not want to do this.* Especially with Erin Moore. But better to get it over with before they continued or he met another employee, like Izzy.

Erin sank into her chair, her pretty face pinched. "But?"

Shoot. She obviously expected him to turn her down flat or ask for more money than she could afford or something. He couldn't disappoint her— she'd had too much already. He swallowed again and wiped his right palm on his jeans. "I... it's easier to show you, I guess."

Ryan put his left arm on the table, unfastened the cuff of his green Kelly's shirt, and pulled it up above his elbow. He wore his "polite" flesh-colored prosthetic today. At a glance, it looked like his other hand, except it didn't move. It wasn't particularly functional, but he could push with it, and he could hook it into the steering wheel on his car, or the Kelly's truck, so it worked well enough for the auto parts store most of the time. But he bet it wouldn't work at a coffee shop. He let his eyes rise to Erin's face, his shoulders rising with them.

Double shoot. Erin's eyes were enormous and horrified. He'd hoped she might understand... Ryan reached for the sleeve to pull it back down, but she put up her hand to stop him. She reached, resting her hand on his residual arm, above the prosthesis. "Ryan, I'm so sorry. I didn't know. I lost touch with Michael's old crews when I left McChord, but somebody should have told me about *this*." Her pretty hazel eyes were shiny, and she blinked rapidly, soft lips pressing together. "Does it hurt?"

She was *touching* him, touching his cut-off arm? Not recoiling in horror? Upset *for* him, not with him? Wait, she'd asked a question. "N-n-not usually. Sometimes. It depends."

"I'm so sorry. So..." Erin gazed at his arm and shivered. She took in a big breath and slid her hand off his arm. "But you can drive a truck and deliver parts, so you ought to be able to run an espresso machine. Might take a few modifications, but hey, mechanics here." Erin pointed between the two of them. "We can do that. No problem." Her smile seemed a bit forced but determined.

She still wanted him for the job? And wasn't going to ask how it happened? He ought to answer her question, rather than stare in amazement. "Uh, sure. I don't know anything about how they work."

"Let's go look." Slapping both hands against the table, Erin stood and strode behind the counter.

He followed, a little dazed and confused at her sympathy and her quick dismissal of his damage. He pulled the sleeve down and fastened it.

"This is Izzy, our Italian espresso maker." Erin ran a hand over the shiny silver metal of the yard-long, complicated-looking machine.

Ryan almost laughed—Izzy was a machine, not a person. Erin didn't seem to notice; she continued explaining. "Izzy can be a little temperamental sometimes, but he makes a mean espresso. The first key is the right grind. We have a very good burr grinder here." She patted a big, black cylinder that narrowed into a funnel sitting on the counter beside the espresso machine. "It's already set for the best grind for these beans and Izzy. If we change roasters in the future, we might adjust, but that's not anything you need to worry about right now."

She flicked her fingers. "Anyway, Izzy works by forcing high pressure steam through finely-ground coffee. The coffee goes in these filters." She picked up a shallow silver bowl attached to a thick black handle. "Load your filter like this." She held the bowl of the small, round filter under the burr grinder and flicked a lever. Coffee poured out, piling high. "Then pack it down with a twisting motion." She put the filter on the counter, picked up a small, dumbbell-looking thing, and poised it above the pile of coffee.

Erin looked at the filter for a few seconds, then at his arm, frowning, and back at the filter. "Now, this might be tricky. We could build a jig to hold the filter so you could pack it properly. Or, mmm, do you have other prosthetics that you could use to hold the filter while you bear down and twist?"

They weren't anything anyone wanted to see. "Maybe. I have others, one with a mechanical-looking grasper that might work better, but it tends to freak people out."

"Really?" She looked up at him, frowning. Then she rolled her eyes. "Idiots. People are idiots. I'm sorry, that sucks."

He still couldn't wrap his head around the idea that *she* wasn't freaking out about the missing arm. "Yeah, it does sometimes."

Erin shook her head sharply. "But a jig to hold the filter, fastened to the counter, would be easy enough. Then you take the packed filter and bring it up to the machine, where it seats with a twist. Izzy puts out a lot of pressure, so you have to make sure it's seated properly, or it will blow the filter out on your foot, hard, and send steam and coffee flying everywhere. But, once you get used to it, most people do this step one-handed." She demonstrated.

"Okay."

"Then you put these shot glasses below the spouts in the filter and flip the switch, and beautiful espresso comes out." She raised her voice over the hissing noise. "Now, I put a double in. I never bother with a single, because there's always a use for another shot, even if a particular customer only wants one. Which rarely happens." She grinned. "People love their coffee. As you see, we can run two filters at a time, so we can have four shots ready to go."

"People drink that much?"

Erin laughed. "Oh, yeah. Some of our regulars want quad-quads, which is four shots of espresso poured into our largest drip coffee."

"I'd jitter for a week." Ryan shuddered.

"Me too, but to each his own." Erin shrugged. "Most hot coffee drinks also take foamed milk. The amount of foam to milk is critical for each drink. Cappuccino is mostly foam, and a latte is mostly milk, with a little foam on top. Customers can order whole or skim milk or cream even. There's a bunch of different styles; I've got a guide. The foaming wand—" Erin patted a long, skinny silver thing attached toward the end of the machine "—shoots steam down into the milk. You get out a foaming pitcher, attach a thermometer to it, raise it up onto the wand, then open the valve here. The motion is circular, and you move the wand from the bottom to the top. The higher up and longer you hold it in the milk, the more foam. And it must reach the correct temperature for food safety." Erin demonstrated.

Which explained the loud screeching noise in most coffee shops. He'd never paid attention before, just got black coffee and got out.

"Now, there's a lot of subtleties that we can get into later, but what I really want to know is if you can do this or if we'd have to design some sort of tool to help you." Erin smiled, her head tilted.

"You want me to try?" *Come on, Walsh, get your act together.*

"If you think this is something you could stand to do." Her tone was tentatively hopeful and her eyes wide.

"I guess we'll see." Her demo was clear enough. Ryan reached up, unscrewed the filter from the machine, and she showed him how and where to knock the old coffee out. Then he tried to fill it with coffee. First, he got too much, then not enough, but eventually he got it. By pressing his prosthetic hand down on the filter handle, holding it in place, he could torque down and compact the coffee. But it wasn't easy, and the correct pressure would take a lot of practice. Maybe he could use a scale.

Getting the filter on the machine wasn't a problem. Ryan clicked and twisted, then let the steam flow. Coffee streamed out, and he smiled. Then he considered the milk pitcher. Balancing steaming hot milk on his fake hand seemed like a good way to get burned. Unless he watched closely, he couldn't be sure his prosthetic hand would stay flat and level, and he couldn't stare at his hand if he was checking the temperature and the amount of foam. "Uh, Erin?"

"Yes?"

Ryan swallowed hard. She'd been cool about everything so far. *Just spit it out.* "I don't think steaming milk with this prosthetic is a good idea. I can't grab it securely. One of my other ones would work okay though, especially if I hold the pitcher in my real hand and work the controls with the prosthetic."

Erin grimaced. "I definitely don't want you getting burned. I'm guessing you've already been burned, and once is enough." Her head tilted. "Do you have one of those fancy bionic arms?"

Ryan frowned, but it seemed like she was interested. Still... "Why?"

Her face shone with enthusiasm. "I think the technology is so cool, and I'd love to see what they look like underneath the covering. The level of engineering and programming is amazing." Erin paused, then frowned. "I hope I'm not offending you by geeking out about the technology. Obviously, it's not a real hand, and I don't want to lessen the severity of what you've gone through and are still going through." She looked at him, lips compressed.

She wasn't freaking out; she could geek out all she wanted. "Uh, that's okay. It's a fact of life. I don't have a forearm or a hand anymore, and a prosthetic doesn't do everything a real one can." He'd learned to adapt. "I have a couple of different ones for different tasks. Maybe I'll get one of the bionic ones someday, but the closest place for something that high-tech is Seattle. I can't have something super-fussy that needs constant adjustment."

Erin glowered. "That sucks too. Montana has a ton of vets. They should have all the services here."

"Montana's got more vets per capita than any other state, but we don't have much capita to start with so..." One of the many reasons Ryan came home—no people.

Erin laughed, the sound so happy he couldn't help but smile. "That's true. But getting back to the job, I don't think you'd want to risk a fancy hand here. Coffee stains pretty badly, and the grounds get everywhere, and I do mean everywhere." She looked at the ceiling for a second and chuckled. "Little tiny gears and motors would get jammed up." Erin shook her head slowly, her mouth turned down. "Which is too bad, 'cause I'd still love for you to have one. Doesn't seem right that you don't."

Ryan shrugged his right shoulder. "Maybe someday." He didn't really need anything high-tech—and more trouble than it was worth.

"Does this seem like something you could stand to do five mornings a week?" She lifted her eyebrows.

"Yeah, I could do this. With the right prosthetic. Is it going to freak out your customers if I've got a pinching-type thing instead of a hand?"

Erin scowled. "If they're freaked, bad on them. They can get their coffee someplace else. Is it going to bother you if people ask you how you lost it, and a whole bunch of other invasive questions?" Both her brows raised. "You know people will."

Ryan snorted. "Can I just tell them I don't want to talk about it?"

"You can." She nodded slowly, with a smirk. "Not sure it'll work, but you can definitely say that."

"It'll work. They might not come back, but it will work."

Erin laughed and held up a hand. "Okay, let me qualify that. You can tell them that—politely."

He shrugged. "I'll be polite. It's hard to keep asking when you keep getting the same answer."

"Hard for some people, not so hard for some ladies who frequent this shop. They're relentless." Erin seemed both amused and resigned. "And if they don't get an answer, they have a tendency to make things up. You have to decide which is worse." She looked at him with a challenging smirk.

"And what stories have they made up about you?"

Erin wrinkled her nose. "Oh, they think I must be a lesbian since I refuse to date the men my mother sets me up with."

Ryan almost spit out the latte he was sipping. "You? No. Not that there's anything wrong with women being attracted to women, but I don't think you are."

She laughed louder. "As you said, nothing wrong with it, but not my thing."

"So why haven't you dated anybody?" He was an idiot to ask.

Erin cackled. "None of your business."

Good thing she took it as a joke. "Guess that will show me. Ask a nosy question..." He grinned to show he was kidding. But he really wanted to know.

"Yup." She sobered. "Would you like to see the apartment, and then we can talk about salary?"

"Sure."

Beaming, Erin led him through the connecting door to the garage, the scent of coffee fading, oil and gear lube taking over. They walked past the long, narrow service counter to the garage's outside entrance. In the little foyer, rather than continuing outside, she unlocked the door marked "Private" and led him up a set of stairs, unlocking another door at the top. Erin motioned him through ahead of her, which he did after hesitating, manners warring with orders.

Ryan stepped into a short, narrow hallway, painted beige, dark brown tile on the floor, with coat hooks fastened to the wall. He turned right, the only direction possible. The hallway opened into a long, narrow room, carpeted in a medium brown. There were two good-sized windows breaking up the expanse of off-white walls—the room looked huge without any furniture in it.

Erin joined him. "We set this up as a studio apartment, but we could put up a wall for a bedroom if you wanted or build some sort of screen." She pointed to his left. "The kitchen has all the appliances, just in smaller sizes."

A small island with two bar stools separated the kitchen from the living area. The kitchen had pale wood cabinets above light gray countertops with a double stainless-steel sink, stove, and dishwasher in a row. A refrigerator stood at the end of the counter, with a water and ice dispenser. It was all high-quality stuff and more than he needed with his lousy cooking skills.

Erin led him through a door on the far end of the kitchen. "And the bathroom is back through here."

Wow, this is prime. A tub and shower combo but not cheap fiberglass. No, it was a light tan solid-surface material. A big vanity and sink, plus a set of shelves, for towels maybe? "This is really nice. I can't believe you've had problems finding somebody for the job with this place on the line."

"A lot of people don't want to live this far out of town, and even more don't want to be a barista." Her mouth quirked.

"A bar-what?" He hated feeling stupid.

"Barista. It's an Italian word for an expert at making coffee-based drinks."

"I guess I've heard it before."

"Starbucks uses it." Erin flashed a grin. "Or misuses it, according to some."

He laughed. She was funny too.

"Are you interested?" The look on Erin's face— tentative hope barely holding back disappointment— tugged at his heart.

Fortunately, he had no intention of disappointing her. "Yeah. This is really nice. Way nicer than anything else I've seen in my price range. And it's quiet."

"Mostly quiet." Erin walked to the far window and opened it.

Ryan joined her at the window. It faced the highway directly. The road was noisy, but it was tires on asphalt, not weapons fire. He turned to the other window, overlooking the coffee shop entrance. That one might be quieter. "Sure, there's road noise, but it's all high-speed travel, not jake brakes or something. Still better than a jetway."

"Good point." Erin bit her lip. "Shall we sit down and talk about money?" There was that resigned hope again...

"Sure. Yeah. This is great." He sounded like an idiot. She must be really desperate to hire him.

She closed the window, then led the way back to the kitchen island and sat down, pointing at the other stool.

"Uh, Erin?" He really didn't want to add on to his disabilities, but...

"Yes, Ryan?" Her brows rose.

"There's one other thing you should know before you decide to hire me. I've got some..." Ryan sighed. She waited. "I've got hearing loss. Tinnitus." He swallowed hard. "Some post-traumatic stress issues. Sudden loud noises send me diving for cover. Sometimes I shut down."

"Oh, I'm sorry to hear that." Erin grimaced. "But I can't say I'm surprised. Michael had some of the same stuff. I came back that way too. Mine eventually went away, but there's still times..." She looked away, swallowing, then back at him. "But you've been okay at Kelly's, right? It gets pretty noisy and chaotic there sometimes."

"Yeah, mostly. Backfires bother me." He held back a shudder.

"But dropped tools don't, do they?" She tilted her head, clearly listening to him, not acting polite.

"No, but if you drop an engine block, it might." He trembled. *Come on, Ryan, you're only talking about it. Keep it together.*

"I try not to do that. It's kind of rough on the engines." Erin chuckled.

Ryan tried to smile back, but he didn't think it was very successful because she frowned.

"Talking about it bothers you, doesn't it?" Erin whispered.

He tried to open his mouth to reply, but nothing came out. His whole body shook.

Erin stood, and before Ryan could move, she stepped up to him, plastered herself against his side and wrapped her arms around him, tight. *Wow.* He should pull away, but his body had other ideas, better ideas. He pulled her in tight, burying his face against her shoulder. She was in great shape but soft in all the right places. He held on and shook, waiting for the terror to pass.

Ryan wasn't sure how long he'd been holding her, but after a while, he wasn't thinking about death and destruction. Her hands ran up and down his back. He was pretty sure Erin was trying to soothe him, but all he could think about was how much he wished those hands were on his bare skin. Erin's scent was enticing; a mix of engine oil, orange cleaner, coffee, and something sweet and spicy. Ryan gritted his teeth and released her. The hug was amazing, but he could never have what he wanted. She wouldn't want him.

Erin stepped away, the corners of her mouth

barely turned up. "Better?"

Ryan had to clear his throat. "Yeah. Sorry about that."

"No problem. Hugs among friends are good things. Anytime you need one, I'm here." She sat down.

Friends—she said "friends," and he'd better remember and be grateful for that. Swallowing heavily, Ryan tried to think about other things, like baseball and drill sergeants. *The Sarge*. That sure did it. All he could think about was the Sarge saying, "And this one is *mine*. Get your own!" He sighed. That wasn't likely, not with the arm. Besides, he wanted *her*.

The Sarge's girl. Ryan sighed again.

"Shall we talk about salary?"

He nodded, not trusting himself to say anything. He listened as she outlined what she could pay him, and how many hours she wanted him to trade for the apartment, but he really didn't care about the details. Nope, he just wanted to be with her. He was such an idiot. No way she'd want him for more than a friend. Then his name caught his attention.

"...Ryan?"

"Sorry, drifted for a minute there." He forced his shoulders down.

"Sure." Erin huffed a chuckle. "I was saying I could help you find a car to restore, and you can keep it here. You might have to keep it outside most of the time, or maybe in the garage at my house, but I'll trade you hours working on your car straight across for hours you help me on my project cars. We can trade off weeks or months or something. How does that sound?"

She was too generous, but it wasn't an offer he'd pass up, either. "That would be awesome. I've always wanted a classic. How about a Superbird?"

She chortled. "Sure, if you've got a couple hundred K socked away."

"How much?" he squeaked. That sounded mature.

"A Superbird goes for over two hundred thousand. But we might find a plain Road Runner, or a GTO, or something like that."

"Sure. That would be cool. I'm pretty open on make and model." Ryan snorted. "I definitely don't have a couple hundred K hiding anywhere."

"Didn't think so; you wouldn't be trading making coffee for my little apartment if you did."

He needed clarification on something she'd said earlier. "Um, if it's none of my business, tell me, but you said *your* garage, like it was separate from this building. Where do you live?"

"I have a small place on the far end of this property, a little three-bedroom house with an oversized three-car garage." She grinned. "You're always welcome to drop by for a beer or something after work."

"Thanks." That was tempting, but she was just being friendly, nothing more. Unless she was lonely, living way out here by herself.

"Do we have a deal?" Erin tilted her head with a tentatively hopeful look. The hope seemed a little brighter, and he wanted, needed, to make it shine.

"Yeah, we've got a deal." She rewarded Ryan with a big, bright, cheerful grin. He held out his hand to seal their deal. Erin took it in hers and shook firmly. Some calluses and a strong, firm grip, but she was a mechanic, so no duh.

She's the boss now, and way, way out of your league. But he couldn't help dreaming as he followed her gently swaying backside out the door and down the stairs.

Chapter 8

Mistakes and Misinterpretations

Rats. No one told her Ryan lost an arm. Or got a TBI. *Poor kid.* And "kid" was the right idea to keep in mind, especially now—she was his boss.

Ryan got in a dinged-up blue Honda Civic and drove away. Erin only meant to comfort him with her hug—he'd been so upset by her questions. But when Ryan crushed her into his rock-solid chest, she'd quickly gone from "poor kid" to "I want to stay." It had been so long since she'd had a fierce male hug, her desire overwhelmed her common sense. And common decency, too. But oh, he felt so good. Ryan was lean muscle—like holding a warm rock with a thin coating of firm foam.

She shifted uneasily. Ryan was at least five, maybe ten years younger than she was. Guess she'd find out for sure when he filled out the tax paperwork. Plus, she was his boss. Taking advantage of the help was sexual harassment. Didn't matter if it was a woman or a man—it was wrong. Besides, she doubted Ryan felt anything for her, other than gratitude she didn't freak out about his arm. She was so much older—and her face reflected both her age and the stress she was under.

When Ryan had shown her his arm, he'd obviously expected her to react with horror or fear. All too often, military members came back from the war-torn lands America sent them to with awful physical and mental scarring. Everyone should understand they owed their freedom to these kids. They should treat them with gratitude and care, not fear and disdain. Even if someone didn't agree with the war—and nobody in their right mind *wanted* war—they still shouldn't take that out on the military members following legal orders. They should reserve their hatred and horror for the politicians who sent the kids there to fight useless, never-ending battles. And the money-grubbing contractors supporting the politicians. Those were the jackasses who deserved disdain and disgust.

But she wouldn't solve America's political problems tonight or any night. Back to the real problem. She had the perfect employee, and she needed to keep him. Ryan wasn't outgoing or super friendly, but he was a bit of a perfectionist; that was already obvious. He'd become a great barista. She'd probably lose some customers who came to see Tiffany, but she would gain true coffee connoisseurs

once he got good. And Ryan would be better than
Tiff in a week or less.

Erin grinned. William was right too—put Ryan in
a tight T-shirt and the ladies would probably triple.
When Ryan realized the silver-haired crowd was
drooling over him, he'd be horrified. She chuckled.
But maybe he'd welcome that kind of attention. If he
played his cards right, he could really luck out and
get himself a sugar mama. Sugar grandma? The
chuckle turned to a laugh. With his "stay away" vibe,
that wasn't likely. And, as his boss, it was her job to
protect him from all kinds of harassment. She'd have
to institute a "look, don't touch" policy. She sobered.
For herself too.

Back to business, Erin. She double-checked the
locks and set the alarm. Trudging down the long
drive, the dust kicked up under her feet, sweat rolled
down her back, and she gratefully passed through
the open gate separating her home from her
business. From the fence onward, tall ponderosa
pines shaded her drive, blocked an amazing amount
of highway noise, and kept the dust down. The big
shop and garage helped too, bouncing noise back to
the road. Even with the trees, the long summer days
were scorching, but the sunshine made the heat
bearable. Winter was long and dark in Montana.

Letting herself in, she sighed with pleasure in the
cool dimness. *Home.* The thick foam-insulated walls
kept heat in—or out—efficiently and muffled the
remaining highway noise. Her wallet and keys
landed on the little hall table with a metallic thud.

She pulled off her boots, sighing with relief. Entering the kitchen, Erin relished the slightly rough, cool slate tile under her hot, tired feet. She grabbed a beer from the fridge, ambled into the living room, and plopped down on her worn but comfy leather sofa, pulling up the footrest.

Hiring Ryan solved one problem, anyway. She had half-a-dozen more to figure out. Erin tipped back the bottle, the sharp citrus flavor of the hops complementing the smooth brew. The stupid lawsuit was probably the most pressing. Sam had sent their official reply off to the opposition and the Court, and they waited for the Adams' reply.

Ryan would help her with the second problem, too. She could spend more time on the Barracuda and get it, and Cust, out of her life. The third problem was stickier. No one could solve her mom. But maybe with Ryan on board, she'd have time for a social life, and she could find her own dates. She snorted. Michael was the social one. Which was strange, since her military career field was public affairs, but it was true. She was a homebody, an introvert. That was one reason she loved her work and living away from town.

Ryan was also going to keep her from going under, at least right away. By agreeing to trade hours of work for the apartment, her cash flow would skyrocket. And with the ridiculous lawsuit, cash was critical. She should spend more time selling coffee than working on cars, for now; the profits were smaller but steady. But she had to finish the 'Cuda and send it far away, along with Chaz. She shuddered, his sleaziness sending shivers of revulsion along her spine.

Taking another swallow, she considered the Cust problem. Maybe Ryan could help with that, too. If she could talk him into going to some of Mom's events with her, maybe Chaz and the rest of them would get the picture that she wasn't interested. She'd get called a cougar, but it was almost fashionable these days.

But she couldn't. She was the boss, and she had to be professional. Ryan was an employee only—less chance of another lawsuit that way.

Maybe she could start her regular afternoon rounds again. She tapped a fingernail against the bottle, the sound ringing in the quiet house. She'd close a little earlier in the afternoon and get a workout in before going to Deb's for the shop's pastry order.

Erin tipped the bottle high and swallowed the last bit. All right, time to stop dreaming and start doing. A salad for dinner, check email and social stuff after, watch a little mindless TV, and go to bed early so she could get up and do it all over again.

#

Three weeks later, Erin waved at a departing customer. "See you tomorrow!"

"Argh!"

Erin spun. "What?"

"I'm never going to get this milk steaming thing right. I always turn it on too high, too fast and end up with milk everywhere!" Milk dripped from Ryan's eyebrows and chin, plastering his shirt to his solid pecs.

She chuckled. "Don't worry, it happens to everybody. You've only dropped the pitcher once. Tiffany did it almost daily." She shrugged and turned to her next customer. When she finished, she shuffled close and whispered, "Besides, your fan club appreciates the view." She nodded at the table of silver-haired ladies sipping coffee and chatting, casting glances and smiling at him.

"Gee, thanks," he grumbled.

"Good tips."

He growled. Erin returned to the drive-through window for another order. William was right. She'd ordered some thin, long-sleeve T-shirts with her logo, a size smaller than he asked for, and her female customers doubled overnight. The loggers still came in, but they didn't stay nearly as long; no, now she had tables of women coming in all morning. And they all bought espresso drinks first, then changed to drip coffee.

And she sold a lot of T-shirts.

A fan club member stood on her tiptoes, trying to wipe his face off. She must have said something too because poor Ryan blushed fire engine red. At first, she'd enjoyed seeing the tables turned, but the objectification bothered her more than a little. She'd have to give him larger T-shirts, although it might not help. But the lectures usually worked—most of her customers took it well when Erin reminded them how they felt about unwanted touching. One lady laughed and winked. "Honey, I still get pinches! But I understand; look, don't touch."

William wasn't the only one who had guessed right about Ryan—he was a perfectionist. After Erin made a jig to hold the filter, he'd practiced compacting the espresso until he got the right pressure, so his shots were consistent, no matter what arm he wore. Their drive-through customers increased as word spread about the quality of the espresso. And despite the milk bath he'd gotten, he was getting much better at steaming milk, too. Soon, Ryan would need help only during the drive-through commuter rush, and then only because there were more customers.

If it wasn't for the lawsuit, Erin would thank Kaylee Adams. She waited for the next car to pull up. The logger who told Erin about Tiffany and Kaylee's fight had agreed to talk to Sam, but he hadn't made an appointment. Every time she reminded him, which was about twice a week, he grimaced and told her he was just too busy. Funny—he was sitting in her shop drinking coffee every morning, not out chopping down trees. Yesterday, she told him if he wanted to drink coffee, he *would* make the time, or the lawsuit would drive her out of business. The threat seemed to make a difference; he'd apologized and taken Sam's card—again. Maybe a miracle would happen and he would follow through.

As orders came in, she called them out to Ryan. Erin wrote them down, but she knew he'd heard and was pulling them now. That was another big difference between Ryan and Tiffany—half the time, Tiff forgot who ordered what, even with a list.

"I see it's true." Old Mrs. Cust was standing at the counter, her tiny body ramrod straight, a permanent scowl firmly engraved beneath her silver helmet-hair and framed by her huge pearl necklace.

Erin sighed internally and crossed to the counter. Ryan was busy enough with Izzy. She'd take on the entitled matriarch. "What's that, Mrs. Cust?"

"You got yourself a boy-toy."

Erin blinked at her for a moment, stunned she would say such a thing. She took in a deep breath to give herself a moment. "Mrs. Cust, Ryan *works* for me. I'd appreciate it if you wouldn't refer to him in such unflattering terms." Poor Ryan was turning red again.

"I wasn't being unflattering, dear. I'm envious." She sniffed.

"Mrs. Cust, I meant unflattering to Ryan. I couldn't, quite frankly, care less what you think about me." She spun to the drive-through window. The old biddy could wait if she was going to be rude.

"Aren't you going to take my order?"

"After I take this one." She turned to the drive-through window and took the order, passing it to Ryan, who was clearly trying, but failing, to hide behind Izzy.

Ryan whispered, "What a horror!"

"Yup. A very rich one."

He grimaced. She went back to the counter. Mrs.

Cust ordered a vanilla latte, skinny. Erin passed the order to Ryan. "You'll probably have to take it to her. She thinks she's too good to come get her drinks like everyone else."

"I guess it will get cold then, because it will sit on the counter." Ryan turned the steam wand off. "I'm not in any mood to wait on her after she called me names." He scowled. "Besides, she didn't even tip."

Erin grimaced. She couldn't agree more. She took more orders.

Ryan called, "Skinny vanilla latte for here." The cup sat on the counter.

They worked to fill a few more orders. "Vanilla latte, skinny, here. It's getting cold."

"Young man, *service* means you bring the drink to me, not yell at me to come get it!" Mrs. Cust trumpeted from her seat.

Ryan frowned down at her, staring over Izzy's bulk. "No, ma'am, it doesn't. Not here. Everyone comes up and gets their drinks. We don't have a wait staff."

"Erin, this young man is rude and clearly doesn't understand what *service* means!"

That woman had some nerve. Erin marched to Mrs. Cust, fists clenched, standing right over her so the harpy had to crane her neck. "Mrs. Cust, I think Mr. Walsh has a much better idea of what *service* means than you ever will."

Mrs. Cust's mouth opened and closed several times. She glared, lips clamped, then curling in a nasty smile. "Clearly, he doesn't, and neither do you."

"I think we do, Mrs. Cust. See, we both served our country. *Military* service. So, I strongly suggest you take your business and your complaints to someplace where they care about *your* version of service!" Erin started calmly but ended shouting. Every face in the room stared at her. She turned away blindly but whirled when she heard a slow clap start. The loggers were on their feet, applauding, and everyone else soon joined. *Oh, no. Too much.* Her blood ran cold. She shouldn't let her temper flare.

Mrs. Cust glared at the standing ovation. She rose slowly, her eyes narrowed and bright red flags across her cheeks. "I don't know what my Chaz sees in you, but I will tell him you are clearly unsuitable. I don't expect to see you with him ever again!"

Her anger returned with a vengeance. "*Please* tell him that. I can't stand him. I've been telling him that for months, but like you, he just doesn't want to listen."

Mrs. Cust gaped at her for a long moment, then turned on her heel and marched out the door. Everyone in the room clapped again, then yacked with their neighbors. Erin sagged against the counter. The old biddy had it coming, but she shouldn't have lost her temper. She'd made an enemy. And Mother? She'd be furious. That thought wiped the remorse right away.

Ryan put his hand on her arm. "Hey, you didn't have to do that. I don't care what some old woman calls me."

"I know. She drives me crazy. She always has."

Erin sighed heavily. "Still, I shouldn't have let my temper get the better of me. She's going to make my life miserable."

"Pfft." Ryan raspberried. "It looks like there's a lot of people here who can't stand her."

She grimaced and returned to the window. No one was waiting—the commuter traffic was dying off. "Ryan, ready to take the stick? The commuters are on their way, and your fan club has switched to drip, so I'm sure you can handle it." Erin smiled at him, putting a little challenge in it. She had to get out of here, back to her cars. They didn't gossip when she lost her temper and yelled.

Ryan shrugged. "If you think so, I'll give it a shot."

"Yup, you'll be fine. Just yell if you need help."

"Okay." He turned away, then twisted back. "What did she mean about her son?"

Erin laughed, but there was nothing funny about it. "The Barracuda out there?" She thumbed over her shoulder. "Cust owns it. For some reason, he seems to think that me working on his 'Cuda means I should work on him, too." She shuddered. "I don't want either one of them. The 'Cuda is paying work, and Chaz is slimy."

"So, this could really be trouble." Ryan frowned.

"Yeah." She shrugged, feeling helpless. "Maybe. Either way, I need to get the thing done. Yell if you need help." She retreated to the garage. The 'Cuda's engine was due in this week. All the other parts were here, so once the engine was in, everything else would go quickly. It would still take a couple of weeks, maybe a month, but it would be out of her garage soon.

It couldn't be soon enough.

Chapter 9

Rich People Turn Trouble into Catastrophe

Ryan scrubbed a table, the bleach making his nose wrinkle. It didn't surprise him when Erin stood up for him, but the vehemence was a little shocking. Obviously, there was some bad blood there. *Chaz* sounded like a real winner. But trouble with rich people was trouble doubled or tripled. The little guy usually got squished. He'd do everything he could to protect Erin, but he probably couldn't do much. He had less clout than she did.

And if it came down to a fight, he was in trouble. A guy with one arm wasn't much of a threat.

The silver-haired crowd finally jittered their way out of the shop, letting Ryan consider Erin's problems and wipe down all the tables without getting his butt pinched. Some of these ladies were outrageous, egging each other on like a contest for

"Grandmothers Gone Wild." He snorted. At least they tipped well.

And none of them said a single word about his arm. He'd gotten a few stares, but they quickly averted their attention, sometimes blushing or grimacing. His terse "Afghanistan" seemed to satisfy the few who asked. But then, most of the older ladies had lived through two or three wars—they'd probably seen worse. Wringing out the cloth, nose wrinkling at the bleach, he moved to the next table.

There were a few like Erin, curious about the mechanics of the arm and why he didn't have one of the fancy prosthetics. He'd toss off an excuse about the difficulties of living in Montana and they understood. Montana was beautiful but remote; that's why people loved it. In his case, it was partially an excuse. He could get one, but Seattle was a nine-hour drive, and that meant hotels, way too many strangers, a multitude of unknown threats, taking time off, and a lot of hassle. Maybe someday. He didn't need anything fancy, so why bother?

The Chaz Cust problem was a much bigger issue. Since Ryan had little money and less influence, he had limited ways to help. Except, he could help her with the Barracuda. No reason not to help her with it, especially in the evenings. He wiped the next table. Not like he had a social life or anything—he watched the idiot box, blew zombies away, and talked with old friends online. And if he helped Erin with the 'Cuda, he'd build up hours to trade for Erin's help with his own muscle car someday. That day was probably a long way off—he had to save some money and find something he liked and could afford. He'd watched some of the car auction shows; most of the classic hotrods were way too expensive. Maybe something a little more modern would be better. One of the early 2000s Mustangs? Or an IROC Camaro? But computers meant more expensive parts and less work he could do himself.

It didn't matter right now; he didn't have money or time for toys. Furnishing his new apartment took priority. He'd bought a good mattress first, a king, arriving Saturday. Then he could move the rest of his stuff in, empty his storage unit, quit paying that bill, and see what else he needed. He'd scour the second-hand stores and save his hard-earned money for important things.

But even if he couldn't afford a stick of furniture, he'd be happier here, sleeping on the floor. He loved his family, but he craved peace, quiet, and a lot less smothering. He'd been on his own for a lot of years. His family was a little too clingy, treating him like he was handicapped—and he wasn't. They didn't mean to make him feel bad or less—but they did. They forgot he'd learned how to live without a lower arm. Erin didn't coddle him—even when he needed an accommodation, she was practical. She worked with him to find a solution, unemotionally and logically; it was such a relief to be an equal instead of a problem child.

He gave the counter one last swipe, the cloth almost dry, and frowned. Erin usually helped close.

Ryan locked the cash register, put up the "ring the bell once only, please" sign and entered the garage. She wasn't in the first two bays, so she must be in the back by the Barracuda. Her voice rose above the constant ringing in his ears. He couldn't understand her words, but the anger was clear. He sprinted around the lift. Inspiring that level of fury in Erin, far fiercer than earlier, was a real feat. She was in trouble.

Near the Barracuda, Ryan skidded to a stop. A short, fat man was plastered against Erin's back, pushing her into the front end of the 'Cuda. Her hands clamped the man's wrists, trying to get his dirty, T-shirt-clutching paws off her waist; the animal was grinding his pelvis into her.

"Chaz, get off of me, or I'm taking a wrench to your head."

She didn't need to. Ryan marched to the idiot, grabbing the back of the man's shirt collar firmly in his good hand and his belt with his grasper. "Let her go, *now*, or I'm going to beat you bloody." When the dummy didn't reply or let go of Erin, Ryan jerked the idiot's belt up and snorted at his gasp of pain.

The dolt squeaked. "Let go of me, or I'll charge you with assault."

Ryan yanked again, harder. "And I'm sure Erin will charge you first. With attempted *rape*. Let go, now!" The man released his grip and let Erin go. Ryan pulled him back two steps, spun him toward the door, and shoved, sending the jackass stumbling to the floor with a thud.

He glared, tossing his thin comb-over back. "You're going to regret that, boy!"

"I don't think so." Ryan stared at him, going for cold and menacing, with his hand on his hip and his grasper ready.

Erin's boots thwacked the concrete, then she stood shoulder to shoulder with him. "That was the last straw, Chaz." She fired each word at the man and sneered his name. "I have told you, time after time, *not* to touch me. We're done. I am canceling our contract in accordance with the unreconcilable differences clause. I will deliver your Barracuda back to you and return the money that remains in your account, along with the final accounting. Today." She glanced at the car, then focused on Chaz, fists clenched at her side, her words staccato. "Charles Cust, you are not welcome on my property ever again. If you come back, I will call the Sheriff and have you charged with trespassing. Is that clear?"

"You'll regret this. You're going to pay, and pay big." Chaz struggled to his feet, brushed himself off, and staggered out the door.

Ass. Hope a truck runs him over. Ryan clenched his fist, desperately wishing he had two so he could pound the idiot into the concrete. With a sigh, Erin locked the door behind him, then returned to the car, sagging against the fender. He scanned Erin, looking for physical damage. "Are you okay?"

She laughed, but despair blasted through the sound like an air horn. "Oh, sure, I'm fine. I'm going to get sued again."

Ryan stepped closer but didn't touch. "I meant physically. Did he hurt you?" He knew better than to touch any woman uninvited, but especially a woman who'd been assaulted.

Erin flipped her hand carelessly and scowled. "I'm fine. Chaz might have been something in high school, but he's a sponge now. A rich, slimy sponge. He probably will charge you with assault." Erin scowled harder. "I'd better call Sam."

"Who's Sam?" A boyfriend or former lover?

"My lawyer."

They might both need a lawyer. "Good idea. Want me to get the phone?"

"Nope, got it right here." She lifted her cell phone.

Ryan walked away, giving both of them some privacy. The confrontation was over, and now he trembled, vibrating like an earthquake. *Great.* He entered the now-empty coffee shop and plopped into one of the dining room chairs, watching his arms and legs quiver. Yep, reaction shakes. He waited it out, playing through the clash in his head. He was totally overreacting to a minor altercation. No weapons, just a little manhandling. If only he'd been able to pummel the jerk.

A hand thumped on his shoulder, and he bounded to his feet, knocking the hand away, ready to defend himself. Erin stood with eyes wide and hands raised. Ryan relaxed his arms, which had come up automatically, and dropped his head. *Sh... oot!*

Erin took three steps back. "I'm sorry, Ryan. I

didn't mean to startle you."

"No, I'm sorry. I didn't mean to attack you." He collapsed into the chair with a thwack. He was as big an idiot as Chaz.

She waved her hands in front of her body. "You didn't. You were clearly in defensive mode. I startled you; it's my fault." She shook her head. "But it doesn't matter. Sam advised me to call the Sheriff and report what happened. So, I did. Can you talk to a deputy now, or do I need to put them off for a while?" Concern creased her face.

"Yeah. I'll be okay. Sorry." Ryan shuddered and shivered. He'd almost attacked Erin. *This is so bad.*

Erin sat down next to him and put one of her hands out, palm up on the table. "Ryan, are you sure?"

He grabbed her hand and hung on. "I'll be okay. Sorry."

"It's okay, Ryan." Erin's face was calm, compassion shining. "This is Chaz's fault, not yours."

He looked down at the table. "Yeah, but I almost attacked *you*. That's my fault."

"Ryan..." She squeezed his hand and put her other hand on top.

The warm, firm grip gave him something to focus on, but the comfort was almost too much. He hung on anyway.

"You were reacting, not attacking. You moved back to defend yourself, not forward into me. Trust me, I know the difference."

He didn't know what to say, so he said nothing,

sitting there shaking, gripping her hand. He was probably holding on too tight, but she didn't object.

The door opened. Erin released his hand, the sudden coolness startling. A white man in a Deputy Sheriff's uniform entered, hand near his weapon, surveying the entire room, then arrowing in on them. "Erin Moore? You reported an assault?"

"Yes, I did. Would you like some coffee, Deputy?" She stood.

The deputy's arm relaxed, and he strode toward them. "Not now." When Erin waved a hand at a chair, he sat with a creak and jingle, probably from the gun belt and bullet resistant vest. "Please tell me what happened. I'd like to record your statement." His long, oval face showed no emotion under the wide cowboy hat.

"Sure."

Ryan listened to Erin's recitation, his anger growing. Chaz was a braying jackass.

The deputy aimed his dispassionate gaze at Ryan. "And you, Mr. Walsh? What happened from your perspective?"

He told the deputy exactly what he'd seen and done. He kept to the facts, keeping emotion and speculation out of his story.

The deputy took notes as he talked, then turned back to Erin when he'd finished. "Mrs. Moore, do you think the attack left bruises?"

Erin jolted, then settled back in her chair. "Maybe." She pulled up her T-shirt.

Ryan looked away, not wanting to invade her

privacy. She'd been attacked; she didn't need him gawking.

Erin said, "Nothing shows yet except some red marks where he pushed me into the car." She'd turned away from both of them slightly and was peering under the bottom of her shirt, pulled away from her stomach.

The deputy turned off his phone, probably ending the recording, and hit a couple more buttons on it. "Could you take a picture for me, please? And if bruises form, come down to the office, and we'll have a female take pictures. Do you want to file charges against Mr. Cust?"

She snapped a photo, then dropped her shirt. "Only if he files charges against me or Ryan."

"I see. Let me check with the Sheriff." The deputy rose, took his phone back, and walked to the far end of the dining room.

Keeping his voice low, Ryan leaned toward her a little. "Are you sure you're okay? He must have grabbed you pretty hard."

She looked down at her stomach again, then at him. "I'm okay. I've had worse just working. He stretched this shirt all out of shape, though."

The deputy came back. "Mr. Cust hasn't called the station to report anything. If he files charges, one of us will be back to arrest Mr. Walsh."

"What? He was defending me." Fury lit her eyes and flagged her cheeks.

"I'm sorry, Mrs. Moore, but that's how it works. I'm sure Mr. Walsh would be released quickly, especially if you file charges." The corners of the deputy's mouth turned up slightly. "And if you do, we'll arrest Cust, too. The Sheriff is going to chat with Mr. Cust and tell him that a report has been made. Hopefully, that will head off all unnecessary legal action."

"Thanks." Erin smiled, but it looked like it took some effort. "I appreciate your hard work and fairness."

"You're welcome." He nodded and pressed his lips together firmly for a moment. "Be careful, Mrs. Moore. The Custs are powerful. Consider a surveillance system, inside and out."

"That's a good idea, Deputy. Thanks." She smiled again, a little more successfully. "Would you like that coffee now?"

"Sure. Thanks." He tucked his phone and notebook away.

She walked back to pull him an Americano, medium size. Ryan noted it for future situations, although he certainly hoped nothing like this would happen again.

The deputy nodded at Ryan's prosthetic grasper. "Afghanistan or Iraq?"

"Afghanistan."

"Sorry, man. That sucks." He frowned. "Spent some time in Iraq myself, but it wasn't in the rough places."

Ryan nodded, but he wasn't sure what to say. At least the deputy wasn't likely to ask a lot of insensitive questions.

Erin called, "Cream or sugar?"

"No, just black, thanks."

She walked back to the table and handed the deputy the cup. He took a sip and raised his eyebrows. "This is good. I'll have to stop here more often."

"Anytime." Erin smiled like she meant it. "I give a discount to law enforcement, firefighters, and military."

He smiled at her in return, with a little more personal interest. "Thanks again, and don't forget about the surveillance system." He lifted the cup to her and left.

"Thanks! Have a great day!" Erin sank into the chair and put her head in her hands. "This sucks. Sam says Cust probably won't file charges against you, but he'll probably try to sue me for breach of contract, which he can't win, but it will cost me a ton of money to defend against, at least upfront. And now I need a security system upgrade, or my business might get attacked."

Ryan dithered, then put his good hand on her shoulder, warm muscle firming, then softening under his hand. Good, she took the gesture as comfort. It was the least he could do. Actually, there *was* more he could do. He hesitated, not sure how she'd take it, then decided it didn't matter. He was doing it for his peace of mind. "I'm calling William and telling him I can't make it in. I'll help you get the Barracuda on a trailer and deliver it, because you shouldn't be anywhere near that guy by yourself."

Erin raised her head. "You don't have to do that."

"I know, but I want to. William will understand." No way he'd leave her alone to deal with that sleaze ball.

"I should say no, but I won't. Thanks." Her smile flickered and died.

"Sure. That's what friends are for." He pulled out his phone and called William, explaining the problem without too many details. William demanded he put Erin on the phone, and she told him the story but softened Cust's attack. She handed the phone back to him.

William said, "Don't worry about work. Do you need a weapon?"

Ryan chuckled but realized he did. His was in a safe at his mom's house. Erin shook her head "no." "Thanks, but I've got one. See you tomorrow."

Erin tapped her fingertips on the table. "I've got weapons; we don't need his. Better yet, I can get a deputy to supervise the delivery." She smiled, a slightly evil smile.

Ryan shrugged. "Yeah, maybe. Do you have a trailer and truck, or do you need to borrow one?"

"Got one." Erin smirked. "It's kind of necessary for the business. It's over at the house. Let me close up, and I'll go get it."

"I'll do the close-up. You go get the trailer." Erin nodded and left. Ryan locked the door and ran the closing checklist fast. He double-checked the door and windows and jogged into the garage. The big door at the end was open, with a trailer positioned in front of the Barracuda. Erin was hauling cable from a winch mounted on the back of her truck.

The garage phone rang, and Ryan answered it. "Coffee and Cars, can I help you?"

"Could I speak to Erin Moore, please?"

"She's a little busy. May I ask who's calling?" He'd take a message. Very few things were as important as getting rid of that car. And the slimy sponge.

"This is the Custs' business manager, Mr. Peng."

That might be important. Erin needed to deliver the car someplace. "Hold on." He took the phone to Erin. "A Mr. Peng is on the line. Says he's Custs' business manager."

She grimaced. "This is Erin." She listened, her frown deepening to a scowl. "You can certainly file and try to make my life difficult, which is what Mr. Cust undoubtedly wants, but I have a very good contract, one that specifies mediation first. Ms. Kerr wrote it for me. You won't win, and Ms. Kerr will get paid—by you. And I reserve my right to counter-sue for emotional pain and suffering. If Mr. Cust wants to cause me monetary and emotional pain, he's out of luck because he *will* pay the bills, and my lawyer will do all the work. I won't even need to be there." Erin smirked, waggling her brows. Ryan grinned, giving her a thumbs-up.

A glare took over. "Mr. Peng, I will not continue working on this car. Mr. Cust will never set foot on my property ever again or come within twenty feet of me anywhere else. Find someone else to finish the car, now. I will email you recommendations. I have already loaded all the parts I purchased into the vehicle and made it ready for transport." She listened, grimacing and pacing.

"Mr. Peng, my lawyer is filing for a protective order against Mr. Cust. I do not want to see him, talk to him, or have anything to do with him ever again. He *attacked* me in my place of business. I have filed a report with the Sheriff's Department, and if he files charges against my employee, who physically pulled Cust off of me, I *will* file criminal charges. Perhaps Mr. Cust downplayed what he did, but I will not be giving him a second chance. He assaulted me and told me he was going to have sex with me. That's attempted *rape*, Mr. Peng. Now do you understand why I'm being what you have the nerve to call stubborn?" She scowled.

If he'd known, Ryan would have pounded the jackass into the concrete, regardless of the missing fist. Rapists were the lowest of the low. Scum.

"I thought so. Let me know where to take the car. I'll give you a week. That's more than generous." She hung up and glared at the floor, her hand clenched around the phone. "I'm stuck with the 'Cuda for now, but I think he understands how serious I am about this. He actually seemed shocked for a moment." She snort-laughed. "I didn't think anything could shock that man. I guess I screwed up your afternoon for nothing." She grimaced, shaking her head. "Sorry."

Ryan waved her concern away. He'd done little, really. But he needed to get her mind off the problem and on to something positive. Neither one of them needed to brood and worry—it was over and done. "Don't worry about it. It's nothing. And since we're not delivering a car, and you already have the trailer hooked up, want to help me get my stuff out of my storage unit?" He smiled hopefully.

Erin smiled, clearly happy to do something else. "Sure. My pleasure. How were you going to do it?"

"Lots of trips and probably asking the guys at Kelly's for help." Buying lots of pizza and beer after, too.

"I guess it all worked out in the end then, didn't it? Come on, let's go." Erin grabbed her cell phone, and they walked out together after locking and alarming the building.

Ryan gave her directions to his storage facility. A comfortable silence fell. He wondered when the consequences of the event would hit her. Or maybe he was the only one who got reaction shakes. He didn't before, when he was whole.

They pulled up to the gate, and he gave her the code. He directed her to the unit, stopping the trailer right in front of the door. Ryan unlocked the padlock and raised the rattling garage door. There was less stuff in here than he remembered. With any luck, they could get it all in one trip.

They loaded the furniture first, put his boxes in the back of her truck, and drove back.

"Ryan, have you put anything else in the apartment yet?" Her voice had an urgency to it that didn't match the question.

"Nope. I've got a new mattress being delivered

tomorrow." He could hardly wait to get a good night's sleep on it. Or any sleep. Bad dreams plagued him.

Erin nodded. "So, you're not staying there tonight, right?"

"Wasn't planning on it, no."

"Good." Her eyes flashed to his, then returned to the road. "Just in case Cust does something really stupid."

He hadn't considered that. "Do you think it's possible?"

"He's pretty pissed off, and the Sheriff hasn't talked to him yet, so yes, I think it's possible." She nodded, a resigned look on her face.

Shoot. "In that case, do you have someone else to stay with?"

"I suppose." She frowned at him. "But why?"

"Because he might go after you or your home, not your business. His car is still in your shop, remember?" The guy was stupid but probably not that stupid. Too bad. If he was, Ryan could take care of the problem permanently.

Erin scowled. "I am not letting that idiot scare me out of my house."

Ryan snorted. "I hope your couch is comfy."

"Why?" She glanced at him, her face puzzled.

"Because you're not staying way out here by yourself, that's why." A lone defender was a dead defender.

She scowled. "Ryan, I can take care of myself. I grew up here, learned to shoot as a kid, got better in the military, and I've never been a shrinking violet."

"Never said you were." She wasn't—not by a long shot. "But you're only one person. How many windows and doors do you have?"

She sighed. "Lots. Maybe I'd better get a dog."

Ryan nodded. "Not a bad idea, but not one that's going to happen today. I'll grab a bag after we unload this stuff."

Erin sighed again, a long, gusty sigh. "If you insist. But I'll be fine."

"Most likely. But no sense taking chances."

"Okay. Thanks." She looked at him again, but he couldn't read her expression.

"That's what friends are for."

Erin smiled, a real smile, which made the possibility of a sleepless night worthwhile. *Wonder what she wears to bed? Whoa, boy.* Guard duty, that's all. She's not offering anything more. No one ever would, not with his damage. He wouldn't ask, either.

They got everything upstairs in an hour, even his lightweight but awkwardly long dresser, which was pretty amazing considering the steep, narrow stairs and his lack of a real arm. Good thing Erin was really strong and could pick up his slack.

At home, he showered and packed a bag for the night, including his weapon. Mom wasn't home, so he left her a note that he was staying at a friend's and drove to Erin's. Leaving his car running, he dropped his stuff off in the apartment, then drove past the shop. He rolled through a thicket of pines and pulled up in front of a house with a three-car garage that looked bigger than the rest of the house. The perfect mechanic's home. Two stories, light brown wood-look siding, dark green trim, and a matching green metal roof blended into the scenery. The front porch was small but had a solid timber-frame and a deck; real classy. He parked in front of the garage, walked up to the door, and knocked. From the rapping, it was a good solid door.

The forest green door swung wide, revealing Erin. "Come on in."

Wow. Ryan choked, "Thanks."

He was in trouble. Big trouble.

Chapter 10

A Different Kind of Trouble

Erin wore a thin, tight, low-cut, light blue top with tiny little straps. If there was a bra under it, it wasn't much of one—the top hugged her like a second skin. Below that, she wore snug gray shorts painted on her amazing thighs. *Smoking hot.*

She turned, sweeping her arm in invitation. He motioned for her to go first. Erin smiled, turning away. Her feet were bare too, the toenails painted sparkly pink. From her feet, he scanned up long, muscular legs to a firm backside, just as good as the front. His fingers itched to touch, caress, even the fingers he didn't have anymore.

That reminder knocked back some of his desire. Erin wasn't for him. He toed off his shoes, kicking them next to hers and pulling off his socks. Hopefully, his feet didn't stink too bad. The stone was nice and cool, a relief after sweating up and down the apartment stairs.

Erin waved her arm. "Here it is. Kitchen and living area here, my bedroom over there, and the guest room is upstairs."

He forced his eyes away from her and examined the room. He was in her house to provide security, not dream about things he didn't deserve. In the kitchen, black and gray streaked granite countertops topped stainless steel appliances, with an island separating the cooking from the living area. Natural dark blue and rust red slate tile covered the floor, with a black fireplace set into the far wall, and floor to ceiling windows at the back, with a sliding door leading to a covered patio.

Knotty pine covered the ceilings inside and out. Most of the living/kitchen area had off-white walls, and the furniture was slightly worn, comfortable-looking leather with a couple of light wood coffee tables. "Wow. This is prime." He had to keep his mind on her house and the need to protect her. Like that huge wall of windows. But that's why he was sleeping on the couch.

Erin glanced around the room, smiling warmly. "It really is. It's not big, but it's just right for me. Want a beer?" Her pretty eyes focused on his.

"Yes, please." He nodded, a little too frantically. He needed something to cool him off.

"You can put your bag upstairs." She tossed her head toward the stairway beyond the kitchen.

Ryan shrugged. "I can, but I'll be sleeping down here."

She tilted her head, wrinkling her nose. "Why?

The guest bed isn't great, but it's better than the couch."

"Because if there's an issue, it will be down here, not up there." He was there to protect her, not have a sleep-over. And he'd better keep reminding himself.

Erin rolled her eyes. "Fine. Suit yourself. It's your back. Still, you might want to put your bag upstairs, since the only other bathroom is up there. Then come out to the patio; I've got pizza ready to go into the oven out there."

"There's an oven out there?" Erin's place was amazing.

"Yes. It's too hot to turn the one on in here."

"Cool. I'll be right down." Blast, he really wanted to take this thing off. He dithered, but she'd been okay with the arm so far. Regardless, his shoulders hunched, and he rotated them. "Hey, Erin."

"Yeah?" She turned on her toe.

"Uh... there's no easy way to ask this..." She raised her brows. "Do you care if I leave off my prosthesis?"

"No, of course not! I imagine it starts to hurt after a while. Do whatever you need to do, Ryan. I don't care what you wear or don't wear." She wrinkled her nose again, looked away, and blushed. "As long as you wear a pair of shorts, anyway. I don't need to see you naked."

Ryan laughed, but at himself. He'd like to see *her* naked, but that wasn't going to happen. "How many of those beers did you drink?"

She glared, but it was adorable. "I'm still working on the first one, thank you very much. Just thought

I'd be clear." Erin turned to the fridge.

Ryan escaped up the stairs before he could make a bigger fool of himself. Three doors opened off the small landing, displaying two smaller rooms, one set up as an office, one as a guest bedroom, and a standard bathroom. It was a lot warmer upstairs—good thing he was sleeping downstairs.

He dropped his bag on the guest bed, took his prosthetic off, and cleaned the socket. *Ah.* Fortunately, his residual arm didn't have any blisters or sores. Bouncing down the stairs, he joined Erin on the patio. She turned away from the outdoor fireplace and pointed at the loungers. He took the one farthest from the oven, figuring the closest was hers. A frosty glass of beer waited on the small table between. He assumed it was his, since she had one in her hand. A dining set sat in the middle of the patio, a stack of plates and utensils waiting on the tile-top table.

He sat, a little hesitant to let his residual arm hang next to her. But from the placement of the glass, she had claimed the other lounger. He tasted the beer—light, crisp, with a slightly lemony tang. "That's perfect, thanks."

"Yeah. One of the local breweries. I like all of their stuff, but this summer ale is particularly good when it's hot." She sipped, savoring and then swallowing.

Ryan forced his eyes off her long neck and looked around the patio. "This is a really nice place, Erin. And it's pretty quiet for being so close to the highway."

"We designed it that way." One corner of her mouth turned up, the other down. "The garage and house are angled to deflect the sound waves. It's not perfect, but it helps. The house is foam insulated, too, which also keeps the noise down, along with keeping it warm in the winter and cool in the summer. But in summer, I have to leave all the windows open at night, so I get a good cross-flow." Erin shrugged. "No air conditioner."

"You probably don't need it ninety-five percent of the time."

"True. And suffering through those few sultry nights is better than spending tons of money on air conditioning I don't need."

A high-pitched beeping made him wince. Erin crossed to the fireplace and hit a button on the timer perched on a high wood mantle. She opened the small compartment door, set above the empty open firebox, blue flames hissing away. Before he could ask, she explained, "The main fireplace burns wood, but the oven burns propane. It's faster and easier than lighting a fire, letting it burn down, cleaning the stone, and then, finally, baking." With a wide, long-handled board, she scooped the pizza out of the oven, slid it on the cutting board at the edge of the table, and transferred a second pizza to the paddle, putting it into the oven with a sharp jerk of her arm. She reset the timer and sliced the pizza, sliding it on plates and bringing both over. The sizzle of hot cheese and the toasty scent of baking bread preceded her.

Ryan's stomach rumbled. He reached up and took the plate from her. "Thanks. This looks excellent. And homemade." He put the plate on his lap and picked up a slice.

"It is homemade. The dough stays in the fridge, so I've got some whenever I want it." She sat on the other lounger.

"That's an outstanding idea." He took a bite and chewed. Delicious. "You're going to regret feeding me."

Erin regarded him with a small crease between her brows. "Why? I like having someone to eat with."

"Yeah, but this is so good, I'll be over here all the time." He smirked. "I eat a lot." Ryan took another bite. *So good. Almost good enough to get my mind off of you.*

"You won't bug me, and if you do, I'll tell you." She chuckled.

"Deal. This is really, really good."

"Thanks."

They ate in silence for a while. They'd probably both built up an appetite with the furniture moving. And all the drama. Erin pulled the second pizza out, cut it, and gave him most of it. "Save some for yourself. You're the one doing the cooking."

"Nah, I usually eat only part of one." She put a third pizza in and refilled his glass from the growler on the table.

He smiled at her, thankful. "You don't have to wait on me."

"I know. But I know where everything is, and you

don't."

"But I do now, so I can serve you next time." *Food, nothing else, idiot.* A strong, independent woman like Erin didn't need a damaged guy like him. Ryan ate most of the third pizza too, then sat back, stomach content. A loud burp rolled up and out. *Crap.* His cheeks burned. "Sorry."

"No worries. Now I know it really was good." Erin winked.

He snort-laughed and took another drink while gazing at the pines behind the house, letting his cheeks cool.

A muffled, tinny version of Darth Vader's theme came from the house. It must be Erin's cell phone. Erin scowled and went inside. She wasn't happy to hear from whoever she pinned with that ring tone. It better not be Chaz Cust.

She didn't quite close the sliding glass door. "Mom..."

Family drama. He rolled his eyes and lifted his beer.

"Mom—" She paced across the patio. "Mom! Did he tell you he tried to *rape* me? Well, he did."

Suddenly, he understood the ring tone.

"So, because he has money, you believe him and not me?" Pained disbelief rang through her words. Then her tone changed, becoming calm, slow, and sharp, like thick ice cracking under a car tire. "I cannot believe this. I can't talk to you." The phone clicked on the table, like she'd placed it carefully, probably so she wouldn't throw it. The phone went off again, but she silenced it immediately. Three times. Erin stomped back out to the patio and dropped into the lounger. Flags of color slashed her cheeks, and her eyebrows practically met above her nose, her mouth clamped tight.

He couldn't blame her. He probably couldn't make her feel better, but he could try. "Family."

"Yeah." She shook her head. "Can't live with 'em, can't kill 'em."

"Yeah." His drove him crazy sometimes, but hers was horrific. He truly hoped her mother's disbelief was a recent development, not a long-term issue.

They sat in silence again. Erin poured the last of the beer into their glasses. She said, "Can I ask you something?"

"Sure."

"Does it hurt?" She nodded at his residual arm.

Shoot. He hated talking about it, but she'd fed him and been cool and hadn't run away screaming, and she clearly needed something else to think about, so he'd talk. "Sometimes. When I wear the prosthetic too long, it aches, and I can get blisters, although I don't much anymore. Sometimes I get phantom pain, but not very often." He took a drink.

"That sucks."

He shrugged. "I suppose, but it's like overdoing it on a normal arm. Too much work and pressure makes you ache. It's a slightly different ache." He snorted. "It's better than the alternative, that's for sure." Early in his recovery, he'd wished he was dead, but with the mandatory counseling, he'd recovered. Plus, so many of the guys and gals with him in the hospital had much worse injuries. A forearm and hand were nothing in comparison.

"True." Erin looked at it again. "Do you have full feeling?"

"Yeah. Sometimes too much. That's what causes the phantom pain." Something he was fortunate to rarely experience.

She winced. "Oh, that does suck. They can't get rid of the nerves?"

"No. They grow back. Some of the research they're doing right now takes those nerves and implants them into the chest wall, and then they hook up the controls for a bionic arm to the nerves on the chest wall to control the arm."

"Really? That's so cool!"

He smiled at her, amazed she could even talk about it, let alone think it was cool. "Yeah, it is. That's cutting-edge stuff, and they've only done it on a few people who have lost arms from the shoulder."

Erin jolted. "The shoulder? Wow, that would really suck."

"I could have it so much worse. I feel pretty darn lucky, most of the time." He should always feel lucky—he had it so much better than so many.

"But not always. I think it would be way too easy to get depressed. Does that happen often?" Compassion shone on her face and in her voice.

Should have known she'd want to talk about his feelings. Women always did. "Not as much as it used to, but probably more than it should."

"Are you in therapy?"

He winced. *Stupid.* After that give-away move, she'd never believe a yes. "Uh, sort of." He was fine. The docs needed to concentrate on the people who really needed them.

She raised and wrinkled her brows. "So, no."

Ryan grimaced. "Yeah."

"Why not?"

His excuses seemed flimsy. "My mom kicking my ass out if I didn't get a job did more."

"She did what?!"

Avenging angel Erin just appeared. She was hot but unnecessary. He held up a hand and shook his head. "Tough love. She was right: it was time for me to get out and be around people and get out of her basement. I've been less depressed since I got a job."

Erin gazed at him, the fury fading slowly. "But it doesn't make it go away, I'm sure. That's not something that's going to disappear, is it."

She wasn't asking. Erin probably knew way too much about this subject. "No." He stared blankly out at the trees. The silence wasn't as comfortable this time.

"You're always welcome here. Talk or not as you want. Just come over. There's usually beer and food in the fridge."

"Thanks." Erin was completely sincere, so the silence was comfortable again. Ryan blanked his mind, concentrating on the trees and the shifting shadows. They sat, drank beer, and watched the sun slowly descend toward the mountaintops. Finally, when the sun was touching the mountaintops, Erin sighed and rose, picking up dishes. He jumped up to help, and they got it all cleaned up quickly.

Erin flipped on the TV but didn't sit. The local news played. She pointed at the couch. "Have a seat. I'm going to load the dishwasher, then join you to watch the news. I'll get you a sheet, blanket, and pillow after that, if you still want to sleep on the couch."

"Want help? You don't need to wait on me."

"No, thanks." She shrugged. "I know where everything is."

"Okay." He plopped down, still amazed after all these months back home at the lack of violent crime and the relatively large number of fatal traffic accidents. Why couldn't people wear their seat belts? And why drink and drive? Ryan shook his head in wonder and despair at the stupidity of people.

After the clinking of dishes, Erin sat down at the other end of the couch. They watched the news together until the sports came on, when she got up and trod upstairs. A minute later, a stack of soft stuff landed on his lap, and he looked up to see her grinning at him. She crossed to her bedroom door. "Even though we're not working tomorrow, I always get up at the same time; way too early." She tilted her head with a half-smile. "My body reacts better that way. Goodnight."

"Goodnight." That was probably a smart tactic. He was tired too—all that emotional stuff did it every time. He put the sheet down on the couch and the blanket at the foot, figuring he probably wouldn't need it. He brushed his teeth, then put on a pair of lightweight cotton pants and grabbed his weapon, returning to the couch.

Putting his .45 on the coffee table, Ryan punched the pillow and lay down. It was a surprisingly comfortable couch but not so comfortable he'd forget where he was. Which, with a possible attack, was a good thing.

Chapter 11

Nights Are Dangerous

Erin woke with a jolt. Moonlight pierced the gaps in her bedroom curtains, but nothing moved, nothing was out of place. Perhaps a deer or raccoon outside made enough noise to wake her. She grabbed her weapon from the nightstand and, leaning on the wall, lifted the curtain away a bit. She peered out the bedroom window, careful not to silhouette herself in case someone was out there. Nothing moved.

A voice. Muffled. Coming from the living room. Ryan was out there, sleeping. Her heart thudded.

Standing to the side, she cracked the bedroom door, letting her eyes adjust. Everything looked normal. Except Ryan, thrashing and moaning on the couch. Erin sagged against the wall. A nightmare. She put her nine mil back on her nightstand and returned to the couch. She moved his weapon to the far side of the coffee table so he wouldn't grab it and sat down on the edge of the table.

"Ryan," she whispered. His arms windmilled, and she barely ducked in time. She put her hand on his shoulder, firmly, ready to jump out of the way. "Ryan."

He grabbed her hand, pulling it off his bare shoulder, but held on and sat up, blinking at her.

"Ryan, are you okay? You were having a nightmare, I think."

He shivered and shuddered like a horse, then blinked a few more times. "Yeah, I'm okay. Sorry." His voice was deep and sleep-roughened.

"No problem." His hand surrounded hers, almost too hot. "You sure? You want to talk about it?"

He shook his head but kept holding her hand. Erin nodded. There were certainly worse things she could do than hold a man's hand in the middle of the night. His hand might be hot, but it was strong and the grip firm, his skin a little rough and callused. *Oh.* She was holding a *sexy* man's hand. Without a shirt, the true extent of his injuries—and hotness—was clear. Scars slashed along his side where he'd lost the arm, but underneath the tattoos of trauma, he'd built a six- or maybe an eight-pack, with firm pecs and solid shoulders. *Mind off the poor kid's chest, Erin. Eyes up.* She looked at his face, but his eyes were on *her* chest. The night air was cool, but suddenly it was way too hot.

He looked into her eyes. She didn't know *what* Ryan was thinking, but it sure wasn't about his nightmare. Erin sucked in a breath, trying to get her emotions back under control, and his eyes returned to her chest. Everything tightened in reaction. *Whoa. Ryan works for you, remember? He's eight years younger.* She stood, and her hand slid out of his; she mourned the loss. She swallowed, trying to wet her mouth. "Sure you're okay?"

"Yeah," he said in a rough voice. "Thanks." He flopped down, turning away from her. She slid his weapon back over to his side of the coffee table and went back to her bed. *It's going to be a long night. A long, lonely night.*

Erin woke for what must be the four-hundredth time but to music instead of hopes, dreams, and recriminations. She scrubbed her eyes. Usually, she was up and running, but not today. She staggered into the shower, hoping it would help, but it did little except make her want to get back in bed. But she had way too much to do. *Coffee. I need coffee.* She dressed, stumbled into the living room, and stopped.

Ryan lay flat on his back, the sheet thrown off, his rock-solid chest fully displayed. She licked her lips, then caught herself. *Focus, Erin. Employee, eight years younger. Not for you.* She entered the kitchen, the rich, bitter scent of brewing coffee snapping her out of her ridiculous fascination. Her programmable coffee pot was the best investment ever. It might not be espresso out of Izzy, but it was lovely, dark caffeine goodness, ready when she was. Pouring a cup, she resolutely kept her back to the living room. She plopped some yogurt into a bowl, added some fruit and granola, and took it to the patio, carefully not looking at the couch.

Erin ate, drank, and tried to enjoy watching the world wake up. But her usual contentment was far away this morning. Her attraction to Ryan was ridiculous. Even without the inappropriate employer/employee relationship, she had no reason to believe he'd want her as anything but a boss. Eight years was a sizeable gap. Especially with a younger man. He probably thought she was nice enough, like an older sister. *Yeah. Think kid brother.*

An obnoxious rap thumped through the house. Must be Ryan's alarm. Good thing they were delivering his mattress today; he could move into the apartment and out of her living room.

But he wouldn't be moving out of her dreams anytime soon.

The patio door opened, and the subject of her dreams flopped into the chair next to hers, coffee in hand but still shirtless. *Eyes on the mountains.*

"Morning," he rumbled.

Even his voice was sexy. "Good morning. Did you sleep okay?"

"Yeah, it's not a bad couch. You?"

"Sure." She shrugged. "Other than getting your new mattress, what are you doing today?"

"Figured I'd get everything organized and put away. Doubt the delivery will be on time. But just in case it is..." Ryan stood up and stretched.

Oh, wow.

"Guess I'd better get going." He lifted his cup to

her and left.

Erin gathered her things and followed, trying not to watch Ryan's impressive shoulders and backside as he walked up the stairs. She shook her head. *Focus, Erin, focus. Coffee.* She poured herself another cup of coffee and returned to the patio. Besides catching up on her finances, she had something else on her calendar... *Oh, rats.* Dinner with Mom tonight. *No.* No, she wasn't having dinner with Mother tonight. Not unless she got one huge apology, and maybe not even then. She'd find her next project car, and research video surveillance systems, and—

The patio door opened. Ryan wore his usual T-shirt and cargo shorts and plopped into the lounger next to hers.

Erin swallowed. "You're welcome to use the shower upstairs."

He waved her invitation away. "Nah, I'll be in the apartment in five minutes. I'll take a shower after I get all my stuff put away." He lifted his eyebrows. "What are you doing today?"

"I'm going to look for a new project car and research surveillance systems. I'm sure my alarm company can do it, but it will be pricey."

Ryan sipped. "I might know somebody who could help you with that. I'd need to check and see how she's doing and if she'd be willing to come out and work with us, but...maybe."

"Someone you knew in the Air Force?"

"Yeah." He grimaced. "She was...injured badly. More mental than physical, although there's some of that too. Then her waste of space husband left her at the very worst of it, and she really spiraled down. She's recovering, but it's a slow process." He shook his head. "She's... it's rough."

"That sucks. I can't imagine abandoning my spouse."

Ryan sighed. "To be fair, sometimes you have to protect yourself. I know some guys who came back, but they're not back." He tapped his temple. "They're dangerous. Mostly because they refuse to admit there's anything wrong. They drink and do drugs and won't do counseling. But that's not the case for Wiz. She's an awesome person, and her ex is a total loser." Ryan scowled and his fist clenched.

Erin hadn't noticed he'd left the prosthetic off until now.

"He didn't even have the guts to talk to her about it, just left her a note saying he couldn't do it anymore. Then a set of divorce papers showed up. Jerk."

Huh, he could talk; the subject had to be something, or *someone*, important to him. Maybe they could heal each other. Then she wouldn't have an inappropriate attraction—he'd be taken. "That sucks. Maybe it would be good for her to hang out here. You know, someplace different, with you, someone she knows well."

Ryan grimaced again. "Maybe. Hard to say with Wiz. She's not good at different. Not anymore. Which is too bad, since she's different, but...anyway, I'll see what I can do." He shrugged, then flashed a grin.

"What are you doing tonight?"

Erin snorted. "I was supposed to have dinner with my mom, but unless she's left a huge, sincere apology on my voicemail, it's not happening. And that will never happen."

"Can't blame you there." Ryan shook his head slowly, lips clamped in a frown. "As annoying as my mom can be, at least I know she's got my back."

"Whereas mine prefers to stab me in mine." Erin shook it all off. "Anyway, I'm not sure. Probably just stay here and watch TV or read."

"You helped me move and then made me pizza." He grinned. "Traditionally, the guy being moved buys. So, if I bring you dinner tonight, would that be cool?"

Erin blinked up at him, surprised. "Sure. But you don't have to."

"I want to." He stared into her eyes, unsmiling. "Do you have a grill out here, too?"

"Over there." She broke his stare and pointed at the counter next to the fireplace on the patio.

He chuckled. "Good. 'Cause about all I know how to cook is protein with fire. And salad from a bag." He laughed.

She laughed with him. Ryan had a contagious laugh; he should use it more often. "Good enough for me. I'll get the bread though."

"Awesome. Hey, lots to do." He stood. "Thanks for the coffee. Let me know if you need help with something at the shop today."

"Sure. And thanks for staying."

He smiled. "Anytime." His smile died. "Sorry about the nightmare."

"Not like you're trying to have them, right? By the way, I heard there's a new therapy for nightmares. You think through the scene and then change it in your mind to a good ending, and you think about it that way over and over, and if you do that enough, you can train yourself out of the nightmare."

His smile morphed to unreadable blank while she spoke. "Huh. I'll have to try it."

Erin couldn't tell if his response was "I don't care" or "I'll give it a shot." She smiled encouragingly. "You should. It's brand new. You might have heard about it if you were still in therapy or a support group."

Ryan scowled. "I have a mom; I don't need another."

"Sorry. I hate to think of you suffering like that. I'll shut up about it now, though." Erin turned and stared at the fireplace, clamping her mouth shut.

Ryan stood there for a moment, then went back inside. She heard the front door open, close, and his car start and drive away. She'd had to try. And now she had confirmation. She was in mom territory, not lover. Erin rolled her eyes. *No duh.*

Resigned to the confrontation, Erin went inside and grabbed her phone. Three voicemails from Mom. Angry, call me. Angry, call me now. Angry, stop being a child and call me. No apology. *Gee, there's a surprise.* Erin checked the time. Mom would be with her Saturday morning ladies' golf group, busy gossiping and slaughtering reputations. Not that she

would ever admit to gossiping. No, her mother
"networked."

Erin sent a text: "Won't make it tonight. Take
someone else."

No way she was going to say sorry, not when
Mother wouldn't. And she wasn't sorry about her
actions. Not one little bit. Erin put the phone down
carefully, even though she wanted to throw it.
Mother wouldn't answer until her golf game was
over because it was "rude to use the phone when you
are with others." Of course, she never kept that rule
with Erin. Erin didn't count. Not for the first time,
she wondered why Mother ever had a child. Dad's
influence? Too bad he died so young. Erin shook
away the faint memories of happier times.

She should channel this anger positively. She
could go for a run before it got too hot. Putting some
workout clothes on, she grabbed her headphones,
warmed up, and walked down her driveway,
breaking into a jog at the highway. The asphalt path
beside the highway was busy. Lots of runners, bikers,
dog walkers, and one roller blader. By the time she
got back to her house, she was sweaty and tired, but
it was a good tired. She added pushups and sit-ups
and called it good enough.

After a shower, she headed downtown in Smoky.
Downtown Marcus was small but cute. One main
street, but the blocks surrounding downtown were
beautiful. A mix of Victorian, log, stone, and brick
homes with huge, old maples and hawthorns
shading the streets; the area between the main street

and the County Courthouse was particularly gorgeous. It was also the location of the weekly farmer's market. She'd pick up veggies for the next week and see some friends. Maybe someday she'd have time for her own garden, but not this year.

Erin wandered the small market, picking up produce and spreading her purchases among the various farmers. She chatted with friends along the way, saving Deb's stand for last. As usual, there were people waiting for cupcakes.

"Hi, Deb!"

Deb waved enthusiastically, blonde hair bobbing, a big grin on her pretty face. "Hi, Erin! Long time, no see. How's the new guy working out?"

Erin stood off to the side so Deb could keep working. "Great. He's not chatty, but he's good with coffee and polite to the customers, and the older women love him."

Deb flashed a grin. "And I've heard he's easy on the eyes, too. That can't hurt, huh?"

Erin laughed. "He is that. Why do you think the ladies love him?" She really shouldn't encourage others to objectify him, even her friends.

Deb's grin died. "I also heard he caused some trouble, or you did, or both."

Erin scowled. The Marcus gossip mill was grinding away. She lowered her voice and stepped closer. "The Custs caused trouble. First, old lady Cust tried to demand special service, when we were really busy, and got all in my face about it. So, I told her she didn't know what service was. I got a standing ovation. But..." Erin swallowed. "I really shouldn't have lost my temper like that. Not over something so trivial."

"She's horrible, Erin," Deb whispered. "Thinks all that money entitles her to special treatment. I always make her wait at my store too. She's rude. But that wasn't the worst of it, right?"

"No. Chaz came in to 'check on his car' and pinned me between the car and his slimy self." She shuddered. "I told him to get off of me for the last time and was about to hit him with a wrench when Ryan pulled him off and sent him flying halfway across the garage."

"Ah. Rescued by the handsome but slightly damaged prince who needs a beautiful woman to remind him that his injuries don't matter." Deb clasped her hands under her chin and blinked her eyes like an old-fashioned cartoon princess.

Erin snorted. "If we were in the movies, sure. He's eight years younger than I am and my employee. Making a move would be sexual harassment, and I'm not going there."

Deb snorted back at her. "You're beautiful, inside and out, Erin. I'm sure he'd be happy to be harassed. Most of the men in this town would be."

"Thanks, I think, but Ryan thinks of me as another mom." She shrugged off Deb's words. "Anyway, I called Sam, and she said to call the sheriff, so I made a formal complaint. I noticed bruises today, so I've got to go over and see if anyone's around the office who can take pictures, in case Chaz tries to file charges against Ryan."

"Chaz isn't that stupid, Erin." She shook her head and sighed. "He'll sue."

"He can try." She smiled smugly. "I had Sam draw up my contracts before I ever opened my doors to prevent stuff like that."

"Good for you. Smart." Deb nodded, lips pursed. "Better to spend the money up front and avoid the legal issues on the backside."

"Yeah." Erin grimaced. "Michael and I learned that one when we were still in Alaska. A handshake doesn't mean a thing in court."

"Too true. The problem is, the Custs have lots and lots of money. And you've got the Adams' on your case too."

"I know. If these both go badly, I might have to declare bankruptcy, but then I'd get a judge from outside the local area, maybe one who isn't drinking buddies with Chaz or friends with the old lady." Erin looked at the mass of people in front of the booth. "You've got customers stacking up. I'll drop by your shop this week or call you. Oh, and here." She put money in Deb's box. "I'm going to grab a baguette."

"Great. Here, try these." Deb shoved a small white box in her hand. "Have fun today."

"Thanks. I'll do my best."

Erin called the sheriff's non-emergency number while she packed her veggies in the cooler in Smoky's trunk. The dispatcher told her a female deputy was on duty today, but she was on the far end of the county; she'd call and drop by Erin's house when she could. Erin hopped in Smoky to head home.

Erin was waiting for the light at the end of town, Smoky rumbling underneath her, when her phone rang. Glancing down, she saw the call was from her security company. That couldn't be good. She answered, pulling off into a parking lot.

"Mrs. Moore, we have an unauthorized entry and a smoke alarm at your business. We've notified 911 — the fire department is on the way."

Erin's heart dropped to the floorboards.

Chapter 12

Smoke and Fire

"Where's the fire alarm coming from?" Erin propped the phone between her head and shoulder and put Smoky in gear. Normally, she didn't drive and use her cell, but she had to get there—fast. And the engine was too loud to use the phone's speaker.

"It's from the coffee shop. Only one smoke detector has gone off, and nothing has triggered the heat sensors yet."

Thank heavens—the sprinklers hadn't started. Maybe they could get the fire under control before her shop flooded. A sheriff's vehicle screamed by, lights flashing. Erin stepped on the gas, Smoky roaring through the gears.

"I'm on my way. There's a sheriff right in front of me. Can you turn off the security alarms, please?" She let the officer pull away—no sense in getting a speeding ticket, even if she could easily pass him.

"I've turned off the security alarms, but the fire alarm has to be reset at the box, ma'am."

"Okay, thanks, I've got it." She hung up, pulled into her driveway, and parked away from the building so the fire trucks, sirens wailing, had a place to park. The deputy sheriff was peering in her front window and pulling a baton off his belt, probably to break a window and open the door.

"I've got the keys! Hold on!" Erin sprinted to the door and unlocked it. The fire alarm blared, but no flames flickered. A haze of smoke hovered near the ceiling, and a pile of dishcloths on her counter smoldered, the smoke plume widening. She was halfway down the room when the cloths burst into flames. The deputy stopped short, but Erin ran behind the counter and grabbed the bleach water bucket, dumping it on the cloths. They sizzled, a blast of nasty-smelling steam rising from the charred mess. Erin swept the rags off the counter into a dish tub, dumped them into the sink, and turned on the cold water. Another hiss, mostly lost in the whoosh of water, and the fire was completely out. Her counter hadn't even scorched.

Erin leaned on the sink, recovering her breath as the sink filled. She turned the water off and jogged back down the dining room to turn the alarm off. The room filled with firefighters, big hoses in hand, the flashing of red, white, and blue lights almost blinding her. She finally entered the right code.

"Fire's out!" the deputy bellowed over the sound

of fire truck sirens. The firefighters turned around and trooped back out but not before knocking over a bunch of tables and chairs with the bulky hoses. Erin leaned against the back wall, trying to drop her heart rate.

The deputy returned, grim-faced, with a man whose helmet proclaimed him the fire chief. "Mrs. Moore, this is Chief Victor. Chief, Mrs. Erin Moore; she owns the place and put out the fire all by herself." Erin finally realized it was the same deputy who came out yesterday after the Cust incident.

"Nice to meet you, Mrs. Moore. I wish it was under better circumstances." The chief was a little shorter than she was, and much slimmer, but clearly tough, with a big handlebar mustache. Probably one of the many rawhide cowboys on the volunteer fire department; she was thankful for all of them. "Before we talk about this, I'd like to have my people scan your building with an infrared sensor and make sure we don't have any other incipient ignitions. If this was arson, there might be additional attempts." The Montana drawl clashed a little with the formality of the words. He might be a cowboy, but he did something else too. Probably another small business owner; lots of those around these parts. Or he could be a CEO.

"Rats, I hadn't even thought about that. Sure, great idea." Erin shook her head in disbelief. "I can open the garage doors from the outside or from right here." She pointed to the side.

"I'll get one guy to scan in here, and we'll get

another one in the garage. If you could come with me and get the locks and alarms?" He punched a thumb over his shoulder.

She followed the chief out, keys and phone still clenched in her fists. The air outside smelled a lot better. She strode to the garage foyer door, unlocked it, and reached for the handle.

"Stop!"

Erin spun to face Chief Victor, puzzled.

"There could be a back draft when you open the door. Please stand away."

"Okay. This is the foyer. The main garage door is to the left."

He nodded and, standing off to the side, used a long metal tool to pull the door open. Nothing happened. She pushed through the firefighters to unlock the garage door and the upstairs apartment, then went back outside. Again, no whoosh of fire, thank heavens. Firefighters tromped in, big rubber boots smacking against the concrete, shining small sensors with red laser beams on the walls. They scanned each wall and ceiling carefully but found nothing. Eventually, everyone but the deputy and the fire chief left.

"I hate to tell you 'I told you so,' Mrs. Moore, but you definitely need a surveillance system." The deputy shook his head.

She grimaced. "Call me Erin, please. I know you're right, but I didn't think I'd need one today. Silly me."

"The Custs are powerful, and Chaz has always been a bully." Chief Victor scowled. "By the way, while I'm very happy you could put the fire out by yourself, please reconsider running into burning buildings. It's not good for your health. If the fire was a little farther along, you could have died from smoke inhalation. It really is our job, and we're equipped for it." The chief's tone was desert-dry.

Erin nodded. "I thought about that when I opened the door, Chief, but when I saw what was burning, I knew there was a little time. Those were cleaning cloths from my dirty hamper—I could see the coffee stains, and I knew they'd be damp. At least for a while. Whoever set this, they weren't too bright."

Both men snort-laughed. The deputy said, "True, that. A tech has already checked your drive-through window for prints—there's nothing but smudges, probably from gloves. The window was popped out; it's not even broken. It wasn't a pro, but it wasn't an idiot either. You need that surveillance sooner rather than later."

"Copy that, Deputy. It's the first thing on my list." An expense she couldn't afford but less expensive than her business burning down.

They said goodbye. She checked Ryan's apartment first—the boxes were pushed away from the walls, but a quick vacuum run had the dirt from the firefighters' boots cleaned up. The stairs, she left for later. With no damage, she didn't need to tell Ryan about the incident; there was no need to worry him more. Although with him living above the shop, he was at more risk than she was. She entered the garage. It was fine—a little more dirt wouldn't hurt anything—and the coffee shop didn't take long to sweep. The nasty burned smell would take longer to fade. She popped the drive-through window back in and resolved to install locking security bars inside immediately.

Finally, she hopped back in Smoky and put him in the house garage. She wanted him with her, safe and sound.

Dragging her groceries into the house, Erin put them away and did a little research on surveillance systems. Mostly, she learned she didn't really want to do it herself, but she could, and it wasn't quite as expensive as she thought The female deputy sheriff called and told her she'd be by later to take the pictures, so Erin gave herself the rest of the day off. She poured an iced tea, put her feet up, and pulled out her e-reader.

Erin awoke to a loud knocking. *Dang—must have drifted off.* "Just a second!" At the door, she looked through the side window. A female deputy sheriff had one hand raised to knock again, so she opened the door. "Come on in. Can I get you some iced tea?" The blast of afternoon heat made the offer automatic.

"No, thanks. Going to snap these photos and get back on the road. Lots of speeding tourists today. I'm Deputy Enich." She was shorter and wider than Erin, but the wide was all muscle—she looked like a real bulldog, a pretty one. The bullet-resistant vest probably contributed to the impression of solidity.

"Nice to meet you, Deputy. Erin Moore." They shook hands. "Where do you want to do this?"

"Wherever you're comfortable. Maybe your bedroom?"

She led the way back, and the deputy closed the door. "Where are the bruises?"

"On my waist and left breast."

"Any bite marks?"

Erin wrinkled her nose. "I don't think so. He was behind me."

The deputy grimaced. "Sometimes, they bite the back of the neck."

Erin snorted. "He's half a foot shorter than I am. He couldn't reach my neck."

"If you can put on a workout bra and low-cut underwear, I'll take pictures of the bruising around your waist first, then I'll try to take close-ups of the breast so it doesn't become a porno-pic. Okay?"

"Sounds good. I've got a low-cut workout bra that will show the thumb print pretty well."

"Perfect." She snapped the photos and let Erin see them before packing up her camera and leaving.

Erin checked—she had enough time for a quick shower. The deputy was very professional and careful, but she felt dirty and slimy, remembering Cust's hands on her. She shuddered and jumped in the shower, then dressed quickly in shorts and a T-shirt but left her hair wet. It would be hot on the patio.

She poured herself another glass of iced tea, made a salad from the greens and veggies she'd picked up at the farmer's market, and sliced the bread, putting them all on the kitchen island. Maybe they'd eat inside after cooking the steaks. It was much cooler.

A knock sounded, and she peered through the side window. Ryan, wearing a T-shirt and another pair of cargo shorts. He had such great legs, despite the scars. "Come on in."

He smiled, but it looked a little forced, and it died quickly. "Thanks. Where can I put this stuff?" His sandals thunked against the stone floor.

"How about the kitchen counter?" She was trying to read his mood, but as usual, he was a vault.

"Thanks." He padded into her kitchen, pulling out a plastic bag with steaks and marinade, a six-pack of local beer, and a bag of salad. Guess he wasn't kidding about that.

"I went to the farmer's market today, so why don't you put the salad and beer in the fridge?"

"Okay." He turned to her with the steaks. "Grill and tongs? And a plate?"

Erin grabbed a plate and led the way out to the patio. "Tongs are out here." She fired up the grill and showed him where everything was.

"Wow, you've got a complete kitchen out here."

"No running water but everything else. Can I get you something to drink while you're grilling?"

He fiddled with the grill. "Just some water, please."

"Sure." She went back inside and got water and ice from the fridge. *Guess we're back to short answers again.* "How's the move going?"

"Okay. Got everything clean and put up." He coughed from the smoke caused by the marinade burning off and quickly closed the grill cover, glancing at his watch.

"Do you need a timer? There's one in the drawer."

"Got it. Medium rare?"

"Perfect." She stood there for a few moments, waiting to see if he'd say anything, but he didn't. "Kind of hot out here, so do you want to eat inside?"

"Sure."

Erin went back inside to get plates and silverware. She didn't know what was wrong, but something was off. But she couldn't figure out a lot of Michael's silences either, especially after his last tour. The tour before he died, anyway. *Enough, Erin. Let's not go back down that road.*

Erin pulled two beers from the fridge and a couple of glasses from the freezer, although Ryan would probably drink it from the bottle. Finishing the salad, she put it and the bread on the table, too. Then she washed up the few things she'd used, to keep busy.

Ryan brought the sizzling steaks to the table. They both sat down, Ryan plopping a steak on her plate and swapping out the clean plate in front of him for the plate he'd used for the steaks.

"No sense in dirtying another plate. Besides, all the juice is on here." He winked and grinned at her, grabbing a piece of bread and soaking it.

She smiled back at him and cut a piece of steak. The knife slid easily through, juices pooling, and the scent made her mouth water. *Tender and flavorful.* "Oh, this is good."

"Should be. Got it from Marcus Meats." He was staring at her. At her... mouth? She wiped her chin, in case she'd missed something. He blinked and went back to his steak.

"They have good stuff." She took another bite. Delicious.

They ate in silence for a while. Ryan abruptly asked, "Are you feeling okay?"

"Yeah. I ended up with some bruises—a deputy took pictures today."

Ryan's hand clenched, and he glared at the table. "Wish I'd done more than pull him off. Should have pounded the guy into the ground." His jaw was so tight he snarled the words.

"I'm glad you didn't because I'd be bailing you out of jail. And you'd be perpetuating the stereotype of the veteran who freaks out and goes ballistic. That's how the Custs would sell it." Erin shook her head. "No, your response was perfect."

His mouth twisted. "Yeah, maybe. But not as satisfying as pounding that rat."

She laughed. Ryan stared at her incredulously, then joined her. She figured he'd see the humor, eventually.

"He is a rat but a rich rat. I shouldn't have taken on old Mrs. Cust either, but it was *so* satisfying to pay her back for the years of arrogance." She shrugged. "I'm sure I'll be paying more for that, but..."

"It was perfect, and everybody else thought so too." Ryan took another bite of steak. "Wait a minute, what do you mean by paying *more*?" The words were garbled a bit.

She'd forgotten to tell him about the attempted arson. That was dumb, except the more she thought about it, the angrier she got. But there was little she could do except spend money she didn't have.

He scowled. "That son of a... I really wish I'd pounded him into dog meat."

"I kind of do too, except it would still end with you and me in jail." That wouldn't help anyone.

"Shoot." He glared off into the distance for a while, then turned back to her. "You know, I'd kinda wondered why all my stuff got shoved around and about all the dirt on the stairs, but I wasn't sure I wanted to ask." Ryan grimaced. "Sorry I doubted you."

Erin huffed. "The apartment is yours, Ryan. I'll only enter it under emergency circumstances, like today, or with your permission. But I should have told you about the attempt right away. Sorry." She grimaced. "I didn't want to think about it, and that's not fair. You're at risk, so you have to know."

"I get it. It's not a problem." He kept eating, including about a third of her steak.

They finished the meal in silence, but it was pleasant. After she cleared the plates, Erin said, "I got dessert, too. Want it now?"

Ryan groaned. "No. Too full. Maybe a little later? We could download a movie."

"Sure. Anything but *Full Metal Jacket*."

Ryan's look of horror was hilarious. "What's

wrong with *FMJ*?"

"Nothing, but I've seen it—a lot." So. Many. Times.

"But it's got such great lines! And R. Lee Ermey. Gotta love that guy." He smiled fondly, like the guy was his grandpa.

She laughed. "He's great. But I've seen it enough."

"Hey, I'm just joking." He winked at her. "Maybe one of the new kids' movies instead?"

"A kids' movie? You?"

He shrugged one shoulder. "Wiz told me she really liked the last few."

"And how is Wiz?"

He shrugged again. "Hard to say, really. She's not willing to leave her Fortress of Solitude, but if you send her blueprints of the building and some pictures, she'll do the design, and then you can buy kits from Costco. She'll only charge you two hundred for the design because she says you must be an awesome person to put up with me." He laughed.

Erin chuckled. "You're no problem. You're the perfect employee, actually."

His smile crashed and burned. "Thanks. Movie?"

"Sure. Pick one out. Another beer, or something else?"

"I got it. Anything for you?"

"Nope. Thanks." She pulled up the TV listing, scanned through to the kids' movies, then sat on the couch in her usual spot. *Wonder why he went blank again?* Maybe he was more worried about Wiz than he said. She didn't feel comfortable asking about it, though.

Ryan sat on the other end, with beer and water on the coffee table.

"There's a footrest if you want one." She handed him the controller. He quickly selected one of the first ones and glanced at her. She nodded.

"Cool." Ryan selected it and leaned back. "Do you mind?" He pointed at his prosthesis. He was wearing the one that looked like a hand. She didn't even notice anymore, and she wasn't sure if that was good or bad.

"No, of course not. Make yourself comfortable." Erin took a sip of her beer, not wanting to stare. But she watched out of the corner of her eye. He put the prosthesis on the coffee table and raised the stump—wait, no. What did he call it? Residual arm. It was important to get the terminology right. Raised the residual arm and massaged the end.

She had to ask. "Are you sure that doesn't hurt?"

"No. Just feels...tight. Constricted." Ryan frowned into the distance for a moment, and her heart sank—had she pushed too hard? But he continued, "Like wearing a ski boot or a hiking boot, then taking it off. You like doing the sports, but it feels so good when you get the gear off."

Good, he wasn't offended. "That makes sense. Do you ski?"

He looked at her with an obviously fake look of horror. "Ski?! A two-planker? I'm a boarder, baby." He held out his arms in a surfer's stance. "You?"

She laughed. "Yeah. I ski. I try to go at least a couple times a month. I'd love to go during the week when it's less crowded, but the business isn't there yet."

"I can hold down the shop. But if you go on the weekend, I'd love to catch a ride."

"Sure. Always nice to have company on the drive. Do you hike?"

"Yeah." He nodded, a thoughtful look on his face. "I used to backpack too, but I haven't gone since Alaska."

Erin paused the movie, which hadn't finished the credits yet. "I go out backpacking with the University of Montana's Wilderness Institute once a year. I'm sure they'd be happy to have you along too."

"Really? What do they do?" He seemed intrigued.

"They have a Citizen Science program for wilderness character monitoring. Trail conditions, what campsites are like, inventorying manmade structures, who's using them, and sometimes trail clearing, campsite naturalization, or weed pulling. They go to lots of different places." She grinned. "This year, they're going to the Frank Church River of No Return Wilderness—it's practically in our back yard."

"I'd love to get out there." Longing was plastered across his face. "When are you going?"

"Middle of August. I'll be shutting down the shop for a long weekend, which I meant to talk to you about, anyway. I can send you the details, and if you want to go, I'll email the director and see if they can fit you in on my trip. We can share most of the stuff they recommend."

"Cool. Yeah. Send me the deets, please." Ryan smiled at her, an excited, happy smile.

For a moment, she could see what he was like before his injury. She smiled back. "Sure. Movie?"

"Yeah."

They watched, sipping beers and cracking up. As the end credits rolled, Erin got up. "Your friend Wiz was right. This was a good movie. Dessert now?"

"Sure."

Erin put the cupcakes on plates, handing one to him. She was unwrapping hers when Ryan moaned. She chuckled at the look of ecstasy on his face. He *really* liked the cupcake.

"That is *so* good. Did you bake this?" He took another bite, leaning over the plate on his lap to catch crumbs.

She chuckled. "No, my friend Deb baked it. She owns the best bakery in town."

"I guess so." He stared worshipfully at the treat. "Is she single?"

"Yes." The way to a man's heart... At least one of them could have a hot hunk of manhood.

"Wow. The men in this town are all idiots."

Erin snorted a laugh. "That's true. Present company excepted, of course."

Ryan flashed a smile at her and ate another bite. She'd tell Deb she had a new convert. She sampled hers and had to strangle a moan of ecstasy. *Wow.* Deb really outdid herself. She licked her lips and glanced at Ryan. He looked at her mouth, then raised his gaze to her eyes.

He leaned toward her, a finger extended—she couldn't look away, trapped by the heat in his gaze. He trailed one finger down her cheek, swiping it across her lower lip. Pulling away, he licked the frosting off his finger, never taking his eyes off of hers. She swallowed. *That was hot. So hot.*

Ryan's voice was low and gravelly. "Yeah. The only way that could be better—"

Three quick raps sounded on her front door, breaking the spell. *Oh, no.* She knew who knocked like that. Erin considered not answering, but Mother would walk around to the patio and let herself in. Talk about lousy timing. Or maybe it was good timing—that moment might have led to all the wrong places.

"I really don't want to deal with her right now," Erin muttered. Rising, she reached the door as three more ever-so-polite raps rang louder. She jerked open the door. "What?"

"That's no way to answer the door, dear. Let me in. I'm not standing here on your porch." Mom's usual haughty annoyance sat on her face.

Erin didn't move. "I have company."

Mother, dressed too formally for Marcus in a beautiful, silky, dark blue shift dress with a short jacket, pushed past her. "Really, dear, I taught you better manners than that. Who's here? Deb?"

Erin closed the door behind Mother and went to face the music.

"Now I see why you couldn't come to dinner with me and my guests." She spun to Erin. "Aren't you going to introduce me?"

Erin sighed. "Mother, this is Ryan Walsh. He's my new barista and lives in the apartment above the shop. Ryan, this is my mother, Sharlene Murphy."

"Mrs. Murphy, nice to meet you." Ryan held out his hand, keeping his left side angled slightly away from her mother. He'd evidently put the prosthesis on while Erin got the door.

"Likewise, I'm sure." Mother turned back to her, ignoring his hand and clearly dismissing Ryan. "Erin, it's not wise to socialize with the help. You should know that."

"Mother, first, that's incredibly rude. The help is standing right there." Erin made the air quotes obvious and swept an arm toward Ryan. "Second, Ryan worked for Michael in Alaska. He's a *friend* and a fellow veteran from my former unit, not just an employee." She glared. "And if you're going to act this way, you can see yourself out. Now."

"Erin! Talk about rude!" Red slashes appeared on her cheeks.

"Funny how clearly you see it in others but not yourself. I, on the other hand, am happy to own being rude right now because you are being intolerable. I think you should go." She pointed at the door. She was so done with Mother's attitude.

"Fine." Mother sniffed. "I came to see if I could mend this ridiculous fuss with the Custs, but I can see you've got better things to do." She minced to the door.

"Mrs. Murphy." Ryan stomped over, brows

narrowed and red highlighting his high cheekbones. Erin tried to wave him off, but he ignored her. "That sleaze ball tried to *rape* your daughter. I know; I pulled him off. This isn't a ridiculous fuss. He left bruises! What kind of a mother thinks the man who attempted to rape her daughter is just a fuss to mend?"

Mother turned back around, eyes snapping, and as she opened her mouth, Ryan added, "Or is it that he's rich? After all, money makes everything better, doesn't it? You didn't even ask if Erin was okay. My mom may not be very successful by the world's standards, but at least she loves me more than someone else's money."

"Your mother?" Mother pointed a shaking finger at Ryan's chest. "I know about your mother, Ryan Walsh, and she's a drunk. She may love you more than money, but she doesn't love you more than alcohol." She spun, her high heels beating an angry staccato across the slate and out the door. A car door slammed, and gravel flew as Mother sped down the driveway.

Erin closed the door gently, then turned to face Ryan. "I'm sorry she was so awful to you." She shook her head sadly. "Believe or not, she didn't used to be this bad. She's always been driven and wanted more than she has, but it wasn't until she made bank president that money ruled every bit of her life. I suppose Dad dying at that same time didn't help."

Ryan slashed his hand through the air. "That's okay. I don't care if she's rude to me. But acting like a rapist is a good guy because he's got money is evil."

"Yeah." Erin scowled. "Nothing like encouraging unacceptable behavior from the same people you had to fight to make it to the top." She returned to the couch, Ryan following.

"What do you mean?"

Erin plopped into her seat, exhausted. "She had to fight hard for her position. A lot of powerful men with big money did their best to keep her out. But most of the board members realized she was excellent at her job and would make a good president. But now? She sucks up to those same rich men who didn't want her there. It's bizarre. I can understand not wanting to lose business, but that takes politeness, not fawning all over them. And I think her behavior pisses them off. It was one reason they didn't want an 'over-emotional female' in the job."

"It seems a little weird." His puzzled look matched hers.

"Yeah. And she does her best to keep other women at the bank out of leadership roles. It's like she thinks they should have to fight as hard as she did, or maybe she's threatened by younger women." Erin sighed. "I love my mother, but I really don't like her much anymore."

"I get that." Ryan nodded. "I love my mom, but I didn't like her very much when I was in high school. She *was* a drunk. My dad walked out, leaving her with three kids to raise on a housekeeper's salary, and she drank every evening, probably to wipe away the memories or the stress. But she got sober after I left." He smiled. "I expected her to go off the deep end, but I guess me leaving knocked some sense into her head. She goes to AA every week."

"Good for her. I wish there was a twelve-week program for 'nasty rich person syndrome.'" Erin laughed, a little despairingly. "I'd hogtie her and haul her there." She sighed. "And thanks for defending me, but I can take care of myself. You don't need to get in the middle of my family problems."

Ryan nodded. "I know you can, but it's kind of nice to have someone in your corner. You did it for me; I'll do it for you. What puzzles me, though, is why she'd know anything about my mom." His eyebrows rose. "Not like Mom is hanging out with your mother's set."

"That is odd. Did she get a loan from Mother's bank?"

"No. She got the house in the divorce. That's why she could raise three kids and drink on a housekeeping salary." He pointed at the remains of her cupcake. "Are you going to eat that?"

"No." Not with the way her stomach churned.

"It's not going to waste." He ate it in a couple of bites, then picked up all the plates and took them to the kitchen. "I'm going to go. Don't forget to email me that backpacking stuff. Thanks for having me over."

"Thanks for the steaks. Do you want the rest of the beer?"

He smirked at her from the door. "No, now I have

an excuse to come visit." He tapped the door frame. "Even if the guy probably won't come after you tonight, since his attempt failed so badly, keep your windows and doors locked, will you?"

She nodded in agreement. He closed the door gently behind him. Erin sank back into the couch. *What a night.*

Chapter 13

Mom: Another Word for Love

Ryan walked back to the shop, gravel crunching under his feet. He was both happy and miffed about Erin's mother riding in like the Seventh Cavalry. He'd almost kissed Erin. He stopped and closed his eyes for a second, remembering the feel of her soft skin. If he'd followed his first thought and asked her to lick the frosting off his finger, they wouldn't have answered the door.

If her mother came in anyway, she might have seen a lot of him. He laughed, the sound echoing off the metal doors of the garage. No, they wouldn't have gone that far. But locked on Erin's lips? Yeah. He'd wanted to, that was for sure.

But if he had, everything would change, and he wasn't sure either of them was ready for that.

They'd both been caught up in the moment, but afterwards, she'd regret kissing him. Ryan would regret it because he'd forget and use his residual arm, and Erin would freak. She might be comfortable seeing him without the prosthetic, but touching her with the ugly stump? No one wanted that. And then everything would be really awkward. No, it was best if they just stayed friends. He didn't have many. It would be stupid to scare her away because he wanted her.

But logic didn't stop his longing. Erin was beautiful, inside and out. He kicked a rock. The men in this town really were idiots. They had gorgeous, talented women everywhere, and rather than wining and dining them, they felt threatened. So stupid. He snorted. If he hadn't gotten to know Erin at work, she'd intimidate him too, even if he had both arms. But if he had both arms, he'd still be in the Air Force or working on a flight line. If he was playing the what if game, the Sarge would still be alive, and they'd be happily married.

He entered the garage, locked it, checked the shop alarms, and trudged up the stairs into his apartment. It was looking pretty good, if a little bare. Everything was clean, neat, and in the proper place. And the new bed was comfortable. Really comfortable. Not that it would help him sleep tonight. No, tonight was likely to be a repeat of last night, tossing and turning and wanting what he couldn't have. Plus, he was worried about an attack on Erin's business, or worse, her home, out there on the back of the property, all alone.

But it would take a lot of guts to attack after such a spectacularly failed attempt, and he didn't see Cust having any courage at all. He was pretty sure they were both safe for tonight. Cust was sneaky enough to know he needed a plan, not another stupid attempt. Not after such a massive failure.

Besides, there was no way Cust could have fit through the drive-through window. He must have paid or threatened someone to set that fire, and now that guy had a hold over Cust. Or Cust had a really powerful hold over the arsonist. Either way, it would take a little more time to set something decent up. Cust wasn't entirely stupid; he had to know people talked, eventually. He'd want to find a pro, one that couldn't get traced back to him. Nah, Erin and the business were safe tonight. But since Ryan would be awake anyway, he'd patrol, weapon in hand.

He flopped onto his bed. The mattress was perfect, except for the lack of a sexy mechanic. He could want all day, but he wouldn't get. He had friendship—it had to be enough. Especially when she needed a friend as much as he did. She spent way too much time out here by herself, when she should be downtown, dancing the night away. And not with Chaz Cust or her horror of a mother. Ryan shuddered.

Even when his mother was drunk, she hadn't been like that woman. Dysfunctional, sure. Pretty much useless after she got home from work and started drinking, check. But Ryan knew Mom loved him— she'd never throw him under a bus for money. Especially money that wasn't even hers. It must be the power of her position. Political and economic power was addictive, they said. Not that he was likely to find that out. He laughed, the sound echoing a bit in the mostly empty room. Not with what he was making. Not that his salary was bad for what he was doing, and this apartment was perfect. But he'd made more in the Air Force, even as a brand-new airman. And he'd had a promotion due when his arm got blown off.

He could go to school, if he could figure out what to study. He had the GI Bill, and he'd saved some for college. Or the VA would pay for training in a new career field, but again, he'd have to figure out what kind of a job he wanted. Nothing really held his interest. He'd make coffee for a while and see what happened. Maybe he'd figure it out. Or maybe he'd spend the rest of his life making coffee and driving a delivery truck. It could be worse. Lots worse. Too many guys came back missing legs or brain cells. Or worse. An icy shiver ran down his spine.

Enough doom and gloom. Time for some mindless entertainment, and then he could sleep in tomorrow. Ryan pulled out his laptop and surfed through all his social media, laughing at some of the stuff his buddies in his old unit posted. He really missed those guys. He missed being in the military. Not the military itself but the sense of being part of something bigger, having a real mission; everyone working together to crush a goal. Yeah, that's what he missed. At Kelly's, everybody was doing the mins, and for what they paid, that's what they got. He was more than happy to work hard for Erin, but it was still just coffee. Necessary to most of the people he saw driving through in a zombie-like state but not life and death, no matter what they thought. And they could get coffee in half a dozen other places if they wanted to.

He pulled up his email and clicked on Erin's name. The info she promised about the backpacking trip. He read the email from The University of Montana's Wilderness Institute. While the "citizen scientist" spiel was serious, the trip looked like a little work and a lot of fun. Attached was an application, medical questionnaire, legalese, and an equipment list. He'd see what he had and what he'd have to find, borrow, or buy.

The first thing he needed was a new pair of hiking boots. His old ones were pretty beat up, and while he could wear his desert camo uniform boots, they were pretty beat up too. His good ones hadn't made it through the medevac. Good hiking boots were pricey, but maybe he could find something on sale.

He'd check Mom's—maybe his old backpack was still there. No telling if it would fit. He had way more muscle than he had at eighteen. He might have an old sleeping bag there too. Clothing was easy; he still had all his military gear, a never-used mess kit, and water bottles, too. Peanut butter and jelly for lunch, oatmeal for breakfast, throw in some trail mix and jerky, and he'd be good to go. Dinners were provided but vegetarian, so he'd get some sausage to add. No alcohol allowed. Interesting, and probably smart.

He closed down his email and put his hand behind his head. The last time he'd been backpacking was with a bunch of the guys from his Alaska unit, after they'd returned from their first overseas deployment. They'd hiked to a lake on the Kenai Peninsula and spent most of the time sitting around the fire, drinking beer. Their packs were a lot lighter on the way out. He grinned. They hadn't seen much other than the trail and the lake, but it'd been a blast. Yeah, he missed those guys.

Tomorrow he'd take Mom to breakfast after church and see if his old gear was still around. He sent her a text, asking, and she answered back 'yes' with hearts and smiley faces right way. Hopefully, they wouldn't run into Sharlene Murphy. Ryan snorted. It wasn't likely. She did "brunch" at expensive restaurants, rather than breakfast at a diner like the rest of humanity. Poor Erin.

And now I'm full circle, back to thinking about Erin. Yep, it was gonna be a long night. He grabbed his Xbox and put his grasper back on. Time to kill zombies.

The next morning, he pulled out a chair for his mom at the Coffee Cup.

"Ryan, how's the new job?" Mom's expression slid from hopeful to worried and back again.

He was tempted to tease her, but he couldn't—not after meeting Erin's mother. A shiver ran up his spine. "It's okay. It's kind of interesting. It takes practice to make a good espresso." Ryan huffed. "It's kind of ruined me for regular coffee. And that's not something I ever thought I'd say."

Mom laughed. Katie Walsh was still a good-looking woman when she smiled, but her addiction and tough life carved some pretty deep lines into her face, making her look older than her forty-nine years. "I never thought I'd see the day my son would become a coffee snob."

He snorted. "Doesn't seem likely, does it? Surprised me too."

"And your boss? You knew her before, right?" Mom raised both brows, clearly curious.

She'd never met any of his coworkers or bosses—the Air Force had never stationed him in Montana. Or anywhere close to Montana. Neither of them could afford tickets to Alaska. The Air Force flew her to Walter Reed, but she'd seen little except the hospital and his broken body. Ryan nodded. "Yeah, she was married to one of my first bosses in the Air Force. He was killed downrange four years ago."

She took in a sharp breath. "That's terrible. I'm so grateful you made it." She leaned across the table and grasped his hand, squeezing once before releasing him.

"Yeah." He'd lost too many friends. Not so many compared to an Army soldier or a Marine, but every single one of them left a hole.

Mom put a hand on his and squeezed. "I'm sorry, dear. Didn't mean to bring up bad memories." She smiled brightly. "How is working there at, what is it, Coffee and Cups?"

He grinned. "Coffee and Cars. I know, it sounds like a weird combination, but it works. I can take you out there and show you my new place if you'd like. If

Erin's around, I'll introduce you."

"I don't want to put you to any trouble." She fiddled with her purse strap.

Ryan chuckled. She wanted to go. "It's no trouble, Mom. I'm not doing anything today except laundry. I want to stop by the house first and see if any of my old gear is still in the attic."

"Sure, honey. It might be." She shrugged. "I haven't done anything with it, but your sister or brother might have. They've been cleaning."

"Really? Why?"

Mom shrugged again. "They thought it was time to get their stuff out of my way and clear out leftover junk. I haven't missed anything up there for the last few years, so I don't think I'll miss it now." Her smile turned down. "I didn't specifically tell them to leave your stuff alone because I didn't think I'd have to, but maybe I should have. Sorry, Ryan."

He shrugged in turn. "We'll wait and see what's still there, Mom. It's a long shot. Even if it's there, it probably won't be in one piece."

"What are you looking for?"

"Some of my old hiking gear."

"I rather doubt it will fit you at this point. You've put on a lot of muscle." She surveyed his shoulders. "I've seen the admiring glances you've been getting."

Ryan glanced down at his prosthesis. "Thanks, Mom."

"Ryan." She sighed. "The arm really isn't as big a deal as you think it is. Sure, it startles people at first, but after that? I bet most people don't even notice after a while, do they?" She leveled her the quintessential "Mom knows best" look on him.

"There's a big difference between 'no big deal' for a friend and 'no big deal' for a girlfriend." He frowned.

"Maybe. If a woman is that shallow, then you don't want her, anyway." The "look" ramped up.

Ryan scowled. "I haven't found out if someone is that shallow. They see the arm and disengage."

"Then you're looking in all the wrong places." She shook her head sadly, then perked up. "You should come to church with me."

Ryan snorted. "Sure, Mom, your friends all want to date me."

"Well, they do, but no, there are lots of younger people moving back here now that there are more jobs."

"There are?"

Mom tilted her head. "A lot of them go to the oil fields while their families stay here. Or they work from home. So many remote-work jobs these days. It's a different world."

"Ah." Ryan changed the subject to his high school friends and where they were now through the rest of breakfast, then drove back to Mom's house. When he poked his head into the attic, it was clear Marie and James had truly cleaned up. There wasn't much left. To be fair, most of his stuff was probably mouse-eaten or dry-rotted, anyway.

Downstairs, he convinced Mom to look at his new apartment. He didn't have to work too hard; she really wanted to see the place. He showed her around the coffee shop and the garage first, then locked and alarmed the shops. They climbed the stairs.

"I'm glad she's got good security. You're not too far out of town but far enough that it probably takes a while for the sheriff to get here." Mom shot a look over her shoulder.

"That's true. We're going to get even better security; I have a friend designing a surveillance system for the place. After the incidents we've had out here, Erin needs a video record." Ryan opened the door and held it for her.

"What's happened?" They entered the main apartment. "Ryan, this is lovely. What a nice place."

Dodged that bullet. Breathing a sigh of relief, he showed Mom around the little apartment and all the very nice amenities that Erin added, like the stacked washer/dryer combo and the built-in storage.

"And she lets you pay by working?" Mom sounded incredulous.

He still couldn't believe it either. "Yes. It's a straight trade, hours for the apartment. And if I find a car to work on, she'll trade me hours working on her projects for hours on mine."

Mom beamed and put a hand on his arm. "That is a very good deal, dear."

"Don't I know it. And it's quiet here. There's road noise, but with the air conditioner on, I don't notice."

"You've done a great job, finding this."

"William brought it up to me."

"Still..."

"Do you want to meet Erin?"

Mom shook her head. "I don't want to bother her, dear."

Ryan knew she was curious; she was being polite. "Let me see if she's busy." He fired off a quick text message and got one back immediately.

"Come on, she's home." He escorted Mom out, locked up, and led her to Erin's house. It was hot, but she wanted to walk, so they walked. Good thing Mom didn't believe in high heels.

She peered around the whole way and caught her breath when Erin's house appeared. "What a lovely home."

Ryan smiled. "Wait until you see the inside."

After he knocked, Erin answered the door, and even with his mom right there, the surge of attraction stunned Ryan. She wore another tank top, yellow this time, with khaki shorts, and it all fit her like a glove. "Mom, this is Erin Moore. Erin, this is my mom, Katie Walsh."

"Nice to meet you, Erin." They shook hands and smiled at each other. Erin offered a tour, while Ryan got her iced tea.

Erin showed Mom the entire house, including the master suite he hadn't seen—yet. When they came down the stairs, they were laughing.

"Erin, what made you think of this business, and how did you become a mechanic in the first place?"

He'd heard the story before, so Ryan tuned out and watched the two of them. They were getting along fine with none of the awkwardness of last night's fun with Erin's mother. He shuddered reflexively, remembering how nasty that woman acted. What made someone go that bad? Abruptly, he came back to the conversation in front of him; Mom was saying goodbye. Probably a long, drawn-out goodbye, but he'd better pay attention.

"Thank you for the iced tea and for the very good care you're taking of my boy." Mom smiled at Erin, clearly meaning every word.

Erin laughed. "Ryan's the one helping me, not the other way around. He's the best worker I've had. He's studied how to make espresso better, and the customers love him."

Ryan snorted. "They love my espresso."

Erin rolled her eyes. "No, no, no. Those women all love you. I've had to tell enough of them 'look, don't touch' that it's getting old." She pointed a finger at him. "They love *you*."

Ryan's cheeks heated, and he couldn't say a word.

"Next, you'll have to learn how to pour the milk in the lattes so it makes a heart." Mom held up her hands, making a heart. "Then you'll have every woman in town out here, not just the blue-haired set."

Ryan groaned and closed his eyes. "That's all I need. A bunch of teenage girls cooing over me putting hearts in their cups."

Both women laughed. "I doubt it will be the teenagers, dear. For one, you don't work the right hours." Mom shook her head slowly, a put-on look of despair. "No, I'm going to guess it's the cougars who will be after you. They'll be moving their meetings out here, you wait and see."

Erin chuckled. "I bet you're right. Good for me, those women spend a lot of money."

Ryan groaned again. They were trying to embarrass him, and it was working.

Mom stood. "Thanks again for taking good care of my boy."

"Ryan is taking care of me more than the other way around. He's got a protective streak a mile wide."

Mom beamed proudly at both of them and walked to the door. "Yes, he does. It's good to know he's using it for the right person. Thanks again."

"Drop by anytime. Ryan's a lucky guy to have you."

They walked back to the car; the sun beat down, reminding him of the desert. The lack of explosions made it far more bearable. He opened the door for Mom and started the car to kick on the air conditioner as soon as possible. "We should have driven over there. It's way too hot."

"Nonsense, dear, it's fine." Mom waved a hand dismissively, then looked at him quizzically. "What did Erin mean by 'a protective streak'?"

Ryan sighed. "I wasn't going to tell you because I know you'll worry, but Erin's had some problems lately. Her last employee got in a fight with another girl, a customer, and that girl is suing. And the guy who owns the classic car in the garage right now attacked her. I pulled him off. Wish I'd pounded him right into the concrete. He's probably going to sue, too. And then somebody tried to light the coffee shop on fire. It wasn't a good attempt, but it could have gone bad."

"None of that sounds good. Are you going to be in trouble?" Her brow wrinkled.

"If he tries to charge me with assault, Erin's going to charge him with assault and attempted rape. We've already reported everything to the sheriff. But it won't stop him from suing, which will take time and money Erin doesn't have."

"Whose car is it?"

"Chaz Cust's."

Mom's face fell. "That is definitely not good. That boy is no good and his mother is horrible. And they have a lot of money and power."

"Yes, they do. That's why we're working on a surveillance system."

Mom shook her head and sighed. "Be careful, honey."

"I will." He dropped Mom off at her house with a hug and a promise to call later in the week, then went home to do laundry. And dream about Erin smiling at him in shorts and a strappy little top.

Chapter 14

Avoidance Isn't a Good Strategy

Erin finished the invoice on a Chevy, blowing her bangs out of her face. She needed a haircut—it was too hot to wear it this long, falling in her eyes, driving her crazy. Problem was, she had no time for a haircut or anything else. No time at all.

It seemed like every older woman in Marcus—and plenty of not-so-old ladies—brought their cars out for oil changes and everything else under the sun; any excuse to drink coffee and drool over Ryan. Ryan's espresso was getting rave reviews, so business was way up in the drive-through, too, even without the cougar contingent. Erin grinned. All of which was great for her bottom line, but not so much for her time. At least the ladies made appointments for car work. And after word got around, she didn't have to give the "look, but don't touch" lecture very often anymore.

With Ryan onboard, everything ran smoothly. He picked up Erin's auto parts before he got off work at Kelly's, so they were sitting in the shop in the morning, and she worked without interruptions, finishing those jobs fast. Tiffany's temper tantrum wasn't a disaster; it was a blessing in disguise.

But in her experience, curses usually balanced blessings. She'd had more than her fair share of curses, so maybe the scale would stay on her side for a while. She sure hoped so.

Erin opened the next car's hood; another oil change, something she could do in her sleep. She inspected the engine, fluids, and the other filters on auto-pilot. She still hadn't found a new project car, and Cust's blasted Barracuda was *still* sitting in her shop. She called Peng every week, but he said Cust hadn't decided on a shop to finish the work. The weekly reminder about storage fees didn't bother him at all. Erin had to ask Sam what she could legally do with the thing; she didn't want it here. Cust might use it as an excuse to visit the shop. She never wanted to see the slime ball ever again, especially not in her shop. Although, if he ever cornered her here again, she wouldn't hesitate to take a wrench to his head.

Sam had nothing more on the Adams lawsuit, either. Erin snugged down the last bolt on the air filter cover, resisting the impulse to take her frustrations out on the innocent, and fragile, plastic case. The logger who'd witnessed Tiffany's meltdown finally talked to Sam, and she'd filed an affidavit, but the Adams hadn't replied. They were on a long family vacation. Erin snorted. It must be nice. She'd be happy for a full weekend off, but even with the coffee shop closed, she had too many cars waiting. Sam told her the logger asked her out on a date after she did the paperwork, but she'd reluctantly turned him down as a conflict of interest. Somehow, Erin couldn't see elegant Sam going out with the flannel-and-dirty-overalls-clad logger. Maybe his personality overcame his lack of style, or he cleaned up for Sam. Or maybe Sam was joking. She certainly deserved to find love again, after the disaster of her first marriage.

But, overwhelming everything else, there was Ryan. Every morning, Erin worked in the coffee shop until the commuter rush was over. Technically, there was plenty of room behind the counter for two or three people to work comfortably. But somehow, she and Ryan constantly brushed up against each other, ran into each other, his hard, sexy body rubbing up against hers, his lips far too close. He drove her to distraction.

Then, add in Ryan's personality, and it got her thinking about things she *really* couldn't have. She slammed the hood closed on the Mazda and checked the time. Well within her estimate; the customer should be happy. She made a note on the paperwork, then leaned against the car fender.

Ryan said little, but his dry and occasionally juvenile sense of humor made her laugh. He was also smart and hardworking and really, horribly wasted as a barista. Or a parts delivery guy.

"Erin?" Ryan leaned through the connecting door.

She forced a smile. "Yeah?"

"Somebody wants to talk to you."

"Who?" Usually, they'd wait in the garage, at the desk.

"Says he's the Custs' lawyer." His lip curled.

"Tell him to call Samantha Kerr, my lawyer. He's got her info. He should know better than to come here."

"Okay." The door closed.

I'd better call Sam. No answer, so she left a voicemail. Sam's office wasn't open this early. If only Cust would give up.

Ryan entered the shop. "I told him what you said. He claimed he didn't know you had counsel."

"Bull. I told Peng, and Sam sent a formal letter." She frowned at the door.

"Yeah, I know." He smirked. "I tell you, this guy had 'slimy lawyer' written all over him. Expensive suit, slicked back hair, gold jewelry everywhere, the stench of cigars—he screamed, 'I'm a sleaze—a rich sleaze.'"

"I left a message with Sam's office, so at least she'll have a heads-up. Sounds like a real piece of work."

"Yeah." Ryan grimaced, then straightened out of his slouch. "Wiz sent a diagram and a parts list for your surveillance system. Do you want to hire someone to do it, or do you want my help?"

"Guess I'll have to take a look first."

"Sure. I've already forwarded the email to you. She said to buy three kits and a computer at Costco, and I've looked up places to buy the other stuff based on her recommendations. We could go to Missoula one of these afternoons and get all the stuff, then install it this weekend. Then she'll do the computer work remotely." Ryan seemed excited about the idea.

"Geez, got my life all organized, do you?"

Ryan took a step back and his face went blank. "Sorry, I didn't realize I was overstepping."

Erin reached out and put a hand on his arm. "You didn't. I was kidding. Mostly." She shrugged once. "I'm not used to someone else caring enough to go the extra mile."

Ryan huffed a laugh. "Get used to it, 'cause I'm not gonna stop."

Erin smiled gratefully. "Thanks."

He turned away. "I'd better get back to the shop. Let me know when you want to go."

She blinked, his caring warming her heart. He should know how much his support meant. "Sure. Ryan?"

He turned back to her. "Yeah?"

"Thanks. Really." She couldn't say more without her emotions overwhelming her.

He nodded and returned to the coffee shop. *Rats.* Ryan was so sweet it was hard to keep the whole employee-employer relationship in her head. Not that it mattered; Erin was sure he'd want someone younger. Ryan was being protective. Like he'd guard his mom. She was simply another old lady to him.

She rubbed her forehead with the back of her hand. She felt ancient today. Old and tired.

Erin finished the car, checked all the fluids one more time. She buttoned it up, drove it outside, and dropped the keys and bill with the owner, who was in a deep discussion with her friends about knitting. At least she thought it was knitting. If the talk about gauges and softness ratings was something else, she really didn't want to know.

She returned to the garage, but she had finished all the outside work for the day, so she did a good cleanup. Then she messed around with a few other things until she couldn't deny she was trying to avoid Ryan. *Come on, Erin, grow up.*

With new determination, Erin opened the coffee shop door. Ryan was getting an order from one of the knitting ladies. She was trying to chat with him; he was polite but kept his answers short. He white-knuckled one of Izzy's filter handles, knocking the old coffee out with more force than necessary.

"You know they're trying to be friendly, right?" She leaned against the doorframe.

He scrunched his face at her. "You're kidding me, right?"

"No. Why?"

"Those women are worse than construction workers on the streets of NYC. They talk about me like I'm a stripper or something," he muttered, his face fire engine red.

"Oh, I'm sorry. Do you want me to tell them to stop?" Erin was trying not to laugh, but from Ryan's glare, she didn't think she was being very successful.

"I don't think that will help. It will probably make it worse."

Erin couldn't hold it in anymore and she burst out laughing. Ryan glared. "I'm sorry. It's so funny for the shoe to be on the other foot. I've dealt with that kind of thing for years. But they shouldn't be doing it, and I shouldn't laugh about it. Two wrongs don't make a right." Her cell phone rang. "Hi, Sam. You got my message?"

"Yes, and I got a visit too. Lucky me." Erin could almost hear Sam's eyeroll. "What a jerk. He evidently thought I'm an incompetent idiot. Tried to hit on me too. Yuck."

"Ew. Sorry."

"Not your fault Chaz's lawyer is as nasty as he is." Sam snorted.

"True. What did he do?"

"First, he tried flattery and slimy innuendo. When I kept going back to the contract instead of responding to his comments, he tried intimidation. When I made it clear that wasn't going to work, he tried to imply they'd win in court because they know all the judges. When I responded that you could file criminal charges, and that we would appeal any civil action to a higher court, *and* he could expect a certified letter specifying Cust is not welcome on your property, he made some lovely comments about women and stormed out."

"What a dummy."

"Yes, very unprofessional." Sam blew out her

exasperation. "Look, I'm calling Peng. I'm telling him that he's got twenty-four hours to give you a delivery location, or you're dumping it in Chaz's driveway. This has gone on long enough. I don't want to talk to that scumbag again."

"Thanks, Sam. I'd appreciate that. When I deliver the car, I will email a final invoice and return the remainder of the deposit. I'm not even going to charge him storage fees for these last couple of weeks; I just want it out of here."

"No, no, Erin, charge the fees. They may not be much in terms of money, but they need to see that you're a good businessperson and not a pushover." She laughed. "As a matter of fact, add in an hour of my time to the bill as a mediation fee. If I've got to talk to his sleazy lawyer, he's paying for it."

"That, I'll be happy to do. Thanks, Sam." She was so lucky to have such great friends.

"You're welcome. I'll let you know where and when, and, just for you, I'll talk to the sheriff's office about an escort."

"Thanks."

"No problem. Bye." Sam hung up.

"Sleazy lawyer man trying to make trouble?" Ryan poured milk into a cup.

"Sam put him in his place." Erin smirked. "Sam is calling Peng and giving him twenty-four hours to give me a place to drop the 'Cuda. She's also sending the lawyer a certified letter informing him that Cust is not welcome on my property, with a copy to the sheriff."

"Good." Ryan scowled. "We don't need any excuse for Chaz to drop by."

"Yes, but now I've *got* to get that surveillance system in. And upgrade with my alarm company. It makes me more than a little nervous knowing you're living here. I don't want you getting hurt because that jerk tries to take out his frustrations on my business. Maybe you should move into my house for a while?"

Ryan's brows knit. "I'm not too worried about being here, especially while the 'Cuda is, but I am a little worried about you being alone back there. Do you have an alarm for your house?"

"No." More money she didn't have.

"Maybe you should." He put another cup on a tray.

"Not sure what good it would do." If she was there, she'd hear someone breaking in. If she wasn't, everything she owned was replaceable.

"If someone breaks in, you'll wake up. Maybe you should move to your upstairs bedroom at least. That way, you wouldn't be so vulnerable."

Erin nodded. "That's probably a good idea. I have to leave the windows open, or it's too hot to sleep, and being on the ground floor with a window open seems stupid right about now. Thanks."

He fussed with the cups. "Good. I'll take your bed."

"You will not!" She glared at him. "That is *not* going to happen, Ryan. I'm not letting you put yourself in harm's way. You're a barista, not a bodyguard. Maybe you should move back in with your mom for a few weeks."

"And leave you out here by yourself?" He glared. "Not gonna happen."

They stared at each other, neither one willing to give in. Erin turned away, trying to get her brain back in gear. *Come on, Erin, think about this logically.* Maybe she should look at the surveillance plan Wiz sent. Cups clinked; Ryan taking the tray of drinks to his customers. At the office computer, she pulled up her email and the schematics from Wiz. Okay, these were clear, and the installation didn't look difficult. Ryan returned to Izzy, cleaning the steaming wand.

"Ryan, did you look at the schematics?" She sent them to the printer.

"Not really. I just glanced at them." He shook his head once, with a frown.

"Wiz added a warning system on the driveway. Since my property is fenced, we can close the gate at night, and if someone opens it, an intrusion alarm will sound. And she's got another set of detectors set closer to the building, so if someone drives in, that alarm will go off as well. Of course, it will also go off if a deer walks between the detectors, but better safe than sorry."

"That's great, unless someone parks off the property, then sneaks along the fence until they get to your house." He tapped the filters out.

"I can email her a set of plans for my house, and she could do that one too, if she agrees." She'd happily pay the design fees.

"Good idea." Ryan nodded sharply. "But I'm still sleeping in your bed for the next couple of nights."

"No, you aren't." Erin glared at him. She could protect herself, and she didn't want to put him at risk.

He stared back impassively. "Yeah, I am."

She put her hands on her hips. "I'm not some helpless wallflower, Ryan!"

His expression remained emotionless. "Didn't say you were. Two people is safer than one."

Giving up for the moment, she threw both arms up. "Save me from stubborn men! I'm going back to the garage." She brushed past him and opened the door.

"Sure. Let me call William and ask him if I can have the afternoon off, and we'll go get all the stuff."

She turned back. "No. Go to work. I'll get it."

He smirked. "But I know where it all is. You'll have to do all the research again."

"You could give it to me."

"I could." Ryan's smile slowly widened to a grin. "But I won't."

Erin glared at him and stomped into the shop. Men were so arrogant. Did he really think she was so incompetent that she couldn't do a little electronics shopping? When the door closed, she stopped. Oh, rats—she had finished everything she needed to do. But the Barracuda still sat there, mocking her. She could load it on the trailer and have it ready to go. She'd get her truck and trailer from the house.

As Erin neared the house, she spotted someone

crouching at her garage door, fiddling with the handle. "Hey, what are you doing?" The person looked back at her, startled, then ran to the back of her house. Erin broke into a sprint, chasing the man.

Chapter 15

When Trouble and Help Collide

Erin skidded to a stop. She was unarmed; following the man was stupid. She dialed 911 on her cell phone and jogged back to the shop while she reported the attempted break-in, glancing over her shoulder. Once safely inside the shop, she locked the door and entered the coffee shop. "Ryan, you have a weapon upstairs, right?"

"Yeah, why?" He stopped wringing the cloth in his hands.

"Because I just scared off someone trying to break into my house. I'm on the phone with 911. Shop's locked. Need to get the customers out of here safely."

"Crap." He pushed past her and into the garage.

Erin grabbed her stack of freebie cards and trotted to the remaining table of women. "Ladies, I'm sorry, but there's a problem at the back of the property. For your safety, I need you to leave." She handed each of them a card. "I'm really sorry."

By the time she herded them out, Ryan was standing in the doorway to the shop, facing her driveway. His arms were at his sides, so she couldn't see his weapon; she appreciated his discretion. When a deputy sheriff pulled up in front of her, Ryan went inside the shop. She and the deputy inspected her shop and house but found nothing.

Back at his truck, the deputy tipped his hat. "I'm sure you scared him off, ma'am. You might want a surveillance system."

"Working on it. Thanks for the help." Erin let herself into the coffee shop and picked up the remaining cups. Ryan was on his cell, weapon strapped to his thigh, pacing. She started on the closing list. It was better to stay busy than think about what might have happened. But she couldn't help considering the possibilities. If she hadn't gone back there, that man could have broken in, stolen her stuff, including Smoky, and lit the house on fire. Sure, everything was replaceable. Except Smoky, the place she felt closest to Michael. She missed him so much, especially at times like these.

Ryan crossed the shop to her, phone still at his ear. "Wiz wants the plans to your house, and if you've got one, a plat, you know, something that shows where your house and business are on the property."

"I've got all that on a thumb drive. I needed it for the bank loan. I can email it to her." The house was only three years old, but sometimes it felt like a lifetime ago. Other times, it felt like she'd accepted the house from the builder just yesterday.

"Great. Wiz already emailed an updated parts list based on what I could tell her about your house, but she needs the plans to do a real layout. How many windows do you have in your bedroom?"

"Two. There's one in the bathroom too."

"Two in the master bedroom, one in the master bath." Ryan nodded and paced some more. "Erin's emailing them to you. Thanks, Wiz, I appreciate it. Are you sure you'll be okay on the drive? Yeah, I'll tell her that. Thanks." He brought the cell down and hit the end call button.

Did she hear that right?

Ryan shook his head, brows raised. "Wiz is coming; she wants to do the install herself. She says in addition to her two-hundred-dollar design fee, you'll owe her gas money and a full workup on her vehicle and some metalwork in the back of her van. I told Wiz she could stay at the apartment or at your house. I hope that's okay?"

"Of course; that's nothing. Are you sure that's all she wants? Doesn't seem like much for all the trouble she's going to." It wasn't anywhere near what that kind of work was worth.

"That's what she said." He shrugged. "Wiz told me to get the stuff today; she's driving out tomorrow, and she'll start the install when she arrives." Ryan grimaced. "I'll have to tell you a few things about Wiz." He glanced away, then back. "She's got some issues."

"Don't we all?" Maybe with Wiz here, the two of them could help each other. Erin ignored her sinking stomach. She was Ryan's boss and too old for him. She'd have to keep repeating it, reminding herself. The attraction was one-sided.

"Not like Wiz does. I don't *know* everything that happened to her, but none of it was good, and she's...well, she's got damage." He ran his hand through his hair. "We'll talk on the drive. Let's go." Ryan slid behind the counter, grabbing his cell.

"Don't you have to work?" Erin followed, warmth blooming in her chest. She was so used to doing everything on her own; having someone who cared was strange. A good strange, but so odd.

Ryan paused with his hand on the door. "I called William. He's asking Craig to work afternoons for the rest of the week."

"I should call him. I'll pay you for your time, of course."

He turned, frowning. "That's not necessary."

"Oh, but it is." Ryan had already done so much, he deserved compensation for his time.

Ryan shook his head. "Don't. William said don't bother calling; he's cool. He also said Craig offered to set up a sniper position for you."

Erin chuckled. She didn't know Craig very well, but that certainly fit his personality.

Ryan laughed too but sobered abruptly. "If things get worse, you should consider it. Craig knows his stuff. Kind of strange when you consider he was a pilot turned space geek, not a Ranger or Recon, but he would have fit right in with the guys doing base defense or even the special forces guys."

"Hopefully it won't come to that." Cust was a lazy, entitled jerk with a huge ego. Even if she'd wounded his pride, hiring bad guys to attack her seemed like too much work, too much risk for way too little payoff. Unless someone was pushing him to act for some other reason. But who would have that kind of power over the richest guy in the valley? Did she wound his mother's ego that much? Or maybe he really was that stupid. Speculation could wait; she had work to do. "Do you have the updated lists?"

"They should be on the printer." He held the door for her and then locked it.

She pulled the paper from the printer while Ryan retrieved his wallet from the apartment. They double-checked the locks and alarms. When they reached her house, they walked around the outside, Ryan first with pistol in hand. Then they entered the house and cleared the interior. Erin emailed the house plans and plat to Wiz, grabbed her nine mil and truck keys, and locked up. They got in the truck and headed north to Missoula. She was thankful she'd applied for a concealed weapons permit shortly after moving home, although she'd never anticipated needing it. She rarely carried a gun, concealed or openly, as Montana law permitted; Marcus was a safe community. Erin called Sam on the way, telling her what happened.

"This isn't good, Erin. I'm going to file an updated request and push the judge to sign the protective order today. He won't want to. Taking on the richest family in town is career suicide, but I'll make it clear the consequences of non-action will also be career suicide."

"Sam, don't blow your career for me. I know how fragile the legal system is in a small town where everyone knows your name."

"Eh, don't worry. I know how to play this game. Bye."

Erin blew out her breath and relaxed into the truck seat. Sam knew what she was doing and how far and hard to push. She shouldn't have to; justice should be blind. But that was Sam's battle to fight; Erin had hers. "Want to tell me what's up with your friend?"

Ryan slumped. "Not really, but I will. A little. It's not my story to tell. Maybe she'll talk to you. Wiz sure needs to talk to someone. She's got some big hang-ups." Ryan scowled at the dash. "I guess I have to tell you something, otherwise it won't make sense." Ryan tapped his fingers on his thigh. "I hate speculating, especially about a friend. I wasn't there, and she won't talk to me about it. What I know is secondhand. But one of our guys sexually assaulted her downrange. And the leadership blew it off and tried to cover it up when she reported."

"You're kidding me!" But Erin knew he wasn't. Too many senior leaders cared more about their careers than their people. Too many jerks only wanted power. They took it, grinding everyone down underneath their slimy boots, too lazy and selfish to do things the right way, the hard way. Taking from their brothers and sisters instead of caring for them. Greedy horrors, every one of them.

"No." He glared, and his hand clenched on his thigh like he was strangling someone. "Wish I was. They tried to blame Wiz because she was wearing workout gear. Official uniform workout clothing." Ryan turned an incredulous look on her. "Can you believe that? You're not allowed to wear civies downrange. What was she supposed to wear? A burkha?"

"No, no, I can't, and yet I can. Blaming the victim happens all the time, and the US military is twenty years behind society on this because men still make up the vast majority of members. Did Wiz eventually get justice?" She peeled her fingers off the steering wheel, one at time. No sense in strangling rubber-covered steel.

"Not really. Some. Because she's tough and brave, she didn't give up, and she had the medical people on her side. In addition to the sexual assault, the rapist beat her badly. The doctor in charge, also a woman, said there may have been more than one man, but since Wiz was drugged and there wasn't much physical evidence, there was no way to prove it. The attempted coverup raised a huge stink, and a bunch of people got relieved of command, and others got reprimands and all that. But it took a long time, and way too much effort, and crappy treatment by almost everyone except the medical folks, and by the time they launched a proper investigation, it was too late. What little evidence existed got 'lost,' so they could prove nothing against the guy Wiz could identify. And her testimony wasn't admissible because of the drugs."

Ryan scowled. "The guy was Security Forces, so you know his buddies were covering for him. Some of his friends actually taunted her, by anonymous email and burner phone. She didn't report the harassment because she knew nothing would happen. Besides, that's partially what let her figure out who the guy was." Ryan's scowl changed to an evil smile. "But she's a computer wiz, thus the call-sign, and she tracked them down, got a little revenge." He cackled.

"Oh?" While she might have done the same thing, revenge rarely made things better and sometimes created big trouble for the survivor.

"Yeah, like social media campaigns outing the guy as a rapist, with evidence. Not good enough for court but other women, telling their stories. And photos of him cheating on his wife. He got kicked out for dereliction of duty, finally, but rumor has it there was more, like theft and illegal gambling rings. He blames Wiz, of course. Slimeball. He tried a counterattack on social media, but Wiz has a lot of online friends. All his accounts got reported and shut down, time after time. He had a secret bank account that somehow got emptied. A couple of his buddies also got targeted through social media. Several of them got kicked out over the next year. One ended up in Leavenworth for assault." Ryan smirked.

"Funny thing, after the rapist's wife finally divorced him, the amount that had been in the secret bank account ended up in her new account. The cops looked at Wiz, but they couldn't pin anything on her. Then, with Wiz's help, the jerk got caught again, a civilian this time. He's doing hard time now."

Ryan exhaled, hard. "Unfortunately, while Wiz was watching him and enacting revenge, she wasn't doing her actual job in the Air Force. She got a medical retirement because her chain of command knew what had happened, but they considered Wiz totally unreliable, which, to be fair, she was. She's got some real bad post-traumatic stress. Her reactions are really extreme."

Ryan turned toward her in his seat. "Wiz goes armed everywhere, with guns, knives, and other stuff. She's learned martial arts too, so if you touch her at all, you'll probably end up with something broken, if not dead. Wiz doesn't say much, and she'll probably startle you, more than once, because she's real quiet, like a ghost. She won't show any emotion, at all." He raised his hand and grasper, like he was surrendering. "Make sure no one goes near her. Don't touch her, at all, ever. Even if she falls or trips. Don't startle her. Don't get behind her."

A gusty sigh, with a slow shake of his head. "Normally, Wiz doesn't leave her house. She does everything electronically, gets her groceries delivered, signs for things through a barely opened door, all that. I think Wiz will stay in my apartment, and I'll stay with you, if that's okay, but she might want to stay at your house and for you to stay with me."

"Whatever Wiz needs to feel safe. Anything at all." What a horrible, awful, traumatic experience. So unfair. So wrong. If those so-called leaders were here now, she'd strangle them without remorse. She'd help Wiz any way she possibly could.

"I figured you'd say that. Thanks." Ryan shuddered. "A lot of this I've pieced together from things other people have told me, and some of the stuff her husband, the piece of dirt he is, told me. I've only talked to her in person once since all this happened. We used to be pretty good friends." Ryan smacked his fist on his thigh. "Wiz trusts me because I don't push her. I know a little about how she feels, so I never bug her to do stuff like go to counseling and things like that, even though it would probably be better if she would. I don't think she'll ever let anyone into her life for real ever again."

"I'm sorry, Ryan. That sucks for you and for her." How awful. Ryan had feelings for Wiz, but she'd never be able to respond. Such a genuine tragedy.

"It sucks for Wiz, that's for sure. I'd like to help her more, but all I can do is listen or chat when she needs someone. Sometimes it's at zero three hundred, but that's okay." He ran his hand through his hair.

"You're awfully patient and selfless to do that."

"No, I'm not." Ryan turned a puzzled look on her. "It doesn't take much to jump on the computer and type, even if it is three in the morning. Even with only one hand."

"No, I meant... never mind, it's really not my business." It wasn't. She shouldn't get involved in someone else's relationship. She knew less than Ryan did.

Ryan stared at her, brow wrinkled. "No, what did you mean?"

Erin swallowed, uncomfortable. "I meant you obviously have feelings for her, so it sucks that she won't let you in."

Ryan snorted. "No, no, no. She's like a little sister or a best friend. I'd like to have dinner with her, but anything more? No." He waved, a negating gesture. "I knew Wiz because her husband was on the flight line, too. We all hung out on the weekends and did stuff together. I always thought he was an ass, and Wiz was way too good and smart for him, but she's really not my type at all."

"Oh. Sorry." Erin ignored the relief sweeping through her.

"No worries. Anyway, she's likely to be really paranoid out here, so be careful, okay?" Ryan definitely looked worried.

"Yeah. Of course. I'm amazed she's coming out at all." Erin shook her head in wonder.

"Yeah, I am too. I think it's because Wiz knows what it's like to be up against power when you're powerless."

Erin scowled at the road in front of her. "I can see why she might think that, but I'm really not powerless. If he comes after me, he's a dead man."

"Cust won't do his own dirty work, and if he does,

it won't be alone. And he's got a ton of money and political power."

"That's all too true." Erin sighed. "Where are we starting?"

"Costco."

"Okay. Got to go there anyway. If there's something you want, add it to the cart; we'll sort it out later." She'd never show him the receipt. Ryan's help was worth more than she could pay.

"Thanks."

They got to Costco, locked Ryan's weapon in the truck since he didn't have a concealed carry permit, and bought everything she needed. After five more stores and a late lunch, they headed back. When they returned to the shop, they checked the building and Ryan's apartment. He packed a bag, insisting she needed his help until Wiz got the alarms in. Erin was too tired to fight about it.

They drove to her house, cleared it, then unloaded everything and relaxed on the couch, watching TV. Ryan didn't ask her about removing the prosthetic; he popped it off. Which hopefully meant he was more comfortable with her.

Ryan texted with Wiz, asking Erin about places on the drive between Missoula and Seattle, some of which she really couldn't answer.

"Erin?"

"Yeah?" Exhaustion weighed her soul.

"You got any fine gauge wire here?" He chuckled at something on his phone.

For the alarm system? "Maybe. I'm sure I've got

some at the garage. Why?"

"Wiz suggested we set up some low-tech alarms." He gave her a half shrug and tiny smirk. "String wire on the trees outside your windows, with aluminum cans or something attached by more wire at the ends, so if someone trips over the wire, the cans make a racket and let you know something's out there."

"Huh. Good idea. Tell her thanks, please, and I'll go look."

"Great."

Erin checked the garage in the house first. She found a roll of safety wire, which was fine enough to be invisible in the dark, and a bag of aluminum cans. Ryan helped her string lines at ten and twenty feet from her bedroom windows. They also fastened a line to the patio door on the inside, one to the front door, and one to the door to the garage.

She inspected their handiwork through the patio door and laughed. "I look totally paranoid."

"Good. It will keep you safe." He yawned, a long, drawn-out yawn with a big stretch. Erin watched, the sliver of abs below the T-shirt enticing. "I'm beat. How about you?"

"Yeah. I'm going to turn in." She walked to her bedroom, but Ryan grabbed her arm outside the door. Erin turned back. "What?"

"You're sleeping upstairs." Ryan jerked his head toward the stairs. "I'll sleep in your room."

"Don't be ridiculous." Erin frowned at him. "I'll sleep in my room. That's why we set up the trip wires. Besides, I'll close the windows, and it will be hot in there."

"So?" He cocked his head.

"It's my house. If someone's going to suffer the heat, it will be me." Erin raised both eyebrows at him and looked at her arm where Ryan's hand held her. He let go and stepped back. She entered her bedroom, closing the door in Ryan's face. She changed into lightweight shorts and a tank top and did her normal night routine. When she opened the bathroom door, Ryan sprawled across her bed, wearing only shorts. She stopped dead. *Oh.* Desire sang from her head to her toes and everywhere in between. "What do you think you're doing?" Her words came out breathless and raspy, instead of indignant. She was making a fool of herself.

"I'm sleeping in your bed. You can sleep upstairs." Ryan looked smug.

And the desire disappeared. She didn't need a big brother or a dad. She could take care of herself. Erin scowled at him. "No, you aren't." She pointed at the door. "Out."

Ryan met her eyes for what seemed like forever, then scanned her body all the way up and down. "You're welcome to sleep in your bed, but I'm not moving." He stared right into her eyes and then let his gaze go back down her body.

Whoa. Erin thought about calling his bluff, but from the way Ryan looked at her, she wasn't so sure it was a bluff. His phone chimed on the nightstand, and he turned away to grab it. Ryan's backside was just as good. *Come on, Erin, get it under control.*

Employee, eight years younger, remember? Erin snatched her pillow from under his head and stomped out. Not that stomping on the thick carpet did much good. She could hear him chuckle. *Men. Always so sure of themselves.* That was better. Righteous anger—yep, that was what the situation called for. Not ridiculous desire, anger.

She grabbed her phone and weapon from the kitchen counter and tramped upstairs to the guest bed, plopping down on it. *Men.* She would never get to sleep, not with her body humming at the memory of Ryan in her bed. *Rats.*

Chapter 16

Old Friends, New Friends

Ryan watched Erin stamp out of her bedroom, her backside snapping back and forth. *Sierra Hotel. So sexy.* And the timing on that last text from Wiz couldn't be worse. He thought, for a second, that she might call his non-existent bluff. He'd tried to make his interest clear without being crude, but Erin left as soon as he looked away. And now he buzzed with desire. He sighed. Another long, sleepless night.

Ryan put his hand under his head, then pulled it away. It never felt right with just one. That must be why Erin left; she saw his residual arm when he grabbed his phone. He looked at his slightly scarred stump. It didn't look bad, really, but it didn't look good either. It definitely didn't look normal. No one could really want him, not in his damaged state. It was good that she'd left. If Erin had joined him in the bed, he'd have rolled on top of her and kissed the breath out of her. But he would have forgotten and touched her with his residual arm, and she might have freaked out. Then everything would go wrong. He'd have to find a new job, and a different place to live, and she'd still be in danger, and he wouldn't be able to protect her. Not that Erin wasn't capable of protecting herself, especially once Wiz got done with her magic, but he'd feel a lot better if he was around to help. Ryan wouldn't be able to forgive himself if something happened while he wasn't around.

No, it's better this way. Harder to sleep, but then he was on guard duty, so that wasn't a bad thing, necessarily. Of course, if she'd stayed, they wouldn't be sleeping either, but they would be a lot more distracted. Ryan grinned. He'd do everything he could to keep her completely distracted. Accomplishing that mission would be fun. But the last time he'd made a woman call out his name, he'd still had two hands. *Shoot.*

At least he still had one. Which was more than some guys had, so he should be content, if not happy. Ryan punched the pillow she'd left and flopped down. The pillow smelled like her—soap, coffee, a hint of citrus from the hand cleaner, and something too faint to put a label on, but it said "Erin" to him. He might not sleep, but he should try. Tomorrow was likely to be a really long day—Wiz would want to get everything done so she could scurry back to her fortress of solitude. Anger and sadness overwhelmed his previous mood—nothing like a real-life horror story to kill arousal. *Poor Wiz.*

The next morning, Ryan watched Erin out of the

corner of his eye. She was touchy, and dark circles underlined her eyes. Maybe she hadn't slept well. He could hope it was caused by frustration like his lack of sleep, but that was unlikely. She was probably worried about Wiz.

He was worried about Wiz, too. What if she broke down in the middle of nowhere? His phone chimed, and he pulled up the text. Relief let him sag into the couch. Wiz made it to Missoula. He texted the address to her again, just in case. "Wiz is in Missoula. She should be here in forty to fifty minutes."

"Whew." Erin's shoulders dropped. "I'm glad she made it. I think we've got everything on her list, so hopefully, she'll be happy." She bit her lip. "How do you want to play this?"

Ryan tore his gaze away from her lips. He'd missed what she said. "Huh?"

"When Wiz gets here. Do you want to go out and meet her, or should I, or should we let her walk in on her own, or what?" Erin spread her hands, a slightly perplexed look on her face. "I don't want to upset her."

"Yeah." Ryan considered how Wiz was likely to react, but he really didn't know. "I think we just let her come in. She knows this is a business. She even knows what it looks like. I took a bunch of pictures for her. If she wants something, she'll let me know, I think."

"Okay. We'll play it by ear."

"Yeah." Ryan went back to putting together some of the equipment Wiz had asked for. Erin was working on another piece. They had almost finished when a tall, white panel van pulled up, one of the fancy Mercedes versions. Wiz got a new vehicle. Surprising.

A few minutes later, Wiz entered, stepped to the side, and scanned the entire room. She walked to the wall, along it, and then to the table they were using. She wore baggy black cargo pants with combat boots and an oversized black hoodie. Beneath the hood, her long black hair was pulled back tight from her pretty, slightly elfin face. A semi-auto was holstered on her thigh, and knife handles peeked from below the hoodie's cuffs. Her belt carried a taser, bear spray, and more knives, all of them black. A small black backpack completed her "don't mess with me" look. Wiz stood to the side of the table so her back wouldn't be to either door.

"Long time, no see, Ryan." She didn't smile, offer her hand, or get close to the table.

He grinned at her, unable and unwilling to hide his happiness at seeing her for the first time in what seemed like forever. "It's good to see you. Really good." He tipped his head toward Erin. "This is Erin. She owns the place."

"Hi, Wiz." Erin smiled but stayed seated and left her hands on the table. "Thanks so much for coming out to help me. I really appreciate it. Please let me know if you need or want anything at all. You're doing me a huge favor."

"No problem." Wiz backed away from them and shot glances around the room, but her eyes darted back to them.

Erin asked, "Do you want me to show you around, or do you want to look on your own? I've got keys to everything there on the table for you, and the alarm master codes are on that piece of paper." She nodded at the sheet in front of her on the table.

"I'd like to look around and then ask you questions. Can I look at your house too?" Wiz glanced at but didn't make eye contact with either of them.

"Absolutely. Ryan and I will be here when you're done. There shouldn't be anyone else around today, unless there's a delivery I don't know about."

"Okay." Wiz backed to the wall, slid off the backpack, and pulled out a tablet, then started flicking her fingers along the surface.

Ryan watched her for a while, then made himself look away. Although it was hard to tell under the baggy clothes, he was fairly certain she'd lost weight, but she didn't have any to lose. Her eyes looked dead, with dark circles underneath, and her deep bronze skin was dull. She was so alert, nervous, maybe even outright scared. Those evil people who attacked and ignored her needed to pay and pay big. Ryan kept his eyes on the equipment on the table, trying to keep his body relaxed, until the door to the garage opened and closed. He let out the breath he hadn't realized he was holding.

Erin twisted to stare at the closed garage door. "Dang. Poor kid. She looks like one of those pit bulls they rescue from dogfighting. Wanting to trust so bad but can't do anything but growl because someone has hurt them over and over."

"Yeah." Rotten slime, taking away something beautiful and bright because they were insecure losers. His fist clenched, Ryan pounded it on the table, once. Then he breathed, counting four in and four out. He had to control his anger—otherwise, he'd make Wiz even more nervous. Gradually, he packed the fury away, breathing slowly and deeply. When he could speak again, he turned toward Erin. "Good call on telling her we'd stay here. I think that will allow Wiz to relax as much as she can in a strange place."

"That's what I figured." Erin peered out through the front window, half-rising in her seat. "Wonder what she wants me to do with the van? It's pretty new."

"You'll have to ask her, I guess. But don't ask until she brings up the subject. When she's doing a job like this, Wiz gets very focused and doesn't want to do anything else until she's done. It will probably be a very late night."

"Great." Erin chuckled. "If it's late enough, we'll pull an all-nighter. It'll be like old times. We've certainly got the right stuff to get us through." She waved a hand at Izzy.

Ryan snorted and got back to work on the last electronic gadget. He wasn't sure what these things did, but Wiz had sent him the schematics, so she obviously needed them. They'd finished when the connecting door opened.

Wiz stood behind the coffee shop counter. "Where do you want me to start?"

Erin shrugged and held up both hands, empty and open. "Wherever you want. You're the expert. But there will be people here tomorrow, so maybe you should start here?"

Wiz nodded sharply. "Okay. I'll do the coffee shop first. I need the stuff on list two. I want it all on the table. Take list one to the garage and list three to the house. Ryan, I'll stay in your apartment if you stay in Erin's house."

Ryan smiled. "Sure, Wiz, whatever you want. The sheets and towels are clean. You're welcome to use anything up there."

"I'm going upstairs. Put the list three stuff on the kitchen table in the house, then come back here. I need to look at a few things before I know if it's better to start here or not."

"Sure, Wiz." When the door closed behind her, Ryan grabbed list three and piled everything into boxes. After taking list one equipment to the garage, Erin returned with a handcart. They wheeled the rest to the house, carefully placing it on the kitchen table. Ryan made sure they locked the door.

Erin raised her eyebrows. "Wiz will think someone might have come in if we left it open?"

"Yeah." The bottom of the ocean was too good for her attackers. She'd been such a bright, vivacious person. She shouldn't have to change so much to survive.

Erin sighed. They walked back to the shop in

silence and let themselves back into the coffee shop.

Wiz popped in from the garage, keeping the counter between them. "It will be at least four hours before I'm done with your shop. If you have shopping or something to do, now would be a good time. Ryan, do you need anything from your apartment?"

"No, Wiz, I don't." He shook his head. Everything he needed was at Erin's.

"Good. Don't go up there." Her tone was fierce.

Ryan slowly held up his hands, the real one and the grasper. "I won't, Wiz. It's yours as long as you're here."

"Okay." She edged back toward the garage.

"Wiz?" Erin took a single step.

"Yes?" Wiz gripped the countertop.

"Would you like some dinner when you're done? I make a mean homemade pizza." Erin smiled gently.

"She does, Wiz. It's delicious." His stomach rumbled.

"In the outdoor oven?"

"Yes."

"That would be good." Wiz's hand was on the doorknob.

"Okay. Text Ryan when you're done, and you can come over if you feel comfortable with that. If not, I'll make you one and bring it over to you."

"Okay." Wiz escaped into the garage.

They both sat there for a few moments, staring at the door. Ryan tried to lock down his rage again. When Erin got up, he followed her down the drive, kicking rocks, trying to work off the anger.

"I've got to pick some stuff up if we're going to have pizza for three. Come along? I'm taking Smoky." Erin stood at the garage door.

"A chance to ride in that car? I'll pay for the groceries." It would take his mind off Wiz for a while. Ryan followed her into the garage, admiring the big silver beast, and slid into the passenger seat. Dang, the vehicle was prime. Every piece fit together perfectly. The seat was comfortable but firm enough for aggressive driving, and the engine rumbled.

Erin drove sedately down the gravel drive to the highway. She shot him a grin and stomped on the accelerator. The engine roared, and they took off like a bat out of hell, the force shoving him back in his seat. *What a fantastic ride.* Erin wore a huge grin, matching his.

Once they were at the speed limit, Erin whooped. "I love this car!"

"It's awesome! What's the redline?" He admired the smooth paint and perfect gauges.

"The torque flattens after 3600, but it will go higher, like to 6000 rpm."

"Have you ever clocked it?" He'd love to have a muscle car or an old truck. But if he had a Smoky, he'd probably get a lot of tickets, too.

"Michael did. He got zero to 60 in 5.5 sec. He could have pushed it faster, but he didn't want to blow the engine."

"Can't blame him there. She's a beauty." He ran his eyes over the car, then the woman next to him. Erin matched the car perfectly.

She laughed. "It's a he. His name is Smoky."

"Huh. Most cars are women."

She snorted. "When Michael first fired the engine, he smoked so badly his dad called the fire department, thus the name. But I think of him as a sexy silver fox." Erin pulled into the bank, making her deposit and getting change for the next day.

They drove slowly through town, then pulled behind a building with a sign proclaiming "Deb's Bakery." The building wasn't huge, but it was two stories high, with beige siding and a red metal roof. It looked like the typical concrete block construction but prettied up. The second floor was smaller, with a tall, pointed roof and windows on at least three sides. The turret-like structure would make a great sniper post. Erin needed one on her shop.

Erin slid out. "Come on, you can meet Deb."

Ryan followed her into a desert-hot, but absolutely delicious-smelling, commercial kitchen. The scent of cake and bread baking made his mouth water; the heat dried it immediately. He followed Erin around cooling racks, huge mixers, some long metal tables, and up to a tall table where a short, curvy woman stood with a pastry bag in hand, decorating a huge square cake. Her dark blonde ponytail bobbed every time she swirled another decoration on the expanse of white. That cake had to be a meter square.

"Deb, I brought Ryan to meet you."

Deb turned, looked him up and down, and

flashed a grin at Erin. Then she met his eyes with a mischievous smile. "Nice to meet you, Ryan. I'd shake your hand, but I'm in the middle of decorating a wedding cake, and I really can't stop."

"No problem. It's nice to meet you too." Deb's slightly rounded face, light blue eyes, and brilliant red lipstick on generous lips gave her a pin-up girl vibe.

Deb turned back to her cake. "Do you need anything but your normal order, Erin?"

"I need three of your cupcakes. Those new ones you gave me at the farmer's market were amazing." Erin put a hand on her stomach.

Deb chuckled. "Aren't they? They've been selling like hotcakes. One woman told me they were better than sex."

Erin choked. Ryan grinned. "I think that's an excellent name—Sex in a Cup… cake."

It was Deb's turn to choke. She turned away from them—probably so she wouldn't spit on the cake. "Sexy and funny. Erin, this one's a keeper."

Heat rushed into Ryan's cheeks. It was one thing to get those kinds of comments from the little old ladies but from someone younger?

"Deb, you're embarrassing Ryan." Erin smirked.

Deb rolled her eyes. "He's a tough guy, he can take it. Besides, I'm sure I'm not the first to say that."

Now his face *and* chest were hot. He must be fire engine red. He'd keep his mouth shut.

"Anyway, help yourself out of the case, and I'll add it to your bill after I finish decorating the wedding cake from heck."

"Thanks, Deb." Erin walked away.

Ryan frowned at the giant cake. "Wedding cake from heck?"

"Yeah. Look at this monstrosity." Deb tossed her chin at the cake in front of her. "White on white, elaborate design, and this huge thing is layer number three. Three of *seven*. I had to order special platforms and boxes for it and get two of my people to work on Saturday for the transport and set-up. And borrow another truck." Her voice was a mix of pride and exasperation.

"Wow. Your hands must really hurt by the end of the day." He couldn't imagine what it would be like to squeeze frosting on cakes for days.

"Not normally, but they will tonight." Deb snorted a bit of a laugh and stretched out her fingers, one hand at a time.

"Sorry to hear that." He couldn't have done that when he still had two hands.

She shrugged. "It's a living. And I'm good at it."

Erin came back with a small bakery box and a big grin. "I took the last three Sex in a Cupcakes, Deb. Hope you have more for tomorrow."

"Baking right now." She nodded toward the ovens they'd passed. "Not too sure I'll have time or fortitude to frost them in the morning, but I guess we'll see."

"You'll get them all done. You always do."

"I'm the superhero of baked goods." Deb sniffed.

"You are. Mild-mannered Deb, who becomes

'Cupcake Woman' under the cover of darkness, bringing delicious baked goods to the world." Erin flourished her hands toward Deb.

Deb struck a superhero pose, one hand brandishing her decorating bag, the other on her hip. "And increasing dress sizes everywhere in her wake!"

All three of them cracked up. After their laughter died off, Deb said, "Out, out, evildoers. You are keeping Cupcake Woman from finishing the wedding cake from the depths of Mordor!"

Erin squeezed Deb's shoulder. "We've got to go. Maybe we can get together soon?"

"I sure hope so. It's been a while since we've had a night out. Let's do it this Friday—no excuses! And bring sexy and silent here with you."

Ryan's skin burned from the inside out.

"Sounds like a plan. Bye, Deb!" Erin caroled. She stopped at a tall refrigerator case at the back, opened it, and pointed. "This one is ours. Can you get it?"

"Sure." Ryan picked up the large white box, grateful for the rush of cold air from the fridge, and followed her to the car. Erin opened the trunk. He gently deposited the box. Then they hopped back in Smoky, both of them smiling at the roar of the engine.

"We'll make a very quick stop at the store because we don't want the frosting to melt. Does Wiz need or want anything special like, oh, Red Bull or something?" She turned into the parking lot.

"Nice stereotype." Ryan snorted out a laugh. "She didn't give me a list. I'll text her." He quickly typed a message. He got a reply immediately, asking for organic carrots and apples. *Huh. Wouldn't have guessed that.* "Okay. You get your stuff, I'll get Wiz's, and I'll meet you back here."

"Good plan." Erin pulled into a spot far from the store, probably to protect Smoky's paint, and they jogged to the store despite the heat. Ryan grabbed apples, carrots, and beer and checked out. He reached Smoky before Erin, but not by much.

Then Erin blew his mind.

Chapter 17

Smoky Rules

"Want to drive Smoky?" Erin jingled the keys.

"Really?" Ryan couldn't quite believe she'd let him drive the silver beast.

"Yes, really." Erin chuckled and tossed him the keys.

Unbelievable. He caught them and grinned. "Yeah. I'd love to." He opened the passenger door for her, then hopped in. He drove sedately through town and put the hammer down when they reached the highway. "Woop!" All that power!

Erin grinned. "Awesome, isn't it?"

Ryan raised his voice over the roar of Smoky's motor. "We all wanted to drive this car so bad. But Sarge wouldn't let us put a finger on it. He gave us the same line he told us about you."

"Line?" Erin wrinkled her brow and her nose.

"A parody of the Marine Rifleman's Creed. 'There are many cars, but this one is mine. Get your own!'"

Erin laughed, a fond smile on her face. "Sounds like Michael." Her eyes narrowed. "But that's about the car. What about me?"

Ryan snort-laughed. "He'd say the same thing about you when we couldn't stop staring. 'There are many wives out there, but this one is *mine*. Get your own.' Sarge never told you that?" *He* shouldn't have told her that. He was such an idiot. At least he didn't say they were drooling, or lusting, or something worse.

Erin laughed. "No, he never told me that. He wasn't ridiculously jealous or possessive, but he was blunt. He'd try to be funny and take the edge off it a bit."

Sarge was more sarcastic than funny. "All of us knew better than to touch anything of his, whether it be his tools, the car, or you."

Erin shook her head, a tender smile lighting her face.

Ryan stopped at the last traffic light before the shop. He was first at the line, and he really wanted to see what the car could do. He shot a questioning look at Erin.

She winked. "Go for it!"

The light turned green, and he dropped the hammer. The tires squealed, so he lightened up on the gas a bit, and they rocketed down the road. He watched the tach, shifting right at 3600 rpm all the way through the gears.

Erin punched his arm. "Are you trying to get pulled over?"

Ryan looked at the speedometer. *Ninety-five! In a seventy-mile-per-hour zone. Oops.* He let off the accelerator to a sedate seventy-two. *Hope there aren't any cops around.* He glanced at Erin, but she was still smiling. "Sorry."

"It's your record and your job you're putting at risk!" She shrugged.

"Thanks for warning me. I was only looking at the tach and the road." A ticket wouldn't be good for his auto parts delivery job.

Erin laughed. "Figured as much. No problem. I've gotten a ticket or two in this baby too." She patted the dash.

"Not with the Sarge in the car, I bet."

"Are you kidding me?" Erin snorted. "If Michael was home, he drove. I only drove Smoky when he was deployed."

"Really? Man, was he missing out." Ryan shook his head slowly. "I thought he was smarter than that."

"Missing out?" Erin's head tilted, her brow crinkled.

"Are you kidding me?" He shot her an incredulous glance. "Sexy woman driving a cool car? That's so hot." Driving this baby was fun, but watching her? Smokin' hot. It would be even better if she'd drive them someplace quiet… *Okay, stop right there, idiot.*

Erin laughed again and shook her head. "Right. You're cute."

"I'm not trying to be cute. I am absolutely, one hundred percent truthful. You and this car? Super hot. I can't believe Sarge was such a dumbass." He should probably shut up. Erin didn't think of him that way, and he really shouldn't think of her that way because there was no way she was ever going to end up with him. Ryan turned into the driveway, rolling slowly to her house and into the garage.

Ryan turned Smoky off and handed Erin the keys while avoiding her eyes. He couldn't handle her pity, so he jumped out. She remained in the car, staring straight ahead, which was odd. He rounded the car and opened her door. The keys still dangled from Erin's hand; something had distracted her. He retrieved the keys, opened the trunk, and carried the boxes inside, putting them in her refrigerator. On his way back to grab the groceries, he almost ran into Erin, holding the bags. He stepped back against the wall. "Is there anything left?"

"No, I got it. Thanks for getting the boxes. You put them in the fridge?" Her words were polite but her face rather blank, somehow distant.

He shook away his puzzlement and answered her question. "Yeah. I can take the big box over with me tomorrow morning."

"Sure. That will be fine." She brushed by him. "I'm going to get the pizza dough out of the fridge so it can warm a bit before I try to shape it."

He frowned at her back. She was acting rather strange. "Need any help?"

"Can you find out what Wiz likes on her pizza?" Erin didn't turn, just spoke louder. "You're okay with pepperoni and cheese, right?"

"Yeah. But Wiz might be fussier. I'll check." He sent Wiz a text, getting a reply immediately. "She says anything is fine, and the classics are best."

"Good. Then I don't need any help. Make yourself at home. I've got this."

"Okay." He knew a dismissal when he heard one and took his bag upstairs. He'd sleep downstairs until Wiz had the install done, but he wouldn't completely kick Erin out of her room. He snorted. He didn't want to kick her out at all. Maybe she'd get in bed first tonight. That would be a dream come true. Followed by a night of no sleep, but who cared? A guy could dream. But that's all it was, an idiot's dream.

Ryan popped off his prosthesis, cleaned it, and inspected his residual arm. Everything looked good. He plodded downstairs. Time for some TV. Although he should work out. And he needed to ask Erin about workout equipment. "Hey, Erin?"

"Yes?" She stirred something red on the stove; maybe homemade pizza sauce.

Wow. She really was the whole enchilada. "Would you mind if I put up a pullup bar in the garage someplace? I can make it easily removable."

"Sure, that's fine." She kept stirring her sauce. "Make it permanent. I'm not sure where to put it, but we can look around and find the right spot tomorrow."

"Great." He sat sideways on the couch so he could watch Erin. He'd work out tomorrow; he wanted to be with her while he could. No matter how futile his longings were.

"Uh, Ryan?"

"Yeah?" He flipped the TV remote in his hand.

"Can I ask a sensitive question? If you don't want to answer, you don't have to." Erin shot him a wrinkled-brow glance.

"Go ahead." There wasn't much he wasn't willing to tell her at this point. He was such a fool.

"How do you do pullups? Can your prosthesis take your weight?"

That question shouldn't make her nervous—it was nothing. "I usually use a strap. I loop it around the bar and stick my residual arm through it, making it the right length so my shoulders are level." He shrugged. "There are prosthetics that strap across the back, and if they're designed right, they can take the weight."

She flashed a smile. "Thanks for telling me. If I ask too many weird questions, please tell me to stop."

He'd answer anything Erin wanted to know, no matter how personal. "I don't mind. Ask what you want. You're not asking to be mean, so it's okay."

"People ask questions to be mean?" Her incredulous look morphed into anger.

"Sometimes. They want to make fun of you or gossip or... doesn't matter. Those are stupid people." Ryan shrugged once. People could be rude and cruel.

"Extremely stupid. You run into any of those in my shop, tell them to leave and not come back— ever." Fury almost shot sparks from her eyes.

Wow. Only a few people cared so much. Better

cool it off, though. Ryan shook his head. "Nah, almost everyone there has been okay. Except old lady Cust, and you already told her where to go." He chuckled.

She grimaced. "Oh, don't remind me. I feel bad being mean to an elderly woman."

He frowned. "No way. She's a nasty old biddy, and she deserved it." Her son deserved worse.

Erin snorted. "She is. Still, I should have a little self-control."

She had the patience of a saint to put up with him. "I think you've got plenty of that. She was asking for it."

"Maybe." Erin shook her head, regret plastered across her face.

Too bad—she'd been amazing. Better than a superhero movie. Ryan's phone chimed. "Wiz says she's almost done. She'll be over in about ten mikes. Should she bring anything?"

"Only if she wants something special to drink. I've got water, iced tea, beer, and wine."

"I'll let her know. I don't think she drinks alcohol. Doesn't like the loss of control."

Erin sighed. "I can understand that. Poor kid."

Wiz was older than he was, but he wasn't sharing that fact with Erin, not yet. He had enough strikes against him already. *Shoot.* He should really get over the fantasy. 'Cause that's all it was.

"Wiz finished the coffee shop a lot faster than she said. Wonder why?" She pulled the pot off the stove, pouring it into a glass jar.

The sweet-spicy scent of tomatoes, basil, and peppers wafted to him. "You can ask. I have no clue. What she does is mostly FM to me." Programming, networks, it was all a mystery.

"FM?"

"Freaking magic."

Erin laughed again. "That's what it seems like to me, too. I can use a computer, but anything else? Nope."

A knock thudded on the door. Erin checked the side window, then opened the door and stepped back. "All done already? That was really fast."

"Yes." Wiz closed the door behind her back, scanning the entire room. She circled the room and sat on the fireplace hearth. "I did a scan while I surveyed your property. The electromagnetic frequency spectrum is very quiet in this area. So I used the wireless system, instead of stringing cat-five cables everywhere. I use multiple layers of encryption and security on my systems, but I don't think there is much of an electronic threat here."

Erin chuckled. "No, Marcus, Montana isn't exactly a hotbed of computer hackers. I know they're doing a lot with big data in Missoula, but since that's many miles from here, I think we're pretty safe."

"Yes. I like what I see here." Wiz nodded slowly. "I may have to move here."

Ryan sat upright but relaxed back into his seat when Wiz jumped. "Really? You'd move from the Fortress?" That would be great for her. And him.

"Maybe." Wiz tilted her head to the side. "Would

you help me build a house?"

"Sure. Don't know anything about it, but yeah, I'd be happy to help." Ryan grinned at her, excited. That could be fun and interesting.

"Thanks." Wiz nodded sharply.

"I'd be happy to help you, too, Wiz." Erin spread sauce on a disk of dough. "I learned a lot buying and building out this place, and I know most of the local builders."

"Excellent. Better to have experts on the ground. Thanks."

"Yep." Erin lifted a pizza peel and a cutting board with plates. "I'm going to put the first pizza in. Grab what you'd like to drink, and then I'd suggest we eat in here, since it's pretty hot out there. There's salad, plates, and silverware here on the kitchen counter. Sit wherever you want. Ryan, can you open the door?"

"Sure." Ryan bounded to the patio door. Wiz recoiled against the fireplace. *Moved too quick.* He slid the door open and followed Erin out. Maybe Wiz could relax with him gone.

Erin opened the pizza oven. "You moved too fast." With a yank, she slid the pizza from the peel to the stone and closed the door.

"Yeah, I noticed. I'll stay here for a while." Ryan carefully avoided looking inside. He didn't want to make Wiz even more uncomfortable.

"Good idea." Erin set a timer. Then she set up the next pizza and gazed off toward the end of the property. Ryan copied her. He was pretty amazed Wiz had shown up at all.

"Do you suppose she'd talk to me?" Erin murmured.

"About what?" She'd probably never talk about what happened to her, which was a shame.

Erin kept gazing at the trees. "Whatever it is she needs right now. I don't think she's going to talk to you. Wiz trusts you but not in person. She glances over at me, but more like she does the rest of the room, just a wary scan. But the rest of the time, she watches you like you're a threat."

"I guess I hadn't noticed that. Shoot." Ryan's heart sank. He couldn't think of anything else except to leave. "Uh, I could go upstairs with my dinner. Fake a call."

"No, I don't think that's necessary." She flipped the pizza peel in her hand. "Move slow. Eat. After dinner, I'll ask Wiz if I can go with her to the shop, so we can bring her van in, and she can tell me what she wants done to it. You stay here."

"Good idea." Erin was perceptive. He probably didn't want to know what she saw in him. "Do you think it's safe to go back in yet?"

The timer beeped. Erin pulled the pizza out of the oven, put it on the cutting board, and put the next pizza in the oven, setting the timer. "You carry the pizza in and take half of it. Wiz and I will split the other half. You saw what I did, right?"

"Yeah." Ryan wouldn't argue about portions; he was starving.

She cut the pizza. "When the timer goes off, come out and get the next pizza, and slide the third one in.

I think you should sit at the table, rather than on the couch."

He glanced inside; Wiz still sat on the fireplace hearth. "But that's behind her."

"Hm." She handed him the cutting board. "Okay, far end of the couch. Move slowly."

"Yeah." Ryan took the cutting board and walked to the door, opening it for Erin. Then he sauntered across the room, put the pizza down, and served himself pizza, salad, and a beer. Erin followed him. He sat at the far end of the couch, like Erin suggested. As he came around the end of the couch, Wiz started, but she seemed to relax once he sat. Ryan kept his eyes on his plate.

"Wiz, come and get a couple of slices," Erin called from the kitchen. "I gave most of this first one to Ryan, since I know he eats more than I do, but the next one will be out soon."

"Okay." Wiz rose.

Erin sat on the other end of the couch between him and Wiz's spot and put her feet up so that her legs blocked him. Smart lady. He nodded at her. She half smiled, half grimaced.

Wiz returned to her seat by the fireplace with her plate in her lap. They ate in silence. Ryan was too hungry; he'd been taught not to talk with his mouth full. "This is really good." Wiz lifted her second slice before chomping the tip.

"Thanks."

"Told you so." Ryan smiled at her but didn't move otherwise. Wiz stared at him, then nodded her head.

Ryan returned to his pizza. Anything he did or said was likely to set her off. He'd stay here, eat, and keep his mouth shut.

"If you move here, Wiz, where would you want to live? Generally, I mean." Erin waved her hand at the patio.

"I need high-speed internet and clear, defendable space. Perhaps on the east side of the valley, on an open, grassy piece of property. Maybe I could get a dog too." Wiz's mouth twisted to one side.

Erin nodded. "This is a good place to have a dog. I've been thinking about getting one. There's a German Shepherd rescue here, and they often have Belgian Malinois too, if you want an even more active dog."

Wiz nodded slowly. "Those are both good protectors."

"Yeah." He'd love to have one, but without a yard, it wouldn't be fair to a big dog. "Very protective of houses and people. Strong herding instinct. They use Belgians for military working dogs a lot because of that, and they're smart, and strong, and very determined. Shorter coats than a German Shepherd or a Dutch Shepherd." Wiz's blank face froze. *Shoot.* He really hoped her assault didn't involve a K9 handler. "All of those dogs need a lot of exercise, though."

"I'd forgotten that." Wiz swallowed hard.

"Sorry, Wiz. Didn't mean to bring up bad stuff." Ryan grimaced. He had to think before he spoke.

She waved a hand at him dismissively. The timer

went off, and they all jumped. Ryan punched the off button, rose slowly, and switched out the pizzas. Inside, he took a piece with him and returned to the couch. Erin got up and got a piece, then Wiz, like a sad little dance.

Erin put down her beer. "Wiz, you can move your van into my garage if you'd like. I don't have any cars scheduled for tomorrow."

"Thanks."

"And, if you don't mind, can I come over to the garage with you after dinner so you can tell me what you want done? That way, I can order the parts tonight online and work on it tomorrow."

Wiz nodded. "Sure. Good idea."

They ate. Wiz asked, "Erin, do you have a lawyer?"

"Yes, I do. Samantha Kerr."

Wiz stabbed her piece of pizza toward Erin. "Good. You need signs warning customers you are using surveillance. Ask your lawyer about the wording. I don't know what Montana law says."

Erin huffed. "Oh. I didn't even think about that. Good idea."

Wiz raised one brow. "I can't activate it during business hours unless there's a warning up."

Erin nodded. "Okay. I'll send her an email tonight, after I order parts."

"Good."

They ate. Ryan tried to think of a neutral topic, but he was coming up blank. The timer went off again. Ryan switched the pizzas outside, then started the pizza dance inside.

From the couch, Erin called, "Ryan, I've had enough. Take my share."

"Really? You don't eat enough."

"I'm fine. I haven't worked out hardly at all this week, so I don't need the extra calories." Erin chuckled. "Besides, I'll probably make up for it tomorrow morning eating the day-old muffins. By the way, Wiz, there're cupcakes for dessert. If you're full, you can take yours back to the apartment for later. You're also free to eat or drink anything in the coffee shop, anything at all."

"Thanks."

"Sure. It's the least I can do since I'm not paying you anywhere near what this work is worth."

Wiz flashed a smile at Erin. The first smile Ryan had seen since she left on deployment. *Go Erin!* Maybe Wiz would talk to her.

Wiz got up. Dishes clinked in the sink. "Erin, I'm going to pull my van into the garage. Will you come over in five minutes?"

"Sure."

Ryan heard the door close softly, and he sagged.

Erin turned to him. "You realize that you being tense makes her worry?"

"Yeah, I can't seem to help it." Ryan grimaced. "I'm trying, but it's hard being around someone so jumpy. I keep wondering if she's hearing gunfire I'm not." Too bad he hadn't figured that out earlier.

"Oh." A long exhalation. "I get it. You guys are negatively reinforcing each other's PTS. That sucks."

"Yeah." Ryan sighed. "I think we're better friends online." Erin sighed and returned to her slice. Ryan got up and grabbed the rest of the pizza. Before he sat, he crunched down. *So good.* He returned to the couch.

Erin's plate clinked on the coffee table. "Maybe you are better online for now. But Wiz came here. Perhaps she's trying to get out of her comfort zone. That's a good sign. We have to make it a positive experience, so she'll do it again. Or even move here."

Ryan nodded, his mouth full. Erin got up and put her dishes in the sink. Water ran, so he chewed faster. "Erin, leave the dishes for me. You cooked; I'll clean while you're with Wiz. Don't forget the cupcake."

"Thanks." The water shut off. "I'm assuming you're going to sleep in my room again tonight?" Her tone was flat.

He stopped with the pizza halfway to his mouth. "Yeah." *Join me, please?* He'd never begged in his life, but for her, he'd do anything. But she couldn't be interested in him; she was way out of his league.

"If you want clean sheets, they're in the closet in the master bath."

No way—the sheets smell like you. "Nope, it's all good. I'll change them in the morning though."

"I can do that. Don't worry about it. I'm going. Make yourself at home."

Ryan watched Erin walk out the door, focused on her backside until the door shut. He flicked on the TV, but if he stayed on the couch, he'd probably nap. Too bad it couldn't be a nap with Erin. Ryan shook his head. He had it so bad. And he was so out of luck. He got up to do the dishes.

Chapter 18

Karma Rules

    Erin left her house, carrying the cupcake. The sun's rays beat down on her aching head. She didn't get nearly enough sleep last night and probably wouldn't get much tonight either because Ryan was sleeping in her bed. And she wanted to be there too. *Eight years. Employee. Mom territory. Get it through your thick head, stupid!*

    Ryan was not for her.

    Erin let herself into the garage, making lots of noise so she wouldn't startle Wiz. After locking the door behind her, she ambled to the office counter and put the cupcake down. Wiz appeared, standing behind the Barracuda. Erin leaned against the counter. "Brought your cupcake. A friend of mine in town bakes them, and they are really superb. We've decided that she has a superhero alter-ego named

'Cupcake Woman' because normal humans can't make these."

"Thanks." Walking toward her, Wiz cracked a tiny smile.

She probably didn't think Erin's little story was funny but smiled out of politeness. Whatever the reason, when Wiz smiled, she went from anime princess pretty to downright beautiful. Maybe that's why she didn't smile. Whoever attacked her better hope Erin never found them or they'd be missing persons nobody missed. Plenty of empty land in the Bitterroot and Sapphire Mountains; she'd shoot, shovel, and shut up without hesitation.

Wiz was looking at her, clearly waiting, so Erin brought her mind back to the business at hand. "Do you have any questions?"

"No. I've planned for a maximum of eight vehicles inside the garage; the system will self-adjust for fewer. The interior sensors are a combination of motion and heat detectors."

"Wow, that's perfect. Hopefully, the Barracuda will be gone soon. It won't be soon enough for me."

Wiz's eyes narrowed. "Ryan told me about the man who owns it. You should have shot him. The world would be better off."

"Probably." Erin shrugged. "But since he only gave me bruises, I probably would have ended up in jail."

"Yeah. The bad guys always get off." Her mouth twisted.

"If they don't pay in this life, they'll pay in the next."

Wiz's head tilted to the side. "You believe that?"

Erin nodded slowly. "Yeah. I do. Karma rules." Wiz flashed another smile. "What can I do for your van?" Erin walked to it. "Can I take a look?" Wiz nodded. Erin snagged the handle under the dash, then lifted the hood and peered into the engine compartment. Tight fit, but every modern engine was the same. She glanced over her shoulder.

"It needs an oil change, and whatever needs services. Can you check everything? I haven't used it much, but that's going to change. Do you weld?" The longer Wiz spoke, the farther away she moved.

Erin took a deep breath and relaxed her body. "Yeah. I'm not an expert, but I do some basic stuff. Anything like bodywork I take to a shop I know."

"I don't need this to look pretty. I want to do this." Wiz manipulated her tablet, put it down on the counter, and stepped back.

Erin strolled over, allowing Wiz plenty of time to move away. The tablet displayed a line drawing of the back of her van. On the driver's side, a short folding table with a stationary table on the passenger side. Cabinets rested on a bracket welded to the van's wall above the stationary table, and on the floor behind the side door, four metal bolts stuck upright, probably for a toilet. Behind the seats, a ceiling track held a sliding panel to close off the living section from the driving area. "You're creating a camper van. This is awesome."

"Yeah. Got the plans from someone I know online."

Erin nodded. Spot welds would work for these fixtures. "Sure, I can do the metalwork for this, but I don't have the raw stock here."

"It's in the van."

She laughed. "Should have figured that—you're very organized." Normally, she'd check raw materials, but she was sure Wiz had everything required.

"Some people call it anal or paranoid."

"Nope, organized." Erin wouldn't put anyone down that way but especially not Wiz. She was like a bird, used to a bird feeder but expecting the food to be snatched away at any second. Or a cat to jump her. Every success brought an expectation of problems.

Wiz nodded. "I'm going to finish your garage, then get some sleep. When do you open in the morning?"

Erin smiled. "Zero six hundred. I'll be here at five-forty if you want coffee or tea."

Wiz didn't smile back. "Latte, double, skim. I should start on your house by seven."

"Perfect. Customers slow down around ten, if you want a refill, or you can use the coffeemaker at the house." Erin took a few steps toward the door, hoping distance would let Wiz relax. "Help yourself to anything at the house. My home is yours."

"Okay. Thanks." She retrieved her tablet.

"Can you email those plans to me or send them to the printer?"

"Both." Wiz swiped at her tablet. "Done."

"Wiz...by the way, is that what you prefer to be called?" Just in case, because while the military was good at tagging people with callsigns, they were often hated by their owners.

"Yes."

No smile or head nod, only a verbal agreement. Wiz was hard to read. "Okay. So you know, you're welcome here anytime. And I'm happy to talk or not as you want. I know Ryan would like to see you more, but we can both see he makes you nervous. I'm sure you realize that you're both triggering each other, right?"

"Yes. A feedback loop." Her chin lifted.

"Exactly. You've got a feedback loop going. We figured it out, so hopefully now that Ryan's aware, we can short-circuit it."

"Okay." Wiz backed away farther. "I'm going back to work."

Rats. Perhaps she had pushed too hard. "Sure. I'll order an oil filter and an air filter tonight and see what else it needs in the morning. I also want to look at the plans in more detail before I weld."

"Thanks."

Erin smiled. "You're welcome. Thank you. You're doing me a huge favor. Anything else you need done on the van or anything else, you let me know." She picked up the plans from the printer, then walked out, locking the doors behind her again. Rustling through the pages, she strolled back to her house. A good, basic campervan. Perfect for one person, and when everything was folded away, there was still plenty of room for cargo. When Erin entered her house, the dishes were drying in the rack, the TV was on, and Ryan was sleeping on the couch. Like he belonged there. *Eight years younger. Employee. Same story, different day.* She closed the door quietly, so she wouldn't wake him. He'd probably be upset, since he thought he was guarding her place, but she wasn't worried. She was sure he'd wake if someone broke glass or forced a door.

Erin grabbed her laptop, ordered the filters, and examined the plans. All of it was pretty simple, mostly spot welds. She might need help to weld the shelf brackets. Ryan would probably be happy to assist tomorrow afternoon, but she wasn't sure Wiz would allow him in the van. Guess she'd ask tomorrow morning.

Sprawled on the couch, relaxed in sleep, Ryan looked even younger, although still very much a man. Erin couldn't believe Ryan called her and Smoky "hot" together. Or that Michael's team believed the same, back in the day. She wasn't anything special. She hardly ever wore makeup or dresses and was taller than ninety percent of men; she didn't draw positive male attention. Especially if she was out with Sam and Deb—they were both prettier. He was probably trying to make her feel better.

Erin clicked on an email from Sam. The Custs were still slow-rolling her on the Barracuda, but the Adams' lawyer said they'd drop the lawsuit soon. He didn't give a specific reason other than Mr. Adams had made that statement after reading the logger's affidavit. Maybe he finally realized Kaylee grew up a spoiled brat rather than a nice young woman. Erin snorted. Not likely. He probably decided he couldn't win.

Ryan stretched, then sat up and looked around. When he met her gaze, he grimaced. "Sorry about that."

"Why? I don't mind if you take a nap." Never pass up an opportunity; that was her motto.

He huffed. "I'm not much of a guard dog if I sleep through you opening the door." He shook his head. "Did you find out what Wiz wants?"

"Yeah. Come look at these plans. Pretty cool. I'll probably need your help, or hers, if she doesn't want you in the van, but it shouldn't be difficult."

He came over next to her, taking the paper plans out of her hand. Ryan took his time looking through them, then grinned. "This is great. Not only is it an awesome design, but this means Wiz is looking at leaving the Fortress of Solitude for more than one trip. This is real progress."

She hoped so. "I wonder where she's going first?"

"Probably not tourist destinations." Ryan snort-laughed.

Erin sputtered. "No, probably not. The van isn't four-wheel drive, but it's got good clearance, so maybe she's planning on doing some remote camping or something?"

"Wiz liked to camp and hike back in the day. She used to come out with us all the time." His fond smile twisted. "More than her loser husband did, that's for sure."

"He was really that bad?" So many bright women ended up with terrible spouses because they hadn't gotten the support they needed growing up.

"Yeah." Ryan glared at the floor.

She might not have the skills to help Wiz, but maybe she could help Ryan. "Offer still stands, you know."

"Offer?" He glanced at her, then looked at the plans.

"To talk about it. Or not. Your decision." *Wiz, you, one of you—talk to me about what's bugging you.*

"Thanks. Anyway, I'll be happy to help with the van. Any news on where to stick the 'Cuda? I know where I'd like to stick it," Ryan snarled.

Erin laughed. "No. Sam says they're still slow-rolling her. We'd both like to drop the thing on their lawn, but they have too much money and influence. They'd probably sue for mental distress. But she had some good news—the Adams may drop their suit."

Ryan raised both brows. "That is good news."

"Yeah." It had cost her more than she could afford, but dropping it now would avoid sending good money after bad. Erin really wanted to know what happened to Ryan downrange, but he had to bring it up. If he wouldn't talk about his experiences, she'd change the subject. "Do you have all your gear for the trip next weekend? Or do you need some help?"

Ryan jumped, eyes wide. "Shoot, that is soon, isn't it? I've got some stuff, but most of my old gear is gone. My sister and brother cleaned out my mom's attic, and they got rid of my stuff too."

"Really? They didn't ask you first?"

"I'm sure it was probably toast, or they would have." Ryan shrugged. "Anyway, I need boots, backpack, and a sleeping bag."

"This might sound a little weird, but I still have Michael's old bag and pack." Erin looked at his build, trying to compare the two of them. "You're not as broad as he was, but you're about the same height. It's torso length, not height, that counts on a pack, but you could try it on."

"That would be great. Good gear is expensive." He rubbed his fingers together.

"Come on, the pack is in the garage. I keep meaning to give it away but haven't gotten around to it." Which was true. First, Erin couldn't bear to give it away. Then she forgot and ignored it, so it collected dust.

Ryan followed her to the garage, past Smoky, to the storage shelves. Erin climbed her step stool, but even on the top step, she had to stretch high to get the big, dark blue pack Michael bought but never had the chance to use. She pulled it down, handing it to Ryan, but he was staring at—her stomach? *Weird.* "Ryan?"

"Huh?" Ryan started, then grabbed the bag. "Sorry, lost in thought."

"Open the door and shake all the dust off, will you?"

"Good idea." He did, while she put the step stool

away. After he returned, Erin closed the garage door, and Ryan followed her back into the house and up the stairs to the office. From the closet, she pulled out a big, unbleached cotton bag. "Here's the sleeping bag. There's a stuff sack in there, too. Let's take this downstairs and see if it all fits."

They walked downstairs, Ryan putting the pack down by the coffee table. He pulled the dark green and beige sleeping bag out of the storage sack. It was a good down bag, rated to twenty degrees. Michael had used it a few times, but not as many as either of them would have liked. There was never enough time.

Then there was no time at all.

Ryan climbed into the bag, zipped it up, and grinned, wriggling around. "Yeah, this is perfect. Sarge was definitely a bigger guy than I am, but a little extra room won't matter in these temperatures." He climbed out and put it back in the storage bag. He fingered the tag on the backpack, then looked back up at her, brows lifted. "This is new."

Erin nodded. "Michael bought it on sale before his last deployment. It's never been used." She couldn't define the mix of emotions swirling in her heart. "Where are we going next?" was one of their favorite deployment phone call topics, but they never got the chance to fulfill most of those dreams. Sometimes she really, really missed Michael.

"Erin, are you sure you're okay with this?"

She stared down at the bag. "It's all good. It needs some good use, some fresh memories." Erin turned toward the kitchen, blinking back tears.

Ryan grabbed her arm. "Hey."

Erin didn't turn back. He didn't need to see her cry. Ryan walked around her and pulled her into a hug, his muscular arms closing around her. She stood stiff for a second, then relaxed into him, shaking a little. *I hate crying.* He tightened his hold, enveloping her securely.

She shouldn't, but she couldn't resist. She rested her head on his shoulder and let the feelings—and the tears—flow. Even all these years later, she missed Michael so much. He should be here with her; it should be his arms around her. When she got the tears under control, she pulled away. "Sorry." She wiped under her eyes with her hands. "It still hits me now and then."

"It's okay. You loved him." Ryan's voice was rough.

"Yes, I did. Still do. But it's been a long time, and I should be over this kind of thing."

"I'm not sure you ever get over it completely." He swallowed so hard she could hear it. "Nothing wrong with missing someone, especially someone who's been taken way too soon. You guys should have had at least sixty years together, and you only got a fraction of that. It's not fair. No reason not to be upset about that."

"Yeah." Erin plopped on the couch, staring out the windows at nothing. "Most of the time, I'm okay, and I try to remember the good times. But he left a big empty space, and I think it's always going to be empty, no matter what I do."

Ryan sat down next to her but didn't touch her. "It probably will be. They all leave holes, especially when they get taken like that. All you can do is try to fill around the empty places and squeeze them smaller. And live life to the fullest. That's the best way to honor them."

Erin couldn't help but meet his gaze. He'd put her feelings into words so well. "That's why I want you to have Michael's stuff. Take it on adventures, get it dirty. I meant what I said. Make new memories with it. He'd want you to have it." He would. Michael was a generous guy.

Ryan gazed into her eyes. "I promise I'll do my very best."

"Good." Erin pushed off the couch and picked up the pack, holding it out to Ryan. "Come on, let's get it fitted."

He took it from her and put it on, twisting and turning so he could buckle and adjust the straps. Erin put her hands behind her back. He didn't need her help and might be offended if she offered. He shifted his shoulders. "Probably needs some weight in it."

"Probably. Hm... Come on, out on the patio." She had some leftover patio pavers around the side of the house. Ryan followed her. Erin picked up a paver. "Turn around." Carefully, she slid a few into the pack. She added more and more. He held up his hand. "Oof. I think that's enough."

Erin laughed. "Turn around, tighten the straps again, and let's see how it hangs." Ryan choked. Erin was about to ask him if he was okay, but he tightened all the straps and strode away. She checked where the shoulder straps met the pack and where the load lifters hit. The torso length was about right. "That looks pretty good. Guess your torso length must be the same as Michael's." Erin chuckled. "Although that hip strap is a lot tighter than his ever was. So is the sternum strap. You're a leaner guy." Not as muscular as Michael, but there was little fat over that build.

He marched around the area, shifting and jumping occasionally. "That's me. Skinny kid." He bent over, then bounded up. "This feels great. Solid." He nodded and looked straight into her eyes. "Thanks, Erin."

"Oh, I wouldn't call you skinny, not by a long shot. But you're welcome." *Kid, yes. Got to remember that.* She looked at the pack, satisfied with how it sat. "Want help unloading those bricks now?"

He pulled the pack off, shrugging it off his left shoulder and using his real hand to slow the descent until it touched the ground. He pulled the bricks out and re-stacked them. "What are you going to do with these?"

"They're leftovers. Maybe I'll add on around the front steps someday." She walked away, back toward the patio, and he followed. "You'll have to find some boots. You can try the local stores, but you might want to hit Missoula one afternoon."

"I've already checked here. They've got some that would be okay, but they're not the best brands. When it comes to boots, I'd rather spend money up front than have foot problems later. I'll go up to Missoula after Wiz leaves. I'll need a sleeping bag pad too."

"I'm not sure what happened to the pad. I've upgraded—maybe I gave both of the old ones away?" Erin shrugged. She really didn't remember. "Anyway, let me know if you need any help." Just inside the house, she paused. She was beat. "I'm heading for bed. It will be another long day tomorrow." Turning toward him, she scowled. "Are you still insisting on staying down here? Like I'm completely unable to protect myself?"

"Yes, I am." Ryan's expression was resolute. "And it's not a matter of you not protecting yourself. It's a matter of getting anyone who is going after you to stop and think for a second." He grinned suddenly. "Nobody is going to mistake me for you, dark or not."

Erin frowned. "I'm only a little shorter, and our hair is about the same length. In the dark? Maybe they would."

Ryan looked her up and down, then focused on her breasts. "Trust me, no man—and it's more likely to be a man—is ever going to mistake me for you. You're...curvy."

"Fat, you mean?"

He glared. "Don't you dare put words in my mouth. You're nowhere close to fat." The glare softened, his gaze traveling over her like warm honey on toast, and his voice rumbled. "Everything you've got is in all the right places."

Erin stared at him, arrested by the heat in his gaze, then remembered why they were having this conversation. *Men are so stubborn.* "Fine." She turned toward her room and spoke over her shoulder. "I'll be out in a minute, and it will be all yours."

She heard footsteps on the stairs. When she came out, he passed her in the living room. She glared at him for a minute, but she couldn't hold it. She was grateful he cared. "Goodnight. Sleep well, Ryan."

He shrugged. "Sure. Goodnight."

Chapter 19

Long Is a Four-Letter Word

Ryan plopped down on Erin's bed. *Yep, still smells like her. Mm.* It was gonna be another long night. Erin clearly didn't believe it when he told her she wasn't fat, but why, he wasn't sure. So many women had such twisted ideas about their bodies, and he didn't get it. He worked hard to stay in shape and happily bragged he had a great body. Ryan snorted. Other than the missing arm and the scars. If it was only the scars, he could probably have any woman he wanted. Maybe even Erin.

He punched his pillow. Yeah, right. He wasn't anywhere near her league. He longed to hold Erin and tell her how wonderful she was, especially when she put herself down. She was everything good in a beautiful package, and he'd love to prove it to her.

But it would never happen.

He turned and spotted the red backpack. Giving

him Sarge's stuff was unexpected and bittersweet. And a little weird. But he couldn't imagine the Sarge being angry, not after four years. The Sarge wasn't a selfish guy; he'd have told Erin to move on years ago. He put on a possessive show for his troops, for good reason. A lot of the guys were immature idiots. But now, he'd want Erin to have a life, a real life, with a husband and a family. Sarge wouldn't consider broken, beat-up Ryan Walsh a good choice for that role.

No sense in worrying about it because it wouldn't happen. He wouldn't get the woman of his dreams. But he could still have a friend, a good friend, and have some fun. He'd endure the frustration. It was a small price to pay. There *wasn't* too big a price to pay if he got to stay close to Erin.

He punched the pillow again, checked his .45 was on the nightstand, and counted sheep. He had to get some sleep—more than the nap this afternoon. *Sheep. 1, 2, 3...*

Ryan's alarm blared. Time for coffee. *Yay. Coffee.* He pried open his eyes and sat up, shocked. Where was he? He was in Erin's room. Erin's *bed.* Water splashed, muffled by a door. Erin's bathroom was next to the bed. He could almost reach out and touch the doorknob.

But he wouldn't. He stumbled away from temptation and into the kitchen. The coffeemaker hissed, finishing the brew cycle, the dark chocolate notes of the Ethiopian blend spiraling up and jump-starting his brain. He poured a cup, sipped, and carried it upstairs to shower. Finished, he put on shorts, his prosthesis, and another Coffee and Cars T-shirt. As he'd asked, Erin got long sleeves but a size too small for such thin material. They breathed better than heavy cotton, and they were super soft, but they fit like a glove. Many customers appreciated the sizing error, but some of them thought he was there for their entertainment rather than making coffee. Probably why Erin chose this size. He'd never been easily embarrassed, but since he started working at Coffee & Cars, he blushed all the time. Some of those "nice" little old ladies had downright dirty minds. Ryan had a whole new appreciation for the harassment women experienced every day.

He plodded down the stairs and back to the coffeepot. It took a lot more caffeine to get him fully awake these days. Erin sat on the patio, sipping from a mug, so he joined her. "Hey."

"Hi. Sleep well?" She sipped. Dark circles under her eyes threatened to drown her freckles.

Her lack of sleep was certainly not the same as his. Maybe she missed her bed; it was comfortable. Although it would be better if she shared—nope. Not going there. "Sure. You?"

Erin wrinkled her upper lip. "Okay. Ready for another day in the coffee trenches?"

"Yeah, bring 'em on. I'm sure Wiz is up." She'd probably stayed up all night, working.

"Whether she is or not, I told her I'd be over there at five-forty, so I guess I'd better get going." Erin rose from the chair.

"Okay. Let me grab the bakery box, and I'll walk with you." Ryan downed his coffee and pried himself from the chair, following Erin inside, trying to look at something other than her. Box in hand, they left, Erin locking the door behind him. At the shop, she let him inside and secured it behind him. If she didn't, they'd have a line of impatient customers at the front counter before they had the morning routine done. If they rushed, they'd miss something and slow the orders down. Ryan had learned that the hard way.

Erin fired up Izzy and opened the safe, grabbing the cash drawer. Ryan pulled them both an espresso and grabbed pastries before he started brewing for the already-waiting customers.

Erin splashed some cream and sipped her espresso. "Oh, Ryan, make a skinny double latte for Wiz, too. I'll take it out to her."

"Sure." He drew the espresso, then poured the milk, trying to imitate the online demo. The milky heart was a little lopsided, but Wiz would appreciate the sentiment. He hoped.

Erin grabbed it off the counter. "Aw, you did it! Awesome. I love it." She carried the cup into the auto shop. Ryan turned to the drive-through for the next order.

As Ryan handed the driver his coffee, Erin returned. The customer pulled away, yelling about stock prices.

"Wiz said cute." Erin made air quotes. "She's already finished the garage and is moving to the house now."

"She's so fast." Her talents had been wasted in the service because she didn't have a degree. She didn't need one—she was brilliant.

"Yeah. She's amazing." Erin nodded. "I'll wait for the oil and air filters to come in, then work on the van. Wiz will probably finish before I can get the van done. What she wants isn't enough to pay for her expertise. Not even close."

"That's what she wants." Ryan shrugged. He wouldn't second guess her. "But even after she's installed the hardware, she'll have programming. That might take even Wiz a while."

They worked together until the big morning rush was over, then Erin went to the garage. Ryan bussed tables, filled more orders, and re-arranged the bakery items to cover the gaps. They'd probably sell out. Fridays were always busy; commuters needed the extra caffeine and sugar to get through the last day of the week. In the coffee shop, everything was clean, nobody was waiting, and the regulars had moved to drip coffee. He put the 'ring for service' sign on the counter, locked the register, and entered the auto shop. Erin might need help. Or that was his excuse, and he was sticking to it.

Under Wiz's van, a pair of long, coverall-clad legs stuck out. He ducked. "Need any help, Erin?"

Her sparkling emerald eyes met his for a second, then she returned to the undercarriage. "Can you call Kelly's, and ask where my filters are? I ordered them last night online."

Ryan snorted. "They probably forgot to check

internet orders. William is off in Missoula for some stupid meeting. I'll call." He returned to the coffee shop and grabbed the phone.

"Kelly's, lowest price always, may I help you?"

"Craig, it's Ryan. Did anyone pull internet orders this morning? Erin ordered some filters last night."

He sighed. "Probably not. I'll get it done and out to you ASAP, man. Sorry about that."

"Happens. Okay, it happens when William is gone."

"Yeah. Can't run the checklist if you can't read." Craig scoffed. "I'll have 'em out shortly, I hope."

"Thanks." He and Craig had far too many conversations about slacker civilians. They couldn't seem to get organized or be efficient. Or actually care.

Ryan pulled a few more espressos for the late commute crowd, bussed tables, and refilled the thermal pots. Unable to stall further, he took a deep breath and checked with the lady brigade. Safely behind the counter again, he tried to cool his burning cheeks by thinking about Alaskan flightlines in the winter. If it was up to those women, he'd be wearing nothing but a swimsuit. Or nothing, period. He shuddered. He'd never been a fan of strip clubs, but after working here, he'd never enter one again. Ryan leaned into the garage; Erin was lowering Wiz's van. "Craig brought you the filters?"

Erin pulled the lift supports away. "Yeah. Said the assistant manager had forgotten to pull the orders, like you thought. Civilians." She sniffed.

"Yeah. That's what he said." They both cracked up.

Erin moved to the far side of the van. "The raw stock for the build is in the back of the van. If you're not doing anything else, can you get it out for me?"

"Sure. I checked everything, and the regulars are all settled in; I'll listen for the bell." He opened the back doors of the van and pulled out lengths of two-inch angle iron, one-inch straight stock, large sheets of lightweight aluminum, and a box with nuts, bolts, and some hinges. Ryan stacked it all on the floor, separated by type, then returned to the coffee shop. He'd have liked to help more, but he had a job to do, and it wasn't welding. He wasn't much of a welder, anyway; his specialty was jet engines.

He wiped tables. Maybe he could get Erin to teach him more about welding, and he could become a specialty welder. Hmm. Or maybe not 'cause that would land him in the oil fields, and he really didn't have any desire to live there, no matter how good the money was. With his part-time jobs, and the compensation from the Veteran's Administration for his arm, he did well enough for now, although he certainly wasn't living the high life. No expensive trips to Vegas, but he could probably swing a decent trip to Reno occasionally. He snickered. He'd been to Vegas enough. Too many crazy bachelor parties before and divorce bashes after deployments. He frowned. Welding sparks would probably do a number on his plastic prosthetics, too.

The door chimed, announcing a woman, but not just any woman. Long, straight mahogany hair swished across her chest, big, dark brown eyes and full ruby lips made promises, while a low-cut silky tank top and a short, tight skirt highlighted every asset perfectly. She strutted on sky-high heels like a model on a runway. Maybe she was a model—a lingerie model. *What's she doing in Marcus?*

As she sashayed to the counter, she smiled; a slow, sultry smile, like she had a secret. She held out her hand. "Well, well, well." She ran her eyes up and down, undressing him more openly than the little old lady brigade. "You must be Ryan. Erin's been holding out on me. She said she had a new employee, but she didn't say he looked like *you*." Her voice was low and slightly rough; a bedroom voice.

Ryan automatically held out his hand but couldn't quite get his brain in gear enough to say anything.

She squeezed his hand, then ran her fingers over his palm when he let go. "I'm Samantha Kerr, Sam to my friends, which you certainly are. I'm Erin's lawyer."

"Hi. Ryan Walsh. Nice to meet you." His voice came out strangled. He cleared his throat.

"Nice to meet you too." Sam chuckled. "But, as nice as you are, I need to talk to Erin. Is she here?"

"Yeah, she's in the garage. If you come through the gap there, I'll take you back." He pointed.

"Thanks." Her heels clicked on the concrete.

Ryan opened the garage door for Sam and followed her in. Erin was trying to clamp some angle iron together. From her scowl, it wasn't going well. "Erin, your lawyer is here to see you." He should probably try to make the title sound more believable.

Erin looked up and smiled. "Sam! What are you doing here?"

Despite Sam's polished beauty, Erin was a billion times prettier, especially when she smiled.

"Erin, I've got some good news. The Adams dropped their suit and, drum roll please, Daddy is paying my bill." Sam bowed gracefully while Erin clapped. "Seems Mr. Adams is absolutely furious that his dear, sweet daughter would lie under oath. He's also not thrilled about his daughter sleeping with this Brad character." Sam rolled her eyes. "We already knew he wasn't bright, but he's got quite the criminal record. Nothing big, yet, but he's headed downhill."

"I'd almost feel sorry for the guy if I hadn't met Kaylee. You don't get that self-absorbed by yourself. It takes a village of servants to get like that." Erin chortled.

Sam laughed. "You're right there. I also brought you the signs you need. One on the coffee shop door, one for the garage door, one at the entrance to the property, and one at the driveway to your house. And I'm guessing tall, built, and handsome here is okay with it?" She jabbed a thumb toward Ryan.

"Ryan suggested it. It's his friend who's installing the rest of the system at my house right now."

"Really?" Sam turned to him. "Is he looking for more work?"

He knew Wiz was incredibly busy. "*She* isn't local, and she's doing this mostly as a favor. She's a computer security expert."

"Good to have expert friends." Sam nodded slowly. "Still, if *she* ever wants to do more in this line of work, or computer security in the area, she should call me. I'm always looking for good people."

"Noted. I can give her your card if you'd like." Wiz would probably ignore it, but if she moved here, maybe she'd want a local lawyer.

"Sure. That would be great." Sam handed two heavyweight cards to him. "And keep one for yourself."

"Nice to meet you. I need to get back to the shop." He had a job to do, and it wasn't dreaming about Erin or chatting with her friends.

"It was *very* nice to meet you, Ryan," Sam purred.

"Sam..." Erin's voice held a clear warning. Ryan slowed his steps, curious.

"You can't keep all the good ones for yourself. Besides, you can't have him, or I'll be defending you in a sexual harassment suit someday."

"I'm all too aware of that, Sam, thanks." Erin's tone was so dry, dust should billow from her mouth.

"Just looking out for you, dear," Sam said in a saccharine sweet voice. "And I'm still trying to get Cust's people to tell me where to put that heap of junk." Her tone turned exasperated. "I've told him over and over to give me someplace or I'm having it dumped in his driveway, but they know I won't do that. He's still paying the storage fees, after all."

"How about Mrs. Cust's driveway?"

Sam's laughter pealed. Ryan shut the door to the

garage. That explained a lot. If Erin was attracted to him, and that was a huge if, she couldn't act on it. And if he made a move, she'd shut him down right away for the same reason. *Shoot. This sucks.* Ryan cleaned up the shop and refilled all the ladies' cups on autopilot, trying to find alternatives. He couldn't quit, that was for sure. No way he'd leave Erin in the lurch. Besides, she certainly wouldn't want anything to do with him then. And he'd have to find some place to live.

He was kidding himself. He didn't have a shot, so why worry? It was all a big dream. Or nightmare. Ryan started the closing duties, since it looked like Erin could use a hand. Good thing she only needed one. He snickered.

Sam appeared in the connecting doorway. "Well, Ryan, if you ever need a night out away from this place, call me." She slid behind him, trailing her fingers above his belt, and Ryan jumped. She chuckled.

He was over the shock and awe. "Shouldn't a lawyer know better than to touch without an invitation?"

She chuckled. "Did you hate it? You can always sue me." She batted her eyes at him. "Didn't think so." She patted his cheek, spun on a toe, and strutted down the room, drawing every eye in the place. Sam must be killer in the courtroom.

After she left, Ryan scanned the room, but everyone was leaving. He locked the door and finished the closing checklist, then returned to the garage, where he wanted to be, with Erin. Sam was gorgeous but couldn't hold a candle to Erin. Besides, high-society balls and expensive dinners seemed like Sam's idea of fun. He'd rather clean Izzy after a month of no maintenance. "Erin, do you need help?"

She knelt on the floor, angle iron laid in a rectangle. "Yes, please. It's really hard to keep this square and weld. The only place I can put a clamp is where the weld has to go. There's another set of welding gloves and a helmet over there." Erin pointed at an acetylene torch rig against the back wall. He grabbed the gear and adjusted the helmet to fit. Erin frowned. "You need a heavier shirt, too. You'll get burned for sure in that. I think there's an old Carhartt coat in the storage room somebody left here. Or you might fit in one of my coveralls."

Ryan looked in the storage room. *Yup, huge, dirty Carhartt coat.* He wrinkled his nose. *Stinky too.* "Okay, but now you owe me welding lessons 'cause this thing reeks."

"Sure." Erin grinned and pointed at the metal stock. "Here, I need this absolutely square. Normally, I'd build a jig, but I don't want to take the time."

"Okay." Ryan followed her directions, holding each piece firmly against the carpenter's square. Minutes later, they had two large rectangular frames.

"Good. I can tack in the aluminum sheet bottoms by myself later. Can you help me with the rest, too?" They finished quickly. "Thanks, that was really helpful." Erin smiled. "I've got the rest. Can you close?"

"Sure." Ryan put all his borrowed gear away, then checked the door and windows one more time and returned to the garage.

Erin stood in the back of the van. She'd already put support brackets in at chest-height. "Oh, good, you can hold these shelves up while I tack weld them. They're supports for cabinets that Wiz will put in later."

Ryan donned the protective gear and grabbed one of the long rectangles, holding it in place while Erin welded. They did the second one, the stationary bench and the folding bed frame, then Erin welded some large bolts to the floor of the van. After lifting her helmet, Erin filled him in. "The floor bolts are for a cassette toilet. Those don't need a waste storage tank. Wiz will have a curtain or an enclosure built around this. No shower, but with a big enough potable water tank," she pointed at the stationary bench, "and a small on-demand water heater, she could drill a hole for an external spigot and have an outside shower."

"Wow, this is really cool. Nice setup." Maybe he'd rather have one of these than a muscle car. He could park at trailheads and get some great hikes in or tour the state. Or the country, even. Erin could travel with him...

"Computer security must pay well. This is not a cheap van." Erin coiled up her welding rig.

"It does." Wiz leaned around the back door.

They both jumped. Wiz bounded out of sight. "Geez, you startled me, Wiz!" Ryan put a hand over his racing heart.

"Yeah. Sorry." She leaned inside again.

"No worries. This is a sweet setup. I'm jealous." Wiz's smile flickered. Ryan's heart smiled in return, but he tried to keep his face impassive. He didn't want to scare her off.

Erin pulled her welding rig to the back. "I hope you don't mind Ryan helping me. I needed it to get these in place."

"No, it's fine. Your house is all done. I put a full security system in along with the surveillance, but it won't go to your alarm company unless you set that up later. I can route it to alert your phone, if you'll give it to me."

"That's perfect. Thanks so much." Erin unlocked and handed her phone to Wiz. "I can't believe you've done all this for what little I'm doing for you."

Wiz tilted her head down, looking up at Erin. She seemed puzzled. "Make sure you don't have your phone on vibrate at night."

"Good point. Thanks again, Wiz. You're amazing." Erin beamed and Wiz looked away. "I think I've got everything you want done. I'll get all my gear out of here and you can check it out. Inspect everything and bang stuff around. If there's anything at all loose, I want to fix it now. I changed the oil and air filters, greased what I could, and checked everything else out, but it looks good. Bring it back when you get enough miles or time for me to change the transmission fluid, or the oil again, and I'll do that for you too." Erin put a hand on the doorframe, and Wiz handed Erin her phone and backed away. Ryan followed Erin out. Wiz had disappeared.

Ryan sighed. Maybe someday Wiz would trust him, but not today. Still, progress was good. He wondered how she'd gotten this far but didn't feel comfortable asking in person. Maybe when they were back in their online relationship. One of the van doors closed with a click. Ryan turned. Wiz must have gone around to get in the front. Inside the van, Wiz swung from the right-hand top shelf. He laughed. Wiz dropped and jumped back. "Sorry, Wiz. Didn't mean to startle you. But that's a great test."

"What did she do?" Erin called from the far end of the garage.

"She was hanging from the shelf." Wiz was tiny; if she'd smiled, she'd look like a mischievous kid. Unfortunately, Wiz would probably never be child-like again.

As she walked back to them, Erin laughed. "That is an excellent test. I didn't plan on that kind of load for those, but you're light. If Ryan did that, they might have come down."

Wiz shook her head. "I don't think so. They seem very solid. Thanks."

"No problem. This was fun and gave me some good ideas. I'd like something like this someday." Erin smiled at Wiz, then tossed her chin. "Ryan, help me put this back?"

Ryan wheeled the welder back to the wall while Erin gathered the remaining gear. Erin didn't need the help, but she wanted him away from the van.

Which was smart. Erin would have made an outstanding leader if she'd stayed in the Air Force. Metal rattled inside the van—Wiz testing everything, as Erin asked.

Erin motioned for him to stay put, while she returned to the van, a clear face shield with ear protectors strapped on her head. "Do you see any rough spots? I took the grinder to the shelves already, but if any of the welds I put in are rough, point them out, and I'll smooth them down."

"There's a couple."

Erin, grinder in hand, jumped into the van. A screech of abrasive on metal made him wince. He plugged his ears, but pressing the grasper against his left ear wasn't very effective. He grabbed the welding helmet.

Erin jumped out before he put it on. "Ryan, Wiz says she'll stay one more night to test the systems and leave first thing tomorrow. If you want to go back over to the house, feel free."

"Okay, see you there." Ryan jogged to the house; he was starving. He made himself a couple of PBJs, grabbed a glass of iced tea, and plopped down in front of the TV. But his mind wasn't on the show. He had one more night at Erin's, then he'd be back in the apartment. Alone again. How depressing.

Ryan put his head back. Living in her house was a short-term deal; he'd known that from the start. He shouldn't be so bummed about moving back into his own space. But until he'd overheard Sam, he'd had hope. He hadn't even consciously realized it, but yeah, he'd definitely planned to make a move at bedtime.

Yep, he could see the scene. They'd get ready for bed, just like last night. When Erin passed the bed to go upstairs, he'd snag her around the waist and pull her in tight. He'd kiss that sexy mouth then... He looked at the brand-new alarm panel near the door and snorted.

With the alarm system finished, Erin could sleep in her own bed tonight. Without him. So much for his grand plans. Ryan laughed and winced at the despairing sound. Sam ruined those plans anyway. Nah, he shouldn't blame Sam—she simply made the situation clear. Besides, Erin wouldn't want him. There were plenty of guys out there with two hands, careers, money, all the things he didn't have. Ryan was a damaged loser. She might think his body was sexy, but only at a distance. He sighed. He had to keep that distance.

He put his plate in the dishwasher and entered her bedroom to strip the sheets. Ryan liked her scent, but she wouldn't feel the same about his sweaty tossing and turning. He smiled ruefully. In his fantasies, she didn't pull back and slap him. And she would if he'd executed his mission according to plan. And then she'd fire him. Even if she'd kissed him back, which was highly unlikely, she wasn't going to fall into bed with him. Erin wasn't easy. And she deserved more than he could give her, anyway. Like two hands and a whole mind.

He sighed and carried her sheets to the laundry.

He'd run the washer tomorrow morning with the guest bed linens. *Wonder if she'd miss a pillowcase?* Ryan shook his head. He had it so bad. He grabbed a clean set of sheets and put them on her bed

"You didn't have to do that, Ryan."

He jumped, his heart racing, then returned to sliding on a pillowcase, keeping his back to her. "Sure, I did." Ryan cleared his throat, trying to sound like a grown-up instead of a teenage boy. "I made myself some PBJs for lunch. Didn't think you'd mind."

"Of course not. I told you to make yourself at home, didn't I? Besides, that sounds good. Think I'll do the same, then I'm heading to the grocery store. Wiz said she'd come over for dinner tonight, so I'm going to get some chicken to grill, and some more greens, and other stuff, and we'll have a Greek-style dinner." Erin's tone was cheerful, if forced.

"That sounds great. I'm going to work out while you're gone, unless you need help. I haven't done a good workout for a few days." He fussed with the pillow.

"Sounds like a plan. Maybe we can figure out where to put your pullup bar tomorrow after Wiz leaves."

"Sure." Ryan finished, turned, and walked out of her bedroom, brushing past her, heading straight up the stairs and into the upstairs bedroom, closing the door behind him. *Whew. Safe.* He plopped down on the bed. *Big mistake. It smells like Erin.* He'd wait until he heard Smoky leave and then work out.

He was finally ready to move ahead with his life, accept that his arm was gone but still go for what he really wanted, and boom, it all blew up in his face.

Again.

Chapter 20

Run Away

Ryan ran up the stairs, stiff with tension. *Weird.* She made her sandwich, scraping the dregs of the strawberry jam from the jar. She needed more from the grocery store than dinner ingredients. A Costco run loomed.

She ate at the kitchen table, making a combined grocery and task list. Once she finished, she grabbed her list and purse and then fired up Smoky. Erin wriggled a little in the vibrating seat. The rumble never got old. Nor did the sensation of sheer power.

She rolled to the highway and, as usual, dropped the hammer until she was up to the speed limit. Only then did she consider Sam's words. Ryan was off limits. He was too young for her and an employee, but she hadn't really accepted the situation until Sam confirmed it out loud. Erin sighed. Clearly, Sam was interested, and Deb admired Ryan, too. He could certainly do worse, and both her friends needed a loyal guy like Ryan. But every time she tried to picture one of her friends with him, all she could see was herself. Letting go was insanely difficult.

But she had to. She had no alternatives.

She would insist Ryan join the three of them for dinner next time. She'd make some excuse to leave early, so he'd have to get a lift home from Deb or Sam. She was sure either of them would be happy to give him a ride—and more.

She squealed the tires coming off the line. She still had Smoky.

Erin pulled into the bank drive-through, turning Smoky off so she could chit-chat with the teller. After taking her deposit slip from the drawer, she glanced at it and grinned. Ryan was good for her bottom line, that was for sure, and she couldn't afford to lose him. Not for any reason, but especially not a reason that would end in heartache for all of them.

He wouldn't want her; even though he'd made comments about her being hot, Erin didn't hold a candle to Deb or Sam. If she made any kind of personal overture, he'd probably recoil in disgust. Or worse, he'd be so offended that he'd sue her for sexual harassment, like Sam suggested. She could lose everything she'd worked so hard to build. She didn't really think Ryan was that kind of guy, but sometimes, people hid their true natures for a long time.

Erin got everything on her grocery list, then drove

slowly through town and pulled into Deb's bakery. Since it was Friday, she didn't have a pickup, but she still had time to see Deb. Which was good because she seriously needed some cheering up. If Deb wasn't happy either, Erin could eat her feelings in cupcakes.

"I'm decorating!" Deb called.

At the front of the shop, Erin gave Deb a one-armed hug, relieved to see a normal-size cake in front of her. "Did you hear the door?"

"No, Smoky." Deb peered around her. "No silent and sexy today?"

"Nope. He stayed home to work out."

"Ooh." Deb leered, her eyebrows bouncing ridiculously. "Now there's something I'd like to watch."

"I'm pretty sure you could if you played your cards right." Erin tried to keep her voice even and unemotional, but she failed.

Deb put down her pastry bag and turned to her, eyes wide. "You're kidding, right?"

"No. Why would I?" She had no choice. Ryan was too young, and he worked for her; the risks were too great.

"Erin, I met the guy all of one time, but it's pretty clear he only has eyes for you." Deb glanced at the ceiling in exaggerated despair. "Ryan glanced at me, took one long look at my chest—which is completely normal; *every* guy looks—then fastened those pretty eyes right back on you. Even when he was talking to me—talking might be an exaggeration; giving me one-word answers—he was mostly looking at you.

And it wasn't just a guy who likes your body type more than mine. Nope. He's got it bad, for you, the whole fabulous package." She stabbed her finger at Erin's chest.

Erin shook her head. "Deb, he's an employee, and he's eight years younger than me. I can't go there."

Deb grinned. "Sure you can. It would definitely be consensual."

"Until it ended, which it would. Eight years, Deb. He's not the 'settle down forever' kind of guy I need. And when it ended, he could easily file a sexual harassment suit against me, and I'd probably lose everything. Sam even told me that." Of course, Sam was attracted to him too. She wasn't exactly neutral.

Deb reared back, scowling. "Sam said what?"

"She dropped by today. The Adams are dropping their suit, thank God, and even paying her bill. Anyway, Sam told me point blank that she was interested in him and that I couldn't have him anyway, because he'd have grounds for sexual harassment. And she's right." She was. Ryan was too dangerous in every sense of the word. In the pastry case, Deb's cupcakes, especially the ones with the big swirls of chocolate on top, were calling her name. She knew delicious goodies, but not men.

"No, no, she isn't. Ryan's not that kind of guy, Erin."

Deb sounded so certain, Erin had to look at her. "Really? You know him so well?"

"No, but you do." Deb nailed her with a mom look. Too bad Deb's ex was such a loser; she should have kids. But Deb's instincts were wrong.

Erin snorted. "Not really. I knew Ryan's name and face, because he worked for Michael, but Michael was prone to talk about the troublemakers, not the hard workers. Ryan came to the house a few times, but he's always been a quiet guy. He's worked for me for a couple of months now, and I can't really say I know him because he doesn't talk much. He won't even tell me how he lost the arm. When he brought his mom out to meet me, she said more in one afternoon than Ryan has in weeks."

Deb raised her eyebrows. "He brought his mom out?"

"He was showing her the apartment and shop on Sunday, so he brought her over. She's a nice lady."

Deb shook her head. "Erin, I think you're being deliberately obtuse. Tell you what." She tilted her head and raised both brows with a sly smile. "You bring sexy and silent out with us tomorrow night. I bet he won't make a move on either of us, no matter how hard Sam plays."

Erin smiled grimly. "I was going to ask him. I figure he spends too much time alone. And Wiz goes home tomorrow, so she won't be around either."

"Wiz?"

"Oh, I forgot. Sorry." Erin shrugged. "A friend of his from the Air Force. She does computer security, and she designed and installed a surveillance system for the shop and my house."

Deb picked up her frosting bag. "Cool. Get her to stay one more night and bring her too."

Erin grimaced. "Not gonna happen. I can't tell you why, but she's got serious issues. Can't stand being around people, real jumpy with only me and Ryan. I think she's reached her people-ing limit for this trip."

"Crap. That sucks." Deb sighed. "Too many kids came back damaged from these ridiculous wars."

"Yeah. The damage that doesn't show is worse sometimes. It amazed Ryan that Wiz left her house at all."

Deb nodded at her cake and fell silent. Then Deb looked back up at her and winked. "But enough Debbie Downer. Bring Ryan with you. You watch. Sam's going to put her best moves on him, and he's not even gonna react. You'll see."

Erin snorted. "I think you're kidding yourself, but we'll find out. I've got to get a move on. Got to make dinner for three tonight. Put three more cupcakes on my bill, please?" Erin moved up to the bakery case, pulled three carrot cake cupcakes out since Deb seemed to have a lot of them and they were delicious, like all of her creations. The chocolate was too tempting—she'd eat all of them before she got home.

"Sure." Deb piped decorations. "See you tomorrow night. We'll meet at the brewery like usual and then go from there."

"Sounds like a plan. I desperately need a night out." Erin left with Deb's cheerful "Bye!" ringing in the air and returned to Smoky. She slid inside and shut the door. Nope, Deb was wrong. The only man in her life was Smoky. At least he was dependable. Usually. And hot. In more ways than one.

She rolled down the window. She probably should drive the truck, but Smoky was way more fun. A guy in a big truck gave her a thumbs up with a mouthed, "Nice car!" Erin grinned. *Yep, Smoky is way more fun.*

Later that evening, the three of them finished their mostly silent dinner. Erin did her best to draw Wiz out about her travel plans with the van, but she wasn't talking. Erin spoke about living in this area and how hard it was to find property at a decent price and recommended a realtor. She told Wiz about some of the unique Montana issues, like making sure the land was in a fire district, and the challenges of drilling wells in the mountains, but Wiz seemed to withdraw even more. Guess she'd had enough. And Ryan wasn't helping; he seemed sunk in his own funk.

Erin made one last attempt. "I have cupcakes from Deb's for dessert. If you're too full, you're welcome to take it with you, Wiz."

"Thanks." Wiz nodded sharply. "That would be best. You're a skilled cook. I ate more than I usually do."

"Thanks. I appreciate that. I've got excellent tools to work with, which helps." Erin put two of the cupcakes on a plate, then placed the box on the kitchen table. Wiz could grab it on her way out. Erin returned to the couch. "Wiz, I know I've already said it, but I really, truly appreciate you coming out and doing all this for me. Whatever I can do on a vehicle of yours in the future is free." She chuckled. "If you have to replace an engine, you'll have to buy it, but I'll give you the labor. I know what you did for me would normally be in the thousands, not hundreds. Thanks. I'll also be happy to land or house shop for you."

"Okay. You're welcome. And thanks." Wiz rose, sidled around the room, grabbed the cupcake box, and walked out the door, facing them the whole time.

Ryan sighed. "Guess she's had enough fun. Back to the Fortress of Solitude. We might see her in another year or two."

He was probably right, but Erin should put a positive spin on her visit. Ryan had enough to bear on his own; he didn't need to carry guilt for Wiz's issues. "She came and stayed several days. Seems like progress. Maybe it won't be too long before she comes back again."

"Maybe." He frowned and shook his head.

Erin changed the subject. "I'm going running in the morning, and then I'm headed up to Costco if you want a ride to Missoula. We could stop by the outdoor stores so you can find hiking boots."

Ryan smiled. "Sure, that would be great. What time?"

"Probably ten, if that works for you? We could hit one of the farmer's markets up there too."

"Cool. I'll come over here."

"Great." Erin tried to think of another topic. "Oh, and Deb wanted you to come out with us on Saturday night. Are you doing anything?"

"Uh, no, I'm not doing anything. Who is 'we'?" Ryan looked wary.

"Me, Deb, and Sam, usually. Sometimes we meet up with people by chance. We start at the brewery, and sometimes we stay there, sometimes we move on to other places. Depends on how we feel."

"I like the brewery. Other places..." Ryan grimaced. "If it's some noisy club or something, I'll pass. I... have a hard time with flashing lights and loud, crowded places." He turned away, swallowing hard.

Poor Ryan. "No problem. We'll hang out and have a few beers and some bad-for-you food."

"Or I can drive on my own." He raised both brows.

"If you want to leave early, you can drive my car home, and I'll get a ride with one of the girls."

Ryan looked away. "Sure."

Back to one-word non-answers again. "Is there something bothering you, Ryan?"

"No." He turned the TV on and flipped through channels.

Classic male avoidance technique: watch TV until the female stops trying. Michael used that one too. Erin sighed, got up, and loaded the dishwasher. Then she hand-washed the few things that needed it and surfed the internet a little. Maybe she'd find a car to work on or something interesting would be in her email.

She clicked on an email from the Wilderness Institute. Rats, she'd almost forgotten the trip in all the fuss. She forwarded it to Ryan. "Ryan?"

The TV sound turned down. "Yeah?"

"I forwarded you an email about the backpacking trip."

"Okay." He nodded.

Erin kept herself from rolling her eyes. Sometimes Ryan reminded her of a teenage boy. The trip leaders would expect her to make sure he was prepared. "Do you have breakfasts, lunches, and snacks figured out?"

"I was going to bring oatmeal, peanut butter and jelly, and trail mix. Are they hardcore vegetarians, or are they okay with people bringing meat?"

"The leaders are fine with whatever you want. Some folks who go on these trips are definitely more on the new-age, vegan side, but then they tend to stereotype us military types, too. Usually we all end up a little more tolerant at the end of the trip."

Ryan snorted.

"I'll email you a website I use for recipes. They've got a great one for oatmeal that you make in a Ziplock freezer baggie." Wait, that was silly. "Actually, I was going to pick up everything for the trip tomorrow, and I can make oatmeal for you, too. Twice as much as I eat, I'm sure."

"Thanks. I'll pay for my share and help you make it."

"Sure. We can do that on Sunday afternoon, unless you have other plans."

"Nope. That's fine."

"We can figure out where to put that pullup bar

too."

"Okay."

The TV volume came back up. Erin sighed again. *Men.*

There wasn't anything in her email that couldn't wait and nothing on social media. No cool cars she could afford that weren't piles of rust. She had to find something to work on. Soon. The coffee business was good, but for a real profit, she needed to restore cars. And a project would keep her busy. Erin looked down at Ryan on the couch. And keep her mind off of things she couldn't have.

Sometimes, when Ryan slumped on the couch giving her one-word answers, it was easy to remember how much simpler life was without a man around. And it was easy to remember how much younger he was when he sulked. But then he'd say something thoughtful, and she'd be off in fantasy land again. Or she'd look at him. His body was worthy of fantasies, regardless of the arm. Erin smiled. Might have to get a little creative, but ooh. Creative with him would be fun. Erin tore her attention away from him, back to her computer. *I need a car.*

There were some 60s Mustangs out there, but everybody did Mustangs, and they were expensive. Erin wanted something unique, maybe a little challenging, but not something that was impossible to find parts for, like an International Harvester. Maybe she should restore a truck, a classic old pickup, like a 50s Ford or something. Those were fun.

Or maybe something newer, like a 70s Bronco? Those were big now. She wouldn't solve the problem tonight. She closed the computer with a snap, picked up her e-reader, and flopped down on the couch. Two could play at this game.

Suddenly, the TV clicked off, and Ryan got up. "I'm headed for bed. See you in the morning. Let me know when you want to leave. Thanks for dinner."

Erin checked the time. Wow, it was late. "Goodnight. See you in the morning." She checked all the doors and walked to her bathroom. Maybe she could get some sleep tonight, but that didn't seem likely with Ryan sleeping upstairs. She really needed to get over her infatuation. With Michael, she'd had it all; she should be happy with what she had and quit moping about what she couldn't have.

Hopefully, it would all look better in the morning.

Chapter 21

Sponges Can Be Dangerous, Too

Ryan rolled over and smacked his phone. Ugh. He'd slept in, but even so, he didn't want to get up. It'd taken a long time to get to sleep—again. He had to get over his infatuation with Erin. Yeah, it would be a perfect morning if he could've followed through on his fantasy and finally kissed the woman. But no. *Argh*. He should go work out. Yesterday felt good, but he'd lose ground if he didn't keep pushing. And they had stuff to do today. Ryan forced himself to get out of bed, putting on running shorts and a shirt.

Erin was going running this morning. Maybe he'd meet her on the trail, and they could run together. He laughed. He had it so bad, and it was so useless. Erin would never be his.

Ryan walked down the stairs, crossed to the coffeepot, and smiled. Sweet—Erin had left him half the pot. He'd need that and more to get moving this morning. Erin's bedroom door was open, so she must

be running the trail already. He poured himself a
cup, made a PBJ for breakfast, and took it all to her
patio. Eating, Ryan gazed out at the trees, enjoying
the peace. Even the highway noise wasn't bad; it kind
of faded into the background with his tinnitus.
Another lovely present from his military career.

Why didn't Erin have kids? She and Sarge were
married six or seven years. She'd said nothing about
kids, so maybe she was one of those women who
didn't really want any? Didn't seem to fit her though.
Or maybe they couldn't have any? Or maybe they'd
been waiting for Sarge to deploy less often? He
snorted. Like that would happen. Ryan suddenly
realized he didn't even know how old Erin was. He
laughed. Like he cared. She could be part of the little
old lady brigade, and he'd still want her.

He didn't even know Erin's birthday. And that
bugged him. He wouldn't want to miss it. Guess he
could ask Deb or Sam tonight if he got the chance.
Hmm. Really, there were a lot of things he didn't
know about her. The backpacking trip might be a
real learning opportunity because everyone else
would expect a basic rundown. Ryan scowled.
They'd want to know about him, too. He'd share
what he wanted to, then stare if they pushed for
more, like usual. Most people couldn't maintain a
stare-down with him.

Okay, enough useless thoughts. It was go time.
Ryan stretched, drank a glass of water, and tightened
his shoes. He locked the door, then realized he wasn't
wearing an arm—and he didn't care. If people stared,

it was their problem, not his. Ryan walked briskly down the driveway, warming up for the run.

Near the shop, a guy peered through the coffee shop window, a shiny black Mercedes parked behind him. Ryan cupped his hands around his mouth. "Hey, we're closed on Saturdays."

The guy turned. *Cust.* Ryan ran closer. "You're not supposed to be here. Leave, or I'm calling the cops."

Cust sneered at Ryan's missing left arm. "And what are you going to do about it?"

Fake it until you make it. Ryan laughed. "I kicked your ass no problem last time. It doesn't take much."

Cust sneered. "Without your bionic arm?"

"Nope. No problem at all." Ryan grinned. "By the way, see the new signs? Smile and wave. You've just given us all the ammo we need to get a restraining order."

"What, 'cause you put up a sign?" Cust scoffed. "Like Erin's got the money for a real surveillance system."

The garage door opened. Wiz held a semi-automatic pistol pointed at the ground. "Yes, she does. Leave or I fill you full of holes."

"Who are you?" Cust stepped back, gaping.

"I'm the person who will kill you if you take one step this way." Wiz's voice was dead flat. She raised her weapon.

This could go real bad, real fast. Ryan backed away so Wiz had room to move. "Cust, she means it. Move your ass or you're dead. You do not want to mess with her."

Cust backed toward his car, got in, still staring at the pistol in Wiz's hand. "You'll regret this. I have dangerous friends!" He drove off, fishtailing and spraying gravel back. Wiz holstered her weapon and stared down the drive.

"Wiz, are you okay?" Ryan didn't touch her—she'd probably react badly.

"Yeah. I was about to leave." Wiz kept staring at the highway, even though Cust's car was long gone.

He wasn't sure what was going on in her head, but talking was probably a good idea. "Thanks for the save. I could kick his ass, even one-handed, but I might have gotten beat up."

Wiz finally looked at him. "No, Ryan, you might have gotten dead. He was packing."

"Really?" Ryan swallowed. He hadn't seen a gun.

"Yeah." She nodded. "Concealed holster, back of the pants. He reached back there a couple of times, then I saw the outline when he turned."

"Wiz, Erin's out running." His heart sped with terror. "I don't know where. I'm getting my car." Ryan sprinted for the house. He had to find Erin before Cust did. He entered the code on the alarm pad and bounded up the stairs. Arm, keys, weapon. He ran back down the stairs and out the door, almost slamming into Erin on the porch. He grabbed her by both arms, his left one glancing off.

"Ryan, what's wrong?" Her friendly smile changed into alarm.

"You're okay, right?" His heartbeat almost deafened him.

"I'm fine. What's going on?" Erin's brows almost met above her wrinkled nose.

Erin was safe. She hadn't even seen Cust. Ryan panted and let go, collapsing against the doorframe. He'd had a death grip on her arm, with keys and weapon jammed into one arm, grasper pressing against the other. "I'm sorry—that's probably going to bruise." He took a deep breath, then another, trying to regain some sanity. "Cust was here, looking in the coffee shop window. I told him to leave. He threatened me, but Wiz came out, weapon in hand. When Cust mouthed off to her, I thought he was dead." He dropped his hands to his knees and took a few breaths. Erin was okay. He stood up. "Cust left, but Wiz said he was armed. I was going to look for you."

Erin stared at him with both brows raised for a moment, then let out a breath. "I'm fine. I saw Chaz; he yelled something at me and shook his fist. But there were a ton of people and cars out there today. He's not going to attack me in broad daylight. He's a bully, but like most of them, a coward." She shrugged. "I had my phone out, ready to call 911. But I'm more concerned about Wiz. I'll check on her. I want to make sure she's all right."

"Good idea. Wiz was scary. It's better that I stay away." Erin jogged to the shop. She was fine; he could stand down, stop worrying. Except he'd better worry about himself—he was acting like an idiot. Weapon and keys jammed into his right hand, left arm on but not quite straight. Which was kind of tough to do. He laughed, but it sounded a little... off. Guess he should start practicing at the firing range again. He'd done some one-handed shooting as part of his therapy but not much since then. He carefully shut the front door and collapsed on a kitchen chair. *Whew*. When he thought of what Cust could do to Erin, out there on the trail... *Come on, Walsh.* There were a billion cars going by, lots of runners and bicyclists too, especially on a weekend. And even if Cust got Erin into his car, it's not like she was some helpless wallflower. Still, the thought made him crazy. He was so screwed.

He stared up at the ceiling. Yeah, he wanted Erin, but it was because he *loved* her. When did that happen? Sure, he'd thought she was hot the very first time he saw her, but he didn't even know her back then. Now, he'd only been around her for a short time, but he couldn't imagine life without her. Guess love didn't take long.

Yep, this is fantastic. He was head over heels, like a teenage boy, and had a snowflake's chance in the desert with her. Ryan laughed, the sound echoing through the house. This time, it didn't sound off, it was downright despairing. *Get it together, Walsh.* If Erin walked in now, she'd want to know why he was upset, and he'd end up blurting out, "I love you." She'd let him down gently and it would kill him. Better to keep his mouth shut, and then he could pretend that he had a chance someday. Desperate, he tried the rhythmic breathing exercises the shrink suggested.

When Erin returned, he'd calmed his breathing, if not his heart. He took one more deep breath, repeating "Erin's safe" to himself, then remembered why Erin had gone back to the shop. "Wiz okay?"

"Yes, she's fine." Erin smiled. "I expected to find her curled up in a little ball somewhere, but she was calmly downloading the surveillance video segments with Cust on them so I could email them to Sam. Which I did. I pressed Wiz a little, and she said she felt powerful and strong for the first time in a long time. All her training paid off. She also said she definitely wanted to live in Montana because our gun laws are better." Erin chuckled. " She's going to look for property or houses, and I told her I'd be happy to check out anything for her in person."

Ryan laughed with Erin in sheer relief. "That is a good sign. I was absolutely sure you'd find her hiding in her van or in the back corner of the shop or the apartment. I wasn't looking for her. I figured she'd hear my footsteps, know they were a man's, and off me. But I guess I wasn't very fair to her."

"Better safe than sorry. Besides, it's my business, my responsibility." Erin shrugged one shoulder.

He nodded. He'd like to share the responsibility with her, but that would never happen.

Erin smiled, a little sadly. "Anyway, Wiz took off for home." She frowned. "She said she was going to research Cust—his remarks about dangerous friends bothered her. I'm sure he's grandstanding." She waved, like she was brushing away Wiz's concerns. "Want to go for your workout or go to Missoula?"

He huffed a laugh. "My heart got enough pounding. Let me change, and we'll go shopping."

"Sure. Take your time." She filled a glass of water. "I need a shower."

He ran back up the stairs, took a fast shower, and changed. He also switched to his "polite" arm, grabbed his wallet, and ran back down. "Let's go."

He'd offered to drive his car, but she said they'd need the truck for her Costco run. He stared at the side of the Sapphire Mountains, trying to find a good spot for Wiz to live, but he kept replaying the morning.

Just before Missoula, Erin poked his shoulder. "We should hit the farmer's markets first. I threw a cooler in the back."

"Sure. Maybe grab something to eat there too." There, he sounded normal.

"Yep, they have great food stalls and trucks." She nodded her head.

Ryan had nothing to talk about. He couldn't get the terror of the morning out of his head. All the cars around them made him nervous, like he was expecting an IED. Which was ridiculous in Missoula, Montana.

A few minutes later, Erin asked, "Traditional farmer's market with veggies and other food, or did you want to hit the more arts and crafts markets?"

He swallowed hard. "Whichever you want. I'm along for the ride, mostly."

"All right, farmer's then. And if you get bored, you can go over to the downtown hiking store while I browse."

"Okay, good idea." It was, but Ryan still couldn't stop thinking about the what-ifs. He had to stop; get out of his head. But he kept reliving the terror of knowing Erin was out there alone with Cust gunning for her.

At the market, fresh problems meant letting the old ones go. In the crowds, he scanned for suicide bombers and found escape routes, edging through the crowd with his head on a swivel. Erin told him about the market's history and found different, delicious foods for him to try. By the time they'd walked the first aisle, her care let him relax enough to enjoy the food and the location next to the Clark Fork River. Erin handed him bags and packages, treating him like a pack mule. But she fed him something with every bag, so it wasn't so bad. They visited the hiking store too but didn't find boots that fit.

Erin went to Costco while he went across the street to REI. He found a great pair of boots on sale and bought a better sleeping pad with the savings. He wore the new boots to break them in. It wasn't much of a walk, but starting short was smart.

Ryan leaned against Erin's truck, the noon sun beating down. He could get a drink, but it wasn't worth the effort. She'd be here soon, and then he could watch her walk across the parking lot. He squinted at a tall stack of big boxes rolling toward him, red hair popping around the side occasionally. He laughed and threw his old shoes in the back of the pickup, grabbing the front of the cart. "That is you behind all those boxes."

"Yes, it is." Erin chuckled.

Ryan helped load and secure the boxes down with a stretchy net, and they headed south in minutes. Once on the road, Ryan asked the burning question. "Erin, when's your birthday?"

"Why?" She frowned.

"Don't want to miss it. You know when mine is."

"That's for taxes, not anything else. Besides, you know the rules. No gifts for the boss." She shot him a raised brow look.

"We're not in the military anymore. Nice try, though." Ryan smirked at her.

"Fine." Erin's lips flattened. "September twenty-seventh."

"Thanks." He'd put it on his calendar later.

"Sure. But don't get me anything. Really."

"Okay." He'd find the perfect gift for her no matter how long it took.

Erin laughed. "Such a guy answer."

"Yeah. Guy here, in case you didn't notice."

"Oh, I noticed." She cleared her throat. "Was there anywhere else you needed to stop?"

Erin noticed him, huh? Maybe there was hope. "Don't think so." Or maybe it was a friendship thing.

"Okay." She kept her eyes on the road.

He really wanted to ask her some other questions, but she'd respected his reluctance to talk, so he couldn't ask without telling her more. And he really didn't want to talk to her about his problems.

"Did you find a pair of boots?"

He lifted one foot, but probably not enough that she could see it. "Yeah. I'm wearing them. On sale even, so I could get a nice sleeping pad too."

"Good. Makes a big difference out there." Her smile turned rueful. "Especially when you get older."

Ryan frowned. "You certainly aren't old enough for it to matter that much." Erin couldn't be that much older. Thirty-something, certainly not forty yet. Not that it mattered.

She chuckled. "You're so sweet. But so wrong."

"I don't think so." He scowled.

"Oh, trust me, you're wrong." She lifted her fingers off the wheel in a little waving motion.

Ryan frowned at her skeptically, and Erin chuckled again. Obviously, she wasn't going to tell him. It didn't matter; she could be eighty and he'd still be toast. He settled back into his seat and remembered he had questions about the backpacking trip.

"This will sound a little weird, I guess, but...what do you sleep in out in the backcountry?"

Her laugh rang in the truck's cab. "Why? Worried you'll have to see something you don't want to see?"

No, worried I won't. Ryan discarded half-a-dozen sexy innuendos. "No, I'm trying to figure out what to bring."

Erin snickered. "I usually bring super lightweight wool long underwear with me, just in case, and sleep in that. But since it's been really hot this summer, and we're not gaining much altitude, I'll probably bring a pair of running shorts and a tank top or something."

That would make sleeping right next to her easy—not. Ryan bit back his groan.

"I might bring a sleeping bag liner or a sheet. Our sleeping bags will be too warm, but it will be too cold to not have something over top."

Cold might be necessary, or he might not sleep at all. "I'm usually too hot."

She glanced at him. "What else are you wearing?"

"My old desert ABU pants and undershirt. My desert boonie hat, when I can stand to wear it. Probably an old T-shirt for around camp with silkies. Couple of pairs of socks. Sandals." He didn't want to carry a bunch of extras.

Erin bit her lip. "My turn to ask a slightly weird question. Umm, which arm are you bringing?"

Ryan laughed. "That's a good question. Think I'll probably bring the grasper I wear for work. It will be more useful."

"Good idea. I don't think anybody will care, and if they do, they can pound sand." Erin scowled.

"Hey, chill. I'm sure it will be fine. Hopefully, they won't freak out if I strap it to the back of my pack while we're hiking." He laughed at the mental picture.

She sputtered, then laughed outright. "Wow, that might be quite the sight for someone running into us on the trail. Which rarely happens."

They pulled into the business garage to unload the boxes. Ryan left his stuff in the foyer, then rode over with Erin to pick up his clothes from her house.

In the kitchen, Erin pulled an oatmeal container

from her cabinet. "I got the breakfast makings and a system, so don't worry about helping. You've got enough to do."

He walked back to the shop, hauled all his stuff upstairs, and looked around. There was no sign of Wiz, except she'd stripped the bed and put the sheets in the washer. He threw them into the dryer and got his other set.

Time for a twenty-minute nap and a shower before going out with Erin and her friends. It was probably a huge mistake, but he had no easy way out.

If he was honest with himself, he'd take any excuse to be with her.

Chapter 22

Danger Brews

Erin pulled in front of the shop, and Ryan exited and locked the door. He must have every color of cargo shorts and every long-sleeve logo T-shirt in existence. But he looked good in them. All too good, since he'd obviously just gotten out of the shower, and his T-shirt clung to all those muscles.

"Hey." He got in Smoky and shut the door, careful not to slam it.

A guy who understood how to treat a classic car was refreshing. "Hey. Ready for this?" She wasn't.

"Night out with hot women? Sure." His smile flickered.

She chuckled at his attempt to psych himself up. He was an adult; he could tell her if it was too much or too boring. Perhaps he would, or he might suffer in silence. If he'd open up a little...

Smoky roared down the highway, making quick work of the drive, and they pulled into the brewery. Not many cars in the lot, so it probably wasn't too busy. Erin pulled into a spot on the far side of the parking lot to protect Smoky from door dings. Inside, there was no sign of Sam or Deb yet. Erin turned to Ryan. "If you get me a summer ale, I'll order some food."

"Deal." He wandered to the bar, scanning the room.

Erin ordered a selection of snacks and found a table in the back. Just like Michael, Ryan would feel better with his back to a wall in view of the door. Around the room, more than a few guys did the same thing. *Okay, no more of that. Tonight's about having fun.* Ryan brought their beers. She waved down Deb and Sam, standing in the doorway. They waved back and walked to the bar. "Let me know if it gets too noisy in here for you, Ryan. I'm not up for an all-night session, anyway. Too much stress this week."

He smiled at her, a small, kind of sexy smile, but said nothing. Deb and Sam joined them, and she exchanged hugs. Both women hugged Ryan too but with a lot more body contact. Erin's spurt of jealous anger shocked her. What was she, sixteen? But when Sam lingered long past politeness, her anger grew. Even when Ryan stiffened and pulled away, she was a little miffed.

"You got sexy and silent here to come out for the night! Good for you." Deb winked.

"Good for us." Sam ran her hand down Ryan's chest. He grabbed her hand and slapped it on the table. Sam laughed. "Oooh, hard to get. I like it."

Ryan glared at her for a second and went back to examining the room. Looking for threats, probably. Erin shook her head. "Lighten up, Sam, or I'll never get him out with us again."

Sam rolled her eyes but then pointed at her. "I got the email with the video. I'll be filing that request for a restraining order, with the video attached and referencing the sheriff's reports from the assault. No promises, but I think that will do it."

"What are you talking about?" Deb's brow wrinkled.

"Erin's told you about Chaz, right?" Sam arched a brow.

"Yeah, but did something else happen?"

"Yes." Sam's face fell. "Did you want me to tell her, Erin? I'm sorry, I shouldn't have said anything here."

Erin shrugged. "It's okay; I don't have any secrets from Deb." And the chatter in the brewery was loud enough to cover their conversation.

Sam filled Deb in, quietly.

"That guy is trouble with a capital 'T'." Deb drew the letter in the air.

Sam grinned, a fierce grin that was more a baring of teeth than a smile. "But no match for Erin's security expert." She sobered. "I'd like to meet her, Erin. That's a woman no man should ever mess with. I have some pro bono clients who could use some help like that."

Erin grimaced. "She headed back home this morning. But she is thinking about moving to the area."

"Good. She'll do well here. Can't imagine she's very popular in a city wearing all that hardware."

Ryan glanced at Sam. "She doesn't go out much."

"Really? Why?" Sam's eyebrows arched.

"Not my story to tell." Ryan bit off the words.

"Sorry." Sam half-smiled and shrugged.

Ryan's smile flickered, but Erin could tell it was forced. Sam didn't mean to be obnoxious, but she'd lived here most of her life—in Marcus, everything was everybody's business.

Sam took a drink. "Well, if she needs any legal help, please let her know I'm happy to help, and I won't ask personal questions. And if she wants to do more of the kind of work she did on Erin's place, I know some folks who would hire her in a second."

Ryan slashed a hand. "It was a favor. She's a computer security expert. Works online mostly, doing design, assessments, and testing."

"Still, I know people who'd like that kind of work too."

Sam never knew when to give up, but that made her an excellent lawyer.

"So you said. I gave her your card." Ryan glared, then turned away.

"Thanks." Sam wrinkled her nose, facing Deb. "Your name fits—he's definitely sexy but silent."

Erin held back a snort. Sam wasn't used to working for attention. Ryan grimaced and studied the room again. A server brought their food. Deb and Sam filled Erin in on all the local gossip while they ate and drank. Ryan focused on a group gathered around a large table near the front. "Someone you know?" Erin asked.

"A bunch of folks from school."

She smiled and tilted her head toward them. "You're not tied down here. Go talk to them."

"Maybe." Ryan shrugged. "Don't have much in common with them anymore." He turned to her. "Besides, the company is better here."

Erin smiled at him but saw movement out of the corner of her eye. A cute little blonde cheerleader-type minced on high heels, a puzzled look on her face. "Ryan? Ryan Walsh?" Her mouth dropped open, then she pushed past Sam and threw herself at him. "It is you! When did you get back? Why didn't you call?" She wrapped her arms around his neck.

"Hi, Starla. How are you?" He tried to push her away, gently, but it was impossible. Starla locked on Ryan like a mountain lion on a deer.

"I'd heard you were back, but you didn't call, so I thought they were lying. Why didn't you call? Or email or something! I can't believe you didn't let me know!" She seemed to latch on tighter with each exclamation, and her voice pitched higher, leaving all of them wincing from the piercing noise. Starla finally let go, grabbed him by the hand, and towed him over to the group at the front. There were a lot of hugs and handshakes.

"She's enthusiastic. I'll give her that." Deb rubbed

her ear.

The girl, Starla, pushed Ryan down in her seat, and sat in his lap. He had his back to Erin, so she couldn't tell if he was comfortable or not, but his back sure was stiff. He held his left arm down at his side. Then all the eyes at the table turned their way, stared for a moment, and most of them turned away. She could see some of the boys' eyes staying on Sam. Erin huffed out a laugh. "Looks like you've made new conquests, ladies."

"I don't think it's just us." Deb chuckled. "But they seem so young. Ryan doesn't."

Erin snorted. "Hard to stay that young when you've been to war. I don't really fit in with most of our graduating class either."

"Well, that's true," Sam drawled. "But neither do I, or Deb." They all smiled knowingly at each other. Or ruefully, maybe. Somebody plopped down a beer in front of Ryan, and the noise grew. "Looks like we've lost sexy and silent, and nobody from our era is showing up. Probably all home with the kids. Do you want to move on somewhere else?"

Erin grimaced. "I don't want Ryan to feel abandoned on his first night out. Let's wait a few more minutes, then I'll text him that he can call if he needs a ride back."

"Sure, Mom," Sam snarked.

"Cute." They were deep into a discussion about how to get deadbeats to pay their bills when a high-pitched, "What?!" silenced the bar for a moment. Starla ran to the bathroom. Ryan's group all looked a little shocked. *Oh. Must have found out about the arm.* The girls followed Starla to the bathroom, whispering amongst themselves and shooting glances back at Ryan. A couple of the guys stared at the girls for a second, shrugged, and talked to Ryan. Everything seemed calm, but none of the girls came out of the bathroom. Eventually, Ryan got up and walked out the door. Erin shook her head. What a lousy thing to do. But it wasn't surprising—they were a bunch of immature little girls masquerading as women. They'd probably never really grow up.

"Uh oh. Doesn't look good. What a bunch of shallow idiots." Deb's mouth twisted.

"Yeah." Erin grimaced and drank the last of her beer. "Think I'll go. Remember I'm going backpacking tomorrow ."

Sam shuddered. "Yuck. But have fun in the dirt."

Deb smiled and gave her a hug. "Be careful and have a great time."

Erin left, looking around the parking lot for Ryan. He paced near Smoky. When she got closer, she lifted her arm to pat his back, but he backed away. "Ryan, you okay?"

"Yeah." He lifted his chin, face blank. "What are you doing out here? Go back and have fun with your friends."

"They're happily attracting every male eye in the place, and you're my friend too, so I thought I'd come see what was up." *That sounded lame.* But it was true.

"I'm fine. I'll wait here until you're ready, or you can give me Smoky's keys and get a ride with one of your friends if you trust me with him."

She waved the idea off. "No, let's go. It's late." Without Ryan, the fun was gone.

"Not that late."

She got in Smoky and rolled down the window. "Are you coming?"

Ryan got in and buckled up, but he didn't say a word until they got back to the shop. "Thanks for dinner. It was nice."

"Set your alarm—Jules will be here early."

"Not sure I feel like going." He put a hand on the door handle.

Erin turned to him, glaring. "You're going, even if I have to drag you out of that apartment. And those stairs will leave bruises." He was going, no matter what. She was *not* leaving him alone and depressed for a week.

Ryan snorted. "Like to see you try." He shook his head, a weird mix of amusement and despair on his face. "But you probably would try, and then you'd strain something and not be able to go, and I wouldn't want that."

She snorted. "Now you're getting the idea. And just because some *little girl* is an idiot, it doesn't mean everybody's an idiot."

Ryan flashed a forced smile.

" You'd better be packed and ready to go when they pick us up, or I'll get everyone to drag you down the stairs." She speared him with a look, making sure he knew he didn't have a choice. There was no way he'd stay and talk, but she wanted a commitment from him, something for him to focus on. She wanted to hug him, but from his stiff posture and hand on the door, she could tell it wouldn't be welcome right now.

"Okay." He hopped out and walked away.

She sighed and drove home. There were plenty of idiots in this world, that was for sure. She'd done all she could for tonight—hopefully he'd still be here tomorrow.

She hated leaving him alone, but she didn't have justification to invade his space. Not yet.

Chapter 23

Wilderness Is Good for the Soul, but a Tiny Tent Might Be a Different Story

Ryan trudged up the stairs to his nice, quiet apartment and locked himself in. The whole thing went exactly as he figured—fine until they found out about his arm. At least he'd reconnected with his old friends, but they were so young. So innocent. So naïve. So undamaged. Bonus—he didn't have to worry about Starla coming on to him anymore; she'd never grow up. That voice—yikes. He peeled off the arm, cleaned it, and made sure his residual looked healthy. He'd gotten so used to people either ignoring the arm or being happy with his barked "Afghanistan" that he'd forgotten how girls reacted.

Erin was right. He'd caught her emphasis on the word "girl." He chuckled; she'd made it obvious enough even for him to catch. He hadn't felt self-conscious around Deb or Sam, even when Sam put her hands all over him. Too bad the guys hadn't seen that part. When he'd pointed the three women out to them, jaws dropped. And after Starla had run away, and he made it clear he wouldn't tell them how he'd lost the arm, the guys had asked him lots of questions about the three ladies and what he was doing next. He snorted. He probably ruined any potential points with the guys by walking out the door instead of back over to the women, but that's the way it went. Not that he cared about making points with those guys anyway. They didn't have much in common anymore. He hadn't really missed any of them; not like he missed his Air Force friends.

Too wired to sleep, Ryan gathered all his gear and rolled, stuffed, and stowed it all in his new backpack. Plenty of room left for group gear. In the kitchen, he checked his food and water bottles and made a sandwich for the long drive tomorrow. The Frank was immense; the few roads were all dirt, so it took a very long time to get anywhere in the interior. And deep as they were going into the wilderness, they were hardly scratching the surface.

Ryan pulled out his tablet and sent a reminder to Wiz that he'd be backpacking for the next five days. To his surprise, she opened a DM and chatted with him. Guess she was feeling better. Wiz showed him some of the property and houses she'd found online. He had to laugh at her annoyance with the property descriptions, but most realtors didn't evaluate real estate in terms of defensive firing positions and evacuation escape routes. He promised to check them out when he returned, and she sent him a smiley face emoticon—the first he'd gotten from her since the attack.

Ryan went to bed early with a smile on his face. The next morning, he woke with a lot more enthusiasm for life. He couldn't wait to get out there, deep in the Frank Church River of No Return Wilderness. They'd hike and search for trails that were still on the map but hadn't been cleared in well over a decade. Finding old, overgrown trails could be difficult, and staying on them could be challenging. And fun.

He dragged his backpack, lunch, and an extra water bottle down the stairs. Erin was locking the coffee shop door when a big, burgundy SUV with the University of Montana logo on the side pulled up.

"Hey, Erin!" The bouncy blonde trip leader, Jules, jumped out of the driver's seat, waving. She hugged Erin, then bounded to him. "Hi, you must be Ryan. How are you this morning?"

"Great." He forced a smile, but all that energy was hard to take at o-six-thirty.

She smirked and shook her head. "Let's get your packs loaded and get this show on the road."

"Thanks for picking us up here." Ryan grabbed his pack.

She led him to the back of the big SUV. "We were driving right by. No reason for you to drive an hour north and then come right back, but you're welcome, anyway."

Ryan put both their packs in the back of the SUV.

They climbed in, bringing their sack lunches and water. He noticed Erin had a thermos of coffee; she'd almost certainly made enough to share. Which was wonderful because he was dragging.

Jules turned in the driver's seat. "We had a couple of people cancel last minute, so we're a smaller group than we planned." She nodded at the man in the passenger seat. "You remember Tyler, my co-trip leader, right? And then we have Dan and Laura in the very back. It's a long drive down the Magruder Corridor into the Frank Church, so kick back and relax."

Erin held up the thermos. "Before we leave, anyone want a shot of espresso? It's got cream in it, and I've got sugar packets." Everyone shoved mugs at her, and she laughed.

Ryan dug the sugar out of her lunch sack, handing it out. Then he handed Erin his mug, too. "You fired up Izzy this morning? Why didn't you tell me? I could have done that."

She poured. "I was up early. Didn't dawn on me until I got over to the shop that I could. So, I did."

Sounds of approval surrounded them. "Wow, we're stopping here first on our next trip." Tyler toasted Erin with his mug.

Erin chuckled. "You should. We open at six."

"I won't have any trouble staying awake on the drive, that's for sure." Jules sipped.

Erin asked about the trips they'd led so far, and Jules and Tyler told them funny stories about all the crazy things people did out backpacking and the strange and cool things they'd seen. Then they talked about music, and movies, and other common topics. Jules drove the huge SUV like a dirt track racer, so it wasn't long before they reached the trailhead. They exited and pulled out gear. Jules and Tyler made last-minute adjustments to the food for the reduced group size, and Erin gave him bags of her homemade oatmeal mix.

Jules pointed at the gear and food spread out by the vehicle. "Grab a couple of things, it's all got to go in someone's pack. When that's done, we'll do a stretch and safety circle, then get moving."

Ryan grabbed some of the heavier items, like a stove and fuel, one of the big group dinners, a pot, and a small folding saw. Everyone was in good shape, but the leaders already had a lot of stuff, and he was younger than everyone else.

Once packed, they gathered in a circle and did some active stretches. Jules pointed at the trailhead sign. "As we told you at the meeting, we've hiked the first part of this trail, and there's a good campsite about four miles in. We'll probably spread out on the trail, so stop at any trail crossings or streams so we can regroup, and make sure no one's been snatched by a sasquatch." They all chuckled, but Ryan was sure they all realized it was to make sure no one got left behind in case of an accident or someone took the wrong trail.

Ryan's amusement didn't last. He'd just ask. With only six of them, it was better to get the freaking out over with. "Uh, I've got a slightly bizarre question."

"Sure, Ryan, what is it?" As he swung a leg to warm up, Tyler's wild brown curls bounced.

He grimaced. He didn't want to but... "I don't want to make any of you uncomfortable, but it's really more comfortable if I don't wear my prosthesis when I'm hiking." He waved his left arm in the air. "Does anybody mind if I take it off?"

Erin chuckled, but the rest of them stared at him wide-eyed. Blast it all, he should have sucked it up. Then Jules and Tyler laughed, too. Eventually, Dan and Laura joined in, although they were shooting looks at each other.

Tyler shook his head. "Dude, I thought I'd heard it all, but that's a new one on me. I certainly don't care. You do you."

Everyone nodded, although Laura still looked a little wild-eyed. Ryan pulled his prosthetic off and strapped it through the pack's shove-it pocket, hiding it from view. Which was good because an arm strapped across a pack was a little weird. It was a little tricky getting the heavy pack on with only one hand, but he'd practiced. He lifted it to his knee, then swung it around, catching the strap with his residual arm, and fastened it up one-handed. The hip strap was challenging, but he'd figured it out.

"That's pretty impressive. I don't think I could pull that move off." Tyler tried to buckle his hip strap with one hand but gave up.

Ryan grinned. "Practice."

"It's probably a good idea. I solo a lot, and you never know when you might break an arm or something." He nodded slowly, his eyebrows lifted.

"You solo out here?" *That's gutsy.*

"Yeah, all the time." Tyler grinned. "Except this year—been busy with this gig—but in past years, yeah. And I'll probably travel to South America this winter. I'll be alone there, at least at first." He smirked. A good-looking, friendly, laid-back guy, Tyler would find a partner quickly if he wanted one.

With Tyler in the lead, they started down the trail. Ryan asked Tyler more questions about his travels. He'd been to a lot of interesting places, and in some downright scary situations, all by himself, both in the US and abroad. At least Ryan had the power of the US military behind him when he'd been in dangerous places.

While they talked, Ryan enjoyed the stark beauty. In places, the builders had literally carved the trail into the jagged, steep, rocky hillsides. A massive wildfire swept through the area a decade ago, leaving dead trees standing in mockery of living groves, the black of the charcoal standing out against the white of the bleached deadwood. Occasionally, they passed small groves of unburned trees, mostly in canyons carved by seasonal streams. They stopped at one of those shady, thickly treed spots for a water break about an hour and a half into the hike. The country was magnificent but scorching in the blazing August sun. Sitting in the scant shade of the tree with squirrels chattering, the tension left Ryan's body for the first time in a long time. Wilderness was good for the soul.

The rest of the group caught up, Erin promising Laura she would share her photos with everyone. Ryan hadn't brought a camera, but he had his phone. He didn't bring an extra battery, though. He put the phone in airplane mode, so it wouldn't look for the non-existent cell signal, and in battery-save mode.

Tyler leaned toward him for a moment, then pulled out his cell phone. "Good idea. I always forget to do that. Everyone, put your cell phone in battery-saver." Suddenly, there was a flurry of swiping.

When everyone had a snack and water, they continued. His pack weighed heavily on Ryan's hips, but the belt was conforming to his body, so tomorrow would be better. The surrounding terrain became impossibly steeper, but the trail remained fairly level, carved into the canyon walls, perched precariously above water-carved valleys hundreds of feet below, with miles of empty territory in every direction. The rocks glowed gold and red, the trees black and white; a rare dark green fir and an occasional light green plant provided respite from the glaring sun. Occasionally, they caught glimpses of the Magruder road as it carved through the wilderness. The corridor was so rugged drivers could rarely traverse it the whole distance, landslides and falling trees blocking it constantly. The chattering of squirrels and the rattle of rocks sliding under their feet were the only sounds. Even under the weight of the pack, Ryan relaxed, leaving his worries behind.

As they hiked farther into the wilderness, the land gradually shifted into gentler slopes. They rounded a bend and crossed a stream, entering an area with a mix of burned and unburned trees.

Tyler stopped. "This is our camp, so take a load off. We'll wait for the others to join us before we do anything else."

The rest of the group trickled in, Jules last. She unbuckled her pack. "Okay, folks, this is our first night's camp. Find someplace to put your tent where a tree won't drop on you if the wind picks up. Look for living wood and look up for loose branches. Those things can kill you. We'll put our cooking site here, where there's already a fire ring and some seats somebody cut a long time ago, so make sure you're at least a hundred yards away from here." Jules dropped her pack, groaning. "Leave the group gear here."

Erin dropped her pack next to his. She pulled the group gear and her food stuff sack out of her pack. He did the same and picked the much lighter pack back up. "Where do you think?"

Erin looked around and then up the trail a bit. "How about over there under those living trees?"

"Sure." They returned to the trail, walked a hundred yards, then entered the small but thick stand of unburned trees. Ryan looked up to make sure there weren't any dead branches overhead while Erin did the same, both of them moving, looking from different angles. They put down their packs, and Erin pulled the tent out of hers.

"You were supposed to give me part of that." Ryan scowled. He should have remembered to ask.

She shrugged. "It's not that heavy, but you can take part of it tomorrow." Erin laid it out and set it up, demonstrating so he could do it quickly in the future. It was a typical backpacking tent, long, narrow, and low to the ground, but both sides had entrances with big rain fly overhangs to keep gear and boots dry.

Erin shook out the waterproof rainfly, laying it over the tent. "It's too hot for the fly, but there's always the threat of thunderstorms in August, so better safe than sorry." They attached it but tied back the door flaps to allow airflow. They pulled out their pads, sleeping bags, and headlamps, putting them in the tent, ready for the night. Their bags seemed awfully close together.

As they pulled off their boots, they both groaned. Hiking was amazing but tough on the feet. Dry air wicked away his sweat and hopefully the smell, too. Ryan tossed his socks over a branch to dry, pulled his prosthesis off his pack, and put it on. As they returned to their cooking site, he spotted three more tents within a few yards of theirs. The circle of green they camped in was one of the few spots without hazardous, burned trees. Not much privacy, but since he didn't have a need for privacy, it didn't really matter. He grimaced. Too bad; backpacking was probably even more fun with the right partner for nighttime activities. Then he shoved that thought away. He didn't need that in his head, not when they'd be sleeping so close together.

Near the empty fire ring, Jules and Tyler were

heating water over a camp stove and chopping veggies for the meal. Erin squatted next to them. "Can we help?"

Tyler waved a hand. "Nah. We got it. Just relax. I already found a good bear hang to store our food, so no worries."

Erin frowned but sat down. Ryan shrugged and refilled his and Erin's water bottles. Then he refilled the big group water filter at the little stream. He sat on one of the log stools next to Erin.

"How are the new boots and pack?" Erin pointed at his feet.

"Good. I wore the boots for work this week, so they're all broken in, and I've been adjusting the pack a little as I hiked." He'd worn the pack for some workouts too. Ryan rolled his shoulders. Sore, but not screaming.

Dan and Laura returned and filled their bottles. While dinner cooked, they chatted about various backpacking trips in the past. Dan went out a lot with trail maintenance groups; Laura had camped with the Girl Scouts and hiked in college. Erin also went out on trail maintenance trips. Ryan was the least experienced traditional backpacker, but he'd been out on patrol in Afghanistan when the base defense and EOD patrols needed help. Not that he'd be telling the group any details. They probably weren't interested in the finer points of setting perimeter patrols or making MREs edible. Meals Ready to Eat; three lies in one package. Tonight's coconut rice and black beans with fresh veggies was so much better.

After they ate, Jules offered tea and cocoa. They cleaned up, brushed their teeth, and went off to hang the food and pots where they would be safe from bears and other critters.

"Wish we could have a fire, but the fire danger is too high." Jules hauled on the last rope, pulling the bag high over a sturdy branch.

Laura tied it off for her. "Too bad. Even when it's hot, sitting around a fire is one of the best parts of camping."

"Yeah, and there are s'mores, which you really can't do over a stove flame. Well, you can; I've toasted marshmallows that way, but it's not the same." When they got back to their camp site, Tyler spread out a large topographical map, about three feet square. "Since we can't do that, I'll show you where we're headed tomorrow."

He pointed at the "TH" symbol near the road. "The trailhead was here, and we're headed southwest toward the Salmon River. We're here now." Tyler pointed at the blue line of the stream. "And we'll be camping around this little lake in the Salmon River Breaks for the next two nights. That's about five miles from here, so we'll hike tomorrow, get all set up, then maybe go for a very short day hike to see if we can find this trail." His finger traced a dotted line on the map. "It's only a half a mile or so from where we're camping, but it will be hard to find because the area was badly burned, and there's a ton of downed wood. We'll be looking for blazes, obvious cut wood, and man-made objects like logs set into the trail to divert water and prevent erosion. Then the next day, we'll try to day hike this loop, starting with the trail or trails we find tomorrow, if we find them at all. Either way, it will be challenging. There's no water on this loop, so we'll have to take everything we need." Tyler gazed around the circle at each of them.

"Then the final day, we'll hike the entire way out, which is farther than we usually go in a day, but you guys are all experienced, and we won't have any food or fuel weight. That means we'll get home rather late, but it was the only way we could make this trip work. We wouldn't have tried with a regular group, but we could tell this hike didn't challenge any of you." Tyler looked around the group again.

Jules nodded. "If any of you are uncomfortable with that idea, we can go out tomorrow as planned, do what we can the next morning, then come back to this midway spot and camp, then hike out the next day. That would put us back in Missoula earlier. And we can make that decision tomorrow. Just let one of us know."

"Seems okay to me." Erin chuckled. "Tuesday's opening will be rough, but I own a coffee shop. I can overdose on caffeine."

Everyone agreed to the plan. Ryan thought Laura looked a little uncertain, but he wasn't the only one to notice. Jules or Tyler would talk to her. Personally, he didn't care what they did and when; he was happy to be outside in the woods with Erin. He'd rather be alone with her, but having people around prevented him from making any stupid moves.

Jules rose. "Normally, I'd hang around with you guys, but it was a rough week, so I'm going to go to my tent, read a little, and sleep. We'll plan on having hot water by eight a.m., and we'll want to be on the trail by nine."

"If we don't see you by eight-thirty, we'll come wake you up." Tyler grinned as he got up. "Loudly."

Ryan and Erin joined the stream of people walking to their tents. Jules and Tyler had separate tents—evidently, they weren't a couple. But then, they might not have been a couple, even if they were sharing. Like him and Erin. He pulled a little trowel from an outside pocket on his pack. "I'm going to find a bathroom spot, so you'll have the tent to yourself for a while."

Looking up from her pack, Erin smiled. "Thanks. Makes that whole discussion go away."

Ryan forced a smile in return. "I don't want to make you uncomfortable. If you need me to disappear for a while, say so. I'll go watch the wind blow or stargaze or whatever. Won't bother me any."

"I'll tell you, but I don't think it will be necessary." Erin shrugged one shoulder. "You can do the same."

"Sure." He walked at least a quarter of a mile away and found a decent spot, then headed back to the camp. He sanitized his hands and returned to their tent. The sun glowed gold, dropping toward the horizon, so he was glad they'd broken up a little early. The first night out was easier in daylight, rather than by headlamp. Especially with a new tent—and a new hiking partner.

At the tent, Erin's pack leaned against the nearest tree, with the rain cover on, and she'd tucked her boots under the right-side tent vestibule. He changed into shorts, pulled off his arm and cleaned it, then put the cover on his pack and put it next to hers. His boots and arm went under the left-side vestibule. He hesitated. Should he ask Erin if he could come in? Nah, she'd say something if she wanted privacy. She could hear him loud and clear through the thin nylon.

Ryan stooped down and unzipped the tent, sitting on his sleeping bag with his back to Erin to take off his sandals and brush his feet off outside the tent. He put his bear spray near the door and his headlamp above it, where he could easily grab either. With nothing left to do, he flipped back the sleeping bag top and turned on his back.

He couldn't avoid it anymore, so he glanced over at Erin. She was far too close and too far away; lying there, reading, cool as a cucumber. She wore a pale green tank top, a skimpy pair of running shorts in dark green, with miles of bare legs below, and nothing else. *Sexy.* The view in the tent was way better than the scenery outside.

Erin looked up from her e-reader. Fortunately, he noticed and met her eyes. She smiled. "How's the pad and bag feel?"

"Good. I like these air pads." Ryan rolled a little back and forth, the pad creaking slightly and giving a little underneath him.

"Yep, they're great. Lightweight and cushy." She smiled again, but it died pretty quickly. With both of them crammed so close together, she didn't seem comfortable.

Ryan nodded and turned on his side away from her. He didn't want to worry her. Plus, something about the way she said "cushy" made him think about other soft things, like her lips. And that was a bad idea in the tight confines of the tent. He pulled out his paperback, but he wasn't reading. Nope, too busy thinking about the woman next to him. They'd set up the tent so that their bags both opened in the center, next to each other. He swallowed hard. Maybe she always slept on the right with the Sarge. The realization hit—these bags were a matching set, meant to zip together. That thought made her even harder to ignore, with a side of guilt.

Ryan lay there on his side, pretending to read, until it got too dark to see the words, then he put the paperback away. Erin's bag rustled as she shifted.

"Goodnight, Ryan."

"Night." It was gonna be a long one, probably without a lot of sleep.

Chapter 24

Tiny Tents Mean Little Sleep

Erin woke, squeezing her eyes shut, blocking the laser-like sun. She moved her head a few inches, then cautiously opened her eyes again. No blinding sun, but Ryan was right in front of her. They were close enough to kiss, and she wanted to lean forward so badly. Those soft lips, open slightly in sleep, were far too tempting, and last night? Last night was worse. She'd hardly slept at all.

She'd badly misjudged the hazards of sharing a tent with him. Yesterday, she'd been far too aware of the man lying so close to her, wearing nothing but silky shorts. She'd shot glances at Ryan from behind her e-reader. When he turned away, she'd given up the pretense and stared. His wide, muscular shoulders tapered down to a narrow lower back, all corded with muscles and decorated by scars. The scars weren't big, but he had both burns and penetration wounds, like hot shards of metal had peppered his left side. How incredibly painful. The less obvious scars on his face must have been corrected by a plastic surgeon, but these hadn't. Erin shuddered. Did his scars still hurt? She really wanted to kiss them all and make him feel better, but Ryan was eight years younger, an employee, and off-limits. She'd turned away from him, toward the tent door, and tried to put him out of her mind, but she'd tossed and turned most of the night.

She rolled away from temptation and picked up her phone. Well before her alarm, but she couldn't go back to sleep with Ryan lying next to her and the sun in her eyes. She climbed out of the tent. Bright blue sky, the sun rising, birds chirping merrily, and not a soul stirring. Erin shivered a little in the cool morning air until she pulled on her lightweight sweater, hiking pants, and hat. She took her e-reader and water bottles to the cooking area, did her morning routine, cleaned her hands, refilled the hanging water filter, and got a pot full of water for breakfast. Then she went to the bear hang, released the food bags, and carried bags and ropes to the cook site. She had to stay busy and stop thinking about the impossible.

Jules was starting the stove when Erin returned with the second load of bags. "Morning. Thanks for getting all this down." Jules motioned to the bags.

"No problem. I woke with the sun in my eyes, and I knew I wouldn't get back to sleep. Faster we get started, the quicker we get there. Miles to go and cool things to do." She grinned at Jules, who gave her a smiling thumbs up, shimmying in place. Erin pulled her mug, coffee, and oatmeal out and did the same for Ryan, getting it ready for hot water. Hopefully, he'd sleep for a while still. She'd heard him tossing and turning during the night, too. Probably not for the same reason, though.

They chatted as the water heated and everyone else trickled in. Ryan was last, stumbling into camp as Erin finished her coffee.

"Good morning, sleepyhead," Jules sang. Ryan winced at her overly cheerful voice, making everyone laugh. His hair stuck up, and pillow wrinkles marred his face. He looked a bit like a bear waking up from hibernation.

Erin prepped his coffee and oatmeal, handing the coffee over when he sat on the log next to her. He grunted, then sucked down a long drink of coffee.

Laura chuckled. "Was that a thank-you?"

Erin nodded. "That's as close as he gets until he's had a significant amount of caffeine. I've learned to interpret his different grunts over the last few months. He's a great barista, but Ryan is not a morning person." He'd never talked much but even less at the beginning of their shifts.

He grunted again and glared at her a little, but she could tell he was kidding. While he spooned up oatmeal, she cleaned her dishes and went to the tent to pack. By the time he arrived, she had the sleeping bags, pads, and tent rolled and in their stuff sacks.

"Thanks. You didn't have to do that." Ryan shoved his bag in the bottom of his pack.

"No problem. I wasn't doing anything else." Erin packed her stuff and put on her socks and boots. She enjoyed helping him, probably because he rarely tolerated it.

"Hey, give me part of the tent." He stood over his open pack, reaching his right hand to her.

Erin patted her pack. "Too late. You can carry it on the way out." The tent wasn't heavy, and she was used to carrying it.

He scowled, and she gave him a challenging stare in return. "Okay, fine. But only because it's too much work to pull out now." He plopped down and put on his boots. Erin hoisted her pack, checking around the site to make sure she'd packed everything. Back at the cook site, she grabbed the same group gear she'd had the day before, tightened all the straps down, and sat down to wait, but it didn't take long.

"Ready for the trail by eight-thirty. This is an amazing group!" Jules led them in warmups. Tyler gave them the same reminders as the day before, and then they moved out. As fast hikers, he and Ryan took the lead, then Erin followed, with Dan, Laura, and Jules bringing up the back. Jules wasn't slow, but she claimed to enjoy being last, so Erin left her to it. It was probably for safety reasons.

They stopped half an hour later to strip off their sweaters and hats because the temperature rose from the 50s to the 90s. As they hiked deeper into the wilderness, the hills rounded off, becoming less jagged, but the canyons were just as deep and steep. The wildfire had burned much hotter, leaving nothing but blackened stumps. The trail was a powdery mix of white and black earth over rock, each step raising small dust clouds. A few low, pale green plants sprouted in small groups on the edge of the trail. The fire had burned hot enough to sterilize the soil, and it was only ten years later that there were enough nutrients to support life. It was still beautiful but harsh and barren.

The trail was firm underfoot and gently undulated with no big elevation changes, so they made very good time. Gradually, standing burned trees became more and more common, along with a few larger green trees and smaller recent growth. They reached their target lake by lunchtime and gathered at a well-established campsite.

The site was lovely, with a large area of unburned trees around it and plenty of logs and rocks for seats. Far less than the required two hundred feet from the water to meet the Leave No Trace standards, but since it was already there, they'd use it. While they ate, Tyler told them he would make the fire ring smaller and naturalize the area before they left, but most likely, someone would rebuild the ring by next fall, despite the rules. "Find a tent site. There's a bunch past the lake. We can spread out a lot more than last night." Tyler winked at Dan, then pointed at the trail along the lake. "Make sure you're at least two hundred feet from the water." He rose, and they all followed. "We'll regroup here in thirty minutes.

Jules and I will find a bear hang in the other direction, so bring all your food back here, please."

Dan and Laura took a side trail, while Erin stayed behind Tyler and Jules until they split off. She continued along a narrow trail across a grassy meadow to a small grouping of young trees in the middle. She followed the light path between two thirty-footers to an area of mostly bare ground inside the small copse, just big enough for a tent. Surrounded by decent size, healthy-looking trees, the site allowed a good view of the sky, with no hazards overhead. "This looks perfect, don't you think?"

Ryan smiled at her, his gaze intent. "Yeah, perfect." He turned away and dropped his pack.

Feeling a little flushed from his regard, she did the same, and the two of them set up the tent quickly. Ryan was all business, so she must have misinterpreted his look. Probably wishful thinking on her part. She had to remember he couldn't be hers—too young and her employee. They hoisted their much lighter packs and headed back to the cook site.

After hanging extra food and gear, Tyler took the lead with a Forest Service GPS unit and map. They hiked less than a mile to the area on the map. "Okay, spread out and look for signs of the old west-bound trail. But don't go more than, say, four hundred yards from here. The growth is too thick to keep an eye on everyone, and we want to find you fast if something happens. Stay in sight of at least one other person." The area had burned in the same wildfire but cooler, leaving thickets of willows and dog hair pines sprouting among burned, mostly downed timber. It looked like a giant dumped a box of scorched logs, covering the ground with crisscrossed trunks. Recent growth sprang up in and around the piles, so thick it was difficult to even see the ground in places.

Erin climbed over the downed wood, slipping and sliding despite her caution, willows and branches smacking her across the face. She panted in the heat. Only a few minutes later, she sat and drank, grateful for the slim protection of her floppy sun hat, and wished she'd done more squats. Her legs ached.

Ryan bounded from log to log, seemingly without a care; she worked hard to keep up. About fifteen minutes into their search, he whooped. "Hey, I found an old water diverter!"

Erin shoved through the willows to reach Ryan, a hundred yards from the trail. "Nice, Ryan." She patted his shoulder, and he shot a grin at her. Then he hugged her, shocking her. By the time she recovered enough to hug him back, he was pushing away. The other hikers gathered around them.

Tyler tied a piece of thin blue plastic surveyor's tape on a branch above Ryan's find. "Yep, that's a water bar, not just a log. Great job, Ryan." Everyone cheered, while Ryan smiled a little sheepishly. "Now that we have a starting point, Jules, Dan, and Laura will head back toward the main trail while me, Erin, and Ryan will go west." Tyler waved the roll of blue tape. "Onward!" He and Ryan jumped from log to log while Erin sweated behind them. But she found the next sign; they'd missed the line of carefully piled rocks on the edge of the old trail.

Tyler tied another ribbon. "Outstanding, Erin. Guess me and Ryan will slow down a bit."

Erin chuckled. "Nah. Leaves something for me to do while you mountain goats make distance."

Tyler laughed but bounded ahead, taking her at her word. He found the next two trail signs, tying more flags. "Let's head back. It's super hot, and we've already done five miles of backpacking today. We got a great start for tomorrow." Even with the flags, going back was slow and arduous, clambering over the log piles and hacking at the undergrowth to clear the trail a little.

At the main trail, the other group had found the intersection and cleared a few feet, marking it on both sides. Jules took off her hat and wiped her sweaty brow. "Great job, everybody. We'll take the rest of the afternoon off and relax. It's way too hot to do this kind of bushwhacking and trail work, especially after this morning."

They strolled back to the lake, refilled water bottles, pulled off their hiking boots, and snacked. After repacking her food bag, Jules stood up. "This is a big enough lake, so if anyone wants to splash a little, go in on the far side, closer to the tent sites. But it's cold, so be careful." She walked away, pulling off her shirt.

Erin gazed at the lake. The cold water would feel so good on her hot, sweaty skin. She couldn't compete with Jules's or Laura's beauty, but she was too sticky to worry about it. She looked at Ryan; his eyebrows waggled above a challenging smirk. "Come on. Let's go."

Ryan smiled, a slow lift of his lips that grew. Then he swept his eyes from her head to her feet and back. He was grinning by the time his eyes made it back to her face. Erin almost fanned herself like a Regency heroine. He jumped to his feet and held out his hand.

Erin forced a grin in return, ignoring the flush of heat his gaze caused, and took his hand, letting him pull her up. He yanked too hard, and she stopped herself with a hand on his firm, muscular chest. *Ooh.* Despite her overwhelming need to touch, Erin stepped back and turned toward the lake. She had to stop thinking about Ryan. He was off-limits. What did she need for the dip? Sandals and her pack towel, fortunately in her pack. Maybe a comb. But with Ryan right behind her, so close she could almost feel his breath on her neck, keeping her mind on swimming was difficult. She *needed* that cold water right now, or she'd combust.

When they reached the far side of the lake, Jules was already in the water, floating on her back in her underwear. Erin breathed a sigh of relief. She wasn't stripping all the way in front of strangers or Ryan. Erin peeled off her hiking pants and shirt, then splashed into the frigid lake. She'd learned to get the initial plunge over quickly, or she'd never submerge. When the water reached her knees, she took a deep breath and dove. Shuddering at the cold, cold water on her hot skin, she emerged, gasping.

She swam a few strokes and then did another shallow dive, coming up at a steep angle so her hair wouldn't fall back in her face. As she put a foot down and opened her eyes, Ryan was doing the same beside her. He wiped his eyes, grinning. Then he shook his head like a dog, sending water flying. Erin shrieked and splashed him back. Then all six of them were throwing water at each other. Ryan held his own, even with one hand. Even with the fight and the scorching sun beating down, the cold water soon made Erin shiver. She waded back to shore with Jules and Laura, toweling off and basking in the sun, watching the guys talk, standing hip-deep in the lake.

Laura waggled her brows. "The scenery around here sure is great."

She and Jules laughed, leering exaggeratedly at each other. Surreptitiously, Erin pulled her phone from her hiking pants and snapped a couple of pictures. A beautiful lake, surrounded by dark green spruce and fir trees, a light green and gold meadow on one end, big red and gray rocks stacked on the other, with three muscular men, water dripping down their chests and underwear plastered to their hips. With Ryan's right side to them, it was a perfect calendar shot. Not that she'd care about getting his residual arm in the shot; it made him more attractive, not less. But the other women might not feel the same.

"You gotta send me a copy of that. It will keep me

warm this winter." Jules pointed at Erin's phone.

"You two will get copies of these, but I don't think I'll let the guys know." Erin snickered. Jules was right; the shot would heat her up, too.

Laura laughed. "Probably a good idea."

They all giggled. The guys waded back to shore, regarding them warily. Tyler put his hands on his hips. "And what are you women whispering about?"

"Oh, nothing." Jules sniggered.

All three of the men snorted. "Yeah, right. That sound is trouble." Dan regarded them with raised brows.

"Trouble for us to know about and you only to wonder at. Brr." Laura shivered exaggeratedly. "I'm putting on something dry." She walked away, presumably to their tent, Dan on her heels. It would probably be a while before they saw the two of them again.

A drop of water rolled down the middle of Erin's back, sending a shiver down her spine. She needed dry clothes, too. Erin grabbed her things, following the narrow trail to their tent site. Ryan was right behind her.

Erin ducked into the tent to grab her clothes bag, plunked at the head of her sleeping bag as a pillow. She pulled out clean underwear and her sleep camisole, then realized Ryan was also gathering clothes on his side of the tent. *Hmm.* She really didn't want to get naked in front of him. Except she sort of did, but no.

Crouched on the other side of their sleeping bags,

he met her eyes, then scanned down. Erin clutched her clothes to her chest and turned away, shivering, but not from cold. She'd go behind the trees.

Ryan said, "Erin?"

"Yeah?" She didn't turn back.

"I'll go over behind these trees and give you some privacy. I won't look."

"Thanks." Footsteps crackled through the pine straw. She glanced back but saw nothing, so she wriggled out of her wet things, dried off, and put on her hiking pants, a T-shirt, and a lightweight sweater, hopefully hiding her lack of a bra. She had another one, but her shoulders needed a break from straps of all kinds. It was still a little warm for the sweater, but the sun would drop behind the trees soon, cooling off the air quickly.

Erin announced, "I'm done." She hung her wet things on tree branches to dry. Good thing she always brought an extra set of undies. A branch broke, and Erin turned. Ryan hung a pair of boxer briefs on a branch. But clearly, he wasn't chilly at all. He wore only the same silky shorts he'd worn last night, displaying his muscular chest.

Ooh, sexy. Erin shook her head to clear away the inappropriate thoughts—*eight years, employee!*—out of her brain and returned to their cook site, Ryan on her heels.

Jules's head snapped up when she spotted him. She looked him up and down, grinning.

Erin cleared her throat. "Do you need some help?"

"Sure. Want to chop veggies? And Ryan, can you

go get me water? About half full." Jules handed a pot to him.

Erin sat down, took the bag of vegetables, a knife, and a plastic pot lid and started chopping, using the lid as a cutting board.

"So," Jules said, slowly, "are you and Ryan together?"

"No. He works for me. That would be sexual harassment." If she said it enough, maybe she'd believe it.

"Would you be offended if I...?"

"Nope. Go for it." Never mind she wanted to push the knife into Jules's chest rather than into the veggies. Erin chopped harder. She had no claim on Ryan, other than his working time. *Couldn't* have a claim. No matter what she wanted or what Deb said.

Erin kept her eyes on the knife as Jules talked to Ryan. Jules flirted with all kinds of innuendo, but he returned his normal one-syllable answers. Erin glanced at them. Jules was smiling up at Ryan, but he was looking at—Erin? Yep. Not looking at Jules at all but at her. Erin smiled at the veggies, then mentally took a hand and hit the back of her own head. She couldn't have him, and he deserved to have somebody. Jules was a nice girl, with a completely different outlook on life. She'd be good for him. But Erin had a slightly guilty sense of satisfaction knowing the younger, prettier, more outgoing girl couldn't get his attention. She finished chopping. "What else?"

"Nothing. It will take about twenty minutes to

cook all this, so hang out." Jules shrugged and smiled at Ryan, then glanced over at Erin. "Wander around, fill water bottles, whatever you want."

Message received. "Perfect. Thanks." Erin smiled at Jules and got up. She'd leave them alone.

"Hey, Erin, I want to show you something. Come on." Ryan beckoned from the other side of the site.

Or maybe she wouldn't, since Ryan didn't seem interested. Erin followed when Ryan motioned again, curious. And the view was delightful too. They trod a faint path—the unofficial trail probably circled the entire lake.

Ryan turned back to her but kept walking. If she tried to walk backward on a trail, she'd trip and fall. "I noticed this end of the lake when we were swimming. I thought about swimming over, but it was pretty chilly water." He turned around in time to avoid a big rock.

"It was. It felt great though, didn't it?" She wouldn't feel guilty at all looking at that picture in the depths of winter.

Ryan nodded. They continued on the trail and came out at the far end of the lake. Layers of stacked gray and red rock reached into the sky. Each rectangular piece was a foot to three feet thick and twenty to thirty feet long, an uneven stairway to heaven.

Ryan looked up, shading his eyes. "Looks like some giant was going to make a wall, and he dropped everything here, doesn't it?"

"It's pretty awesome." No doubt there was a

technical explanation of deposition, erosion, uplift, and glacial action, but who cared? It was amazing. She snapped a picture.

"Hey, let's see if we can get to the top." Ryan grinned at her, his challenge clear.

Erin looked between him and the top of the rocks, letting her skepticism show. "Without killing ourselves, you mean?"

He mock scowled. "We'll be fine. Come on."

Erin shook her head but followed him anyway. Ryan was hard to resist when he turned on the charm. "It's not the up that gets you, it's trying to get back down."

Ryan scoffed. "Yeah, yeah. Live a little."

She laughed. "Pot, kettle."

"Okay, but come on." He bounded up the slabs of granite. Their side seemed safer than the other side, which had risen almost straight up from the lake. Erin followed him up the extra-large, odd-sized, slightly tilted staircase, moving more cautiously, and it wasn't long before they got to the top.

Ryan whistled. "Incredible view."

"Yes, it is." Erin snapped a few pictures, carefully stepping back to take a couple with Ryan in the foreground. There wasn't a single man-made object in sight, the landscape fading into folded hills and then hazy mountains beyond. "We should get a selfie up here."

Ryan turned, beckoning her with a crooked finger. Holding her breath, Erin took the two steps and joined him, not looking down. The edge was close, but she trusted Ryan. He slung his arm around her shoulders, turned them both to look over the lake, and pulled her back against his hard chest, his face next to hers. "There. Perfect."

Erin held her phone up at arm's length and snapped the picture, amazed her hand was steady. His warm, muscular frame pressed against hers in all the right places, made her want to turn into him and forget all about pictures, phones, and everything else. But she couldn't.

"One more." Ryan's warm breath coasted over her cheek. As she hit the button, he kissed her ear. She couldn't breathe. Her heart pounded in her chest. Erin pulled away and tried to smile at Ryan, but he wasn't smiling. He was looking at her mouth. Erin caught her breath again. *Employee, eight years younger.* She forced herself to turn, put the camera away in her pocket, and look for a safe way back down. *Nothing about this is safe at all.* She clambered down, with Ryan following.

Moving carefully, Erin thought about the kiss. It wasn't a quick press and go, like a cheek-kiss greeting among friends. No, Ryan's lips lingered for a moment, pressing soft and warm against her skin. But maybe it was for the camera.

Ryan couldn't be interested in her. She was too old, his previous supervisor's widow, and his boss. But he wasn't interested in Jules, a beautiful, active woman closer to him in age, or in gorgeous Sam, or pretty Deb. However, lack of interest in other women didn't mean Ryan was interested in her. It wasn't possible.

Erin swallowed hard. But what if Deb was right? What if Ryan was interested in a romantic relationship? Was she missing out on something real because she was too scared to try? Too worried about lawsuits and legalities to see a real possibility?

Erin stepped off the last rock and onto the narrow trail. Or was that possibility a trail to nowhere, petering out in the forest, leaving her lost and desolate?

When they arrived at the cook site, dinner was ready, so they served themselves and sat down on the rocks around the fire ring. Erin was starving but not as hungry as Ryan, who was shoveling down food at a rather amazing rate.

"This is outstanding, Jules. What is it?" Erin tried to make amends for their earlier conversation. She had been so sure Ryan would welcome Jules's attention.

"Veggies and rice noodles in Thai peanut sauce. I'm really glad none of you are allergic to peanuts!" Jules beamed around the group, shimmying in her seat.

"Me too." Erin was grateful Jules didn't seem to take Ryan's rejection too hard. "Life without peanut butter wouldn't be worth living."

"Couldn't have survived all these years without it." Ryan held up his spoonful, nodding at Jules. She grinned but returned to her food.

The conversation shifted into favorite foods, favorite movies, weird places they'd been, and other general topics. When night fell, everyone was ready for bed, yawning with full bellies. Tyler reminded them of breakfast time.

Erin led the way to the tent. Good thing they'd made the trek several times, so they could find the trail in the narrow headlamp beam. Ducking into the tent, she took off her sandals and hiking pants and put on her shorts. "I'm done if you want to come in."

"Okay."

Erin grabbed her book and turned on her side, away from Ryan. She'd meant to switch sides, but somehow, she'd ended up on the right side again. She snorted softly. Old habits die hard. The tent zipper rasped, and Ryan rustled in the sleeping bag far too close to hers. She couldn't face that bare chest until the lights were out. Maybe not then either. *Rats.* Erin put up her book and clicked out her headlamp. She'd had slept little last night, so hopefully she could tonight.

But that kiss. How was she going to sleep, thinking about that kiss? She was probably over-thinking it, making things up. Ryan couldn't really want her.

She shifted uneasily. But what if he did? That kiss might mean as much to Ryan as it did to her. She might miss out on a second chance, never dreaming she could find another man like Michael. She'd had it all, the best kind of love and lover.

Although Ryan wasn't anything like Michael, except in their attitudes toward duty, honor, and sacrifice. Michael was a big, booming, outgoing man, quick with a joke or a story. He made friends everywhere he went. Ryan was withdrawn and quiet, preferring to stay in the background. Some of that might be his injuries; not only the arm but the head injury he'd suffered during the attack.

Erin tried to recall what Ryan was like at the Alaska crew parties so many years ago. He'd been pretty quiet and unobtrusive, but she dimly recalled he seemed to have fun, smiling and joking with his friends. That meant the injury changed his personality, which wasn't unusual. But it really didn't matter because it was the Ryan of today she cared about. And she cared a lot. More than a boss, more than just a friend.

She huffed. Here she was, back at step one, wanting more but unsure if Ryan wanted more too. Erin closed her eyes and concentrated on her breathing, feeling every breath going in and out. She had to stop this merry-go-round and get some sleep. Maybe everything would be clearer in the morning.

Chapter 25

Wish We Were in that Tiny Tent...

Ryan shifted in his sleeping bag, way too aware of the woman next to him. *What was I thinking, kissing Erin?* Which was a stupid question. He knew the answer. When he'd pulled her back into his body, she'd felt so good he couldn't stand it. At least he hadn't done what he really wanted; kissing across her face to capture her mouth under his.

Erin's reaction wasn't what he expected. He'd imagined either a slap or a joke, but he got wide eyes, a weirdly tentative smile, and lots of glances as she climbed down and walked away. Probably better than the slap but a lot more ambiguous. He couldn't figure out what her reaction meant.

Ryan used to be confident with women. If he wanted someone, he went for it. And he usually got what he wanted. If he didn't, he moved on. But since he lost his arm, he hadn't tried, anticipating a reaction like Starla's. He didn't get a negative reaction from Erin, but he wasn't looking for neutral. He wanted it all with her. Too bad he didn't know what she wanted. Not a clue.

Well, nothing would happen tonight. Not that he'd expected anything. He turned on his side and started on his standby—counting sheep. Hopefully, it wouldn't turn into a nightmare.

"Ryan, wake up. Ryan! Hey, wake up, Ryan." Erin's voice rose.

"Huh?" He blinked and tried to rub his eyes, but his good arm was under something.

"Ryan, wake up," Erin snapped. A hand shoved his shoulder.

The command voice startled him. He shook his head, trying to jar his brain into motion. "I'm awake. What?" The darkness told Ryan it was still night.

"Will you let me go, please?" Strained patience and breathlessness.

What is she talking about? Ryan lifted his head off his pillow. He lay on top of Erin, his head on her chest, his waist snugged between her legs, his arms around her, too. *Oops.* He rolled off, even though leaving the comfort of her warm embrace was the last thing he wanted to do. "I'm sorry, Erin. I must have been dreaming." She probably thought he was a total pervert. He winced.

"I think you were having a nightmare. Are you okay?" Her tone conveyed quiet concern.

He only remembered the way she felt in his arms—better than any pillow. "Yeah, I'm fine. Are you okay? I'm not exactly light." Erin was soft but firm, and he'd wanted to cuddle with her in the worst way. He wasn't usually a cuddler, but Erin expanded his horizons in a lot of different ways.

She laughed, low and husky. "I'm fine. You're not that heavy. Do you remember what you were dreaming about?"

Her laugh made him think of other things. But he couldn't—not in the tiny tent, when he didn't know how she'd react. He couldn't even look at her. "No. I don't remember my dreams. Sometimes I wake up, sometimes I don't, but either way, I don't remember specifics, just danger, the sounds of explosions and screaming." Ryan tried to keep his voice unemotional, but recalling those particular dreams made him shudder. This one had been much better.

"That sucks. I'm sorry to hear that, Ryan."

Her sleeping mat creaked, then her hand closed over his and squeezed. He returned the gesture. "It's okay. It could be worse."

"Can you go back to sleep?"

"Yeah, sure. My heart's not racing, so it should be easy." Although, her hand in his caused his heart to beat harder.

"Okay, goodnight." Erin squeezed his hand again but didn't let go.

"Goodnight." Ryan didn't release hers, either, relishing the feel of her slightly callused fingers on the back of his hand, her palm against his. He'd rather have her back in his arms—or arm—but the simple gesture made him ridiculously happy.

\#

Ugh, happy music. What is that? Off, off, off! Ryan blinked in the sunlight and rolled, reaching to swipe his alarm off. But he didn't want to get up. He'd dreamed he was holding Erin, her back against his front. Looking down, he was lying on Erin's sleeping bag, and he'd had to flip and stretch to find his phone.

Ryan's cheeks warmed, and his stomach iced. Maybe he had been wrapped around Erin. If it was true, she hadn't elbowed him to get away or screamed or anything. But he'd had a nightmare earlier, so she probably thought waking him abruptly was a bad idea. Which was true. So she let him hang on. Or maybe she'd been asleep, too. Or maybe it was all a dream, and he'd slid onto her bag after she got up. Too bad he didn't remember for sure.

Either way, Erin wasn't here now, and they had fun stuff planned. Ryan got up and dressed, pulled everything he didn't need for the day out of his pack, and left it in the tent. Then he walked to the cook site. It was sunny but still cool, without a cloud in the sky.

"Good morning, sleepyhead." Jules snickered. "How did you sleep?"

"Okay." Ryan accepted the cup of coffee Erin handed him. "Thanks. I definitely need this."

"When don't you need that?" Erin smiled, but it seemed a little dim.

"Never." He sat next to her and bumped her shoulder with his. "You know that."

"I sure do. Here." She handed him oatmeal.

"Thanks again. You don't have to do that."

Erin looked a little flushed. Strange for a cool morning. "I know."

He shoveled in oatmeal; everyone else had finished. Erin still sipped coffee, probably to keep him company.

Tyler stood. "We'll split into two teams today. The first team will go back to the start of the trail we found yesterday and mark it as we hike. The second group will go farther on the main trail and look for where the loop comes back. That should be about half a mile farther. I'm sure it will be just as challenging to find as the first half. Then that group will follow and mark." He grinned and shrugged. "With any luck, we'll meet in the middle, and we'll come back here on whichever half is clearer. There's no water on this loop; it goes up a high ridge, so fill your bottles now. And bring your rain gear; there's always a chance of a thunderstorm in August. Does anybody have questions?" He looked at each of them.

Seemed pretty straightforward to Ryan, and everyone else seemed to think so too from the nodding.

"Grab your gear, and we'll meet back here in a few and get going. The sooner we start, the sooner we finish, and maybe we'll get another swim."

Ryan grinned. *Another chance to see Erin in next to nothing? Sign me up.* His grin turned down. Tyler said thunderstorms. That wasn't good.

"Ryan? Are you coming?"

He jumped. Only Erin still stood there. "Sorry, lost

in thought." Rising, he put his dishes in his food sack and followed Erin to the tent. She threw excess items on her sleeping bag and cinched down her large backpack so it wouldn't sway awkwardly as they hiked.

Ryan tightened his boots and pack straps, then hoisted the light bag to join the group. But Erin stooped, tightening the tent straps and the rain fly. Thunderstorms—a tight tent was a dry tent. Slack meant water could gather and possibly drip through. He tightened his side, mirroring her actions. "Anticipating trouble?"

"Tyler said possible thunderstorms." She glanced across the tent at him, stomping on the tent stakes, making sure they were firm. "Have you ever tried to sleep in a wet down bag?"

"No, my old bag was synthetic. But I'm sure it doesn't work well." He'd gotten his down jacket wet in Alaska a few times, and it was miserably cold.

"No, it doesn't. I also don't want to chase my tent across the lake or pull it out of the trees." Erin chuckled.

They finished securing the tent and returned to the cook site. "Have you done that?"

Erin twisted and flashed him a grin. "No, but I've heard of it happening, and on one of my trips, a guy had to chase his tent across a meadow. It was really windy, and he'd gotten the rain fly on, but he hadn't set the stakes, and of course, there wasn't anything inside yet." She laughed. "A gust of wind caught it, and it tumbled end over end across this huge meadow, and every time he'd almost get a hand on it, it would take a weird bounce, and he'd miss. It was hilarious to watch, but if it had been stormy, it could have been terrible." They entered the cook site.

"Are you talking about the flying tent escapade?" Jules made a tumbling motion with her hand.

"I was telling Ryan about it, so he understood why I was checking our tent."

"That's an excellent point." Tyler shot a finger gun at Erin. "Did everyone zip and securely stake their tents? If we get thunderstorms..."

Dan and Laura looked at each other, dropped their packs, and jogged away. "Be right back."

Tyler and Jules laughed. "I guess that solves that problem."

"Yep." Tyler nodded. "Okay, Ryan and Erin, you're with me. Your water bottles are full?" Ryan nodded, and Erin did too. "Let's go. Hopefully, we'll see you this afternoon on the ridge, Jules."

They hiked at a brisk clip while it was still cool enough to enjoy the fast pace in the bright sun. They neared the supposed intersection of the loop trail, but no obvious sign appeared. Haphazard piles of logs covered the land, interspersed with brush and small trees. They dropped their packs, spread out, and looked for signs of the trail.

Erin whooped. "You're not going to believe this!"

He and Tyler clambered over to Erin, who stood about twenty feet off the main trail on a large log. She pointed down at her feet. "Look!"

Right below her feet, still fastened to the downed

tree, was a badly scorched wood sign, the kind the Forest Service used to mark trails. Ryan could barely make out the words "on Ridge Trail" in the middle of the sign.

"That's amazing. Nice work, Erin." Tyler snapped a picture. He put a piece of surveyor's tape on the sign. "Now let's see if we can find more of the trail."

They walked along the log to the stump. Remnants of trail tread were worn on both sides. Tyler marked that, then they traced back to the intersection with the main trail. Then they continued up, climbing over, under, and around logs to find the trail. Ryan was happy he'd put his grasper arm on that morning because there were several times when he needed it to stay on top of a log or move branches out of the way.

They climbed steadily, and the hill became rockier and steeper. The downed trees and brush thinned, making the trail easier to find, but there was less and less shade. The sun beat down on them, a reminder of his days in Afghan deserts, loose shale crunching under his feet, sweat streaming down his body. About two hours later, the hill walk became a steep mountain climb, with a sharp drop-off into a canyon on one side, greenery crowding the very bottom. The views were amazing—Erin snapped pictures constantly.

The trail was easy to find because there weren't many trees on the ridge, so they climbed at a steady pace. They stopped for lunch at noon, sheltering in the scant shade of a giant rock thrusting from the ridgeline like a spearhead.

"I hoped that we'd meet up with Jules, Dan, and Laura by now, but it took us longer to get through all those tangled trees and bushes than I thought it would." Tyler waved at the mess of downed logs. "They probably ran into the same problem."

"Hopefully, they didn't have any other trouble. Those logs are tricky." Erin took a long drink from her water bottle.

"We'll go up to the top, and then we can decide whether to come back this way, since we've marked it, or continue to look for the trail back their way. I'm a little concerned because I see there are already some clouds gathering." Tyler pointed into the distance at big, white clouds on the horizon. "They don't look like storm clouds yet, but they could become one. If there's a thunderstorm, we'll go back the way we came. It's marked, so it will be safer than trying to find the trail in the pouring rain or, even worse, in lightning. And we'll head back at the first sign that it might turn into a thunderstorm. There's no shelter out here, and we really need to get back to living trees for safety." Tyler's mouth twisted. "Not that it's ever safe to be out in a lightning storm."

"I've been caught in some before. It's scary." Erin peered at the clouds, shading her eyes with a hand.

Ryan grimaced. "Most of my backpacking was in Alaska. You don't get thunderstorms up there very much. Rain, yes. Lots of rain." He did not want to be in a thunderstorm; he reacted oddly to loud noises.

"And mosquitoes the size of eagles." Erin's nose

wrinkled.

Ryan shuddered. "Don't remind me. I hated showering in bug spray."

They packed their food and continued up the steep ridgeline, making it to the top in an hour. The views were even better, and Erin took a ton of pictures, including some of the three of them, but there was no sign of Jules and her group.

"Guys, I don't like how this looks." Tyler pointed toward camp. "We can see down this ridge for a long way, and there's no sign of Jules. And the clouds are getting thicker. As much as I'd like to complete this loop, I think it would be safer if we went back the way we came. Agreed?"

Ryan nodded, Erin's head bobbing too, so they started back down the ridge. It was tougher going down than up because the heat of the fire had caused many of the rocks to shatter, and they slipped and slid on the shards constantly. All of them ended up on their backside more than once.

They took a water break before heading into the heavy downed trees. The wind picked up. Tyler's face was grim. "Make sure your rain gear is accessible. I think we're in for it. Be careful on the logs; they're going to be really slick when they're wet. Slow and steady is the safest. And if we're out here and lighting hits, crouch down, preferably under some trees, on top of some sort of insulator, like your pack. If you can see taller living trees, run for them."

They headed into the maze of dead trees and brush, moving as quickly as they could from marking tape to tape. Thirty minutes later, Ryan jumped down onto a rare open piece of ground, relaxing for a second on solid earth. A bright flash of light—BOOM—a mortar? They were under attack! He flattened to the ground under a large, downed tree. *Where's the bunker? There should be one right here!*

Chapter 26

Trouble Inside, Trouble Outside

Lightning flashed, Erin jumped, and a boom of thunder followed far too quickly. She looked up. *Rats, it got really dark, really fast.* She looked down the trail; Tyler climbed over a tree about twenty feet in front of her. Ryan had been right behind Tyler, but he was nowhere to be found. She climbed up and over the pile in front of her, pushing through the thick brush.

Ryan was face down on the ground under a log, with his hands over his head. *Oh, no.*

She jumped over the log between them and dropped to her knees next to Ryan. "Ryan, are you okay?" He didn't move. She yelled over the booming thunder. "Ryan!" Still nothing. She put a hand on his upper arm, and he looked up at her with unseeing eyes. "Ryan, it's a thunderstorm. Come on. We need to keep going."

He curled into a fetal position, facing away from her. Tyler bounded off a log, landing next to her. "What's going on?"

"Ryan's out of it. I think it's a post-traumatic stress reaction. Go ahead—I'll get him out of it." She wasn't sure how, but she'd think of something. At least Ryan knew her well—sometimes people could come out swinging.

Tyler crouched. "Can I help?" He put a hand out but didn't touch Ryan.

"No, and there's no sense in all of us getting hit by lightning. We need to spread out! Go! We'll catch up later."

Tyler grimaced. "I don't like leaving you here, but you're right. I'll go down the trail a couple hundred yards. See if you can get him on top of his pack! After the storm blows through, I'll come back and find you." Tyler pressed a few buttons on his GPS unit, climbed back over the tree, and disappeared.

"Ryan, come on." Erin pulled on his arm, but he didn't move. "It's a lightning storm! We have to get in position!"

He rolled toward her and grabbed her arm with his real hand, pulling her down across his chest. She ended up on top of him, with her face only an inch away from his. His eyes stared blankly—he didn't see her at all. "Ryan, it's lightning. We need to get off the ground!" Erin patted his face. She could slap him, but he might misinterpret that as an attack, and then she'd be in even bigger trouble. "Ryan!"

Was he stuck under attack or in the situation where he lost his arm? She had to show him, make him feel he wasn't downrange, that he was safe. But how? She could give the Sleeping Beauty method a try—most guys wouldn't interpret that as an attack. She fastened her lips on his and kissed him.

He didn't respond. Erin pulled away. A complete failure. So much for that romantic notion.

His hand cupped the back of her head, knocking her hat off, his other arm pulled her tightly against his chest, and he kissed her back.

Erin sank into his embrace. All that mattered was Ryan's lips on hers, and his hard arms wrapped around her, crushing her to his solid chest.

Frigid water pounded on her legs. Erin screeched, rolled off Ryan, and crouched above his head under the log, pulling off her pack. "Ryan, it's a thunderstorm. Come on, we've got to get ready!" She yanked her rain jacket and pants out, trying to stay under the shelter of the log as much as she could. Thunder rolled and lightning cracked, the two coming closer together, the deluge increasing.

Ryan lay on the ground, blinking up at her.

Erin shook his shoulder. "Come on, Ryan. Get your rain gear on!" Lightning flashed and thunder boomed almost simultaneously. Comprehension came back into Ryan's eyes. He looked around, then sat up, pulling off his pack.

Finally. Erin put on her rain gear and pulled the rain cover on her pack, cinching it down as tightly as she could to protect the pack. Ryan was struggling into his rain pants. Erin pulled his pack cover and put it on. They threw their packs on the ground, rain cover down to protect the packs from the rapidly growing puddles.

"There's not enough room under this log to spread out!" Ryan looked at her, then down at his feet.

"I know!" Erin peered through the sheets of rain, turning to look behind them. All they had was this little gap under the big jumble of logs. "I think we're stuck here until it passes."

"You're right." He shoved his pack away from hers and climbed on top.

Erin turned, pushing hers as far as the gap would allow. Grimacing, she duck-walked on top of her pack, avoiding the pack lid where her headlamp was. There wasn't a lot in the pack's main bag, but she really hoped nothing broke. She turned so she could see the sky and Ryan, crouched on his pack. "Watch your head." Erin patted hers, happy there was an inch of clearance between her and the log. Which might not be enough, but it was better than nothing.

Ryan looked up and almost hit his head. He crouched a little more, grinning with a little shrug. Erin smiled back. She could cry, anticipating the worst, or laugh, hoping for the best. Looked like they both thought laughter was the better choice. But as they waited, they glanced at each other. Erin wasn't sure about Ryan, but her tension rose with every look.

Finally, the lightning, thunder, wind, and rain tapered off until only sprinkles remained. The storm had rolled on. Erin took a big breath and blew out, deliberately relaxing as much as she could, while crouched in a little ball. "I know the storm isn't far enough away to be really safe, but do you think we're safe enough?"

Ryan shrugged, craning his neck to look up. "It's moving away fast." He scooted from under the log and stood, turning and looking. He bent down with a smile. "I think we'll be okay." He reached a hand to her.

Erin grimaced. "Give me a second." She sat down on her pack and stretched her cramped legs. *Ow, ow, ow.* She rolled out from under the log and snagged her pack, brushing the dirt off. As she put the pack on, she searched for the storm. It was moving away fast, but lightning still flashed in the distance, and rain showered down. "We should find Tyler and get to live trees as fast as we can. Ryan, you go first and get ahead of me. That way, if one of us gets hit, we won't both go down."

He shook his head, glaring. "Negative. You go first."

"No, you're faster, go!" She pointed toward the camp. Both he and Tyler could make it to the trees faster than she could.

He frowned for a moment, then nodded once and climbed over the logs in front of them. She let him get over the first group of logs, then started climbing herself. He'd get farther and farther away. And give her a chance to catch her breath after that kiss and all the tension of the storm. She snorted. The personal storm was more dangerous than the real one.

Setting off, Erin's personal troubles slipped away. All she could think about was finding the next piece of surveyor's tape and bashing through the nightmare of wet branches slapping her in the face and slippery logs trying to throw her off. Occasionally, she caught her breath on a rare spot of level ground. But the standing trees groaned as they swayed in the winds, so she didn't stay in one place for long. She prayed they didn't come down on her head. Despite her need for speed, she tested each step before committing her weight to a log and tried to make sure she had solid handholds too. She kept Ryan in sight, but she was sure it was because he was stopping and looking back for her, not because she was fast enough.

Ryan whooped. "Tyler! Hey, Tyler!"

Erin climbed onto a log. Tyler waved at them, and she waved back. "You're okay?" Tyler yelled.

Ryan waved, urging him on. "Yeah! Keep going!" Tyler turned away and clambered over the logs ahead of them.

After an eternity of slipping, sliding, falling, and whipping of branches, Erin reached the main trail. As if it was waiting for her, the rain stopped and the sun shone on their wet, beat up, and bedraggled bodies. They all looked at each other and up at the sky, chuckling. Before long, they were laughing hysterically, collapsing to sit shoulder to shoulder on the last log they'd climbed over.

"Can you believe that? What are the odds?" Tyler

shook his hand like he was rolling dice.

Erin slumped on the log. "No, I can't believe it. I think I got run over by a truck." She'd love to simply sit there, but she was hungry, tired, and wanted her sleeping bag. She peeled off her rain jacket, leaving her rain pants on so the soaking wet brush along the trail wouldn't get her hiking pants wet. Tyler and Ryan did the same. Ryan took Erin's jacket, shaking the water off and putting both of them in the shove-it pocket on the back of his pack, along with his pack cover. She left her pack cover in place. They shouldered their packs and hiked back to camp.

They got to the cook site—with a tarp over it, sloped to act as a windbreak—just in time to see Jules fastening her pack. As they walked in, everyone cheered.

Jules wiped her brow. "Whew. I was going out to find you. I'm so glad you're all okay. Dinner is almost ready, too." She chuckled, shucking her pack.

"Yeah, we're good. It was a rough trek, and we're bumped and bruised a bit but nothing more." Tyler shrugged one shoulder.

Erin collapsed on a rock, and Ryan dropped next to her. They peeled off their rain pants. Since the storm had passed, the temperature was rising.

"Good. I really didn't want to go looking for you guys." Jules plopped down by the stove, taking the spoon back from Dan. Tyler grinned at the group, relief still shining on his face. He turned a circle, looking into the distance and then down at all of them. "This might be a quick break between storms.

It would be better to eat early and then hunker down for the night in our tents. Good thing you kept cooking, Jules. Thanks for stepping in, Dan."

Erin agreed. She'd rather be safe, dry, and warm in her tent rather than crowd under a barely adequate tarp that might get ripped away. She pulled her rain cover off her pack and draped it over a rock behind her. Then she fished her bowl and mug out of her pack. At first glance, it looked like everything survived her weight. Erin handed the bowl to Jules, who was already dishing out food. Tyler poured her some hot water after she got out a tea bag, and she shoved in a bite, suddenly starving.

After shoveling in a couple of bites, Ryan asked, "So, what happened to you guys, Jules?"

"We struggled with the brush and trees, and we got low on water before we got to the clearer area that Tyler told us about, so we turned back." Jules shrugged and smiled. "I'm sorry we didn't get to meet up with you, but I'm thrilled we got this tarp up before the thunderstorm and got dinner cooked."

"Yeah, you were smarter." Tyler chuckled.

Erin ate seconds as Tyler and Jules discussed the trail. Ryan scraped the remainder from the cookpot into his bowl and chowed on a meat bar. *Guess escaping death by lightning strike makes you hungry.* Dan and Laura took on water duty, making sure everyone's bottles were full. She'd return the favor tomorrow morning.

Jules poured hot water in the cook pot and scrubbed. "Same morning routine tomorrow but an hour earlier. We need to get on the trail early. We've got nine miles, longer than we normally go, but our packs are lighter now, and you're all in great shape. Any questions or issues?"

It would be a long day, but Erin was sure they were all capable. No one objected, so they all helped clean up, put rain pants back on, hung the food bags, and headed off to their tents. Erin shook off the tree branches surrounding their tent and then shook the tent, tightening the guy lines and letting it drip while she found the driest spot to put her pack and put her pack cover back on. Ryan helped her, then pulled his pack cover, shaking it out.

Tyler said they might have another storm, and darkness was falling. "Ryan, can I have my jacket back? I want to put it right under the vestibule, in case it's raining, and I have to get up."

"Sure. Good idea. Speaking of going, I'm going. Be back in a few." He handed her jacket over and took off through the trees.

That was a smart move. Erin changed into her normal sleeping attire but put her lightweight sweater on over the camisole and her rain pants back on. It was a little chilly out here with all the wet foliage. Then she headed out for a bathroom run. As she walked back, it took more and more effort to keep moving. All she wanted to do was collapse.

Reaching the tent, Erin took off all her gear, carefully placing her boots well under the rain fly, and put her rain gear around the boots, making sure it wouldn't blow away or block the airflow into the boots. She zipped up the tent and relaxed back on her sleeping bag and pad, exhausted but not quite able to fall asleep. Gradually, she warmed up. Exhaustion hit her again, hard. Ryan came back as she was closing her eyes. Material swished, but he said nothing. Even if she'd been awake, Erin didn't want to discuss their kiss, not now. She let herself drift off.

Chapter 27

Storms Inside and Out

Ryan watched Erin sleep. *She is so beautiful.* Even with her hair in tangled, damp ringlets around her face and red marks from tree branches smacking her lightly freckled skin, she was gorgeous. *And that kiss. That was a real kiss.* He wanted that again. Immediately. He flopped onto his back, knowing that if he kept looking at her, he wouldn't be able to resist, and he'd pull her over on top of him and... nope. *Can't go there. Shoot.*

Ryan put his good arm under his head. Erin kissed him. But she'd only done it because he'd been so lost in his mind that she couldn't think of any other way to wake him. She should have slapped him, but she was too nice to do that. She should have left him there and moved away, saving herself. He would have come out eventually, probably when the rain poured on him. But Erin wasn't that kind of person. No, she'd done what it took to save him, like she'd done time after time.

But he needed to know if she'd kissed him only to bring him back to reality, or did she return his feelings?

He was no longer content only being Erin's friend. No way—he *knew* what he was missing. If she hadn't kissed him, maybe they could have stayed in the gray area between friends and relationship, but not anymore. He had to know, for sure. And the only way to discover the answer was to make a move, put himself out there. He might crash and burn, but his only remaining question was when. He snorted softly. Too many questions, not enough answers.

The wind picked up, rustling the nylon, and the tent darkened. Tyler was right: they were in for another thunderstorm. Ryan wouldn't flash back this time. He knew the storm was coming, and he had the memory of that kiss to keep him right here, focused on Erin, hoping for another one. Planning on another one. Would she kiss him back or turn away? Or worse yet, give him the "let's just be friends" line? That never really bothered him; there was always another woman out there to meet, but Erin was different. She was it. End of the line.

Lightning flashed, and twenty seconds later, the thunder boomed. Erin started awake, rolled up on her elbow, and looked down at him. He couldn't see anything but a vague suggestion of her head. But he knew she was beautiful without seeing a thing.

"Are you okay, Ryan?"

"Yeah. I knew this one was coming. Wind's been

picking up, and it's getting darker." Temperature dropped, too, but his pounding heart kept him warm.

"Oh." She plopped back down on her bag, her shoulder next to his. "But we knew the last one was coming."

Ryan shuddered the memory of that day away. "Yeah, but I was concentrating on my footing and the trees and moving as quickly as I could, so the sound shocked me. Sent me right back."

She paused. "Will you tell me what happened?"

Ryan swallowed the sour taste in his mouth. He'd known he had to tell her eventually, but he really didn't want to. But she had to know all of him to make a relationship work.

"It's okay if you don't want to, but I'll listen if it helps."

Erin never judged, even when she probably should. He sighed. "I don't really want to talk about it, but you deserve to hear it. Especially when you risked your life to stay with me."

She held up her hand. "Ryan, it's okay. You don't owe me anything. The chances of being hit by lightning would be the same if I stayed or left, but I would have stayed, regardless."

"I know. That's the kind of person you are." Ryan gathered his courage, staring up at the tent. Talking about this was much harder than it should be even after all the therapy he'd had. "I was in Afghanistan; our base was under attack. The thing is, I don't remember much. It's more like a series of impressions and emotions and flashes all jumbled together that I've pieced together into a story."

He took another deep breath. *Come on, Walsh, have some guts.* "They had attacked the airfield before. There'd be a few mortars or rockets, we'd dive for the shelter in the hangar, hunker down for a few minutes, then go back to work. Every time they'd hit us, my crew had been working in the hangar. We'd been lucky. The day it happened, I was out on the flightline, doing the final checks on the bird, and I was about as far from a bunker as you could get. The siren went off, and we all ran for the shelter. Then I was flying through the air, and everything was silent. There was no noise at all. I hit the ground, hard, and it was incredibly loud, like someone turned the mute button back to 'on'. Somebody was screaming their head off, and it wasn't until the rest of my crew ran up to me that I realized it was me. *I* was screaming. I was on my side, curled in a ball, and there was blood all around me. My hand was in front of my face, but the angle was all wrong. It was palm up, and twisted, and bloody. One guy put a hand on my shoulder, pressing me down into the tarmac, and then there was this excruciating band of fire around my arm."

He shuddered and swallowed. Erin rolled over on her side, putting one hand on his shoulder. He grabbed her hand with his good hand, pulled it down to his heart and hung on tight. He spoke louder, so she could hear him over the rain pounding on the tent, the lightning and thunder crashing around them. "I'm pretty sure I passed out at that point. I don't think I realized my hand wasn't attached to my arm anymore, but I knew something was wrong. It must have been the tourniquet that hurt so bad. Those guys saved my life. I would have bled out if they hadn't acted so quickly." Ryan snorted. "It was the Sarge who saved my life. He's the one who trained us in emergency response. But I thought I'd be saving someone else." He shivered the helpless feeling away, holding Erin's hand.

"Anyway, I remember flashes of being in an ambulance, and then in the medical unit, and being transported on one of my C-17s." He snorted. "I definitely remember asking the nurse for the tail number because I wanted to check and make sure all the maintenance was done. Which makes me laugh now. Pretty sure I was on the good stuff by then." Ryan glanced at Erin, trying to smile, but he gave up. "Anyway, I woke up for real at Landstuhl, Germany, and they told me what happened. I finally realized I'd lost my hand and most of my forearm. They shipped me off to Walter Reed pretty quick, and I started physical therapy and getting ready for the prosthesis and all that."

He took a few deep breaths while the lightning cracked simultaneously with the thunder, booming all around them. Good thing the tent was deep in living trees. Erin said nothing, but she held his hand and squeezed it lightly. In the bright flashes, Erin's compassion was clear on her pretty face. "Anyway, most of the time, it's okay. I don't freeze up or flash back very often anymore. I've gotten used to not having an arm and a hand and used to the reactions. Most people are cool about it, and they don't stare or scream. Women do." He shrugged. "Starla's reaction is pretty common."

Erin squeezed his hand, tight. "Girls do. Stupid little girls who have never grown up. *Women* are fine with it and admire you."

He snorted. "That's a nice thought but not what I've found."

"Oh, come on. Sam and Deb both called you sexy, remember?"

"But neither one of them touched me, now did they?" The storm rolled away, but the rain didn't let up, and the wind still howled.

"Sure they did. And as I recall, you were the one who took Sam's hand off your chest." She poked his chest with one finger.

"I guess I did." Ryan stared up at her, trying and failing to read her face in the gathering gloom. "But I don't want Sam touching me. I want *you* touching me."

"Ryan..."

There was something in her voice, but he didn't know what. And it didn't matter—it was go-time. Ryan rolled onto his side and let go of her hand. Her hand slid across his chest, and he shivered, goosebumps rising. *Nothing—and everything—to lose.* He slid his hand up her arm, along her shoulder, and up into her hair. Then, watching her eyes, waiting for a no, he leaned toward her.

He fell face first, putting his hand down to catch himself. He'd forgotten he didn't have a hand to lean on, just a stump.

Erin gasped. *Probably pulled her hair. Argh. Got to do this right.* Ryan quickly got his residual arm positioned and brought his good hand to the back of her head, lowering his lips to hers. He moved slow, giving her plenty of time to back away and slap him.

His mouth touched her pillowy lips. For a heartbeat, she didn't respond, and his stomach dropped to his feet in despair. Then her lips moved against his—she was kissing him. His stomach rocketed up, floating in zero gee joy and ecstasy for a second. *Yes, yes, yes! So good, soft, warm.*

He ran his hand through her hair and over her back to her waist, pulling her toward him. He groaned into her mouth at the wonder of her in his arms. Pulling away from her lips, he ran his mouth down her neck to her pulse point and back up to her ear, nipping at the lobe lightly. Erin moaned his name; the most beautiful sound he'd ever heard. She ran her hands over his chest and shoulders, her slightly rough hands rasping over his skin, spreading heat, so he nipped her again. He captured the moan in his mouth, meeting her lips again. *Perfect.*

The feel of her hands on his skin, clutching his shoulders, drove him insane. Something cold hit the back of his neck and he jolted. Another frigid drop hit his neck and rolled down. He pulled back. A big drop splatted Erin's forehead, and she gasped, wide-eyed.

"Argh!" Ryan rolled away from Erin and grabbed the pack towel he'd put by the door. "The tent is leaking!" He sat up. Erin did too, pushing her sleeping bag down. He shoved his, trying to keep it in the middle and not let it brush up against the sides of the tent, knowing pressure would eventually wick moisture inside.

She peered at the roof of the tent, then prodded it gently, water running down her arm. "Oh, I see what happened." Erin wiped her arm off, unzipped the tent door on her side, put her rain gear on, and unzipped the fly. She stood in the pouring rain, the light from her headlamp bouncing and scattering in the deluge. Then she re-zipped the fly and disappeared.

Ryan kept his towel under the drip and grabbed his headlamp, looking for more. That was lousy timing. The fly popped up off the mesh of the tent, then the whole tent shook. The flapping of nylon quieted as Erin tightened the lines. Ryan ran his towel over the mesh of the tent to catch the last of the drips. Then he moved Erin's bag underneath him so it wouldn't get wet when she came back in.

The fly opened and closed, and Erin carefully took off her wet gear, trying to avoid getting more water in the tent. Ryan ran the dry end of his towel over her hair, neck, and back where she'd inevitably gotten wet pulling the pants and coat off and the tent and pad underneath her. She finally brought her feet into the tent, wiped them off, and zipped it back up. She hung her headlamp above them, light shining down, and flopped back on her pad.

Then Erin turned to him. "A branch fell on the fly, and it was just heavy enough to press it against the tent." A smile flickered. "It was condensation dripping. Glad it didn't tear the fly." She paused, then her smile flashed again. "It's always a bit of a contortionist act to get back in the tent when it's raining. Thanks for drying my back off." Her brows rose. "Can I have my sleeping bag back?"

That's all she's going to ask? He propped himself up on his shoulders and feet and pulled her bag out from under his legs and handed it to her. He rolled on his side, and after she twisted away from him to slide the bag underneath her, he reached up and slid his arm around her waist, pulling her back into him on top of his bag. "There, now you can arrange it easily."

Erin gasped a bit when he snuggled her in, then huffed out a laugh. "Oh, I don't think there's anything easy about any of this."

"No?" He kissed the back of her neck. "Why can't it be easy?"

She wriggled back into him. "Ryan... we can't do this."

Her words didn't agree with her body, not one little bit. "Why not?" He moved his mouth farther down her neck to her pulse point, and she sucked in a breath. She responded so passionately, and unless she pulled away, he was pushing on—it was all or nothing time. He slid his right arm, which was trapped under her, tighter around her waist. She put her hand over his and squeezed. He couldn't do more without full spoken consent, so repeated his question. "Why not? You want me, I love you, so why not?"

She stiffened, her hand clenching almost painfully around his. "What did you say?"

"I said, you want me, and I love you." Unable to resist, he nipped gently at her neck.

"You love me?" she whispered.

"Yeah, I do." Ryan kissed along the top of her shoulder. "Fully realized it about a week ago, but I think I've known for a while now. I know you probably don't feel the same, but that's okay. I can be patient." He squeezed her tight. He didn't want society's logic or laws overruling her real feelings. If she didn't want him, she'd have pulled away. "Usually I can be patient. You want me, so that's good enough for now. Hopefully, I'll grow on you. You already put up with me and haven't threatened to kill me yet, so that's a good sign." He ran his tongue around the outside of her ear.

"Ryan." She gasped when he lipped her ear lobe. She pushed back into him. "Oh. Ryan, stop that. I can't think when you're doing that."

Ryan sighed but stopped kissing her. He didn't let go, but he loosened his arm so she could pull away.

Erin arched against him, then pulled his hand off and rolled away. He couldn't help but reach for her. She took his hand in hers, and his residual arm in her other hand. Ryan jumped, shocked. She was touching him... there? His eyes must be as big as the tires on the jet.

"Ryan... you work for me. You're eight years younger than I am. *Eight.* You're not even close to thirty, and I'm on the downhill side of it." Under the glaring headlamp, her flushed face and intent stare were clear.

Her thumb gently rubbing across the end of his residual arm made it hard to think, but he did the math. "Wrong. I'm closer to thirty than you are to forty."

She laughed, but it wasn't a joyful laugh, and she didn't seem happy. "So? It's still eight years. I'd be robbing the cradle. And you work for me. It's called sexual harassment for a reason."

"I'll beg you to sexually harass me. Please?" He smiled, trying to lighten the mood.

"Ryan... this isn't a joke."

He sobered and looked straight into her eyes. Time to put all his feelings out there. "I'm not laughing, Erin. I love you. I don't care how old you are, and if I have to quit and work for free, that's what I'll do. I'm not going away now. I *love* you. If you'd pulled back from the start, then this would be a different discussion. But you didn't. You want me as bad as I want you, and that's a decent place to start. If it all falls apart later, I'll deal. At least we'll have tried. Really tried."

Erin looked at him. He stared back. He wasn't giving in without a fight. She was thinking too much about other people, not them.

"What happened to the silent, withdrawn Ryan

Walsh I've gotten to know? When did Mister 'I'm all that and a bag of chocolate too' replace him?" Erin's brows wrinkled above a small smile.

Ryan relaxed. They were okay. "When you kissed me back."

She smiled wider. "Then what took you so long?"

He reached out and pulled her on top of him. She laughed, a joyful sound.

"Doesn't matter. You're here now. I'm here now." He gazed into her eyes. "And someday, I'd really like to show you how much of me is right here, right now. But we can go slow. I know you've got doubts, and I'm more than willing to take the time to prove them wrong."

She nodded. "Slow is good. We'll have to navigate the garage and coffee shop a little carefully. But..." Erin cupped his face with her hands, her calluses snagging a bit on his three-day beard. "You need to know now. I love you too. I didn't want to, and I tried not to, but it happened anyway."

What? No. It couldn't be. Ryan snapped his open mouth shut. But he had to be sure. "You... you love me? Really?"

"Yeah. Really. I love you." Erin smiled straight into his eyes.

He stared back at her, completely stunned by her for at least the fiftieth time that day. "Sierra Hotel. How in the world did I get so lucky? Who cares? Show me."

Erin brought her mouth down on his, and the words didn't matter anymore. Nothing mattered anymore but her and him, together.

Erin pulled away. "I love you, Ryan."

He'd never, ever get tired of hearing that. "I love you too, Erin. I'll prove it every day." His heart burned in his chest, and happiness surged through him like oil through a racing engine, fast and hot.

She slid her hands behind his neck. "You don't have to prove it; I know it already."

Her faith in him caused him to blink back sudden tears. "Then I'll live up to your love, Erin, forever."

"Forever." She smiled tremulously and kissed him passionately. There was no more room or need for words.

Chapter 28

Coffee, Cars, and Happily Ever After

Erin laughed at the quip Ryan tossed off to a customer. Their big backpacking trip was only a few weeks ago, but in those weeks, Ryan had come out of his shell, and not just with her. He was still quiet most of the time, and he struggled with depression and anger, but he was showing a little of the self-confidence he'd had before he lost his arm.

They were taking it slow, getting to know each other better, but he was at her house so often he might as well live there. And she wanted him there, despite her grocery bill quadrupling. She missed him too much when he was gone.

They were still learning each other's habits and preferences and occasionally stumbling over things that triggered bad feelings in one or the other of them. But being together was precious to both of them—they talked before their emotions spiraled out of control. Ryan went back to therapy, and she went with him occasionally, so she understood him better. He was also hanging out with a veteran group using her shop, and he'd gone to a couple of veteran events and joined a service organization. He was considering school but still wasn't sure what he wanted to study.

Ryan's mom was thrilled. Katie Walsh claimed she'd known that they were meant for each other the moment she'd met Erin.

Erin's mother, on the other hand, was appalled. And horrified. And every other description one could use to say Sharlene Murphy wasn't happy. Erin tried to be nice, and be the bigger person, but it was hard. Eventually, Mother made it impossible.

Mother invited them to a concert and dinner, and they'd gone, remaining respectful while Mother made nasty, snide comments in her ever-so-polite way. During the concert intermission, Erin reached out to hold Ryan's hand, needing the contact to keep from yelling at Mom. Mother pointed at their clasped hands and hissed at them to stop "making a scene."

Ryan stared narrow-eyed at her for a moment, then smiled very sweetly and told her—loudly—that she didn't know what the word "scene" meant. Then he swept Erin into a blistering kiss in front of everyone. When she'd forgotten all about the audience and couldn't breathe, he'd swept her up in his arms like he was carrying her across a threshold.

As he took her out the door, with her trying to

keep her not-inconsiderable weight on his shoulders rather than his prosthesis, he yelled over his shoulder. "*Now* you should understand what the word scene means." They'd gotten more enthusiastic applause than the musicians. Mother hadn't spoken to her for weeks. They were both pretty happy about that.

Erin might invite her to the wedding, but she wasn't willing to promise. Not that he'd asked yet, but they'd talked about it. When it happened, the only people with guaranteed invitations were Deb, Sam, and Wiz. And Ryan's family and old crewmates.

Another good thing had happened when they became a couple. Chaz Cust got the message, loud and clear, that Erin wanted nothing to do with his car or him, and he'd had somebody pick up the blasted Barracuda. Finally. It probably had more to do with Sam filing the protective order request, totally infuriating the Custs and Mother. Again.

Chaz was still skulking around, hitting on Deb and Sam, but he was very careful to avoid Erin. Nasty old Mrs. Cust took every opportunity she could to complain about Erin and her business, but it hadn't affected her bottom line at all. The Marcus City Bank notified Erin they were reevaluating her loan, but when their assessor finished his report, Mother's attempt backfired—Erin's business was worth more than ever. Mother didn't say a word about it, probably because they weren't speaking by then.

She still sent invitations for Erin to come to events, but friends told Erin that Mother was still bringing those same iffy-looking "gentlemen" to every performance. Erin turned her down via text message. But she was getting worried. Mother looked stressed, but when Erin had asked before their big blow-up, she brushed Erin's concerns away or said she was imagining things. But every time Erin drove to the bank, it seemed more of those "wise guys" were around, either waiting in cars outside or in the lobby. Deb kept turning down offers to invest in her bakery, too, reporting several of the men had warned her that not accepting their "help" was dangerous. Two of them had heavy accents; Deb thought it was Russian but couldn't be sure. Mother wouldn't tell her what was going on, so there was nothing she could do.

Since her mother couldn't be helped, Erin concentrated on Ryan and her business. She filled the empty spot in the garage with a 1972 Ford Bronco and was tricking it out with a hot engine and a very nice, but practical, interior. Ryan's advice was making it a true man-mobile, and he thought they were going to make a very good profit. It was really his Christmas present; she could hardly wait to see the look on his face when she gave him the keys.

Ryan quit Kelly's and was working the coffee shop full-time, but eventually, they planned to find someone new to exchange the apartment for work, and then Ryan could work with her in the garage in the afternoons. Hopefully, they could find another veteran to fill that opening, preferably a friend transitioning from military life.

Wiz asked them to look at some property and houses, and they thought they'd found the right one. It sat above the valley in the Sapphire Mountains, bordered by Forest Service land on one side and vast ranches on the other sides, all of which had conservation easements and other protections in place so they couldn't be broken up into subdivisions. The house was bigger than Wiz needed, but it was easy to add the things she wanted, like metal security shutters, a safe room, and a twelve-foot chain-link fence with razor wire at the top surrounding the house.

The property was hugely expensive, but Wiz was loaded and never spent money on anything but security and weapons, so that wasn't a problem. Besides, her Fortress of Solitude back in Washington would sell for a ton of money, so she'd probably break even. And Wiz wouldn't put any of her money in Mother's bank. She said their cyber security was completely inadequate. Erin happily relayed that tidbit to Mother the last time she'd called to complain about Ryan and Chaz Cust.

But three days ago, Wiz called her, warning Erin her mother was dealing with dangerous people. Wiz had discovered that new investors in her mother's bank were members of the Russian Bratva—the mob. They weren't "wise guys" like the movie mobsters— they trafficked drugs and people and killed with little provocation. But since Mother wouldn't talk to her, and she was a fully capable, independent adult,

Erin could do nothing.

Other than her worries about Mother, her life was amazingly good. Erin gazed at all the happy customers in her immaculately clean coffee shop. Ryan was joking with the older ladies but smiled and raised his brows at Erin. He said something to the ladies, making them all laugh as he walked away. But they aimed envious stares at Erin. She grinned at the women, aware her expression was terribly smug.

Reaching her, Ryan grasped her hand and tugged her into the garage. He locked the door behind them and pulled her to Smoky and into the back seat, where he kissed her wildly. He moved to her ear and neck. "Have I told you how beautiful you are today?"

"Yes, you have, but I don't mind hearing it again," she gasped out.

"And did I tell you I love you?"

"Yessss."

"Good. Don't want to make the boss unhappy with me. She might stop sexually harassing me. And that would be terrible."

She slid her hand down his chest. "Don't worry, I have every intention of taking advantage of you in every way possible. But I'll reward you appropriately."

"Yes, you will." He kissed the other side of her neck.

"Sure. All the coffee you can drink." She ran her hands up to his solid shoulders.

"I'll need more than that."

She tried to concentrate, but his hand distracted

her. "Ooh, umm. No, you can drive Smoky sometimes, too."

"Something else, 'cause I'd rather watch you drive Smoky. It's hot." He nipped at her earlobe.

"Oh, wow, do that again." Thinking was overrated.

He did. "What else?" Ryan nibbled down her neck.

Why was he still talking? "Your own classic car?"

"I'd rather have something else."

She cupped his face in her hands, pushing him away and ignoring his moan of protest. Erin gazed straight into his beautiful eyes. "How about every bit of my love?"

"Perfect. Coffee, cars, and Erin. There are many out there, but this one is mine. And I'm yours. Forever."

"Forever." They locked lips, and nothing else mattered.

The End and Happily Ever After

Want more stories about veterans in Marcus, Montana? Wiz's book, *Bitter Retreat*, is out now!

Sign up for my email newsletter to get notifications about new releases, plus bonus stories and extra scenes! https://sendfox.com/amscott

Author's End Note

Marcus, Montana isn't a real place, but it's based on Hamilton, Montana, where I live. You can find pictures on my Instagram at annemscott_author. Sadly, there isn't a *Coffee & Cars*, but we have lots of great espresso shops and bakeries and the Bitterroot Rodders, who show off their cars during Daly Days every August. Marcus Daly, The Copper King, was real—he helped build much of Hamilton, and you can tour beautiful Daly Mansion. They host festivals, craft sales, and high tea, too.

The auto parts store stories are real. My husband, The Amazing Sleeping Man, worked for a national chain store in Hamilton for five years—all of those things happened to him, plus more. Moral of the story? Be nice to retail workers, or you might end up in a book.

The Wilderness Institute Citizen Science program is also real; they're part of the University of Montana. Erin and Ryan's backpacking trip into the Frank Church River of No Return Wilderness was a trip I took several years ago, and I went back the next year to clear the loop trail we rediscovered. We didn't get caught in any thunderstorms, although I've experienced several on high mountain peaks, and it's rather terrifying. I've gone backpacking with the WI for many years, but sadly, I haven't seen any romances bloom on the trips. My husband, The Amazing Sleeping Man, is not a fan of backpacking, so I don't have anyone to hold me in my sleeping bag, either. But our reunions at home are always sweet!

I realize some of you may think there's too much backpacking information in this novel, but I hope it inspires some of you to get into the wilderness, even if it's a short day hike or a drive through a wild corridor. It's good for the soul, and we need more advocates for quiet places that are minimally marred by humans. I'm fortunate to live in a place where wilderness is so accessible; I hope you can experience it, too!

On a more serious note, if you are a sexual assault survivor, there are resources available to help you. In the US, RAINN is one of the largest; call their hotline at 1-800-655-4673 (HOPE). There are similar organizations in many countries. Get help now; don't wait, please.

If you experience post-traumatic stress, please reach out for help. Don't give up—we need you! In the US, the National Suicide Prevention Hotline is 988; you can call or chat. The number for military veterans is the same. There are similar hotlines in many countries; again, don't wait, reach out for help, please.

Biography

After twenty years in the US Air Force, Anne M. Scott traded her sword for a pen. Well, a laptop. She writes about strong women and men, love that grows slowly in small western towns, with a little suspense, action, and adventure—anything more than kisses and hugs happens behind closed doors. Anne is lucky to live, hike, and ski in the Bitterroot Mountains of Montana. On the rare occasions she leaves, Anne volunteers with Team Rubicon, a veteran-led disaster response organization. She also writes exciting science fiction as AM Scott.

Check out her small town, slow-build Montana romances at: www.amscottwrites.com/romance and signup for her newsletter at: https://sendfox.com/amscott for a free ebook.
Find her:
Web: www.amscottwrites.com/romance
Facebook: facebook.com/AnneMScottAuthor
Instagram: Instagram.com/ annemscott_author
Merchandise: LightwavePub.redbubble.com
Email: romance@amscottwrites.com

Acknowledgements

First, I'd like to thank God for sending me on this amazing writing adventure. If you'd told me 20 years ago I'd be a writer, I'd have laughed. Loud.

Second, I couldn't do this without my husband, The Amazing Sleeping Man. He's fabulously supportive and guards my time better than I do. Love you!

Third, my sister Lia Huni, rom-com writer. Thanks for reading all my novels, especially that first terrible one!

Fourth, my sprint group. Thanks to Lia, Irene Micheals, Sara Ivy Hill, Marcus Alexander Hart, Tony Slater, Lou Cadle, and Kate Pickford, along with all their pen name alter-egos! Y'all are awesome!

Fifth, my crazy German Shepherd, Zoe, for getting me away from the computer regularly. No matter how annoying it may be at the time, it's important to remember there's more to life than writing!

Sixth, my Team Rubicon friends. Thanks for supporting my writing journey!

The final and biggest thank you is to all of you lovely readers! Without you, I couldn't afford to publish. Thanks!

www.ingramcontent.com/pod-product-compliance
Lightning Source LLC
Chambersburg PA
CBHW021412310726
48971CB00005B/1304